THEY WE[RE] ... CHANCE—A[...]

SHELDON RICE, the ruthless billionaire developer behind the world's most incredible playground: He ignored the warnings. Now he must pay the price.

WESLEY DAVISON, the young genius who dreamed up The Park's spectacular rides: He's a class-A nerd, but now he's their only hope.

DR. TAYLOR McKENNA, the head of The Park's medical facility: Her medical degrees are worthless against the forces of evil.

CELESTE DONATELLI, the tough, inner-city fourteen-year-old brought to The Park as part of a PR program for disadvantaged youths: She hadn't thought anything could be worse than the horrors of the streets.

JESUS "JOEY" RIVERA, the eight-year-old orphan smuggled across the border: Accidentally recruited into this fantasyland, little Joey's practiced eye has already spotted all kinds of secret hiding places.

THRILLERS BY WILLIAM W. JOHNSTONE

THE DEVIL'S CAT (2091, $3.95)

The town was alive with all kinds of cats. Black, white, fat, scrawny. They lived in the streets, in backyards, in the swamps of Becancour. Sam, Nydia, and Little Sam had never seen so many cats. The cats' eyes were glowing slits as they watched the newcomers. The town was ripe with evil. It seemed to waft in from the swamps with the hot, fetid breeze and breed in the minds of Becancour's citizens. Soon Sam, Nydia, and Little Sam would battle the forces of darkness. Standing alone against the ultimate predator—The Devil's Cat.

THE DEVIL'S HEART (2110, $3.95)

Now it was summer again in Whitfield. The town was peaceful, quiet, and unprepared for the atrocities to come. Eternal life, everlasting youth, an orgy that would span time—that was what the Lord of Darkness was promising the coven members in return for their pledge of love. The few who had fought against his hideous powers before, believed it could never happen again. Then the hot wind began to blow—as black as evil as The Devil's Heart.

THE DEVIL'S TOUCH (2111, $3.95)

Once the carnage begins, there's no time for anything but terror. Hollow-eyed, hungry corpses rise from unearthly tombs to gorge themselves on living flesh and spawn a new generation of restless Undead. The demons of Hell cavort with Satan's unholy disciples in blood-soaked rituals and fevered orgies. The Balons have faced the red, glowing eyes of the Master before, and they know what must be done. But there can be no salvation for those marked by The Devil's Touch.

Available wherever paperbacks are sold, or order direct from the Publisher. Send cover price plus 50¢ per copy for mailing and handling to Zebra Books, Dept. 3142, 475 Park Avenue South, New York, N.Y. 10016. Residents of New York, New Jersey and Pennsylvania must include sales tax. DO NOT SEND CASH.

PATRICIA WALLACE

THRILL

ZEBRA BOOKS
KENSINGTON PUBLISHING CORP.

For Andy
and in loving memory of
Doris Waudby Mansker

ZEBRA BOOKS

are published by

Kensington Publishing Corp.
475 Park Avenue South
New York, NY 10016

First printing: October, 1990

Printed in the United States of America

Who has seen the wind?
    Neither you nor I
                    —Christina Rossetti

Prologue

The night sky had retreated, and the first pale light of daybreak elicited the plaintive cry of a mourning dove. For a time thereafter, there was no other sound, not even the wind.

Ezra stood motionless, waiting, his senses primed by the unnatural quiet. He moved his head fractionally, listening, but heard only the beating of his own heart, quickened by the climb.

Even this high up, the air tasted of the sea, and his lips were salty when he licked them. Fog clung to the base of the hills, hiding the shoreline below, and muffling the pounding of the waves.

The silence had a presence, he thought, not unlike that of the fogbank, except that it couldn't be seen . . . which didn't mean it wasn't real.

Seventy-nine years of hard living had taught him never to dismiss a possibility, no matter how remote it might seem to be.

From the corner of his eye he saw a squirrel in a stunted elm, its bushy tail held straight up, one forefoot poised an inch above the branch. The squirrel, too, was listening.

Ezra shifted his weight and lowered his body until he was sitting on his heels.

The mourning dove cooed again. A second later it took wing.

Beneath him, the earth trembled just slightly. He pressed his right hand against the ground, palm flat, fingers splayed, and it seemed to him that a tingle ran the length of his arm.

A tremor?

It hadn't been long ago that San Francisco had caught the tail end of a 7.1-magnitude earthquake, which had originated in the Loma Prieta Range near Santa Cruz. McKenna's Creek was a fair distance north of the fabled City by the Bay, but now and then the town had been subjected to a mild aftershock.

If this was indeed another aftershock, it was so minor that Ezra doubted anyone besides himself would have felt it. It was less a tremor, he thought, than . . . what?

A disturbance?

He straightened abruptly and peered down the hillside, narrowing his eyes to make out the roadway through the fog. Or more accurately, to make out what was coming up the roadway.

And there it was. The lumbering weight of the thing swirled the mist around as it headed up Old Mill Road, and as he watched, its form was revealed: a huge tractor-trailer hauling an earthmover.

So. The first of the construction equipment had arrived. The yellow monstrosity was too far away for him to read the name printed in black letters on its door, but he—and everyone else in town—knew it well enough: Rice Enterprises.

Ezra spat.

He enjoyed life as much as the next man, but he had truly hoped that he would have gone on to meet his Maker before *progress* came to McKenna's Creek. And yet, here it was, in all its glory, in the form of Rice Enterprises, and in the person of Sheldon Rice.

6

A second tractor-trailer emerged from the fog, and then a third, and a fourth. They continued to come, on and on, so many of them that he lost count. The heavy equipment parade finally gave way to a line of pickup trucks, filled, no doubt, with hard hats.

In the name of progress, Rice and his damned Enterprises were planning to decimate the countryside, and defile the land.

Trees would be felled, the undergrowth cleared, and the very hills would fall victim to the bulldozers' blades. From the gentle swell of land they would carve out building sites. Then the rich dark soil would disappear beneath asphalt and concrete.

Where once there had been beauty, soon there would be The Park.

What kind of a man, Ezra wondered, would destroy nature to build an amusement park?

"Asshole," he muttered, answering his own question.

Part One

March 1992

Chapter One

Sheldon Rice walked slowly around the scale model of The Park, comparing it in his mind's eye to the real thing in McKenna's Creek.

For years now, this model had been the nucleus around which all of his plans had revolved, and it had held a kind of magic for him. He had studied it from every angle, memorizing the layout so precisely that it was as though the image had been burned into his brain.

The rides were something of a marvel, mechanized and fully operational. Water flowed along the blue-bottomed canals which crisscrossed the grounds, and there were tiny lights which were programmed to come on at twilight. The landscaping too was astonishingly realistic: Rice would have sworn that on occasion he could smell the scent of fresh-cut grass.

But lately, with The Park only weeks away from completion, the miniature, despite all of its charm and meticulous attention to detail, seemed more and more like a child's toy.

A *rich* child's toy, but a toy nonetheless.

"Excuse me, Mr. Rice?"

Annoyed, Rice turned toward the doorway, where one of his junior assistants — Rice wasn't good with names unless

11

there was a financial reason to be—stood, all but wringing his hands.

"What is it?"

"The helicopter will be here in—"

"It's not here yet?"

"No sir, but—"

"Then why," he asked with what he felt was remarkable restraint, "are you bothering me? When the damned thing gets here, *then* tell me it's here."

The young man took a step backward. "Uh . . . yes sir, I'm sorry, sir. I didn't mean to bother you—"

"—sir," Rice finished for him. "I'm not the damned welcoming committee, you know."

"No sir, I wasn't . . ."

This time the words died in the young fool's throat. Rice nodded his satisfaction and turned his attention back to the model. A few seconds passed before the junior assistant apparently was able to discern that he'd been dismissed, and then Rice heard the door close.

He made a mental note to look into the company's hiring practices. He hadn't nurtured Rice Enterprises into a multi-billion-dollar company by suffering fools gladly, or at all. Perhaps his director of personnel had forgotten that little fact.

Then again, perhaps his director of personnel was also a fool.

The intercom buzzed, interrupting his train of thought, and he crossed the twenty or so feet to his desk. "Yes, yes," he said, "what is it?"

His secretary's voice sounded harried. "Your two o'clock appointment is here."

A glance at a crystal wall clock revealed that it was five minutes to two. The last time he'd looked, it had been 9:00 a.m. Where did the hours go?

"Show him in," Rice said, circling the desk and taking a seat in his calfskin chair. He barely had time to settle in before there was a tap at the door.

The door opened and Loretta Billingsley leaned in, peering over wire-rimmed glasses at him, her brow furrowed by her perpetual sguint. "It's *Miss* Chan, from the *San Jose Beacon.*"

Another newspaper reporter, at least the twelfth this week. Was there a factory out there somewhere assembling them? He sighed.

Loretta was uncommonly good at blocking visitors out until he gave the final okay, but Miss Chan was a slip of a girl and she ducked under Loretta's arm and into the room. She was nearly to the desk before either he or Loretta could so much as blink.

"Mr. Rice," she said, extending a slender hand. "Nancy Chan. Thank you for making time for me."

Rice took her hand. Nancy Chan was perhaps twenty-five, quite pretty in her diminutive way, and was bold enough to meet his eyes, appraising him as he appraised her. He approved that she wore her hair short, and her skirt to her knees.

"Not at all," he said finally. He motioned to the chair opposite his and signaled with a slight nod to Loretta that all was well. The door closed with a soft click.

"I know you must be busy," Miss Chan began, flipping open a stenographer's pad, "so I'll cut to the chase. Mr. Rice, how do you justify charging three hundred dollars a day for an amusement park when people are going hungry in the in the streets?"

Rice gave her the faintest of smiles. "To the kill, you mean."

"Excuse me?"

"You've 'cut' to the kill." He toyed absentmindedly with his gold cuff links. "How do surgeons justify charging sixty thousand dollars for a liver transplant when there are people dying in their beds?"

"It isn't the same at all," she said.

But he could see that he had her flustered. "Isn't it?" he asked archly.

"No."

"Really. I would have thought otherwise. How fortunate it

13

is for me—for all of us, I suppose—that you're here to correct my misconceptions."

A hint of color appeared on her high cheekbones. He wondered how long she'd been out of college; not long enough, he thought.

"I'm sorry," she said, straightening her shoulders. "We've have gotten off to a bad start."

Rice said nothing. He was curious whether or not she'd be able to extricate herself from what had the potential to be a thoroughly unpleasant situation.

"My journalism professor warned me that I have a tendency to be overly aggressive. Even . . . confrontational." Her smile appeared genuine, made up of equal parts chagrin and challenge.

An intriguing blend. He'd expected a more feminine reaction . . . tears, or at the very least, a pout. Either would have irritated him. If women were going to compete on male ground, they'd better be ready to compete on male terms as well.

"No doubt your professor had reasons for issuing his warning, but unless I'm mistaken, aren't reporters supposed to be confrontational?"

"The good ones," she agreed, and laughed.

Rice surprised himself by joining her. "So we're not as different as you might expect. I've been known to go for the throat when the necessity arises."

"Yes, I've heard."

There was something in the tone of her voice that suggested to him that she didn't entirely disapprove. He steepled his hands and looked over his fingertips at her. "Then I'll answer your question. I justify the cost of admission by the value of the product. The Park is unlike any other amusement park in the world today."

Nancy Chan leaned forward, the notebook forgotten in her lap. "How so?"

"To begin with, the rides are state-of-the-art."

"Excuse me, but everyone says that."

"Granted, but in this case, it's true. Maybe I should tell

you what the rides are *not*. They're not for little old ladies and cardiac invalids. They're not 'theme' rides with cute little characters singing sweet little songs. And they're not passive."

Miss Chan frowned. "Passive?"

"A number of the rides are interactive, in that the guest is called upon to make decisions which will affect the outcome."

"Interesting."

"And, unique among its brethren, in this park, there will be no lines, no crowds, no waiting."

"Is that possible?"

"It is. Admission is by reservation only. The guests stay on the premises for seven days, and I guarantee it will take seven days to see everything."

"Seven times three hundred dollars a day—"

"Times the number of guests."

"Can you—"

"Make a profit that way?" Rice smiled again. "What do you think?"

She didn't disappoint him. "I think that was my last stupid question for the day. When has Sheldon Rice ever *not* made a profit?"

"Very good, Miss Chan. The other parks sell tickets until the guests are packed in like sardines. No matter to them that the folks have aching heads and backs and feet from standing in lines all day. Or that the kiddies are fussing and whining because just how exciting is it to look at some old lady's backside for half an hour while you're waiting to board a three minute ride?"

Nancy Chan wrinkled her nose. "I hadn't really thought about it, but there's nothing like a slow-moving line on a hot day to make a kid—"

"—want to puke."

She laughed again, and in spite of her youth there was nothing girlish or coy about her laughter. "Mr. Rice," she began.

"Sheldon," he interrupted.

15

"Sheldon. I have to say, you aren't at all what I expected."

"That's how I've gotten to where I am in life, never being, never *doing*, what others might expect. Catch someone off guard, and you have the advantage." Rice's glance strayed to the broad expanse of tinted glass across the room behind her.

He stood abruptly and began to take off his jacket, then walked to a small closet to the right of his desk. After hanging up the jacket, he removed his cuff links and began to roll up the sleeves of his white shirt.

If Miss Chan was unnerved by his actions, it didn't show in her eyes.

"Would you care to accompany me on a short trip?" he asked, loosening his tie.

"A trip?"

He nodded in the direction of the glass wall. "My helicopter looks to be on final approach. I have some business I must attend to at The Park; I'm on my way there right now. You can come with me and have a look for yourself, if you like. Decide if it's worth the price of admission or not."

For the first time since she'd arrived in his office, she appeared at a loss.

He shrugged his way into his leather flight jacket. "I'll have you back in the city by five."

"I . . . I have another interview scheduled."

"Ah, well, of course if duty calls."

"Although maybe I could cancel. . . ."

Rice read her and knew what it would take to bring her along. "You *would* be the first member of the press to tour the grounds."

"Then yes," she said quickly. "I'll go."

Sometimes it was all so damned easy. He smiled at her. "Good."

Five minutes later they were airborne. Shortly thereafter the San Francisco skyline disappeared as the silver-and-blue helicopter followed the coast north. The Pacific Ocean sparkled with reflected sunlight, and whitecapped waves pounded the shore.

It wasn't often that he noticed such things, but for a few moments at least, Sheldon Rice admired the view, both of the California coastline, and of the contour of Nancy Chan's legs.

Chapter Two

The Park

His sneakers squeaked as he hurried down the hall toward the Computer Command Center, but Wesley Aloysius Davison was so absorbed in thought that the sound didn't register.

The passenger loading time for the Water Devil ride exceeded his projections by a full ninety seconds. A minute and a half didn't sound like much, but over the course of a day, it would add up. Perhaps enough to impact the ride and violate the prime directive: Thou shalt not allow a line to form.

With his tongue, he shifted the jawbreaker he was sucking on from one side of his mouth to the other, then experimentally positioned it between his molars to see if it was of a size he could bite into.

Nope. But getting there.

He worked it around between his cheek and his back teeth. There it protruded like a peculiarly symmetrical growth of some kind.

"Hey, Wes," a voice called.

He raised a hand in acknowledgment, but continued onward without breaking pace. Anyone who wanted to talk to him knew where he could be found.

Wesley reached the door to the Center and entered his access code into the lock panel. The light switched from red to green and the door whished open.

NASA's Mission Control had nothing on 3-C; the nerve center of The Park rivaled anything the big boys had to play with. All that was missing was the view from space . . . and the cost overruns.

A contingent of five engineers turned en masse as he entered. "There you are," Perkins said with more than a hint of exasperation. "You know the boss is due in any minute, don't you?"

Wesley felt the door closing behind him as the cool displaced air found its way through a tear in the seat of his jeans. "I know."

"And you know that he'll want *all* of us here to answer his questions—"

"Hold that thought," Wesley said. He'd noticed a caution light flickering on the main operations board and headed in that direction. The others parted like the Red Sea to let him through.

He stood on tiptoe with his face mere centimeters from the pertinent sector of the board and contemplated his options. The light indicated that the air pressure in the pneumatic lines was hovering at just below normal. They'd had similar problems with the pressure readings before, but he had a gut instinct that in this case it might be a faulty sensor rather than a true malfunction.

Wesley thumped the caution light with an index finger, but the damned thing continued to flicker. "Can someone go underground," he asked, "and check out the gauges at the compressor?"

"Is that really necessary?"

"I think so, yes." He sucked the jawbreaker reflectively while scanning the rest of the board. When he was satisfied that nothing else was out of order, he turned. The five of them were standing there with their arms folded across their chests, watching him with narrowed eyes, their resentment almost palpable.

"Now?" Perkins asked. Perkins was the senior engineer among them, and their apparent spokesman.

19

Wesley looked from face to stony face. To a man, they were daring him to pull rank, to make it a direct order. He was tempted to call their bluff, if they were bluffing, but reason—or caution—prevailed. "Never mind. I'll take care of it myself."

He moved so quickly to the door that it couldn't open fast enough and he was forced to stand for a few seconds until there was space to squeeze through. Neither did it close in time to cut off the not-so-whispered remarks that followed him.

". . . smart-ass kid . . ."

". . . snot-nosed brat . . ."

". . . young punk . . ."

". . . damn know-it-all. . ."

Ready or not, Wesley bit down on the candy hard enough to make it crack, then chewed the remains. He couldn't even taste the jawbreaker's center—the best part—and that made him mad.

Right, sure, that's why you're mad.

He rounded the corner, heading for the staff elevator, and hoping that he wouldn't run into anyone just now. Once there, he jabbed the call button with a bit more force than necessary.

He shouldn't let them get to him. It wasn't the first time he'd been called those names, or worse. And with the way his life was going so far, it probably wouldn't be the last.

The funny thing was, he kind of understood how they felt. Here he was, twenty years old last Valentine's Day, and he was their supervisor, second in authority only to Rice.

True, he *had* been in diapers when two of his "team" started work for the company, and he had leapfrogged over them to take the top job. Not that it had been a power play on his part; Sheldon Rice hired him out of Cal Tech a month prior to graduation.

At the tender age of seventeen, he'd joined Rice Enterprises as project manager, director of operations, facility design coordinator, supervising engineer, and chief executive officer.

He'd missed out, or so the company joke went, on being named crossing guard.

"I want the best," Rice had said the day the contracts were signed, "and you, my boy, are the best."

All modesty aside, Rice was right. He was the best. He had breezed through high school in two years, graduated *magna cum laude* from Stanford with his engineering degree at the age of fifteen, and had been vigorously courted by the Massachusetts Institute of Technology before deciding on Cal Tech.

During the spring break of his first year at Cal Tech, while the other students were drinking themselves blind and pissing off hotel balconies down in Palm Springs, he'd designed a corkscrew roller coaster for his independent study assignment.

The ride was faster, sleeker, and had a tighter spiral than any roller coaster in operation. It incorporated lasers in an innovative pattern of light that could only be called surreal. It was dazzling, dizzying, and disorienting. In short, the perfect ride.

He called it the Death Spiral.

Unbeknownst to him, his adviser had worked as a consultant for Magic Mountain in Valencia, as well as for Knott's Berry Farm. The adviser showed his design and specifications to someone—Wesley still wasn't sure exactly who—and before he knew what had hit him, the Death Spiral was the subject of a savage bidding war and he was being acclaimed in *Time* and *Newsweek* as the Boy Wonder of the industry.

The rest was history: Rice had won the war by outsavaging the competition.

Now Wesley had a huge corner office on the fourteenth floor of The Park's Place, the headquarters-hotel which overlooked the 1,001-acre grounds. He lived in a penthouse suite which occupied the entire fifteenth floor. *And* he earned a seven-figure base salary, which was subject to doubling via bonuses.

No wonder the others resented him.

The elevator finally arrived—with the flurry of activity go-

21

ing on, it must have stopped at every floor — and he stepped inside.

"Where to?" asked a timid-looking woman he recognized as one of the clerks in accounting.

"Into the belly of the beast," he said, unwrapping another jawbreaker and popping it into his mouth. "Sublevel Two."

The underground, too, was swarming, attributable no doubt to Rice's imminent arrival. Technicians in white jumpsuits roved throughout the maze of machinery, checking off items on the sheafs of forms on their clipboards. A supervisor in a silver-and-blue electric minicart drove along the main aisle, stopping at intervals to confer with his charges.

The decibel level of the turbines and generators was near deafening. Wesley took a hard hat off a rack and put it on, adjusting the padded earflaps.

The protective gear reduced the noise, but made him feel almost as if he were swimming underwater, able to hear his own breath sounds and the beating of his heart. The effect was eerie, isolated, unsettling. . . .

He grinned at his own willingness to be frightened, then took a quick look at the schematic etched onto the brass-plated wall to confirm which was the most direct route to the air compressors.

Someone tapped him on the shoulder and he flinched in spite of himself.

"He's here," the supervisor mouthed.

Wesley held his thumb and forefinger in the okay sign to show he understood, then pointed to the schematic and the area he was going to.

"Ten minutes," he mouthed back.

The supervisor shrugged elaborately and tapped the face of his watch a couple of times before gesturing toward the ceiling above them.

Don't keep him waiting, Wesley interpreted. He searched his repertoire of pantomime for a suitable reply, but when he couldn't think of anything simply shook his head.

The supervisor drew an index finger menacingly across his throat, laughed, got into his little cart, and drove away.

Wesley was wrong on two counts.

First, it took thirty minutes to locate the problem, and second, gut instincts or not, the problem proved to be caused by a series of pinpoint holes in an air-line. He found it using a trick he'd learned at a neighborhood gas station as a boy, by applying liquid detergent along yard after yard of rubber hosing; the escaping air produced tiny soap bubbles.

He cleaned off the detergent, wrapped duct tape around the hose as a temporary measure, then flagged a six-foot length for replacement.

When he finished, Wesley retraced his steps, heading for the elevator. The supervisor looked surprised to see him, and putted along after him in the minicart.

The noise hadn't diminished one whit, but the supervisor was determined to be heard. "Better your ass than mine," the man yelled, coming up beside him.

"I can't tell you how touched I am by your concern," Wesley shouted back.

He arrived at 3-C to find the workstations deserted. He'd left the door to his office locked, but it was standing wide open and he heard voices coming from within. He walked a bit hesitantly in that direction.

His ears were ringing but not badly enough to keep him from hearing what was being said. Wesley stood to the right of the door where he could listen without being seen, trying not to think of the times as a child when he'd done the same. Trying to forget that never once had he overheard anything good. . . .

"It's not *only* that he's young, Mr. Rice, but how god-damned young he is. There are times I'd swear he's fresh out of grade school."

Wesley heard Rice's distinctive laugh, which started as a

23

bray before ending in a snort. "There's a lot to be said for youth, Perkins. Particularly for brilliant youth, which the boy is."

"Brilliant I'll give you, but he doesn't fit in, doesn't seem to want to. He's not a team player. Hasn't a clue how to act. Plus, he's self-absorbed, always off doing his own thing—"

"That's what I hired him for. His 'own thing' is gonna make me a rich man. Make that, an even richer man."

"Well, I'm not in a position to argue that. But all the designing's been done, and I think . . . that is, we all think . . . his presence is counterproductive."

"Oh?"

"To be perfectly frank, he's something of a slob, and worse than that—"

Wesley realized with a start that the Center wasn't as deserted as he'd thought. He detected movement out of the corner of his eye, and saw a young oriental woman standing a few feet away.

When their eyes met, she gave him a tentative smile, then held her hands out toward him, palms showing, as though urging him back. He took the cue and crossed among the computer consoles to the main door. When he stepped into the beam of the electronic eye, the door opened.

"Oh, hello," she said as if he'd just arrived. This time, the voices in his office fell silent. "You must be Mr. Davison."

"I am." He was grateful for the implied respect in her use of 'mister' but even that was overshadowed by his relief that his own voice did not betray his aggravation. "And you are?"

"Nancy Chan, of the *San Jose Beacon*."

He admired her style; she said her name as if he should know it, but having lived in the area while at Stanford, he was well aware that the newspaper she worked for was a weekly throwaway that depended on its outrageous personal columns for whatever readership it had.

"Are you here—" he suddenly had to clear his throat— "doing an interview?"

"Actually, I'd like to talk to you if—"

Sheldon Rice chose that moment to appear in the doorway.

At six foot four and two hundred pounds, he took up most of it. "Wesley, We were about ready to send out a search party for you. You had us worried."

"You don't have to worry about me," Wesley said, addressing Perkins, although he couldn't see the back-stabbing weasel. "I can take care of myself."

Chapter Three

Nancy Chan turned toward the window, ostensibly to admire the view of the late afternoon sun over the ocean, in reality to hide a smile.

This young genius she'd heard and read so much about, this wizard of high tech, this one-man brain trust, could serve as national poster boy for the Associated Wimps and Nerds of America.

Not that he was an unattractive kid—he had puppy dog brown eyes and a head of sandy blond curls—but he was slight of build and was only a couple of inches over five feet tall. His jeans were a tad too long, and the cuffs were frayed where they skimmed the ground.

The laces of his tennis shoes had broken in numerous places and had been tied in a bevy of knots rather than replaced. He had the requisite row of pens and pencils in his shirt pocket, *and* also a couple of small screwdrivers, a wire stripper, and one of those pointy things she remembered, not too fondly, from her high school geometry class. A compass, that was it.

Apparently, like any good scout, Wesley Davison believed in being prepared.

More tellingly, though, he had a keen, attentive look on his face, as if he were concentrating and didn't want to miss anything. When their eyes had met, she'd imagined that she could feel him searching her soul.

That had given her a shiver.

Even now, with her back turned, she could sense his energy and intensity. It reminded her of a photograph she'd been shown a year or two ago of a smiling young woman whose hair was literally standing on end from a buildup of static electricity in the air. A few seconds later, a lightning bolt had struck her dead.

Nancy would wager that the atmosphere in this room, at this moment, was every bit as charged.

The boy might be brilliant, as Sheldon Rice had said, but was he ever *wired!*

"—make a few calls and then I'll show you around, as promised."

She realized belatedly that Rice was speaking to her, and she nodded as though she'd been listening all along, which she should have been. Luckily, the voice-activated microcassette recorder in her purse would have caught what she'd missed. "That will be fine," she said, turning to face them with her warmest artificial smile.

The third man, Perkins, made a show of checking his watch. "Excuse me, Mr. Rice, but I need to call about those processors before the close of business—"

"Whatever," Rice said dismissively, and put his hand on Wesley's shoulder. "Why don't you accompany Miss Chan to the executive lounge and see that she's comfortable while she's waiting?"

Again, the young man's eyes probed hers. "Sure, no problem."

Superman and his X-ray vision were nothing compared to this kid.

"So, Wesley," Nancy said as they walked down the hallway side by side, "tell me what it's like working for 'Minute' Rice?"

He looked at her curiously. "How'd you know they call him that?"

27

"I'm an investigative reporter. It's my job to know what the employees call the boss, and why."

Wesley shrugged. "It's pretty obvious why. Everything he wants, he wants right this minute. He hasn't a lot of patience."

"That's exactly what my exhaustive, painstaking, and thorough research uncovered." She'd hoped to amuse him by making fun of her own efforts, but he remained poker-faced. "But answer the question. How do you like working for the man?"

"Didn't your research uncover that?"

"Well, that's the interesting part. In all of the interviews you've given, you've never been quoted on that particular subject."

"No one's ever asked."

They approached a four-way intersection, and turned left into a corridor which led to a set of double doors. Wesley unclipped his company photo I.D. card and slid it through a card reader; the doors audibly unlocked.

"I find that hard to believe," she said.

"What's unbelievable about it?" he asked, holding the door for her.

"I know reporters. And everyone knows Rice's reputation, that he's not an easy man to work for. Put two and two together and what do you"—she paused, taking a look around—"get?"

The executive lounge was decorated in a southwestern style, with warm earth tones and clay pots and kachina dolls. It was a far cry from the sleek glass, brass, and leather motif she'd taken note of throughout the rest of Rice's enterprises.

"Whoa, what is this?"

The whiz kid bounced on his heels. "Amazing, isn't it? The third Mrs. Rice did this. They were divorced last year, but apparently she had it written into the final settlement that the room would stay as is." He dropped onto one of the couches. "I guess he's not an easy man to be married to, either."

Nancy did a three-sixty, taking in the decor. It wasn't impersonal the way the more modern stuff was, but had a very distinct character. It was warm, welcoming, comfortable, everything Rice was not.

"I like it," she said finally. She took a seat opposite him, crossed her legs, and rubbed absently at her ankle. "But back to more important things . . . where were we?"

"You were asking how it is to work for Sheldon Rice, and I wasn't answering."

She had to admire his bluntness. A nerd but not a typical nerd. "Why not?"

"Because," he said with a grim smile, "I don't bite the hand that feeds me."

"There are a lot of hands out there that'd be more than willing to feed you," she countered, rather ingeniously, she thought.

He shook his head. "Miss Chan, if all you want to talk about is how difficult Mr. Rice is, you've got the wrong guy. I'm happy here."

She wondered if he knew how miserable he looked. Had he forgotten that she'd overheard what Perkins had told Rice? Did he think she hadn't seen the stricken expression on his face?

Maybe he thought Rice's defense of him was the result of something other than extraordinary greed. Maybe he thought Rice was on his side.

If so, the kid was in for a rude awakening.

And what was it he'd said? That he could take care of himself?

Not likely, she thought. Not damned likely.

"All right then," she said, changing tactics, "why don't you tell me about the stipulation in your contract with Rice Enterprises that requires the company to cover a week's stay at The Park and all travel expenses for five disadvantaged kids per month?"

Wesley Davison astonished her by blushing. "Is there anything wrong with that?"

"No, not at all. But I'd like to know the story behind it. It

29

is an unusual matter, contractually speaking." She glanced around at the decorating efforts of the third Mrs. Rice. "Although perhaps not unprecedented."

"Let's just say, it was something I wanted to do. Okay?"

Was she imagining that she could hear the crackle of static electricity, could smell ozone in the air? Of course she was, but . . .

"Okay," she said. "We'll leave it at that."

Chapter Four

Boston, Massachusetts

Dinah Fremont had slipped off her shoes, the better to feel the warmth radiating from the space heater. One of the hazards of working late was that the building superintendent turned down — or maybe turned off — the central heating after five o'clock.

In either case, it made for chilly after hours. Some nights it was so cold she could see her breath. Some nights ice formed on the *inside* of the windows.

She shivered even thinking about it. Dinah curled her toes, luxuriating in the waves of heat, and thought longingly of going home to sit before a roaring fire and sip hot mulled cider. Or maybe she'd stop at Legal Seafood for a bowl of their New England clam chowder. . . .

"I know that look," a voice said from the doorway. "Wishing you'd taken that Florida job?"

Dinah smiled at Peter Abbott and shook her head. "It hasn't even crossed my mind."

"Right. Why would it?" He came into the office and sat on the corner of her desk, pushing aside the take-out chef's salad she'd bought but hadn't had time to eat. "And if I believe *that*, you've got some swampland you want to sell me."

"Yes, in Florida," she said, and laughed. "What are you

doing here? I thought I had the place to myself."

"Trying to catch up on paperwork, what else?" He held out a bulging manila folder for her inspection. "These are from August, if you can believe it. August!"

She patted her own stack of files. "September."

Peter was co-chairman with her of Get A Way, a private philanthropic organization funded initially by a grant from the Dukakis administration, but which now relied primarily on donations. She, Peter, and their part-time secretary, Joanne, were the only ones remaining from what had once been a twelve-person staff.

But things were looking up.

"Did Joanne tell you what came in this afternoon's mail?" she asked. The precious envelope was locked in her drawer, less to keep it from being misplaced than to keep her from reading it over and over again until the paper disintegrated.

"I haven't even seen Joanne today. I had a meeting over at Social Services at ten, so I went straight there—and only just escaped with my life, I'll have you know. Brutal, that place. What came in the mail?"

Dinah smiled, savoring the anticipation of telling him the good news, but not quite ready to do so. "You'll never guess."

"The landlord's changed his mind and isn't raising our rent?"

"No. Better."

"Hmm." He opened the cellophane pack of saltines that had come with her salad and stuck one whole into his mouth. "Hmm."

"It's something we thought we didn't stand a chance at getting."

He chewed thoughtfully and swallowed. "Season tickets to the Celtics games?"

She reached across the desk and gave him a little shove. "Be serious."

"Okay, not the Celtics. Certainly not the Sox. What does that leave?"

"How about . . . The Park."

Peter blinked. "You're kidding. You are kidding, aren't you?"

Dinah unlocked the drawer and pulled out the envelope which she held so that he could see the return address with its silver-and-blue logo.

"I'm not kidding. Get A Way has been chosen to—*we* have been chosen to—administrate the Disadvantaged Youth Program for The Park."

His jaw dropped. He took the envelope from her, his eyes searching hers as he withdrew the letter and unfolded it. Then he began to read, silently scanning the paragraphs she had committed to memory.

"This is incredible," he said a minute later. He turned it over, as if expecting to find *April Fool* printed in huge letters on the other side. "I didn't think we stood a chance in hell of getting this."

"Me neither."

"I mean, Make A Wish gets most of the media notice, I thought for sure they were the front-runners. Or if not them, then Dreams Come True."

"I thought so too, but maybe they're overextended. Whatever the reason, it doesn't matter." She gently took the letter from him, refolded the thick ivory stationery, and returned it to its envelope, which she put safely back in the drawer. "We got it."

They grinned at each other almost drunkenly. It had been a tough couple of years, but administering the DYP would change all of that.

"We can have an impact," Peter said, "make a difference, both for the kids and Get A Way. We won't be anonymous anymore. Shit, we made it!"

"Don't forget it'll be a lot of work," she cautioned. "We'll be getting thousands of applications and it's only three months till The Park opens. We have to choose the first five kids, arrange their transportation to California, hire a chaperone to accompany them—"

Peter stood abruptly and began to pace. "We can do it. We'll switch Joanne to full-time, hire a couple of temps to help us get up to speed, and—"

"—and I have an idea."

"See? You have an idea, already. This is so . . . so . . . great!" He held his arms up, as though to embrace the heavens. "An idea!"

"Pete . . ."

He stopped, turned, and gave her a sheepish look. "I'm getting carried away, aren't I?"

"You might say that."

"Well, don't worry. I won't blow it for us." He sat again on the desk, then immediately stood and half danced across the room.

Dinah leaned back in her chair. "Pete?"

He seemed oblivious, shadow boxing and huffing like an old steam engine.

"Pete? Could you sit down for a minute? It's tiring me out, watching you."

"Huh?"

"Sit down." She got up and went around the desk, grabbed an armful of files off the second chair, dumped them on the floor beside it, and motioned toward the seat. "Sit," she repeated.

"Yes boss."

She padded in her stockinged feet back to her chair. "Anyway, as I was saying . . ."

"Exactly what *is* this perspicacious idea of yours, Miss Fremont?" he asked, doing a rather lame William Buckley impersonation.

Dinah stuck out her tongue.

"I'm sorry." He ran a hand through his thinning hair. "I'll come back to earth."

"Good."

"Good," he repeated. "You were saying?"

"My idea is, since we have such a short time to get the program in place, we should have a kind of lottery to help us pick the local programs we'll draw from."

Pete shook his head. "I'm not sure I understand what you mean."

34

"What I was thinking is, we can choose five states, and only review applications from programs in those five. Right off, we've cut the review process tenfold. In theory, at least."

"Not bad. How do we choose which five states?"

"Do you still have that dart board in your office?"

Pete nodded. "How do you think I keep in such fine physical condition?"

"Playing darts?" Dinah laughed. "No, forget I asked. Anyway, you have darts and I have"—she gestured toward the wall—"a huge map of the United States."

"Gotcha. I'll get the darts."

While she waited, Dinah crossed over to the map and with her finger traced a line from Boston to San Francisco, and, more slowly, back again. If only, she thought, there was a way . . .

"Here we are." Pete gave her three darts and kept two for himself. "You go first."

"This one," she said, holding the first dart by the barrel, "is a ringer."

"Excuse me?"

"Maybe I shouldn't do this, but there's a girl I have mind who really has to go on this trip." She stuck the tip of the dart neatly into the large black circle representing Boston.

"I can live with that." He scratched his nose. "Who is she? Anyone I know?"

Dinah took a step back and admired her handiwork. "I don't even *know* her, and I've been working with her on and off for a number of years now. She's a tough little cookie, but I think there's a chance that this . . . this will help."

"The first of many tough little cookies, I'm sure. Now, it's my turn. Step back and watch the master at work." He moved into position, took careful aim, then closed his eyes and threw.

The second dart landed in California, missing the Mexican border by the width of the point. A fraction of an inch separated the dart from the Pacific.

"San Diego," he said, almost triumphantly.

"Wait a minute, what's this?" Dinah knew he'd grown up

35

in the area. "Another ringer?"

"You wish." His smile was self-congratulatory. He buffed his nails on his wool sweater. "I got mine fair and square."

"So be it. But the rest have to be truly random, agreed?"

"Agreed."

In the end, they had two specific cities, Boston and San Diego, and the states of Iowa, Colorado, and New Mexico.

"So," Pete said, helping her into her coat as they prepared to leave a little while later. "How does it feel, Miss Fremont?"

Dinah glanced at the map, where the darts remained, and thought of Celeste. "Not bad, Mr. Abbott," she said. "Not bad at all."

Chapter Five

"Child, don't be telling me you're going out alone tonight, not out on *those* streets. Those mean streets will chew you up and spit you out. I can barely hold my own, and I wasn't born yesterday, I'll have you know."

Celeste Donatelli refrained momentarily from applying another coat of mascara, and glanced from her own reflection in the mirror to that of her Aunt Violet who was pacing in the background. "No kidding," she said flatly, "and you look so young."

For once, though, her aunt ignored the taunt. "You know your father doesn't want you out running around on a school night."

"I don't see why not." She used the tip of the mascara wand to separate the eyelashes which were sticking together. "I'm not going to school tomorrow anyway—"

"Oh yes you are, if I have to take you by the hand and walk you there my own self."

Celeste said nothing. It wasn't worth arguing, mainly because going to school and staying at school were two different things. Cutting class was easy—all the kids did it—and the teachers didn't seem to care if there was one less animal in the zoo. Or maybe they cared but realized they couldn't stop it.

She squeezed a fat drop of the new liquid rouge she'd

bought onto a fingertip, then dotted it along her cheek. The color, as she blended it on, was slightly pinker than her usual shade. She wasn't sure she liked it, though; with her café-au-lait complexion, she thought maybe the dusky rose tones looked better.

Aunt Violet, still looming in the background, put her hands on hips made ample by bearing five children. "Are you listening to me?"

How could she not? Her aunt's voice was loud enough to raise the roof.

"I am," Celeste said, "and so are the neighbors."

"My, girl, but you have a smart mouth."

"Runs in the family," she said, and then ducked as her father's eldest sister swatted in the general direction of her head. "Watch the hair."

"Oh, the hair is important, but this"—Aunt Violet leaned forward and rapped on her temple—"this is what? Space for rent?"

"Ouch!" Celeste pushed her aunt's hand away. "What's it to you, anyway?" She grabbed a tissue to wipe the excess rouge off her fingers. "You're not my mama. No one's my mama."

That had been her trump card since she was six years old, and as usual, it worked. The angry expression faded from her aunt's face, and was replaced by a look of sorrow. Or pity.

"I may not be your mama," Aunt Violet said in a near whisper, "but we are blood kin and I care about what happens to you."

"Nothing's happening to me—"

"Isn't it? I've seen the trash you've been hanging around with—"

"They're my friends."

"Then your friends are scum."

Celeste raised her eyes to the water-stained ceiling. "Help me, Mr. Rogers, but I'm living in the wrong fucking neighborhood—"

"Watch your mouth! "

"—and there aren't any fucking *nice* kids to play hopscotch with."

Her aunt's hand flashed again, this time connecting sharply. "I never abided with that kind of language from my own kids, and I won't be listening to it from you, young lady."

Celeste touched her fingers to her cheek, somewhat amazed that she could feel heat coming off her skin. She returned her glance to the mirror; a red mark was beginning to form.

"If I'd known you were gonna do that," she said with all the chilled nonchalance she could muster, "I wouldn't have bothered with the rouge."

Her words and attitude had the desired effect; Aunt Violet gasped, and her eyes widened in shock and disbelief, the way someone might look if she'd picked up a rock and found some awful thing wriggling beneath it, plump and dead-white.

Which should teach them, Celeste thought, not to pick up rocks.

Her aunt looked pained. "What on earth's gotten into you, girl?"

Celeste didn't answer. The truth would get her slapped even harder, and this time she might not be able to keep the tears from her eyes.

"You didn't used to be this way. You were the sweetest little child. . . ."

"And what did being *sweet* get me? A mother who ran off and a father who's never home."

"I won't listen to you talk bad about your daddy. You know he's got to work," Aunt Violet said, but her voice was kind of faraway and distracted, as though her mind wasn't on what she was saying. "Well . . . I guess I'd better be on my way . . . got to get dinner on . . ."

In spite of herself, Celeste felt a pang of sympathy. All five of her cousins were grown and living away from home, busy with their own lives. The dinners Aunt Violet made these days were servings for one—a soft-boiled egg and

39

toast, or soup and half a sandwich—which she ate in front of the TV in the living room.

Photographs of the "children" covered an entire wall, and Celeste suspected that Aunt Violet relied on the pictures to keep her company.

If there was anything Celeste understood, it was how it felt to be lonely.

That was why there was no way she'd be staying home alone tonight.

Boston had enjoyed a relatively mild winter, only to be surprised by a sudden snowstorm the night before. Always restless at night, she'd gotten out of bed to watch it fall, and it had soothed her.

A fresh blanket of snow made everything beautiful.

But in the city, snow didn't stay white for very long. Now it was just one more depressing thing to consider as she went to meet Darla in the Zone.

The Combat Zone was the city's infamous red-light district. Since she'd grown up within walking distance, it held little fascination for her. She'd seen it too many times in daylight to be fooled by the neon lights, and knew the filth that the darkness hid.

By the time she was eleven, it had gotten to where she scarcely noticed the whistles and catcalls.

Tonight, as often happened, she had unintentionally picked up a sidewalk Romeo, a guy who followed a step or two behind her issuing an urgent invitation.

"Fifty, you want fifty? I think I've got fifty for you, honey."

Celeste kept walking. Here the snow had turned to a brown slush and it seeped in through the ventilation holes in her aerobics shoes. She had dressed tonight in her fitness freak clothes—a black leotard, faded skin-tight jeans, black leg-warmers, and a denim jacket—but now wished she'd worn something warmer.

"Seventy bucks, huh?" The man was close enough that she could smell the booze on his breath and the cheap after-shave he wore.

"Get real," she said, breaking her own rule of never speaking.

"Come on, seventy is a lot of money. You know how many hours I gotta work for seventy dollars?"

She had to stop at a corner for traffic and she practically broke her thumb pushing the crossing button. "Change, damn you," she said.

"You a virgin, honey?"

Somehow, he had snaked his arm under her jacket, and she felt the clamminess of his hand on the bare skin of her back. Disgusted, Celeste twisted away.

She ran out into the street, dodging the cars which honked and splashed her with the icy remains of the melting snow. A taxi driver leaned on his horn and swerved to avoid her, missing her by inches.

When she made it to the other side, she whirled and gestured obscenely at the creep who'd nearly gotten her killed, but he'd already turned his attentions to a striking miniskirted redhead whom Celeste knew to be a man. Or a male, anyway.

"Pervert," she said, and laughed uneasily. Once she'd dreamt that she'd yelled that at a sleazoid who was annoying her, and every person on the street had turned and said in unison, "Yes? You called?"

So, with her jeans soaking and her feet near frozen, she continued on her way.

Up ahead in the distance, she could see the pink neon cane that accented the black hat of the Top Hat Club, the strip joint where Darla worked.

"Hey, what happened to you?" Gus asked when she came up to the bar.

"Nothing." She leaned across the counter and gave him a quick hug; as usual, he smelled of beer and pepperoncini and feta cheese. "Am I late? Has Darla been on yet?" The runway lights were off.

41

"She's changing for the second show." Gus tilted her chin up. Fine dark hair formed curlicues on the backs of his plump fingers. "What's the matter? You look like you lost your best friend."

"How could that be?" She touched her hand to his face. "I've got you and Darla."

That she had pleased him showed in his eyes. "I take care of my girls," he said.

Tony, one of the regulars, made a kissing noise. "All this tenderness is like to make me gag."

"Choke instead." Tony, she could live without.

"You're a clever girl," Tony said. "Let me ask you a question. . . ."

Celeste groaned. He'd been asking the same old question since she'd first started coming to the Top Hat. Still, he didn't seem to mean any harm—he kept his hands to himself—and Gus said he'd been a customer since before she was even born, so she humored him by playing along.

"What it is . . . I been wondering . . . are you Russian?"

"No, Tony, I'm not."

"Are you Irish?"

She took the free Pepsi Gus pushed across the bar to her and sipped at it before giving the standard answer: "Irish? No, I don't think so, Tony. Why do you ask?"

"Well, I've heard of Black Irish and Black Russians, but until you showed up, I never in my life had heard of a Black Italian, Miss Celeste Donatelli."

For some reason, it cracked him up to say that. In fact, her skin was lighter than his and she wasn't Italian at all. Her mother was white, of German heritage. Her father was black and two generations removed from Jamaica. Her surname had been chosen because, her father said, she didn't belong in either world, and she was better off knowing that from the start.

None of this did she feel inclined to explain to anyone. Instead she laughed with the guys at the bar long enough to be considered polite, and then excused herself to go talk to Darla.

Darla's new costume looked suspiciously like the uniform of one of Boston's better private schools. Except it was unlikely that the little girls who wore them also wore black lace G-strings underneath. Or had butterflies tattooed on their tushes.

"What do you think?" Darla twirled and the plaid skirt flared as intended.

"An A plus." She sat on the edge of the makeup table and watched as Darla strapped on black patent leather shoes over her white anklets.

"You won't believe it, I could hardly believe it, but I found another pair of these exact shoes in Rosalind's size. I had to buy them, of course. You should see how cute she looks."

Rosalind was Darla's two-year-old daughter, and she really was a living doll. "How is she feeling? Did she get over her cold?"

"Oh yeah." Darla rummaged through her jewelry box and pulled out a tiny cross on a silver chain. "She's tough, like her mother."

"I guess." Darla was having problems with the clasp and Celeste motioned for her to come over so she could help with it. "What's it like, being a mom?"

"Fun sometimes. Other times not so fun."

"Huh." Celeste chewed on her lip as she untwisted the small catch and fastened the chain. "There you go."

"Thanks."

"Darla, do you ever . . ."

"Ever what?"

She pretended to be preoccupied with a spot on her jeans. "Never mind."

"Ever what?" Darla persisted.

"It's nothing. Forget it."

"No, come on. You were going to ask me something."

Celeste hesitated, and then attempted a smile. "Do you ever see Rosalind's daddy?"

43

"That bum? No. Why would I?"

"Well, for one thing, he could give you money to help out—"

"Fat chance. Every dollar he gets his hands on goes up his nose."

"But doesn't he want to see his own daughter?"

Darla gave her a hard look, very much like the look she used to warn off those customers who might be tempted to reach out and touch. "What's up, Celeste? This isn't about me or Rosalind or her dad, is it?"

Celeste crossed to the window overlooking the alley. For some reason, the businesses on the block kept their trash cans locked behind iron gates, but the ripe smell of rotting garbage defied containment. She shut the window and then turned, sitting on the narrow sill.

"I'm late," she said.

"Not again. I thought you were using something?"

"Yeah, well, shit happens."

Darla raised her eyebrows but didn't comment. She took a cigarette out of a crushed pack on the dressing table and lit a match with her thumbnail. She took a deep drag, held it for a second or two, and exhaled. "So what are you gonna do?"

"Have it, I guess."

"Oh, Celeste."

"You did it."

"I haven't done *it* yet. I mean, I had Rosalind, but that's only the start of *it*. Raising a baby alone's not easy."

Celeste thought of her father working two jobs and shook her head. "I was thinking, you and me could share a place, and take turns watching the kids. I could maybe get a day job—"

"Doing what?"

"Something, I don't know."

"You'd better know." Darla flicked her cigarette in the general direction of the ashtray. "It's not like playing house."

"I didn't say it would be."

"And have you thought about what *he's* gonna say when

44

you tell him the good news that you're quitting on him?"

"Neville?"

"Yes, Neville."

She had thought about it—he would not be pleased—but what was she supposed to do? Turning up pregnant was one of the hazards of the trade. She couldn't take the Pill. And condoms broke.

"You want my advice, you'd better, you know, get rid of it—"

"*Not* an abortion." Not again.

"—or plan on giving the baby up. Fourteen's too young, girl, way too young."

"I'd be fifteen by then—"

"And I was sixteen." Smoke curled from her nostrils. "Shit. It feels like forever since I was sixteen."

The wistfulness in her friend's voice brought Celeste up short, and for a moment, neither of them spoke.

The intro to Darla's music drifted up. Darla crushed out her cigarette, grabbed her props—a jump rope and a hoop—and started out.

"I may not be, you know, pregnant." Celeste said. I got one of those kits, the kind you do yourself, but you have to do it in the morning."

Darla hesitated at the door even though the whoops and hollers could be heard from down below. "I'll keep my fingers crossed for you. You gonna hang around? We can have a burger afterwards."

"Why not? I got nowhere else to go."

Chapter Six

Jesus Rivera pressed his back against the corrugated aluminum siding that made up the walls of the shack where he lived with his mother, drew his knees up to his chest, and hid his face in his hands.

He wished fervently that he could disappear through the wall, or into the hard-packed dirt of the floor.

He dug his knuckles into his eyes, which stung from the burning of incense, and from the scent of peeled onions, and maybe from tears. His nose was running too, but he had given his kerchief to his mother, who now lay dying in her bed, the priest and Señora Morales at her side.

Their shack had no windows, and only a thick canvas curtain served as the door. He could hear voices from outside, other children yelling and laughing, the soft clucking of the scrawny chickens that were almost, but not quite, too tough to eat.

He heard as well the murmured prayers of the priest, the click of Señora Morales's beads, and his mother's labored breathing.

There had been a dog once which had come into their neighborhood, so thin its ribs showed, one eye clouded

46

blue. Jesus had always wanted a dog—he had no brothers or sisters—and so he had offered the dog a small piece of dried salted beef he'd been chewing on, to try to make the dog follow him home.

The dog seemed interested, and had walked stiffly along after him, trying now and then to wag its tail, but when they reached his home and he gave it the meat as a reward, the animal let the dried beef drop from its mouth, and had begun to chew instead on its tongue.

Specks of foamy blood fell into the dirt, and when they saw this, the other children cried.

Nothing Jesus did would make the dog stop chewing. It had, one of the adults said knowingly, a sickness of the brain. Soon bits of flesh were dropping into the dirt and the crying had turned to screams.

Jesus shouted and chased the other children away, angry at them and the dog and at himself for having such a foolish idea.

The dog died some hours, later, but before it stopped breathing, it had made the sound that had haunted his dreams. Wet, rasping, terrible.

The same sound his mother was making now.

Jesus trembled, in fear and shame. Fear because he didn't know what would become of him, and shame because he was afraid for himself and not for his mother. She had taught him better, but he hadn't learned.

His failure was all the worse because he had been the man of the family since his father had disappeared into *El Norte*. He was eight years old now, and there'd been no word from his father or his father's brother since before his sixth birthday.

The money had stopped coming then, too.

Lupe, the young wife of his father's brother, believed that both men had died or been killed. Everyone knew that beyond the border, the streets were full of bad people who would slice open your throat for a few pesos. Everyone knew at least one person who had not returned from the land of opportunity.

47

Still, they went.

At this moment, Jesus would be willing to offer his throat to their blades, if only to end his misery and that of his mother.

He wiped his damp face on the sleeve of his shirt. The priest was now merely standing by, hands crossed over the battered Bible he held in front of him, his head bowed, and his lips moving silently.

Señora Morales, who had summoned the priest and whose onions stung his eyes, was kneeling beside the cot. Her prayer beads were clenched in her fist, her fist was pressed against her chest.

"Why doesn't he come?" she whispered angrily. "I said I would pay."

The priest shook his head. "There's nothing a doctor can do for her now."

"No? And he can tell that without ever stepping foot from his door?"

"Perhaps he can. Señora Rivera is not the first to die."

Jesus felt his throat tighten at hearing the word from the priest's mouth. He thought they must have forgotten that he was in the room, to speak so bluntly.

"He is afraid," his mother's friend said, not bothering to hide her scorn. *"Hijo de puta."*

The priest held a finger to his lips. "Ssh. There are better times to talk of such things. Elena should pass without harsh words in her ears."

"I would have paid—"

Without warning, his mother's eyes opened, and her body lurched slightly upward off the thin mattress. A trickle of blood escaped from the corner of her mouth and the rasping sound grew louder.

Jesus covered his ears, but doing so left nowhere for his eyes to hide and he saw his mother's face twist in agony, saw her frothing, the way the dog had, and saw a fine spray of blood erupt from her mouth.

He tried to close his eyes, tried to lower his head back to the safety of his knees, but he couldn't move, unable

48

for the moment to even take a breath of his own. Then his own body shuddered and he gasped.

"Mama," he whispered unbelievingly.

And then, by God's grace, his mother's ordeal was over. Her body slumped bonelessly back to the bed. The terrible rasping had stopped.

The priest gave a final blessing. Señora Morales crossed herself and slipped her well-worn prayer beads into the pocket of her apron. Neither of them looked in his direction.

Outside, the children played.

"Jesus?"

A hand touched his shoulder and he raised his head groggily. Had he fallen asleep? It was darker than it had been, but the lamps had been extinguished and it was always dark inside without them.

"Come," Señora Morales said. "You can stay the night with us."

He got clumsily to his feet and nearly fell; his left leg had gone numb and refused to obey. *"Un momento,"* he said. "My leg. . . ."

Señora Morales seemed to understand. She had the pan of peeled onions braced against her hip, and she took a bite out of one of the small ones. "You hungry?" she asked, offering him the onion.

"Sí . . . no . . ." He shook his head. In truth, he didn't know whether it was hunger or fear that was twisting his stomach.

"It's good for the blood."

Blood, he thought, and the images of the afternoon returned to his mind.

He wiped his eyes with the back of his hand and glanced cautiously around the room. The bucket he'd used to get their water was still by the doorway where he'd left it. He hadn't spilled more than a few drops on his way from the water truck.

49

Nearby, his mother's sandals were tucked beneath one of their two straight-backed chairs. He remembered how many times she'd sat on one of those chair, stitching together the straps of her sandals with a large rusty needle he had found for her at the dump.

"So many good things they throw away."

Jesus swallowed and forced his eyes to continue their journey.

Even in the dim light he could see that his mother's cot was not empty. The blanket was drawn up to her neck; she might have been sleeping.

"Come now," Señora Morales said. "They will be coming for her soon."

The Morales home was built of plywood and, with three rooms, was quite grand. The floor was bare earth, but a woven rug covered the ground in the large room where Señora Morales cooked the burritos that her husband sold to make their living.

The air here was fragrant with the scent of roasting beef and pork. Whole potatoes boiled in a huge metal pan on the wood-burning stove. When the potatoes were cooked and cooled, they would be shredded and mixed with the meat and onions.

Early in the morning, the mixture would be fried in lard, spread on fresh flour tortillas, rolled into burritos, and wrapped in brown paper. Señor Morales would pack them into the metal-lined boxes attached to his bicycle cart, and go out to where the people gathered in the fields near the border to sell them.

So good were Señora Morales's burritos that some of those who crossed the border and were caught joked that they had turned themselves in just to taste another one.

The Moraleses were still poor, but not as poor as they had been.

There were six children in the family, all younger than Jesus, and they looked at him with solemn eyes when he came in with their mother.

"You sit down," Señora Morales said, "I must get to work or there will be no food for anyone tomorrow." She placed the onions on the table and went to her stove.

A few minutes later, she handed him a plate of sliced roasted pork and tortillas. "Eat," she commanded, and wagged a finger at the other children. "You don't bother him. Your bellies have never been as empty as his."

Jesus felt his face grow hot, but the smell of the food was overwhelming and it drove other thoughts from his brain. He folded a tortilla around a thick slice of pork, swallowed hard, and began to eat.

Jesus pretended to be asleep, but through the slits of his eyes he watched Señor Morales pace. With the beds full, he had chosen to sleep on the floor by the door of the room the children shared. He could see very clearly into the larger room.

"You cannot be a mother to every child," Señor Morales said. "You were a good friend to Elena Rivera, but being a friend does not mean you must raise her son."

"Jesus is a good boy."

"Good or bad, he is a mouth to feed—"

"There is plenty of food," the señora said. "One burrito less to sell will not matter."

"I am not as sure of that as you are. Even if it is true, Bonita, there are no children older whose clothes he can wear."

"Then what do we do? Lupe is his only family, and she is not fit to care for him even if she would find it in her heart to take him in."

Señor Morales shrugged. "Nothing. We do nothing. In the morning, take him to the church."

"The church?"

"They will arrange for him to go to the orphanage—"

"Even such places run out of beds."

"That is not our concern. We take him to the church

51

and they will see to him."

"But tomorrow? What would it hurt to keep him with us for a day or two more?"

"What it would hurt, my wife, is you. You are already fond of the boy and in two more days it will bring tears to your eyes to send him away. I know the softness of your heart."

Señora Morales did not speak for a moment, and Jesus could tell that she was looking at him. "He is so young to be without a mother."

"He will not be young for long," her husband said, placing his hand on her shoulder. "And that is for the best."

When all was silent, Jesus crept from his makeshift bed. He strapped on his sandals over bare feet—Señora Morales had taken his prized socks which she said could walk on their own—and brushed his hair out of his eyes.

He considered taking one of the blankets. *She'd want you to have it,* a little voice in his head said, but he knew it would be wrong to repay the señora's kindness by stealing from her.

So he crossed the large room, took a final quick look around, and then carefully opened the door. It squeaked a bit, but no one came, and in a heartbeat he was outside in the cool air of night.

He gazed in the direction of what had been his home, but knew there was nothing there for him. The men who had come for his mother's body would have taken anything of value, and who could blame them? Carting the dead away was not a job that anyone envied, and the men could not be certain of being paid for their trouble.

In any case, it was the way things were done. Even at his young age, Jesus understood that.

So he turned, and began the walk toward the border. He would not reach it, he knew, before morning, but he had a plan for getting across in the daylight, a plan that maybe would keep him out of the clutches of the *coyotes*.

He had seen with his own eyes the sly old *coyote* his father had found to smuggle him into America. The man had smiled frequently, and laughed with little reason, but a look in those eyes and it was as though a cloud had passed in front of the sun.

His plan *had* to work.

And if it did not?

He would live in the streets of Tijuana before he would let himself be sent away. He had heard whispered stories of what went on in the orphanages, and he would rather take his chances on the outside. . . .

Jesus walked on. He felt sad that he would not be here when his mother was buried, but when the letters had stopped coming from his father, and there had been no word in a very long time, she had explained to him that even if his father *was* dead, their love and prayers for him would find him no matter how great the distance between them.

He remembered all at once the touch of her fingers on his forehead when she'd stroked his hair, and a lump formed in his throat. Soon he began to cry, but at this late hour there was no one to hear or see him, and he let his tears fall onto the dusty road.

Chapter Seven

McKenna's Creek

The clouds had hidden the moon, and in the darkness, Ezra passed among the trees. He had taken this path so many times before that he didn't need the light, relying instead on memory to find his way.

He walked quickly but softly, so that not even a twig snapped beneath his moccasined feet. Brushing aside the low-hanging branches, and ducking now and then to avoid those limbs too heavy to move, he made it up the incline to the clearing in less than five minutes.

Ezra had always preferred to do his tending at night when it was cooler — and there were fewer watching eyes — but tonight the air was barely stirring and he was perspiring from the climb. He sat on an old tree stump to catch his breath.

It was as quiet as it was dark.

Ezra frowned. At this time of year, there was usually a cacophony of sounds to be heard in the woods. Crickets and frogs, of course, but also the chir of the pine beetles and the annoying drone of mosquitoes which bred in the stagnant pools of water left over from the spring rain.

And usually, too, there would be the calls of the owls who hunted their prey after nightfall, the flutter of wings,

nd the cry of whatever small rodent was being swept up
nd away to its death.

The leaves whispering in the wind, and the wind itself
ighing . . .

It wasn't his presence which had silenced the woods. As
nany years as he'd spent in these hills, he'd become a
art of them. Of course, there was a momentary hush
vhen any one or any *thing* came upon them, but this stillness, this utter silence, was more than that.

The hush, Ezra knew, was the result of instinct, an
wareness on the part of every living creature that some-
hing around it had changed.

This silence, he believed, was different, more akin to
ear than caution. Fear of what, he couldn't say.

But it bothered him, this silence, and so he broke it.

"A fine night," he said, getting up from the stump, us-
ng the handle of the shovel to brace himself, "for tend-
ng."

The ways of tending had been taught to him by his
randmother, dead now for more than seventy-five years,
nd he'd been following them ever since. Most folks might
nd it odd, if they knew about it—another reason he pre-
erred the night—but as far as he was concerned, it served
purpose.

Nothing went to waste.

This night, he had but one to tend to, a young doe
e'd found by the side of the road a month or so ago.
he animal had been struck, he was certain, by one of
ice's big trucks. It was still alive when he came upon it,
s eyes showing white, and trying, even with an obviously
roken back, to regain its feet. He had kept his distance,
nce he knew of few things more dangerous than a mor-
lly injured animal, and waited.

When the doe died, he used a winch and sling to load
into the back of his old Ford pickup, and brought it

here, where the tendings were done. With rope, a pulley, and the sling he was able to drag the limp body up to the clearing. He'd grunted at the effort, and cursed his heart for laboring so.

Then he had staked the doe out, skinning it, and then slitting it open from throat to rectum to hurry decomposition and, eventually, the drying of the bones.

The scavengers native to these woods had been at the carcass, and within two weeks, most of the meat had been eaten away. Ants and flies and maggots had completed the process of stripping flesh from the bones.

Now the bones gleamed a ghostly white in the dim light as the moon peeked from behind the clouds.

Ezra stood above the skeletal remains and brought the shovel down with as much force as he could muster on the slender bone of a leg. The bone, dried and made brittle by exposure to the sun, cracked and splintered.

The time had come, then, to break the bones down to size, and carry them back to the cabin. There, with a stone mortar and pestle, he would grind the fragments into dust, which he would scatter to the wind, so that the earth would be replenished.

He set to work.

Chapter Eight

The Park
April 1992

Wesley Davison stood at the back of the room and surveyed the crowd. There were at least a hundred reporters
in attendance, all waiting for Nancy Chan, The Park's
new public relations chief, to convince them that the up-
coming opening qualified as *news*.

A news story cost essentially nothing. If she succeeded
in piquing the media's interest and convinced them to
cover the story as a genuine matter of interest to their
readers and/or viewers, it could save Sheldon Rice more
than a few bucks in advertising and promotion.

Judging by the looks of practiced boredom on the majority of faces, it would require a hard sell. They knew
they were being set up.

Rice, on the other hand, knew reporters. His personal
chef had provided a lavish display of food on two six-foot-
long tables and with nary an item repeated. There were
the de rigueur items—caviar, pâté, and other hors
d'oeuvres—as well as the more substantial fare, including
huge jumbo shrimp, cracked crab, oysters on the half
shell, a savory roast of beef, thin slices of honey-drizzled
ham, smoked turkey, *and* Peking duck.

There were also immense silver platters of various cheeses, a round of melted Brie, freshly baked breads and rolls, vegetable trays, and an exotic array of out-of-season fruit.

Champagne was being served by waiters in white jackets who circulated constantly and poured discreetly. Coffee and tea were available for the more prudent at a separate table to the left.

The desserts had yet to arrive, but anticipation was running high and there were rumors of spiced pears with a white chocolate sauce, imported Italian rum cakes, and wild blackberries in heavy cream.

Even more impressive than the food—at least in his opinion—was the design of the press room itself. Instead of the customary rows of straight-backed folding chairs, there were three levels of plushly upholstered built-in seats. A fold down arm enabled the user to take notes comfortably. A recessed shelf provided space for an ashtray or, more elegantly, a glass of champagne.

The aisles were wide, and the view of the podium was unrestricted from anywhere in the room. The paneling was real wood, the carpet thick enough to sink into, and the acoustics, fantastic.

Not bad, Wesley thought, for a man who had given up design when he went into development.

Rice himself had not made an appearance, but he was enough of a showman to know when to make the most effective entrance.

Not so Nancy Chan. She had entered through a side door, and for the past five minutes had been fussing with her notes at the dais. The microphone picked up the rustling of the pages.

Wesley glanced at his watch, which confirmed his suspicion that the press conference was to have started by now. Was she stalling or just plain scared? Perhaps her former job at the *Beacon* was becoming more attractive in retrospect.

She looked up finally and quickly scanned the room, one hand shading her eyes against the spotlights. When she turned her head in his direction, he stepped back into the shadows of a service alcove where he knew he couldn't be seen.

Her gaze swept past him, and he breathed a sigh of relief.

He hadn't come to be introduced to the press. In fact, he wasn't supposed to be here at all; Rice wanted to save him for the Grand Opening. But here he was, and for now it suited his purpose to remain anonymous.

That way he could hear what they had to say about his rides.

He grabbed a glass of champagne from a passing waiter—who didn't even flinch at a hand suddenly reaching out from the dark—and drank it down.

"First of all, I'd like to thank all of you on behalf of Sheldon Rice and Rice Enterprises—"

"What's your name, sweetie?" a voice called. "And spell it, please."

"I'm Nancy Chan," she said without missing a beat, "as in Charlie Chan, and I am equally as inscrutable, thank you for asking. I'm also the director of public relations for The Park. We've invited you here today for a preview of an amusement park that is like no other in the world."

Behind and to the right of her, the rear-projection screen lit up with the silver-and-blue Rice logo. The silver shimmered. A nice effect, Wesley thought.

"The Park encompasses a thousand and one acres," she said, and everyone in the room groaned.

"We've got the press kit, honey, so if all you're gonna do is recite *statistics* to us, we've got better things to do with our time."

"I don't," someone else said, "until the champagne stops flowing."

Others laughed, but several of the reporters were getting to their feet.

Nancy, somewhat wide-eyed, first motioned for everyone to take their seats, and when they didn't obey, she put her index and little fingers in her mouth, and whistled like a longshoreman.

"Hey," she said, "sit down or I'll call your managing editors and tell them you never showed up. Then see if you can get reimbursed for mileage—"

For some reason Wesley couldn't fathom, that made everybody laugh. And, surprisingly, it worked. Those who were standing sat down, and for the moment, she had their full attention.

"Okay, you don't give a damn that it's ten times the size of Disneyland or four times the acreage of Magic Mountain—"

"Statistics," someone called out, but this time the word had a friendlier ring to it.

"Can't put anything past you, can I?" Nancy Chan and shook her head. "Still, you can't blame me for trying. Okay, no more statistics, not even if you *beg* for them. And you will."

The screen went dark for an instant, and then was filled with what he knew was the view from the top of the Death Spiral. They'd used a wide-angle lens, and slow motion, to allow the viewer to take in the magnificence of the ocean, the mountains, and the crystal blue sky.

Even though he'd seen it many times, the sight made his breath catch in his throat.

Then the film switched to real-time, and there wasn't time to notice anything but the sensation of speed and motion that nearly induced vertigo. Dimly, he heard the gasps of the others in the room, but that became lost in the sound of rushing wind. He imagined the coolness of the air, felt it flow over his face.

The ride went on and on, shooting through its tight spirals, up in elevation and quickly down. Then, just as it seemed as if the ride were nearing an end, it descended into the interior structure. Here, after twenty seconds of pitch black, the ride was suddenly bombarded by laser light, in a myriad of colors, as it went through another series of spirals.

"Wow," someone whispered.

"Ssh."

Then the coaster pod began the climb for the final descent. Because the ride was electronically powered, there was only a slight lessening in speed as it ascended. And ascended. And kept on ascending, more than two hundred feet above the ground.

The film returned to slow motion, toying with them, allowing them a few extra seconds to realize that what goes up must come down . . . and come down it did.

A breathtaking ten minutes after it began, the Death Spiral glided smoothly to a stop.

The room erupted in applause.

Wesley closed her eyes. Thank the Lord, they liked it.

Nancy Chan had been right; the reporters begged for statistics. She recited them graciously, but not without the hint of a smug smile.

"The top speed is seventy-five miles per hour. The ride changes elevations thirty-one times, there are eighteen spirals in each of the five sets, and a total of six vertical loops. At its tallest, the Death Spiral is some two hundred and thirty feet above the ground."

"In other words," a male voice said, and a curtain parted to reveal Sheldon Rice, bathed in blue light, "the Death Spiral makes Magic Mountain's Viper look like a kiddie ride."

The man really knew how to enter a room. Of course it didn't hurt, Wesley thought, that he was accompanied by one of the robots from the Nebula ride, its red eyes gleaming malevolently.

"But I can promise you, ladies and gentlemen, that the Death Spiral is only the beginning . . . get set for one hell of a ride. . . ."

Chapter Nine

Charles City, Iowa

Miss Sutton looked up from her desk as they came into the office and Nicholas Cole saw immediately that she was not in any way amused.

"What's he done this time?" she asked in a nothing-can-surprise-me voice.

The cop gave him a little shove. "He was *doing* ninety out near the Whitaker place—"

"In what?"

"I didn't take your car, Miss Sutton," Nick said, knowing the thought had occurred to her. In fact, her old heap could never make ninety miles an hour. . . .

"Shut up," the cop said, and shoved him again, this time harder and in the direction of the chair. "Sit down and don't say another damn word, or I'll change my mind and take you in."

"Ooh, I'm shaking—"

"Hush now, and I mean it," Miss Sutton said. "Where did he get the car?"

"Stole it out of a parking lot somewhere. Hot-wired it, like the last time."

Miss Sutton's reproving look made him want to laugh, but he fought the urge. Besides, if he did, either one of them was purely capable of knocking him upside the head, and with his hands handcuffed behind his back, he wouldn't be able to defend himself.

"Nicholas," she said with a sigh, "why do you do these things?"

"I don't know."

"Bullshit," the cop said.

He tried to appear contrite. "Something comes over me," he said.

"I catch you out hot-rodding again and something will definitely come over you, and you can take *that to the bank, boy*."

The answer to that, of course, was not to let anyone catch him. Which meant he'd have to start stealing faster cars, something that would leave the cops eating his dust, except he doubted there was such an animal in all of Iowa. The last he'd heard, John Deere wasn't into building sports coupes.

Maybe he should just rip off a cop car; at least then it would be a fair chase.

"Well," Miss Sutton said, "I do want to thank you, Officer, for bringing him out."

"Sure thing." The cop motioned for Nick to stand up and turn around, then stepped over and unlocked the handcuffs. "You behave now, you hear?"

With one wrist free, he raised his hand to swear to it, but had no more than opened his mouth when the cop waved him off.

"I've heard it before, Cole." He tucked the handcuffs back in the case on his gunbelt and snapped the case shut emphatically. "Don't waste your breath, kid, and I won't have to waste mine. Just believe this: you've had your last warning."

"Why," Miss Sutton asked again when the cop had left, "do you do these things?"

He pretended to consider it, making as if he had an idea in mind, opening his mouth to speak, and then shaking his head in mock sorrow at the realization that he just didn't know. It wasn't easy keeping a straight face.

Miss Sutton didn't have that problem; her face was expression-less, her eyes eerily blank. "You aren't a dumb boy," she said.

Nicholas made a face. He hated being called a "boy" even though at twelve he knew most everyone considered him one.

"So why," she continued, apparently oblivious to having annoyed him, "do you do stupid things?"

He gave her his best shit-eating grin. "Why not? I want to fit in with all these cornhuskers."

"Do you really, Nicholas? Want to fit in?"

"Oh, sure, why wouldn't I? I mean, isn't that why I'm here?"

"Is it?"

"You tell me." He folded his arms defiantly across his chest and leaned the chair back so that it was balanced on two legs. "Why am I here, Miss Sutton? What am I doing here?"

But Miss Sutton, as with every social worker he'd ever met, never answered a direct question if she could help it. "Why do you think you're here?"

He quirked his head. "I don't know, but while we're on the sub-ject of dumb-ass questions, what is the meaning of life?"

Miss Sutton pursed her lips and shook her head, but didn't answer. Instead, she made a cluster of dots on the desk blotter with her pencil, examined the point and found it wanting, then stuck it in the electric sharpener. When the pencil was sharpened to her satisfaction, she opened his file, flipped through the pages, and, after glancing at him once again, made a notation.

"Is that it?" he asked. "Does the condemned get to choose a last meal?"

"I haven't condemned you," she said quietly. "As a mat-ter of fact, I've decided to do something rather nice for you."

That alarmed him. The last time anyone had said they were going to do him a favor, he'd wound up here. A halfway house in the middle of nowhere was not his idea of a good place to be.

He narrowed his eyes at her. "You're selling me into

white slavery."

Miss Sutton's mouth twitched in what might have passed in some quarters for a smile. "They aren't," she said dryly, "that hard up for slaves."

Nick came dangerously close to a smile himself, but covered by letting the chair sway and drop forward, and pretending to be startled by the noise that it made. "Sorry," he said.

"Do you know what I have here?"

She was holding what his baby sister used to call a "vanilla" envelope. The memory of his sister was a painful one and he immediately blocked it out. "I'm not sure, Miss Sutton. Is it . . . could it be . . . after all these years . . . my Academy Award?"

"Can you be serious for a moment?"

"I *thought* I saw some guy from Price Waterhouse hanging around outside—"

"Nicholas . . ."

"It's such an honor just to be nominated. There really are so many people I'd like to thank." He stood up and took several mincing steps toward her desk, but saw that she had no intention of handing the envelope over to him. "First of all, I have to thank my loving parents, without whom I would never have gotten to where I am today. . . ."

That caught her attention. She blinked slowly, in the manner of a lizard warming itself in the sun. Misery was her sun, was all of their suns, except they wanted to warm themselves on *his* misery, and he couldn't let them do that, because it was the only thing he had left in this world that was truly his own.

So he bit back the words that she—they—wanted to hear, and bent over in a deep bow.

"Thank you," he said, rising. He could feel beads of sweat forming on his brow with the narrowness of his escape; with luck, she wouldn't notice. "Thank you very, very, very, very, *very* much."

"Are you through?"

He shrugged. "For now." He sat down just as his knees were ready to give out on him.

"Anyway, as I was saying, it so happens that we have the opportunity to send one of our boys to that new amusement park in California when it opens this June—"

"Just one?"

"I'm sorry, what?"

"Just one of us is going?"

"Yes. And I've chosen you."

"Why?"

Miss Sutton laughed, and oddly enough, he didn't find it repulsive, as he would have thought. "You can be trying sometimes, but despite that, I think that of all the boys, you would get the most good out of it."

"Meaning what?"

"Exactly what I said. It would help you to put a little distance between yourself and your . . . circumstances. Maybe it'll help you find a proper perspective."

"Perspective," he said, and snorted. "You mean you're going to hold this trip thing over my head like a worm on a hook and see if I'll take the bait."

She sighed, and rubbed at her temples with her fingertips. "What is it you want, Nicholas?"

"Nothing," he said. "I mean, I don't know. I only know what I don't want."

"And that is?"

I don't want to be invisible, he thought, but it was too close to the truth for him to say it. "I'm not a little kid," he said instead.

"And you feel we treat you like one?"

"Yes, kind of."

"I see. And of course you always behave in a mature fashion. . . ."

"Well, maybe not *always*."

Miss Sutton opened the envelope and withdrew the contents, including, he noticed, several brochures for The

Park. He'd seen several commercials for the place, including one ad in which the camera was mounted on the Death Spiral, and it was so awesomely fast, so spectacularly breathtaking, he'd actually had to close his eyes.

The Death Spiral was his kind of ride.

He was interested, he admitted to himself, in going to this place. He sat forward, his elbows on his knees, his fingers itching to get hold of one of the brochures.

"This," she said, holding up a sheet of paper, "is the official notification that we have been awarded a reserved space for one of our boys for a full week during the Grand Opening."

"A week? Seven days?" Nick could feel his cool deserting him, and he tucked his hands between the seat of the chair and his thighs to keep them from assuming the begging position.

"There's a blank here for me to fill in a name."

His mouth went dry. He wouldn't be able to spit even if he were to spontaneously burst into flames and his life depended on it.

She put down the pencil and picked up a pen. "Shall I write in your name, Nicholas?"

Why did he have the uneasy feeling that if he said yes, he'd be making a pact with the devil? Why did he have a sense that something alien was looking at him with Miss Sutton's eyes?

Why didn't he care if either was true?

"Yes," he said.

She held the pen poised above the paper, and it seemed to him that a glint of light sparked off the metal tip. Seconds passed.

"Please," he added.

Their eyes held for the briefest of moments, but long enough for him to imagine that her pupils were elliptical, like those of a cat.

Miss Sutton touched the pen to paper and wrote.

His fate, he thought, was sealed.

"Don't disappointment me, Nicholas," she said, and clicked the ballpoint pen to retract its tip.

"I won't."

Chapter Ten

Mountainair, New Mexico

Betsy Parker twirled a strand of dark red hair into a ringlet around her finger as she listened to the principal talk. She was trying hard to keep an open mind, but she could feel what her daddy called her "mule look" come over her face.

"But we're not poor, Mr. Torrance," she said when he paused for breath.

"I didn't say that—"

"What else would 'disadvantaged' mean?" She didn't wait for an answer, but turned, grabbed the coffee off the hot plate, and looked down the counter and toward the booths for a mug that needed topping off. Unfortunately, Mr. Torrance was the only customer—afternoons were always slow—and today he was drinking tea.

She hated coffee, but rather than standing there like a fool, she grabbed a mug off the shelf and poured half a cup for herself. Then her hands were shaking so bad that she nearly dropped the glass carafe as she returned it to the warmer.

"I can see that I've upset you," he said. "I'm sorry. Would you let me explain?"

"I'm not sure that you can." Betsy lifted her chin in defiance. "I'll have you know, I'm working here solely for the experience, Mr. Torrance. My family doesn't need the money."

"I didn't mean to imply—"

"Raising the seven of us kids hasn't been easy for my parents, but they'd never take charity."

"It *isn't* charity."

She grabbed a damp cloth and wiped the already spotless counter. "My daddy would split a gut if he knew what you're suggesting."

"Actually, he does know."

"I mean, we're not rolling in money," Betsy said, deliberately not hearing him, instead echoing what she'd heard her daddy say time and time again, "but we sure as hell are getting by."

Mr. Torrance gave his familiar tight-lipped smile, then lowered his eyes, seeming to study the murky contents of his mug. His hands were wrapped around it so tightly she thought it might burst.

Her heart kind of felt that way, too. "You know there are other folks hereabouts who are worse off than we are," she said, "and for heaven's sake, I'm the third kid in my family to be named valedictorian—"

"And the only one who won't be going off to college," he said quietly.

Betsy frowned. "That isn't the point."

"I think it is."

"I could go to college if I wanted to; I have a scholarship. You know that. You were the one who helped me get it."

Mr. Torrance reached across the counter and covered her hand with his. "What I know is that you *do* want to go, but you won't."

"They need me at home."

"Tom went to college. David went to college. Scott's in college now. Are you saying they weren't needed?"

"It's different with me."

71

"Why is it? Because you're the youngest? Or because you're the only girl?"

"It isn't that," she said, pulling her hand away. His touch was making her nervous, and she reminded herself that he was a married man.

"Then what?"

Betsy ran her finger along a vein in the fake marble countertop. "Mama needs me. My brothers aren't any help in the kitchen."

"They could learn," he persisted.

It was common knowledge that with his wife confined to her sickbed—and even though they'd hired a rather uppity private nurse from Albuquerque to help out—Mr. Torrance was the one doing most of the cooking and cleaning at their house.

"Well, they won't," she said, and forced a laugh. "But it doesn't really matter—"

"It matters to me. You're the brightest of the bunch, and it's criminal that you won't have a chance to go out and see a little of the world."

She felt a blush coming on and damned her redhead complexion. "Mr. Torrance—"

"Steve."

Betsy looked up quickly to meet his eyes and knew in a minute she'd be red as a beet. "I can't call you . . . you're my principal. . . ."

"I hope I'm more than that." His voice was soft, almost a caress. "That 'Mr. Torrance' stuff makes me sound like an old man. I'm only thirty-two, Betsy."

Why was he telling her this? She wished desperately that a customer would come in, but as far as she could see, there wasn't a soul moving on the streets of Mountainair. Usually about this time of day one of the town's four sworn police officers could be counted on to show up for coffee and a piece of pie, but both of the black-and-white Dodge Ram trucks were parked and idle in front of the station across the way.

She tapped her fingernails nervously on the counter and prayed for deliverance. Or, failing that, a delivery man of some sort.

"Do you know," he said a bit wistfully, "that I can remember the very day you were born? I was fifteen, and you'd think a boy that age would have had other things on his mind, but you were the first girl born in the Parker family in three generations, and the whole town was buzzing over the news."

"Really, Mr. Torrance . . ."

"And they were right, because I've watched you growing up, and you turned out to be the sweetest, gentlest, brightest, and most beautiful young lady this town has ever seen."

"You shouldn't be saying these things," Betsy whispered, but all of a sudden she was glad there was no one to come in and wonder what had brought the color to her face.

"It's the truth."

"Maybe . . . maybe you'd better go."

"Don't worry, Betsy. I'd never do anything to hurt you. Or my wife."

Their eyes met again, and this time what she saw in his made her heart pound like a trip-hammer. The sun was low in the sky and its rays slanted through the dormer windows to cast shadows from the ceiling fan. Dust motes danced in the air.

"I'm sorry," he said, "you're right. I shouldn't be saying these things. It's just that I think you've given up enough by not going to college."

"I don't mind, really."

"But I do. I mind like hell. I hate to think that this"— he indicated the diner and by extension, she understood, the town of Mountainair— "this is all you've got to look forward to."

"I won't always be working here," she said.

"I know." His smile was sad. "You'll marry one of these

73

cowboys, and raise a houseful of red-haired, blue-eyed children, who one day will come to my school and break my heart because they should be mine."

"No . . . please."

"Don't worry, Betsy. This is the last time I'll say a word about how I feel."

She put her hands over her ears, but the terrible thing was, she wanted to hear more. At seventeen, she'd had a grand total of two dates, both with boys her own age, and they hadn't a clue how to be romantic.

Most of the boys in this town had only a nodding acquaintance with how to act civilized, much less how to turn a girl's head.

"Steve," she said, and felt a thrill at the sound of her voice saying his name. She couldn't help but say it again: "Steve. You know what would happen if my daddy got wind of how you're talking to me."

"I expect that your daddy and your brothers would find a way of making their displeasure known. But we're alone now, and I may never have another chance."

"If only . . ." Her momma had brought her up better than to take after someone else's husband, and she left the rest unsaid.

"Yes. If only."

He rested his hand on the counter, palm upward, and after a moment of indecision, she placed her hand lightly on his. It surprised her how natural their hands looked together.

"There are things, many things," he said, "that are beyond my control. I am, however, in charge of this program, and I want you to take the California trip."

"But—"

"I understand how you feel, but it isn't really charity. And I did talk to your father about it; he thinks you should accept."

"That doesn't sound like my daddy."

"Let's just say, I convinced him."

She shook her head. "My daddy is a man sorely in need of convincing at times, but I've never been a witness to it in my life."

"Then you ask him."

"I will."

"And go to California. If your future is a cowboy and half a dozen kids—"

"Not me."

"—then at least you will have had something special for yourself." He raised her hand and kissed the back of it. "I wish I could give you more. . . ."

Across the way, the doors to the police station swung open, and fully fifty percent of the town's law enforcement officers were heading their way.

It wasn't against the law, as far as she knew, to hold hands with a married man, but Betsy felt a sense of panic. There were worse things to consider, like sharp-tongued gossips with eagle eyes. "Mr. Torrance," she said urgently, "somebody's—"

"If you find magic there, and don't come back, I want you to remember, Betsy, that I loved you enough . . . to let you go."

In spite of herself, she laughed. "If you love someone, Mr. Torrance, you'd be a fool to let them go. I may only be seventeen, but even I know that."

Then the door opened, and whatever else he would have said was lost to her.

Chapter Eleven

Denver, Colorado

Max Brown stood on the corner, hands in the pockets of his Denver Nuggets jacket, and savored the freedom that came from having his mother switch to working evenings at the phone company.

"We need the shift differential, what with the rent going up again," she'd said this morning when she told him the news. "You'll be on your own most nights, so you'll have to get dinner for yourself, and I won't be around to remind you to do your schoolwork, but I'm counting on you to be responsible—"

In his eagerness, he'd forgotten his attitude of indifference and interrupted. "I will be."

Doubt had showed in her eyes. "Heaven knows you're big enough and I guess old enough to look out for yourself. Just stay out of trouble."

"Hey, don't worry. This is the new and improved Maxwell 'Smart' Brown you're talking to."

"You'd better be improved," she'd said, "because I got too much to worry about already, keeping body and soul together, to be losing sleep over how you're spending your free time."

Free time.

God, how he liked the sound of that.

Things could absolutely not have worked out better than they had. Here he'd been wondering how he would manage to take care of some outstanding business he had to attend to and still make it home on time this afternoon, and *wham!* The problem was solved without so much as a white lie on his part.

School let out at a quarter to three, he'd taken care of business by four, and had come home to an empty house at five. Dinner was a couple of frozen chicken dinners—he was a growing boy at five foot nine and two hundred solid pounds—and now he was looking forward to an entire evening on his own.

Free time.

He bounced on his heels and idly watched the people passing by as he considered his options. He did have math homework, but that would be taken care of; he'd muscle the answers out of one of the Poindexters in his first period history class tomorrow.

He'd promised old Leroy down the block that he'd lift a set of sockets that Leroy needed to work on the Plymouth Duster he'd won off some dim bulb in a crooked poker game, but Max really wasn't in the mood for skimming an auto parts store.

No, if he was going 'shopping' he'd much rather look for a gift to take along when he visited O'Toole in the hospital later tonight.

Max smiled, imagining the look on O'Toole's ugly face when he gave him a present. It would be memorable, Max thought, for sure.

That, then, was the plan. Visiting hours were from seven to nine—he'd called the hospital while he was waiting for his chicken dinners to heat—and that would give him plenty of time to carefully select and steal an appropriate gift.

Maybe he'd even pay a buck or two to get it wrapped. Maybe.

Max stepped abruptly off the curb, causing an oncoming car to swerve in order to miss him. The driver leaned on the horn and gestured obscenely.

If he didn't already have plans for the evening, Max would have retaliated in kind by throwing a few of the metal ball bearings he always carried with him. The driver might have been stupid enough to stop the car and get out. And then Max would have taught the asshole to show more respect for the youth of America by knocking his teeth down his throat.

Oh well, he thought as he watched the car's taillights disappear into the growing darkness, life can't be all fun and games.

He started off in the direction of the mall.

Max knew that he was making the saleslady nervous, but didn't give a damn. She was a dried-up old bitch, hardly more than wrinkled skin over creaking bones, who even from a distance stunk of stale cigarette smoke and too much perfume. She hadn't said anything to him, but he knew if she did, she'd sound kind of raspy, what his mom called "whiskey voiced."

She'd been eyeing him since he walked in, and trying to make it look like coincidence that she was staying within a few feet of him as he wandered back and forth through the men's department.

The thing was, there was no one for her to call for assistance. Business was slow in most of the stores around dinnertime, and that generally resulted in there being only a skeleton crew working the floors. If the old witch stopped following him and went over to the checkout counter, she could probably call and get a manager to come down, but then that would leave him pretty much free to tuck something in his jacket and split.

It was one of those no-win situations as far as he could see. Except so far he hadn't found anything he wanted to boost.

So they continued their silent dance through the merchandise, with her shadowing him, and he flashing her his nasty smile.

Shopping was *hard* when you cared enough to give the very best.

Briefly he considered taking a leather wallet, one of the tri-fold kind with special slots for credit cards and a place to hide money that wouldn't fool a kid in kindergarten, but it occurred to him that O'Toole never had any cash on him, and it was unlikely that American Express was gonna issue him a gold card anytime soon, so what the hell good would it be?

He also contemplated an amazingly expensive pair of gloves, but since O'Toole had landed in the hospital with a broken arm in addition to his broken leg, he would no doubt be wearing a cast, and that would mean that one of the gloves would be useless. Plus how would he get the glove on his good hand?

Use his teeth, Max supposed.

Not such a good idea, considering that O'Toole wore braces.

Finally, after his third pass through the accessories, he spotted the perfect gift among an arrangement of executive toys: a tape recorder.

It was so simple, he wondered why he hadn't thought of it before. O'Toole could use it to take notes in school — it was his right arm that had been broken — or, more likely, to keep track of who was doing what to whom so he could squeal to the teachers and earn Brownie points for being a good little boy.

Max wheeled suddenly, and stared hard at the old biddy, who looked as though she just might faint. With their eyes locked, he reached down and slipped the recorder into the pocket of his jacket, then deliberately zipped the pocket closed.

"Have a nice day," he said, and left.

No one followed him.

There was a line at the place where they wrapped stuff and it was already after seven, so Max decided not to bother with that particular nicety.

He caught a bus that would take him to the medical center, and while he rode, he recorded a little message for O'Toole on the tape recorder. That gave it a personalized touch, he thought with satisfaction, in addition to taking the place of a get-well card.

Sometimes he was astounded by his own ingenuity, and this was one of those times.

He replaced the recorder in his pocket, folded his arms across his chest, and watched the miles roll by. The bus was doing about forty, and he wondered what it would be like to fly at hundreds of miles per hour.

He'd never flown on a plane—his mother was deathly afraid of them and as for his father, well, the friendly skies didn't extend to prison yards—but that would change, and soon.

Max located the information desk and gave O'Toole's name to the old gent in charge, who ran a gnarled finger along a column to find it.

"He's in 412, that's Orthopedics."

Wasn't that where women went to have babies? "Ortho . . . you said . . . orthopedics?"

"Broken bones," the old man said. "Room 412. You go down that hall to the left there, and follow the green line. Take the elevator up to the fourth floor. You can ask at the nurse's station on four and they'll direct you to your friend's room." Max thanked him and headed off.

As promised, a nurse on the fourth floor pointed out O'Toole's room.

"He's a little groggy from his medication," the nurse called after him. "He may want to sleep."

"That's all right," Max said, "I won't stay long. Hit and run, that's me."

He pushed open the door to 412, but the smile on his face faded when he saw that not only did O'Toole have a roommate, but a visitor as well.

"Mrs. Brennan," he said, genuinely surprised. She was the youth counselor at the Center, and about the last person he'd expected to see. He narrowed his eyes at O'Toole; what had the punk been telling her?

"Maxwell," she said, "how nice."

Apparently nothing, yet. He hefted the tape recorder in his hand, uncertain whether to give it to O'Toole now or not. It would be totally uncool to have Mrs. Brennan hear the message, but on the other hand, it was something he thought the dude shouldn't miss.

"How you doing, buddy?" he asked O'Toole, returning the recorder to his pocket. He'd give it to him later, when they were alone.

"Not great," O'Toole said.

Medication or not, there was a glimmer in those blue eyes that needed to be dealt with. "Yeah? Well, I knew a guy who got it worse than you. Much worse. Busted both legs and both arms." He nodded and raised his eyebrows for emphasis.

81

"Oh Max," Mrs. Brennan said, "how terrible! This was a friend of yours?"

"A very good friend."

"How did it happen?"

Max felt O'Toole's eyes on him, but ignored him. "An accident. He fell down a couple flights of stairs. Broke his collarbone too. Cracked like pretzel, *snap*."

O'Toole turned gray.

Message received.

"How awful." Mrs. Brennan smiled weakly at O'Toole. "You see, Kevin, as bad as you feel now, it might have been worse."

"Absolutely," Max agreed. "Things can always get worse. Trust me."

O'Toole had closed his eyes, and Max saw that he was crying. Funny, he thought, that the little asshole would cry *now*, after the fact.

Mrs. Brennan also noticed his tears, and she sat on the side of the bed to comfort him. "I know you're in pain, and you're disappointed about not being able to go to The Park, but everything will work out. . . ."

"It's not fair," O'Toole sniffed, "I should be the one to go. I earned it!"

"I know, Kevin, but you heard what the doctor said. If you'd only broken one or the other, you might be able to manage, but with both an arm and a leg in casts, you won't even be on crutches by June."

"But a . . . a wheelchair?"

O'Toole was nearly blubbering, and Max crossed to the head of the bed and gripped the boy's shoulder. "Take it easy, pal."

"Now that wouldn't be fair to the other kids on the trip, would it? Someone would have to push you around, and you probably couldn't go on half of the rides." Mrs. Brennan brushed the hair back from his sweaty brow. "There will be other opportunities, Kevin."

"It isn't fair. . . ."

"Hey," Max said, leaning over so his face was only inches from O'Toole's. "You'll live. You'll get over it. Hmm?"

"Maybe we should let you get some rest," Mrs. Brennan said. "It'll all look brighter come the morning, I promise you."

O'Toole appeared unconvinced. Max squeezed his shoulder again, pressing hard enough to bruise. Then he reached in his pocket for the recorder, and set it squarely on O'Toole's chest.

"I brought you a present," he said, and winked. "The least I could do."

O'Toole looked at the recorder as if he feared it might explode. Or bite.

"Take care, buddy, and be careful," Max said, swallowing a laugh. He turned to Mrs. Brennan. "Can I walk you to your car?"

"Why, thank you, Max, that's very considerate of you."

At the door, Max glanced over his shoulder at O'Toole, who hadn't moved and may not have breathed. "I'll be back tomorrow, *Kevin*."

Kevin O'Toole groaned.

"Actually," Mrs. Brennan said on the way down in the elevator, "I'm glad I ran into you. Since Kevin is unable to make the trip, you'll be going in his place."

"Me?" He feigned surprise.

She nodded. "I was planning to phone your mother in the morning, but since our paths have crossed, if you'd ask her to call me?"

Max took the card she offered. "Sure thing. Gee, Mrs. Brennan, this is . . . well . . . I mean, it's too bad Kevin can't go, but . . . wow! And I . . . I had no idea I was next in line for this trip. Talk about your coincidences. It's just, you know, a shame that somebody had to get hurt so I could go, but . . . wow!"

"It's all right to be excited about it," she said. "Kevin is disappointed, but I'm sure later on he'll be glad that you got to go."

Max smiled. "I'll send him a postcard every day."

Chapter Twelve

McKenna's Creek, California

Sheriff Adam Young took his coffee out onto the breezeway to enjoy the sunset. Daylight saving time had sprung the clock forward last night, and there was something almost sinful about it being light out this close to 8:00 p.m.

He leaned against the wood railing and watched the sun hover above the horizon before it began its disappearing act into the sea. The sky was awash with color, gold and pink and purple as well as several shades of blue, but the colors quickly faded as the sun sank.

He sipped his coffee, savoring the peace and quiet; it had been hectic today, unusual for a Sunday. Now it was nearly time to begin his patrol.

The phone rang in the office behind him and he heard Mary Beth's efficient greeting:

"Sheriff's Office, jail, and county morgue."

It was quite a mouthful, but before they'd moved into the new facility eighteen months ago, she'd also had to include the town hall, records office, and tax assessor. Now those offices—and those officials, thank the Lord—were in a separate building across the way.

Mary Beth had been given her choice of which switchboard she wanted to run, and he for one would be eternally grateful that she'd chosen his. She was a real crackerjack of a dispatcher, cool under fire, and worth her not inconsiderable weight in gold.

"Oh my, at it again, is he?" he heard her say. "Well, I'll ask the sheriff to swing by, but you know there's no law that says a man's got to wear clothes in the privacy of his own house. Or pull the shades down. On the other hand, why don't you pull *your* shade?"

Adam smiled and shook his head. The 1990 census had counted 2,644 people in McKenna's Creek, and most of them could have listed their persuasion as "free spirit."

Of course, the town had grown at an alarming rate in recent months, and he would estimate they'd topped the three thousand mark some time back. And even that figure didn't take into account the folks living and working out at The Park.

Thus far there hadn't had been much contact between the locals and them—those people kept to themselves and spent little time in town—but with opening day getting near, he figured all that would change.

He wasn't looking forward to it; there was bound to be some friction when all at once the quiet streets of McKenna's Creek were filled with tourists on their way up to the amusement park.

He prided himself on having learned a thing or two about human nature during the thirty-four years he'd spent as sheriff, and even though the townfolk were glad to take money from Sheldon Rice for so-called civic improvements, he'd bet the gold fillings in his teeth that they'd be royally pissed when some upscale yahoo in a BMW cut them off on Old Mill Road. . . .

Or sooner or later one or more of the locals Rice had hired as maids or busboys or groundskeepers would take a look around and realize that guests who could afford such luxury might have something worth stealing. . . .

Or one of those well-to-do yahoos might think that a pretty young maid was yet another attraction he could buy a ride on. . . .

And the trouble would start. Already there'd been some heated words exchanged between the rent-a-cops Rice had hired to provide security and a few of the local bucks over just who had authority over whom, and who could shove what up where—

"Sheriff," Mary Beth called, "have y'all grown roots out there, or are you still planning on making your rounds tonight?"

"I'm going." He gulped the lukewarm coffee as he went inside. He handed her the empty cup and accepted the mobile radio she offered in return. "So who's revealing his shortcomings this evening?"

"Who's always number one on the dip-shit parade?"

"I'm sorry," he said, strapping on his Sam Browne belt, "but I haven't been keeping track."

Mary Beth sighed and resumed her needlework. "It's Newton."

"That figures." Newton Duffy had crossed the line between eccentric and pain-in-the-ass a good while ago, but since his uncle Mason headed the town council, everyone was resigned to putting up with him. And he was harmless, really.

"Tell him *I* said put on his boxer shorts"—she waved a crochet needle at him—"or else."

"What 'else'?"

"You don't want to know."

Judging by the way she stabbed that hooked needle through the yarn, he figured she was right.

Although twilight was lingering on, the town seemed to have settled in for the night, and he drove through the twisting, narrow roads for a good half hour before he came upon another vehicle, a beat-up Ford truck that flashed its headlights and then slowed to meet him at a wide spot in the road.

"Ezra," he said when he'd rolled down the window, "how's it going?"

"To hell in a hand basket," Ezra answered.

That was what he always said. With his head of white hair and his dark searing glance, the old man looked, Adam thought, like a prophet from biblical times. "Do tell. So what's brought you out this fine evening?"

"Did you know they've dug *into* the mountain?"

Adam blinked. "What?"

"They've actually tunneled into the mountain," Ezra said, and reached across to grab Adam's arm. "Someone has to stop them."

Belatedly, Adam realized what the old man was referring to. "At The Park, you mean."

"Yes, yes."

"Well, Ezra, you know Rice bought the land, and he's entitled to build on it—"

"Destroy it!" Ezra's bony hand encircled Adam's wrist. "You can stop them."

"Now wait a minute, I can't—"

"They have plundered the mountain, undermined it."

Adam freed himself from the old man's grip. "I understand it bothers you that they're building on the mountain, but there's nothing either one of us can do about it."

"You're the law in McKenna's Creek."

"That's not the point. They haven't broken any laws, or done anything illegal, leastways, not that I've heard tell of."

Ezra made a sound like cold water hissing in a hot skillet. "Illegal? Immoral! It's wrong what they've done, what they're doing."

Personally, Adam was inclined to agree, but he knew that to say so would only further incite the old man's passions. He could see that Ezra was barely maintaining his composure; the muscles of his chiseled face were tight with fury, and the impression he gave was of a venomous snake coiled to strike.

"Listen," he said, "Ezra. As it happens, I have business out there in the morning, and I promise you I'll take a look around."

"Ask them how many tons they've hauled away. They'll lie, but ask them."

"Sure, I'll ask."

"And how far down they've dug."

"All right."

"The damned fools think they know how to shore up a mountain, but they don't, I tell you. The whole thing could come crashing down. . . ."

Adam nodded as if he understood. The thing was, old Ezra wasn't an engineer, or a geologist, or anyone other than a man who loved the mountains and had lived in them for longer than anyone could remember.

There were those who said that Ezra had been here first, and the mountains had risen up around him. He was, they said, the last of a breed of mountain men.

He was also a self-proclaimed mystic, who seemed at times to appear out of thin air. He was known to predict a year's rainfall to within a hundredth of an inch, to tell at a glance that a tree was diseased and dying before the first yellowed leaf, and swore that he could hear the earth "speak" to him.

What he wasn't was the kind of a man someone like Sheldon Rice would ever listen to, not once in a million years.

And Adam, though he shared the old man's concern for the mountain, couldn't blame Rice for that.

"It's the stress, you see," Ezra was saying. "It weakens even the rock."

"Don't worry—"

"He is the one who should worry." Ezra's eyes narrowed. "He has made the mountain bleed, and the land does not forgive."

"Now, Ezra—"

"Tend to it, Sheriff. Tend to it, or I will."

Chapter Thirteen

The Park

Dr. Taylor McKenna removed the gauze dressing and touched the wound gently with a gloved finger. Blood oozed from the laceration, which almost looked as if it had been incised. It was approximately four centimeters in length and extended from the base of the right thumb along the palmar crease toward the index finger.

"You've really laid it open," she said. "How'd you do this?"

"On the Graveyard."

She glanced up to meet the young man's eyes. "I hope you mean the ride."

He smiled but he was looking a little pale. "Yes, the ride."

"Can you move your thumb and fingers?"

He complied, although somewhat gingerly. Everything worked.

"Any numbness? Tingling? Loss of sensation?"

"No."

"Well," she said, "you definitely need stitches. When was your last tetanus shot?"

"I don't remember. No, wait . . . I had a booster right before I started graduate school, so that would make it five years ago."

Taylor glanced up in surprise; she'd thought he was in his mid-teens, and had assumed he was the son of one of the engineers. But now it was evident who he must be. "You're Wesley Davison, aren't you?"

He nodded.

"I'm Taylor McKenna," she said. So this was the boy genius everyone talked about.

"Is that McKenna as in McKenna's Creek?"

"The same." She turned from the gurney and went to the cabinet for a suture set. "My great-great-grandfather, Lucian McKenna, couldn't stand all the hustle and bustle of San Francisco—in 1880 the population was something like two hundred and thirty thousand—and he came up the coast to find a quiet place to raise his family."

"It's quiet, all right."

She inclined her head in agreement. "Anyway, he found the area to his liking and settled down. The family's been here ever since."

Taylor didn't add that she was the last McKenna; even two years after her father's sudden death, it was painful to think about.

"Okay," she said, pulling the procedure table to the side of the gurney, "now we begin."

"We? What do I do?"

"Hang in there." She had filled a small stainless steel basin with sterile water, and now added Betadine to it. "This is for you to soak your hand."

Wesley hesitated. "Will it sting?"

"That depends on who you ask. It's not supposed to sting, but I've heard truck drivers swear on their mothers' eyes that it did, and five year olds who say that it doesn't."

Again, that slight smile. "I guess I'll have to take my chances," he said, and lowered his hand, palm upward, into the brownish water.

"Good." She unwrapped a disposable syringe and drew up ten cc's of Xylocaine. Noticing that she again had his undivided attention, she asked, "You're not afraid of needles, are you?"

"Me? Are you kidding? No," he said, none too convincingly.

Taylor could tell he was tensing up, and thought of a way to relax him. "Me neither," she said, and winked. "As a matter of fact, some of my best friends from medical school are pricks."

Wesley laughed, and blushed, which was good because he'd gotten nearly as white as the sheets.

She capped the syringe and placed it on the tray, then handed him a sterile towel. "Pat your hand dry and then put it on the table here."

He did as he was told. She draped his hand so that only the palm was exposed, and positioned the goose-necked lamp to provide the best lighting.

Taylor looked straight into his eyes, which were warm and brown and as trusting a those of a cocker spaniel puppy. "I'm not going to tell you that it isn't going to hurt when I anesthetize the wound, but I promise it won't take but a minute until it's numb. Okay?"

"Sure."

"Good." She hesitated, and then smiled. "You might want to look somewhere else while I'm doing this . . . it's not pleasant to watch."

He stared up at the ceiling, and she deftly inserted the needle subcutaneously, quickly injecting the Xylocaine into the wound and the surrounding tissue. She felt him flinch, but he said nothing, and more importantly, he didn't try to pull his hand away.

"The worst is almost over," she said, selecting another injection site. The bleeding was insignificant now, and she was better able to examine the wound, which was clean edged and free of foreign bodies. The deep palmar fascia had not been cut.

A third injection site, and she had nearly emptied the syringe. After withdrawing the needle, she squirted the remaining few millimeters of anesthetic over the wound to irrigate it.

"There you go," she said. She walked to the counter and, after crimping the needle to render it unusable, disposed of the syringe in the red contaminated-materials container. "How's it feel now?"

"It doesn't." Some of his natural color had returned, and he was looking at his draped hand as if it belonged to someone else. His expression was one of sick fascination. "I didn't realize I'd cut it this bad."

"Hmm." She took the needle forceps from the surgical pack to grip the curved suture. "How exactly did it happen? I mean, when I think of graveyards, I don't imagine anything *sharp*. . . ."

It was as if someone had flicked a switch to suddenly animate him. His shoulders straightened and his eyes fairly glowed.

"The Guardian of the Graveyard," he said eagerly. "It's a robotic skeleton—"

Taylor had begun suturing, but she looked up. "This skeleton carries a knife?"

"No. But the bones are held together with metal rods, and I guess some of the edges were exposed. I was putting him through a range-of-motion check, and he, well, he kind of startled me by reaching his arm out further than he should have."

"That could be dangerous," she observed. As clean as the laceration was, the metal edge that caused it had to be very sharp.

"He didn't mean to do it."

Taylor laughed. "Now you sound like a defense attorney."

"Do I? Anyway, it's my own fault, really, because I'm the one who programmed him. And I should have stepped back when he came at me, instead of putting up my hand. *That* was stupid."

She tied off a suture and clipped a loose end. "I'm not

sure I'd call anyone stupid who could design a place like this, but I sure hope you can get the bugs out before opening day—"

"I will."

"—because otherwise I can envision a waiting room full of bleeding guests, and"—she smiled up at him—"not all of them will be as forgiving as you."

It took the better part of an hour and more than thirty tiny stitches to close the gaping wound. When she finished repairing the laceration, she applied a dry sterile dressing and taped the hand.

From the drug cabinet, she dispensed six Tylenol with codeine to be taken only if needed for pain, then wrote a prescription for twelve more.

"Don't take these if you're going to be working around, what did you call him? The Guardian? Or any other machinery," she warned, and finally sent Wesley Davison on his way.

It was nearly midnight, but as he left he muttered something about adjusting a pulley.

The kid clearly loved his job.

Taylor cleaned up the procedure table, put the instruments in solution, and threw the linens in the laundry cart. Then she walked around the department turning off lights.

The Park's Medical Aid Center was officially closed for the night.

At the gate, she rolled down her window as the security guard approached.

"Quiet night?" he asked, accepting the ID card from her and inserting it into a slot. Somewhere deep in the brain of The Park, a computer registered the time of her departure.

"Actually, it was more interesting than most," she answered honestly. In the two weeks since she'd started work, there'd been little more than the usual assortment of colds and minor stomach ailments.

The guard retrieved the card and handed it to her. "Have a safe drive home, Dr. McKenna." The barred gate began to glide silently open.

"I'll do my best," she said, and accelerated through the passage.

The house, of course, was dark and empty when she arrived; she'd forgotten again to leave the porch light on. If this had been Los Angeles, or Houston, or any other of the big cities she'd lived in during college, medical school, and her subsequent residencies, she'd have cause for concern. But this was McKenna's Creek, and neither the lateness of the hour nor the relative isolation of the house was reason for alarm.

The crimes of McKenna's Creek tended to be those of small-mindedness. There'd never been a murder—or at least, not an obvious one—and there were far too many eyes peering from behind curtains for any of the lesser crimes to go unnoticed.

Occasionally someone might be arrested for being drunk in public, or for driving in the middle of the road and refusing to yield, but even those desperadoes had only to serve a night or two in jail to recognize the error of their ways.

There were repeat offenders, the recidivism rate was high, but even so, it was safe here, almost as if the town had developed an immunity to the ills of the twentieth century, or the fevers of mankind.

Taylor got out of the car and locked it from force of habit, then walked along the gravel driveway up to the porch. The front door was also locked—some habits died hard—but her father had kept a key tied to a string in the mailbox, and she used that to get in.

The ticking of her grandfather clock was the only sound that greeted her. Rather than be reminded of the emptiness, she left the lights off, and made her way in the dark through the living room and the dining room to her bedroom at the back of the house. She stopped only briefly for a decanter of sherry and a glass.

In the bedroom, she slipped off her shoes and hung up her white lab coat. She unbuttoned the front of her dark blue dress, eased the sleeves off her shoulders, and stepped out of it.

A moment later, wrapped in her old flannel robe, she curled up with a glass of sherry, and gazed out the window at the trees whose silhouettes were as familiar to her as the house itself.

The nights were often breezy here, and the sound of the wind rustling through the leaves was also familiar, and oddly soothing. Each of the windows was lowered an inch at the top—her father had always insisted that fresh air was necessary for a good night's sleep—and she could hear as well the frogs down by the creek.

McKenna's Creek.

She took a sip of sherry and felt its warmth begin to ease her.

The problem was, it should feel good to be home, and it didn't, mostly because she was alone. But there were other reasons, including her suspicion that her father's death had been hastened, if not caused outright, by the aggravation he'd had to endure after selling one-third of the family land to Sheldon Rice.

Not all of the townspeople had approved of the sale, and those who were most opposed had made their feelings known. In some instances, from what she'd heard, their objections were related verbally, in a series of altercations that were heated, if short lived.

Less innocent were the phone calls in the middle of the night during which no one spoke, or the hate letters which were never mailed but tucked under the door, or the other untraceable forms of harassment which after awhile began to take a toll.

None of this was overtly illegal, although when she'd advised him of what was happening, Sheriff Young had made a vague reference to it maybe, possibly, constituting a "nuisance."

A nuisance.

Later, when her father had a massive, and ultimately fatal, heart attack, she had questioned Dr. Chambers about what part the harassment might have played in bringing it on, but the doctor's loyalties evidently lay elsewhere. He'd steadfastly refused to acknowledge that the anxiety and pressure of being hated by his neighbors had brought on Benjamin McKenna's death.

"I may be just an old country doctor," he'd said in that infuriating drawl of his, "but I do believe after forty years of practicing medicine, there may be a thing or two I know that you don't."

She'd been tempted to enlighten him about all of the research being done on the relation of emotions to physical well-being, but realized that she would be in effect shouting into the wind.

He wouldn't hear her, because he didn't want to. It was as simple as that.

Regardless, she suspected that her father's death had been hastened by the hostility he'd had to endure. A gentle man, he had no experience at being hated, and it had killed him.

She held the town responsible. Because *she* knew that someone knew who had been harassing him. Someone *had* to have seen who'd delivered the letters, or who'd thrown red paint at the front door. In a town this size, there weren't many real secrets.

Which was one reason she'd taken the position at The Park; she knew it would annoy those who had blamed her father for selling to Rice. Going over to the enemy camp was the rough equivalent of thumbing her nose at them.

Maybe they would come after her, or try to harass her as they had her father.

If they did, she'd be ready. Medical school had given her a harder edge, and dealing with life-and-death matters on a daily basis had imbued her with a calm assurance that she could indeed handle herself, and could take anything they dished out.

She wasn't as tender a soul as her father; she was entirely capable of returning in spades whatever they might do to her.

In an odd way, she was even looking forward to it as a kind of catharsis, a way of releasing the anger she'd felt for the past two years.

A way of letting go.

Taylor finished the glass of sherry, turned out the bedside lamp, and let the whisper of the wind in the trees lull her to sleep.

Chapter Fourteen

Wesley had intended to clean up the blood—*his* blood—that had splattered over the Guardian's gray-white bones when he'd cut his hand, but when he turned his flashlight on the menacing creature, he rather liked the way the bloodstains looked.

Two of the Guardian's fingers were nearly covered with the stuff, which had dried to a disgusting red-brown. There were spots and streaks of blood on the long bones of the arm as well, and there was a fine spray, almost like an arterial spray, of blood drops running in a diagonal line across the skeleton's pelvic bones.

The effect was righteously scary; he couldn't have done better if he'd tried.

It might be, he thought as he surveyed the area, that adding a little blood and gore here and there would enliven the Graveyard.

"Except you," he said to the Guardian. "You're lively enough."

The Guardian gave a toothy grin, but its eye sockets were shaded, and he couldn't tell if it was watching him or simply staring into the night.

"Now let's see if I can adjust the extension of your arm so you don't nail anyone else."

At 2:00 a.m., Wesley gave it up for the night. His hand was throbbing—the anesthetic had long ago worn off—and he had a headache on top of that. Besides, he had run out of jawbreakers some time back.

He secured the iron mesh gate to the Graveyard, locked the computer control module, turned off the colored lights, and began the long walk through the dark and deserted grounds toward The Park's Place.

The corporate headquarters which occupied the upper floors of the Place was brightly lit, even at this hour, although he was reasonably sure that only members of the janitorial crew were still at work. His own crew, minus Perkins, who'd been fired, had clocked out promptly at five thirty.

With the lights blazing, the building, which hugged the side of the mountain, was an impressive sight. It looked, he thought, like the modern version of the Anasazi cliff dwellings in the Southwest.

Except . . . weren't the Anasazi Indians the tribe that had just up and disappeared one day? Or had that been the Mayans? Or was it the Incas? Hell, maybe *all* of them had disappeared.

He should have paid more attention in his anthropology class, but even as a college freshman, he'd been preoccupied with things instead of people. People had always been a mystery to him.

Someone had once suggested to him that the reason he was so fascinated with machines and design and the way things worked was because he had so little in common with the human race.

That someone had probably meant to insult or hurt him, but he'd taken it as a compliment. All he'd ever gotten out of associating with others was disillusionment; people were seldom who they pretended to be.

101

In any case, it didn't really matter. The Park was what counted. People came and went, but what he'd built had permanence, and in some form it would remain.

Perhaps in a thousand years, an anthropologist would discover this place and wonder at the reasons behind its tri-level design, and puzzle over what had become of the tribe that had created the serpentine shapes, and whose totems included skeletal remains, red-eyed robots, and mechanized spiders.

The thought made him smile. Wesley Aloysius Davison, tribe of one.

He'd seen no one on the grounds, nor was security manning the entrance on the lobby level. He accessed the duty roster and determined that the guards were patrolling the perimeter of the park.

There'd been some trouble in the last few weeks with vandalism; a nascent expressionist had thrown gallons of paint on some of the ride housings near the edge of the property. Another creative mind had poured bubble bath into one of the circulating pump reservoirs.

For a time it had seemed that perhaps the Water Devil ride would be forever blowing bubbles, but he had ordered the use of Triton X-100, a chemical dispersing agent, followed by a complete draining and a thorough cleaning of the water works. He had also jury-rigged an aerated cover for the reservoir system.

Still not satisfied, he artificially increased the mineral and salt concentrations in the water—making it in effect "hard water"—thus reducing its susceptibility to foaming agents.

He then devised a new maintenance schedule to compensate for the corrosive properties of harder water, and instructed a junior engineer to investigate the feasibility of using more plastic parts in the pumps.

102

And after all that, he'd jokingly suggested installing electric fences and barbed wire to keep those who would trespass out.

"Maybe we could plant a land mine or two," he'd said. "Nothing spectacular, but just enough to get and keep their attention."

"In a war," Rice had said with a grim smile, "you either fight to win or you might as well stay home."

Winning in this instance apparently required armed security guards. Wesley wasn't sure which bothered him more, the vandals or the pseudocops.

In a battle of wits and cunning, both sides were sorrowfully unarmed.

He stopped on the fourteenth floor so that he could pick up the load-time evaluations for the second-level rides—he'd programmed the computer to compare "continuous loader" versus "interval loader" versus "cycle" rides—but found himself instead in the Video Monitoring Center, or, more familiarly, VMC.

Cameras were mounted in hidden locations all over the park, and the real-time displays were fed into a bank of video monitors which took up an entire wall of the huge room. A master control board allowed an operator to tape any signal using one of twenty VCRs.

The cameras were pre-set to specific areas, but the operator could direct them to track a person throughout the park by keying in on the ID badge issued to each guest on admission. Employees could likewise be tracked using their photo ID cards.

There were, of course, blind spots here and there, but big brother *was* watching, or so it would seem to anyone who'd seen the inside of this room.

As for the badges, they also had another, less questionable purpose. The same microchips which allowed for tracking were used in the financial accounting; purchases of any nature were automatically charged to the guest's master account. No cash ever changed hands. Money, then, had no value.

That had been Rice's idea. He was a staunch believer in the credit card creed: that the use of plastic encouraged spending. Spending naturally increased profits. Profits made Sheldon Rice a happy man.

Wesley had no reason to doubt Rice's reasoning on that count, but in the back of his mind he was bothered by these cameras, although he couldn't deny that they fascinated him as well. It just seemed wrong, somehow, to be spying on everyone.

Rice justified it by saying he was protecting his investment *and* the guests. After all, the camera which watched to make sure no one damaged Park property might also detect a patron falling suddenly ill.

More than likely, a camera had witnessed his own mishap in the Graveyard.

Actually, he thought, surveying the rows of screens, he wouldn't have minded having had that incident recorded; he could have seen with his own eyes whether the Guardian had lunged at him, as he imagined it had.

But then, sometimes it was better not to know. He'd *enjoyed* the cold adrenaline rush he'd gotten when the Guardian kept coming at him, and coming at him, and just wouldn't stop. The hair on the back of his neck had bristled, and his skin crawled.

He'd been scared half to death—for a few seconds—and he'd loved it.

That creepy crawly feeling was what people were willing to shell out three hundred dollars a day for. His job was to make sure they got their money's worth.

He didn't intend to disappoint them.

The pain medication Dr. McKenna had given him was finally taking hold. Wesley lay on the couch in the living room, the computer printouts forgotten on the floor beside him, and tried to work up the energy to get up and go to the bedroom and sleep in a real bed for a change.

Last night, and every night for at least the past week, he'd fallen asleep on the couch and woken up with a kink in his neck.

This morning he'd promised himself he wouldn't do that again.

Right now, though, he found it difficult to care. The pills—he'd taken four tablets instead of the prescribed dose of two—made him feel as though he were encased in a cotton cocoon.

"Cotton cocoon," he said, experimentally. His tongue felt too big for his mouth.

That might prove to be a problem. His stomach was kind of queasy and if he had to vomit, he didn't see how anything would be able to get around that tongue. Consequently, he might choke, although on what he didn't know, because he hadn't eaten in a long time.

Wesley frowned. Even thinking about throwing up was making his stomach worse.

Now his ears were ringing.

No, wait. That was the phone.

The phone? He squinted at his Rolex—a gift from Rice and determined after a moment that it was a quarter till four in the morning. The sky outside was pitch black and seemingly endless. . . .

The phone continued to ring.

Who would be calling him at this hour? If he had anyone he cared about, a call in the middle of the night would scare him. But he'd been estranged from his family ever since he'd taken his parents to court—

It had to be Rice.

He started to get up, but the sudden movement and the

pills he'd taken combined to knock him for a loop, and the sky became even blacker until there was no light and no sound at all.

Chapter Fifteen

San Francisco, California

"He's not answering."

Sheldon Rice looked up from the prospectus he'd been reviewing in preparation for a 7:00 a.m. meeting. "But he's there?"

"Yes. The computer shows that he entered through the main lobby at two twenty-seven. He made a couple of brief stops, at his office and the VMC, then went up to the penthouse."

"Hmm. He hasn't left? Maybe to let the cat out or something?"

"He hasn't got a cat," Nancy Chan said, and tapped a command key on the computer. "And the elevator hasn't left the fifteenth floor."

"Well then, he's simply not answering the phone."

"That's not like him."

"The boy's been working hard," Rice said. He tossed the prospectus into his open briefcase, then reached his arms overhead in a sorely needed stretch. "As we have been. What time is it, did you say?"

"Nearly four."

He rubbed his eyes, which felt gritty from the lack of sleep. "Damn."

"Shall I let it ring?"

"No." If Wesley hadn't answered by now, it was unlikely he'd pick up at all. At this moment, Rice couldn't blame him; it was an ungodly hour.

"I can ask Security to send someone up to his room and check on him."

"No, never mind. It'll keep." He had wanted to verify with young Davison that the moving sidewalks they'd installed between Level One and Level Two were fully operational before he gave the go-ahead to the advertising agency to begin filming the final promotional spots for the grand opening. But what the hell; a few hours' delay wouldn't make that much of a difference.

"I wonder if he's all right," Nancy said, returning the handset to the cradle.

"Wesley? Of course he's all right. Why wouldn't he be?"

"Maybe you haven't noticed, but he's been working almost around the clock."

"So? He's young. He can take it." Rice grimaced as he rose from the chair. "I, on the other hand, am definitely running on empty."

"He looked pale when I saw him last."

"Nancy," Rice said, "you're much too young to be playing mother hen to the boy. Moreover, it's not a role that suits you. Don't worry so much."

She sighed. "Fine. Whatever you say."

"Now don't be like that." He came up behind her and began to massage her neck. "I only mean that it's not a good idea to coddle the boy—"

"I don't *coddle* him."

Rice could feel the tension in her; the muscles of her neck were as tight as the suspension cables on the Golden Gate Bridge. "Relax," he said, bending over to whisper in her ear. "You've been stretching yourself thin these past few weeks. You can't be all things to all people, except perhaps to me."

"Sheldon . . ."

"Come on," he whispered, "you know it will relax you, make you feel better."

"No, it won't." She got up abruptly and crossed to the window, but her body language made it clear she wasn't admiring the view.

Rice sank into the chair she'd deserted; it was still warm from her. He was much more tired than he'd anticipated. Jet lag, he supposed; only a few hours ago, they'd flown in from Washington, D.C., where he'd met with the senior partner of the law firm he'd retained to look out for The Park's best interests.

He closed his eyes and rubbed at his temples. "What is it now?"

"I don't know what you mean," she said, keeping her back to him.

"You do. You've been distant all day."

"Have I?"

Deja vu. Rice could have sworn he'd had this exact conversation with each of his former wives at some point in the relationship. "You have," he said, swallowing a sigh of his own. "And I want to know why. Have I done something to annoy you?"

"No."

Ah, he'd reduced her to a monosyllabic response. It was worse than he'd feared. "Then have I *not* done something and that omission has annoyed you?"

She merely shook her head.

Women, he thought. How was it that they managed to pick the absolute worst times to have their little tantrums or to stage their little scenes? Or was the timing an integral part of their strategy?

"You know, Nancy," he said reasonably, "I'm not a mind reader." *And if I was there might be a shortage of reading material.*

Not even a flicker of interest from her. One would have thought she'd been carved from ice.

She was better than average at game playing, he had to

give her credit. She'd piqued his interest in spite of his years of experience with countless other women.

"If you tell me what's bothering you, I'm certain we can work it out."

"There's nothing *to* work out."

"Oh?" No doubt he was supposed to be cut to the quick at the implication that their relationship hadn't substance enough to qualify as more than "nothing." He knew he would regret it, but he had to ask. "Is there anything I can do to change that?"

"You can—"

Here it comes.

"—marry me."

Firewalkers had never stepped so carefully as they crossed the burning coals. "But Nancy, we agreed when this all started that neither one of us was looking for anything . . . permanent."

"When *this* all started?"

He hated it when a woman quoted his words back to him. Whatever he said never sounded the same; a feminine inflection changed the whole tone of a man's words, made them seem somehow inadequate. Even feeble. "Well, yes," he said, more cautiously.

"And just what is *this?*"

The game was now twenty questions, and it was impossible to win.

But he had given her the ammunition she needed. "And while we're on the subject, what the hell do you mean, permanent? You've been married three times, and none of those marriages were permanent."

"Exactly my point." As exhausted as he felt, he knew it was required of him to go to her now. He did, placing both hands on her upper arms and giving her an affectionate squeeze. "I would hate to see you hurt the way Mary and Debra and Susannah were."

She lifted her chin, and actually sniffed. "They may have been hurt but at least when it was over they could

110

afford intensive care."

Rice pulled her back against him and wrapped his arms around her slender body. "Now Nancy, don't belittle what we have. Money isn't everything."

She shifted slightly, looking up at him. "I can't believe you said that."

He raised his eyebrows. "Neither can I." And he laughed.

That was a mistake. All at once it was as if he were holding a writhing, thirty-foot-long boa constrictor, and then she pulled free.

"I don't think this is funny," she chided, going back to the chair and flouncing into it.

"No, no, I wasn't laughing at you—"

"This is serious, or at least it is to me."

"And me. It's just, I'm so damned tired."

If he'd hoped to appeal to her sympathies, it flat out didn't work. She glared at him. "Then go to bed."

One more try, he thought. "Not alone. Come with me and we'll work this out another way."

"Not likely."

"Nancy . . ."

"I'm not a plaything to be used at your convenience and then tossed aside."

"What you really mean is that if I toss you aside—which is not to say I would—you expect to be remunerated at the going wifely rate. After all, you've given me, what? The best *month* of your life?"

"You bastard."

He stifled an urge to yawn. "I'm a businessman," he said. "It's only natural that I prefer to approach this in a way that's familiar to me. You want, apparently, to renegotiate our deal—"

"Deal? Did you say deal?"

"Ssh, keep your voice down."

"Why? This is a fucking penthouse, there's no one to hear."

"Granted. But when you raise your voice you sound like a common fishwife." He made no attempt to hide his distaste. In fact, all of the women he knew shared an unfortunate tendency to shrillness when excited, but up until this moment, Nancy had held hers in check.

He noted with some amazement that her body seemed almost to quiver with rage, and wondered if she were thinking of throwing something at him. Debra, his second wife, had both the arm and the instincts that if she'd been a man would have made her a baseball legend.

"I don't think I want to talk about this right now," she said, finding control from somewhere.

"Good." He began unbuttoning his shirt. "Set the alarm for six, would you?"

Nancy said nothing.

Rice slipped between the satin sheets, luxuriating in the feel of them against his bare skin. Perhaps after his morning meetings, he would come back and get a few more hours of sleep.

He sensed rather than felt Nancy get into bed beside him. His impression was confirmed first by the scent of her perfume and then by her hand.

As small as her hands were, she certainly could cover a lot of ground with them.

Rice shifted in the bed to welcome her, and her hot little body soon was molded to his. He entwined his hands behind his head and let her work out her frustrations, which it soon became clear were quite extensive.

He knew better than to assume this meant she wasn't still angry with him. Rather this was her way of showing him what he'd be missing if he lost her.

It wasn't a bad move on her part, and neither were the other moves she was making. Whatever her faults, the girl could really get *into* making love.

Soon they were both sweating, and between the slickness of the satin sheets and the slipperiness of her lithe body, he forgot all else.

When the alarm went off, he had gotten no sleep, but he no longer cared. He left Nancy in a tangle of black satin, and went in to shower.

The brightness of the light made him wince when he switched it on, and so too did his reflection in the full-length mirror.

"You're getting old," he said, and ran a hand through his thinning hair. He had always thought that the streaks of gray he had made him look distinguished, but there was nothing remotely distinguished about the rest of the aging process.

He wasn't fat, but the muscles of his chest and belly had begun to sag, to lose the definition he'd had as a young man. Likewise—and strangely, he thought—his calves. They looked the way old men's calves looked, milky white with blue veins showing amidst the patchy hair.

He needed more time in the sun.

You've had your time in the sun, a nagging little voice said.

Then again, wasn't it the sun that had aged his face? Sure, he hadn't slept in a day and a half, but wasn't every one of his forty-nine years there on display? Each day and every minute?

Rice sucked in his stomach until it was flat, but after a minute it was too much effort, and he let his breath out in a sigh.

Maybe Nancy could keep him young. Or more accurately, keep him from feeling old.

"Either that," he said to his mirror image, thinking of how he'd spent the last couple of hours, "or she'll kill me outright."

There were worse ways to die.

But no . . . what was he thinking? His focus had to be

on The Park. Too much was at stake to allow himself to be distracted from business by her petty female complaints. If she couldn't deal with the ambiguity of their affair, the hell with her.

Opening Day was drawing near.

Nothing else mattered.

Chapter Sixteen

McKenna's Creek

Ezra had become aware, over the past week or two, of a marked increase in the insect population, most strikingly apparent in the woods on the hills above that abomination of an amusement park.

Among others, he'd noted, were katydids of various families; snowy tree crickets which had come, apparently, to feed on a bumper crop of aphids; and the predatory— and cannibalistic—California mantis. And he had come across a congregation of ladybugs, thousands upon thousands of them, dripping from the trees like a bright red moss.

He'd seen, as well, an enormous colony of web spinners whose silken environs wrapped around the bases of at least thirty trees, and looked from a distance like a shimmering fog. The insects' plump yellow bodies could be seen within the web, where they pulsated with the effort of producing even more silk.

That fevered activity disturbed Ezra in a way he would be hard-pressed to give voice to. Maybe it was because he had thought the web spinners to be harmless . . . and he wasn't sure anymore if they were.

Only it wasn't the web spinners he was concerned about

today, but rather a brood of sexton beetles.

The beetles were seekers of carrion, with a preference for snakes and frogs, as well as the smaller mammals—mice, primarily—which they buried to serve as food for their larvae. As such, he had quite naturally encountered them now and then as he tended, but of late they had become aggressive.

No longer were they limiting themselves to small creatures; yesterday at dusk he had returned to the clearing where he had staked out a wolverine who'd wandered well south of its habitat and evidently starved. When he approached the carcass, he'd found it heaving with the black and orange beetles.

Somehow—and he didn't want to know how—they'd untethered the wolverine and were actually *moving* it, which he would have thought an impossibility. Above them, a dark *cloud* of flies buzzed angrily, denied their share of the feast.

When he'd taken a hesitant step toward them, the beetles had rustled their stiff front wings, making a sound that, given their numbers, made the hair on the back of his neck stand on end.

He knew very well that they wouldn't bite a human, but that didn't mean they might not swarm him. Ezra could envision himself being suffocated, with beetles crawling into his mouth and wriggling down his throat as he tried to scream.

He'd retreated, but the ungodly sight had stayed with him, and last night, his dreams had been visited by the insects.

Web spinners attempted to encase him, as he slept, in a chrysalis of silk.

An outsized mantis stalked him among the trees, its insectile head swiveling as it searched for him with glowing green eyes.

But what had brought him awake drenched in sweat

116

were the sexton beetles, whose numbers had multiplied until they covered the ground as far as the eye could see in an undulating mass. And though they were incapable of intelligence, in his dream they had a purpose, and that was to punish him for allowing the earth-moving equipment to crush their larvae, their young.

Once awake, with his heart pounding, he'd gone to the cabin door to look out at the night and reassure himself that it had been only a dream. The only insect he'd seen was a single moth which had been caught between the screen and the door.

He'd set it free.

This morning, with the early pale sunlight filtering through the trees, Ezra meant to find the beetles, if he could, and destroy them. He had come to the conclusion, during the seemingly endless night, that he had no other choice.

The air was fragrant with pine, but he could also smell the gasoline vapors from the gallon jug he carried. He had pumped it from the underground tank he used to fuel the five horsepower generator, which in turn kept him from having to rely on the electric company for power.

He hoped that dousing the beetles with gasoline would be enough to kill them outright, but he was fully prepared, if worse came to worse, to set them on fire. He had brought a shovel with which to dig out a fire line, if necessary, or to shovel dirt on the flames.

Fire was an old enemy of his—back in 1933, a lightning strike had set the hills ablaze and he'd almost lost his life when the firestorm had unexpectedly changed direction—but somehow, he was more afraid of the beetles.

It took longer than he thought to find them, and when

he did, his first instinct was to turn and walk away. Walk because if he ran, they would know his fear and hunt him down.

There were more beetles than his mind could comprehend at first glance. They were in a constant state of motion, swarming all over a mound on the ground which was too large to be the wolverine.

The shape of the mound left little doubt as to what it was . . . or had been.

Human. It had to be human.

A tightness took hold in Ezra's chest, forcing the air from his lungs. Pain radiated from his sternum through his ribs, encircling his body to meet in a dull throb at his backbone.

A tendril of pain extended down his left arm, and he dropped the shovel with a thud. Without taking his eyes from the beetles, he leaned over and put down the gas can as gently, as quietly, as he could.

The sexton beetles, thank the Lord, ignored him in their frenzy.

For several seconds, his vision blurred as the hot pain tightened its grip on him. He felt himself break out in a sweat, felt it bead up on his forehead and run down his face to drop from his nose and chin.

With strength from somewhere deep within him, he took a few hesitant steps backward, each one costing him dearly in the constriction of his ribs. . . .

I will not die here, he thought through the pain. *I will not.*

Ezra stumbled backward, away from the brood. When he'd taken a dozen steps, he felt something on his right hand, and looked down to see a single sexton beetle, shiny black and orange, crawling up his arm.

He could have crushed it, but he did not. The beetle dropped off him, landed on the ground, and began to make its way back to the others.

118

Part Two

June 14, 1992
Sunday

Chapter Seventeen

Boston, Massachusetts

"Oh no," Dinah Fremont said into the phone as soon as her sleep-fogged mind was able to decipher what she was being told. "You've got to be kidding, but if you are, this isn't funny. You are kidding, aren't you? Please tell me you're kidding."

"I'm sorry, Dinah, but I'm not."

She groaned, falling back onto her pillow and covering her eyes with her arm. The voice that had woken her—from what promised to be a very interesting dream—belonged to Adele Brody.

The same Adele Brody who, up until sixty seconds ago, had been the chaperone for the disadvantaged youth program kids who were going to The Park. And who until sixty seconds ago had been scheduled to fly out of Logan International Airport this morning at ten o'clock, en route to the West Coast with Celeste Donatelli, the first of her five charges.

"Do you know," Dinah asked despairingly, "what this means?"

"Of course I do, and I am sorry, truly I am, but I'm sure you agree that in an emergency, my own family has to come first."

121

She wasn't at all sure that she agreed, although she knew it was small of her to feel that way. But *damn*, this threw a wrench into the works. "Yes, well, I suppose I understand."

"I knew you would. Anyway, I'll be glad to messenger the tickets over to you if you'll tell me where to have them sent."

Dinah recited her home address, and listened absently as it was read back to her. Accurately, of course; Mrs. Brody was nothing if not precise.

It did not escape her notice that the woman was using the same commonsense tone that had weighed so heavily in her favor when Dinah had interviewed her last month. This was a rock solid, somewhat matronly woman with a no-nonsense attitude.

Adele Brody had what Dinah thought of as "the look." Others, including herself, might talk themselves hoarse trying to make a recalcitrant child or teen see the error of his ways. Adele Brody could do it with a single silent, disapproving frown.

Perfect for the job.

Except Mrs. Brody was backing out, and all because of an *in-law*, for crying out loud. And a mother-in-law, at that. Dinah had never been married, but most of her friends were, and she'd heard plenty of stories from them. Weren't mothers-in-law always finding fault with the wives of their sons?

Leave it to her to find the one woman in Boston who had a warm relationship with her husband's mother. And certainly the one woman in all of Massachusetts whose husband's elderly mother was foolish enough to take a spin on a grandchild's skateboard, crazy enough to venture out into one of the city's famed cobblestone streets, and clumsy enough to fall and break both wrists.

Dinah considered herself a nice person, with a kind heart, and under normal circumstances, she would be

122

genuinely sorry to hear of anyone getting hurt, but at *this* moment, under *these* circumstances, with her own emergency staring her full in the face, she found that she was running short of sympathy.

"Adele," she said as calmly as she could, "what am I supposed to do? The plane leaves in"—she peeked at the clock—"three hours. Do you think I can find a replacement for you in three hours?"

"It won't be easy, I know. But . . . my place is with my family."

"There's nothing I can say or do, or *pay* that'll make you change your mind?"

"No, I'm sorry. Have you thought of trying some of the others you interviewed?"

"I haven't had *time* to think of anything," she said through clenched teeth. Then she took a deep breath. It wouldn't do any good to lose her cool. "But I guess I'll find someone. Thank you for calling, Adele. I hope your mother-in-law feels better soon."

But the moment she hung up the phone she admitted to herself that it was hopeless. The applicant files were at the office, a good twenty minutes away. Even if she headed out the door in her pajamas this very instant, it would be seven thirty at the earliest before she could make the first call.

There was no reason to believe that she would find a willing replacement on such short notice. She might make a dozen calls, and not get a taker. But say that by eight fifteen she'd found someone. This saint would have to dress, pack, perhaps make arrangements with a neighbor to pick up the mail, stop the newspaper delivery, feed the plants, and water the cat.

Or something of the kind. By now, even in the best-case scenario, it would be 9:00 a.m.

The chaperone would then have to find his or her way across town to Celeste's to pick her up, presumably in a cab, and head for the airport. Even a kamikaze cabby in an Indy racing car would be hard pressed to run that circuit in less than an hour.

If by some miracle they made it to the airport before the plane took off—and flights were *never* delayed when you needed one to be—there was still the foray through the terminal maze to contend with. She couldn't recall that any of the applicants had demonstrated an ability to leap over rows of seats and small children to make it to the boarding gate in time.

Moreover, the airline insisted in its imperious manner that passengers check in no less than half an hour before boarding, and had been known to release unclaimed seats to those flying standby.

The simple solution would be to rebook the flight for a later hour, but then she would also have to rebook the connections in Des Moines and Denver, *and* notify those kids of the change in plans. She'd have to call New Mexico to change that flight to Denver, and the fifth child, flying up to San Francisco from San Diego, would no doubt need to be shuffled as well.

It had taken the travel agent, Peter, Joanne, and herself a couple of weeks to coordinate everyone's schedule and to work out most of the bugs—and still the plan, though intricate, was far from perfect—but the domino effect resulting from a single change could wipe everything out in the blink of an eye.

Dinah had no choice, then; she would have to substitute as chaperone, at least for today.

Maybe today while she was busy ramrodding the kids through four, count 'em, *four* airports, and getting everyone settled in at The Park tomorrow morning, Peter would be able to find someone willing to fly out and take her place for the rest of the week.

Failing that, well, it had been a few years since she'd been to an amusement park. She might try to relax and enjoy it.

At eight thirty, the cab pulled to the curb in front of Celeste's building.

"You going in there?" the cabbie asked, squinting in disbelief.

"I won't be but a minute." Before she'd left her apartment, she'd called and spoken to Celeste's father—she had apparently awakened him—who promised his daughter would be ready to go when Dinah arrived.

She had been rather hoping that Celeste would have chosen to wait out on the stoop, so that she wouldn't have to go inside. She didn't consider herself a coward, and it wasn't as if she'd never been in even worse places—there was no way to avoid it in her line of work—but she had thought it might embarrass Celeste to have her see how the family lived.

"I hope you got a gun, lady," the cabbie said as she climbed out.

Dinah didn't bother answering. She closed the cab door, which the driver promptly locked, pulled her sweater down around her hips, tucked her purse securely under her arm, and started up the stairs.

The front doors opened into a vestibule which had long ago been stripped of anything decorative or, she supposed, that could be pawned. The windows were narrow, grimy, and curtainless, the linoleum of indeterminate color and worn down to its black base in various spots. Dozens of cigarette butts littered the floor.

There were no furnishings, but why would there be? She couldn't imagine anyone wanting to sit down in here and while away an afternoon, if for no other reason than the smell. Someone had emptied a few cans of Lysol in a failed attempt to mask the pungent blend of urine, vomit, and stale smoke. Mingled in with that was the slight but

125

unmistakable odor of alcohol fumes that were given off as a kind of by product by habitual drinkers.

Noxious was the word for it.

But she wasn't here to inspect the premises for the health department *or* the Environmental Protection Agency. Besides, the meter was running, and precious minutes were ticking off the clock.

The building had an elevator, which looked to be out of order, and she headed for the stairs. When she reached the first landing, she could hear footsteps from above her, coming down. She paused and peered up into the poorly lit stairwell.

"Celeste?"

Her voice echoed and lost clarity in the enclosed space so that it sounded distorted and unfamiliar, even to her. There was no answer. After a brief hesitation, in which she considered going back down and pretending she'd just arrived, she resumed climbing.

On the third floor landing, she turned a corner and came face to face with Celeste.

"Oh God," she said, her hand at her throat. "You scared the life out of me."

In the dim light, Celeste's expression was unreadable. "Yeah?"

"Yes." Dinah noted that the girl had only a single piece of luggage, and that was a carry-on bag. "Are you ready? Have you got everything?"

"Pretty much."

"Then let's go."

Amazingly, the ride to the airport was going well. Traffic was moving smoothly and the cabbie had run only a couple of yellows and one red light.

Celeste had little to say, obviously preferring to stare out the window. She wore a thin white sweater, skin-tight blue jeans with holes in both knees, and black ankle boots. Three silver earrings dangled from one pierced ear, while the other sported a solitary pearl.

At least twenty bracelets adorned each of her slender wrists, jingling softly in accompaniment when she moved but also hiding the scars from when she'd tried to kill herself last.

Dinah frowned, remembering how pale and defiant Celeste had been when she'd visited her in the hospital afterward. A man was there in the room with her, and it hadn't taken more than a look at him to realize that he was her pimp. He wasn't what she might have expected, in his Italian suit and Gucci loafers, although the diamond stud in his left nostril might have been a tipoff.

Dinah knew from a contact in the police department that the man went by the name Neville. He had carved a niche for himself in the market by providing young girls to much older men. He had recruited Celeste when she was twelve with a promise that he would take care of her.

What he took was half of what she earned, and her clientele paid very handsomely. Neville supposedly invested most of the rest, giving her only a modest allowance for clothes, makeup, and other incidentals. It was Neville who'd arranged and paid for the two abortions that Celeste had had to date.

Despite the fact that Neville was white and in his midtwenties, Celeste told the nurse that he was her father, or rather, "My sweet daddy." He had brought her a dozen roses and a stuffed bunny.

When he left, Dinah looked surreptitiously at the floor for the slime trail.

As far as Dinah knew, the girl still was turning the occasional trick, although never out on the street. She was too valuable to her "manager" to be endangered by working in the rough trade.

Which reminded her. "You're not in any trouble because of this, are you?"

"Hmm?"

"You were able to get time off from . . . work?"

"Sure, no problem," Celeste said. She dug through her leather handbag and pulled out a piece of bubble gum which she unwrapped and put in her mouth. "I get vacation just like anyone else."

"Oh."

"Two weeks, even, so when I get back maybe we'll go somewhere, New York or some place nice."

"We? Your father and you?"

"The other 'we'," she said, and snapped her gum. "You don't like him, do you?"

"I won't lie to you, Celeste. I detest the man and what he does."

She shrugged. "Darla—she's a friend of mine—doesn't like him much either, says his percentage is too high, but he says he's not in no fucking popularity contest, and it no sweat off his—"

"Celeste," Dinah said, seeing the cabbie was taking an interest in their conversation. "Maybe we can talk about this on the plane."

"Whatever." Celeste positioned the bubble gum between her teeth and pulled at it with her fingers, stretching the gum until it looked as though it might snap. Then she stuck out her tongue and reclaimed it.

As innocent and even childish as playing with her gum might seem, Dinah had seldom seen anything so deliberately provocative.

The cabbie nearly ran them off the road.

At the airport, Dinah was further enlightened as to how the male animal reacted to Celeste.

A couple of men in the terminal most likely had a self-induced case of whiplash, judging by how quickly they

128

heads had turned to watch Celeste go by. Another nearly walked into a wall.

Someone else whistled.

And one guy, younger and bolder than the rest, had trailed them all the way to the gate, in the process making admiring remarks which Celeste completely ignored. It was almost as if she accepted the attention as her due.

The girl showed more composure than Dinah would have at her age. Her fifteenth birthday was a week away, and yet just how old was Celeste, really?

Fourteen going on twenty-five?

From Dinah's adult—and female—perspective, the girl was a walking fashion disaster, in the style of borderline trashy but flirting with out-and-out cheap. Even so, there wasn't one man in the lot of them, she thought, who wouldn't make a complete ass of himself at a chance to stroke the girl's exposed *knees*.

And worse than that, there wasn't one of them to whom it had occurred or would probably matter that, despite her appearance, Celeste was legally a child.

The child took full advantage of the spacious first-class seats, bringing her long legs up and wrapping her arms around them, then resting her chin on one bare silken knee.

"Well," Dinah said, unbuckling her seat belt and looking out at Boston below, "we're on our way."

"Yeah."

"Next stop, Des Moines."

"Des *Moines?*"

"And then Denver—"

"Oh wow, the hot spots. Will we make it to Peoria? Then I can die happy."

Dinah regarded her, wondering how much of the girl's indifference was feigned and what was real. Although

129

she'd met Celeste almost four years ago, she had no real sense of having made a connection.

That bothered her, because she was generally quite successful at bonding with the kids she worked with. And she did care about this girl.

"Celeste?"

Celeste gave her a sidelong glance. "What?"

"May I ask you a question?"

"You always do."

Dinah smiled slightly and nodded. "I know. But this is something I haven't asked before."

"Go ahead."

"You don't have to answer if you don't want to, but . . . I've been wondering for a long time. Why would a twelve-year-old girl . . . why did you . . . become a prostitute?"

Celeste frowned and plucked at the loose threads bordering one of the holes in her jeans. "Why," she said flatly. "Why."

"I'm not condemning you, please understand that, but I never could figure out why anyone as young as you were would do such a thing. And at *twelve*."

"What else could I do?" she said, and shrugged. "And as for being twelve when I started . . . what can I say? I guess I'm just a late bloomer."

Chapter Eighteen

San Diego, California

The arrival of the garbage truck signaled that it was time to get up.

Jesus Rivera shifted on the piece of cardboard that served as his bed, and peered out at the street. The garbage man was whistling as he went about his work, in a good mood today, and Jesus considered briefly crawling from beneath the porch and greeting him.

But no. It had only been a few days since the last time, and he should not expect the garbage man to give him money just because they came from the same neighborhood in Tijuana.

Besides, the man was legal and he was not. If Jesus annoyed him, there was no telling what might happen. He'd risked too much coming here to be sent back.

And even if the garbage man would not think to turn him in, it was better that he be unaware that this was where Jesus slept. Safe sleeping places were hard to find, and a careless word might cost him his bed.

The bad men out there had big ears.

With the decision made, Jesus watched silently as the garbage was dumped into the gaping mouth of the truck, and then had to cover his ears at the noise when the truck began to chew it all up.

Someone on the street had told him once that a man who'd sought shelter in the rain and fallen asleep in a dumpster had been crushed by those monster jaws, his screams unheard in the din of the powerful motors.

Jesus did not know if that was true, but in case it was, he kept well clear of the dumpsters, even though they were a source of treasure for others more brave than he.

He had his own sources, anyway. He'd learned a lot in the three months since he'd first come to *El Norte*, and had discovered many good places to scavenge.

Here, as in Tijuana, there were restaurants where people ate at tables outdoors. When the people left there was often food remaining on their plates.

He was very quick; it was easy to grab a half of a sandwich or fill his hand with tortilla chips from a woven basket left wastefully full.

At one or two small cafés in a poorer part of the city, kindhearted waitresses would direct him to the back kitchen door, and then let him choose what he wanted off the plates before they were scraped clean into the trash. In the trash the food would be mixed with paper and cigarettes and coffee grounds, and while there were some on the street who were hungry enough to dig it out and eat it anyway, he was grateful for not having to do that.

If he was unable to get to those places, he went to a store that he knew of. Sometimes he had to wait for a while, but sooner or later, the men working the loading dock would disappear inside, and he would clamber up and dig through the piles of dented cans and torn packages that were being thrown out.

And if he didn't find anything he liked, he could always trade whatever he had with someone else on the street. There was one toothless old woman who would give him chocolate for cans of soup.

Jesus supposed it was all she could eat.

He tried when he could to grab at least one can of soup for her.

Today, though, food wasn't the problem. He had a box of crackers, three small tins of meat—which were called, oddly, deviled ham, as if *el diablo* were a friend to be welcomed—and several pieces of bruised but otherwise edible apples he'd found under a tree. Enough, he knew, to last two days, or maybe three.

Today, Jesus needed to look for clothes.

He had grown since leaving Mexico, and though his pants were loose around his waist, they were too short by the width of his hand. His shirt had lost most of its buttons. And never in all his wanderings had he ever come across another pair of socks that would fit him.

Yesterday he'd overheard two *abuelas* talking about a place called "the goodwill" where clothes could be had for free, if one showed up on the right day.

From what he understood, the Americans gave their old clothes to this, "the goodwill" place. Some of these clothes were better and some worse. The better clothes were cleaned and mended and then sold in the store. They did not cost much, according to the grandmothers; a shirt might cost two U.S. quarters, fifty cents, but who would spend money for something they could get free?

The clothes that were not so good were tossed into big wooden boxes behind the store. These clothes were bought by women who would take them across the border and sell them in Tijuana.

But first, these women threw out the clothes that were too ugly for anyone to wear.

The ugly clothes could be had for free, then, on the right day.

And Sunday—today—was the right day.

Although it was summer, the mornings were gray and

133

cloudy, and Jesus shivered as he began the long walk across town to get his new clothes. He only hoped they were not so very ugly.

He had found a thick plastic bag blowing down the street some time ago, and he brought it with him to help him carry the clothes and anything else he might find. It was bright yellow with the words *Tower Video* in red letters on both sides.

In the bag he had his comb, a sliver of blue soap, a toothbrush with a broken handle, a plastic fork, and a can opener. These were too precious to be left behind, even for a few hours.

He also had a bus pass he'd found in the gutter. Sometimes, when many people were boarding, the bus driver would not take the time to look at it closely, and he would have a free ride. If the driver protested, Jesus would turn and run. No one could catch him.

Today, though, he had to walk; the buses were nearly always empty on the Lord's day.

Still, it was not unpleasant. He liked to look in the windows of the stores, imagining what things he would buy if he had money *and* a place to hide them. Walking past the houses, he thought what it would be like to live in one again.

Not too much different, he told himself, than sleeping underneath an enclosed porch.

The street went uphill, and Jesus became a little out of breath, but he was no longer cold. Up at the top was a church whose white steeple nearly reached the clouds. It had beautiful windows made of colored glass, and a neat green yard.

The name of this church, which he had seen before, was Saint Francis. Services were being held, he knew, because the parking lot was full of cars.

One woman, though, was standing on the brick steps in front of the closed doors. She was looking this way and that, and when she saw him, she waved.

"Thank heavens, there you are," her voice drifted down to him.

Jesus smiled and waved back. It amazed him how friendly some people were. She didn't even know him and yet she was starting down the stairs as if to greet him when he walked by.

"Hurry," she called.

Why should *he* hurry? Jesus turned to see if he had made a mistake and she was speaking not to him but to someone behind him. The sidewalk, though, was empty.

"Come now, don't dawdle."

He was far enough from her that he could turn and run without her being able to catch him, but the smile on her face reassured him, and he continued on toward her and the church.

She had reached the sidewalk and now stood there, hands on her hips, watching his slow progress and shaking her head. "My word, anyone who didn't know better would think you were walking the plank instead of going to The Park."

"The plank?" he said. *"Que es* the plank? What is the plank?"

"Never mind that now." She extended her hand. "Come with me."

Jesus looked at her hand. "I'm sorry, I do not understand."

The woman sighed. "Where is your mother?" She shaded her eyes and looked down the street. "Didn't she come with you? She was supposed to come with you."

"My mother is dead."

"Oh!" The woman blinked and frowned. "No one told me. Well."

But why would anyone tell this woman his mother had

135

died? He didn't understand and, becoming more uncomfortable by the moment, he started to back away.

The woman noticed; she reached out and captured his right hand. "No one told me," she said again. Her hand was warm and soft and gentle. "I apologize, Joey, for the misunderstanding—"

Joey? "Jesus," he said, but quietly, because it was wrong for him to correct her.

"—but we really have no time. If you haven't anyone to see you off, we'd better be on our way."

Jesus could easily have escaped, but there was kindness in the woman's blue eyes, and he saw no harm in going with her to the park. And on the way back, he would ask her to leave him off at "the goodwill."

He had been to Balboa Park only once, and had thought it at first to be a good place. There were trees, and trails that led through the canyons, and he saw at once that many of the people who lived in the heavy brush were from his country.

Jesus stayed through the day, and had even considered finding a place to sleep in the bushes, but then he saw the policemen on horses riding through. A minute later, many, many police cars had driven up, their red lights flashing and sirens wailing, and he had watched as they led off a man wearing no shoes and no shirt, but who was smeared all over with blood.

The man was screaming and yelling and swearing, mostly in Spanish although Jesus had never heard many of the words. Someone said the blood was not his, that he had cut another man with a knife.

The other man had died.

Jesus wondered if the bloody man had the same sickness of the brain as the dog who had followed him home. The thought frightened him.

He was scared also of the police, and when they turned their attention to the crowd that had gathered, he slipped away. He went to stand at the bus stop, feeling very much alone and lost. Finally a sailor in uniform happened by and took pity on him, paying his way back downtown.

The lesson he'd learned was that Balboa Park wasn't safe after the sun went down, but now it was early in the day, and he wouldn't be alone. Besides, the woman taking him there was a *gringa*. She had a big car with windows that went up and down at the touch of a button.

No harm would come to them, and the police would surely not bother anyone with such a grand car.

"Here we are," the woman said.

Jesus did not recognize Balboa Park, which seemed to have sprouted buildings and was closer to the ocean than he recalled it being.

"Let's see, which gate do I take?"

"Gate?"

"I always get lost here," she said. "I don't know why I let them talk me into this."

Jesus realized that she was talking to herself and not to him, but felt it polite to respond in some way. "I've been lost before."

"Hmm."

"Can you see the zoo?"

The woman laughed. "The zoo? Heavens, no. We're miles from the zoo."

"But . . . the park is near the zoo." This he knew, having seen it with his own eyes.

"You're thinking of Balboa Park," she said, and reached across to pat his leg. "The place you're going is much nicer than that."

"Yes?"

"Absolutely. You'll love it—"

Jesus sat up straighter, and felt his eyes get big. They were at an airport. A plane took off and the sound was so loud it seemed to rattle his teeth. It was *much* louder than the garbage truck. The woman pressed a button and the windows glided up.

"You'll be going on a plane just like that one," she said.

Jesus touched a finger to his chest. "Me?"

"And someone will meet you at the airport in San Francisco, and you'll spend the night in a nice hotel, and then tomorrow, Joey"—she paused and looked directly into his eyes—"you'll be there for the Grand Opening of The Park."

Chapter Nineteen

Denver, Colorado

Max Brown could not recall an hour in all of his life that had lasted as long as the one he was now sweating through.

Mrs. Brennan had accompanied him to the airport, which he could handle, but the plane coming in from back east with two of the other kids and the chaperone had been delayed in Des Moines, and even though he'd told her he was fine on his own, Mrs. Brennan had insisted on plunking herself down and waiting with him.

An hour of being on his best behavior was skirting the known limits of his endurance.

To make matters worse, the girl from New Mexico and her escort had arrived, and though she was by no means hard to look at, this Betsy Parker was a little princess, a squeaky-clean straight arrow.

Things were looking up in Albuquerque if this was what they considered "disadvantaged."

Dressed in a white dress, and with her dark red hair twisted into one of those French braids, she looked like a sacrificial virgin. All that was missing were the maidens who sang and threw flowers into the volcano, as appetizers, he supposed.

The guy who'd come with her kept giving Max the evil eye, as though *he* were the volcano, primed and ready to erupt.

As if this girl were his type.

Still, it tickled him to watch the old guy—Torrance was his name—bristle whenever he spoke to, looked at, or breathed the same air as Miss Betsy.

"So," he said, "Betsy. You've graduated?"

She looked at Torrance first and then at her hands. "Yes. Last Friday."

"Huh." He tried to think if any of his friends had actually left high school with a diploma in hand instead of a foot in their behinds, but the guys he ran with weren't exactly scholars. "I'll bet you're glad."

"Glad?"

"You know. School's out for *ever.*"

She smiled a bit wistfully. "I think I'll miss it, really."

From the corner of his eye, Max saw that Mrs. Brennan was nodding in approval, and so he leaned closer to Betsy. "Me too," he whispered loudly.

Not that there was any real danger of him graduating before he reached middle age. If O'Toole opened his big yap about that day in the alley, he might get kicked out yet. Then again, why would O'Toole speak now, what with all the time that had passed? And after having been warned to forever hold his peace?

Max shook his head and focused his attention on the girl.

Torrance reached over, took one of Betsy's hands, and squeezed it. "The school," he said, kind of deep in his throat, "is going to miss you."

Betsy blushed and bit at her lower lip.

Max arched an eyebrow, one of the many skills he'd learned from Leroy. And just what nasty business was going on here? Some extracurricular activity? He glanced at Mrs. Brennan, who seemed oblivious.

Naturally. Her eagle eye was trained on *him*.

He grinned at her.

"Max," she said, "why don't you check and see if the plane is in yet."

"Sure." He got to his feet, took a step, then stopped and turned around. "You wanna come?"

Betsy froze like a deer caught in high beams. "Me?"

"Yeah, you. We're gonna be spending the next week together"—that was for lover boy's benefit—"so we might as well get to know one another."

"Go along, Betsy," Mrs. Brennan urged. "Don't be shy."

After a moment of indecision, she got to her feet. Torrance reluctantly released her hand.

Max *felt* the eyes on his back as they walked off toward the ticket counter. He put a little sass in his step, and made certain that his arm accidentally brushed against the prom queen.

"Betsy," he said before they were out of earshot, "I hope you brought your bikini. . . ."

The flight from Des Moines finally arrived, an hour and a half late.

In the crush of people, it took Max a couple of minutes to get it straight in his mind who was with their party and who was only passing by, but when it all jelled, he liked the way things were shaping up.

Mercy!

The chaperone looked young for the job, but she immediately took charge, making introductions all around. "Max Brown?" she said when she came to him.

He saluted. "Present and accounted for."

"I'm Dinah Fremont, and this is Nicholas Cole, from Iowa—"

The kid stuck out his hand and Max shook it, his grip a degree or two firmer than was called for. Cole winced,

141

but said nothing.

Good. They understood each other.

"And from Boston, this is Celeste Donatelli."

"Ooh," Max said, "*hurt* me."

Celeste, who was totally hot, acted as though she hadn't heard him. She ignored his extended hand; her own hands were in her back pockets, hugging her fine little ass. Her eyes met his for a split second and then she looked away, her glance finally coming to rest on Betsy.

Checking out the competition, Max thought. But if Betsy was a pure and refined Miss Sugar and Spice, Celeste was *everything* nice.

And the bitch knew it.

"I hope you weren't terribly inconvenienced," the boss lady was saying to Mrs. Brennan. "These layovers can be murder."

Torrance, who had deliberately missed his return flight to Albuquerque, shook his head. "It was no trouble at all." His hand had found its way to the small of Betsy's back. "Just take good care of my girl."

"Don't worry," Dinah Fremont said, and smiled warmly. "I will."

Max wondered what it was with adults. Here this old guy Torrance—who was thirty at least—was putting his hands all over Betsy, who was probably half his age, which *had* to be a felony, as well as revolting, and no one so much as blinked. Yet let someone his age do some penny-ante, half-ass thing like spit on the sidewalk, and the kid would be thrown up against a cop car so fast his head would spin, spreading 'em and being patted down.

There was no justice in the world.

He sighed.

"Max?"

Dinah Fremont rested her hand on his arm. The lady got familiar fast, he thought.

"Would you mind going with Nick to the men's room?

This place is a madhouse, and I don't want him wandering off and getting lost."

So that was part of the gig; playing wet nurse. He looked at the twerp. The kid's blue eyes with their long dark lashes were nearly as pretty as Betsy's. Maybe he wasn't small-town enough to get lost, but with those eyes, he might attract an admirer.

He didn't see any way out of it, so Max nodded. "Come on."

Max hoisted himself up to sit on the counter while he waited for the kid to do his business. A gray-haired old buzzard who looked like he'd swallowed a few pits with his prunes frowned fiercely at him.

The geezer opened his mouth to say something, but Max, anticipating, slid off the counter and started his way. Before he'd taken two steps, Pops was hightailing it out the door.

Too easy, he thought, and leaned down to peek under the doors—the kid had gone into a stall—to see if there might be any other takers.

Not that he really wanted there to be. Mrs. Brennan could still yank him from this trip, which he would deeply regret after all the trouble he'd gone to. Of course, if she did, she might come to regret it later.

The problem with retribution was that *some* people didn't get the point, didn't learn from the experience. He figured Mrs. Brennan for one of those; she no doubt would sic the cops on him.

On the other hand, he had two more years as a juvenile. Juvie violations were nothing to sweat, and the big, bad Hall adults liked to threaten kids with, was, to him, a minor league social club.

He did want to avoid the jail, though. Go into jail as a juvie, and it was the same as having USDA Choice stamped on your forehead. Fresh meat for the inmates, and it was "dinner is now being served."

A toilet flushed, and after a minute Cole reappeared. He went to the sink to wash his hands like the good boy he probably was. Not quite a Poindexter, Max thought, but damn close.

"Hey," he said. "How old are you?"

"Twelve."

He'd guessed right on the money. "What do twelve-year-old kids do in Iowa?"

Cole made a face at the mirror. "Listen, I'm not *from* Iowa. I mean, I don't live there."

"No?" He pulled half a dozen paper towels from the dispenser and handed them to Cole.

"No. We were just passing through and—"

"Who's we?"

"My folks, my little sister—"

"Talk about little sisters . . . sister Celeste is welcome in my family any time."

"Yeah, she's okay."

Max had been interested in girls at twelve—he'd been born interested—but he could tell the kid wasn't on his wave length. Better to change the subject, he thought, than get caught corrupting babyface. "Where are you from then, if not Iowa?"

"Nowhere."

"How the shit can you be from nowhere?"

The kid had wadded the towels into a tight ball and he made a bank shot into the trash. "We travel all over the place, that's how."

"But you must've started from somewhere."

"I don't think so."

"What about school? Where'd you go to school?"

"I didn't."

Max was intrigued. "Not ever?"

"Not until I landed in Iowa, anyway."

144

"So what the hell happened there? Did they bust your parents or something?"

All at once, the kid clammed up. He shook his head and started for the door.

Max reacted without thinking. He grabbed fists full of the kid's jacket, lifted him off the ground, spun, and slammed him against the mirror, which cracked.

"What the fuck is your problem?" he asked through clenched teeth, still seeing the film of red that colored his vision whenever he got mad. "I'm making conversation, here."

To his credit, the boy didn't flinch. "Sorry, I thought I heard them calling."

Max blinked. "Huh?"

"Miss Fremont and the others."

He relaxed his hold. "Shit, I forgot." He put the kid down and looked at himself in the mirror. The crack split his face in halves, neither of which looked too damned cool. He made an effort to relax, but he could *feel* the blood pumping wild in his veins.

"Hey," he said to the kid, "no hard feelings."

Cole shook his head and tried a smile.

The release of tension made his muscles feel kind of warm and, what was the word? Spent. Sort of the way he felt after getting off.

"Shit," he said, "it's a good thing you used the can before, or we'd really have a mess."

The kid gave a weak laugh.

"You know, you're all right." He draped his arm across Cole's shoulders and headed for the door. "But you did make me break the mirror, so you've got seven years of bad news luck coming to you."

"What's seven years?" the kid said, and to Max he sounded old.

"I hear ya," Max said.

Finally it was time to board the plane. Max had heard about the security drill and when it was his turn to go through the metal detector, he emptied his pockets, placing his wallet and a couple dozen of his ball bearings into the little tray.

"What are those?" the dude from Security asked.

"Steelies." That brought only a blank look. "You know, marbles."

"Marbles?"

"Yeah. You know, cat's eyes, purees, steelies."

The dude gave him a skeptical look. "A little old for kid games, aren't you?"

"Man, I got two years left of kid games," he said as he collected the bearings on the other side, "and I intend to make the most of it."

Chapter Twenty

The Park

"Watch it," Wesley said, looking up from the section of electronic track he was adjusting.

One of the Web's four-foot-tall black spiders lumbered by, and its jointed metal foreleg very nearly hit him in the head.

"Oops," the operator said. "I didn't see you working there."

"You shouldn't be running him that fast anyway." Wesley gave a final turn to the screw and glanced after the spider, which was rapidly nearing one of the nests.

Dozens of baby mechanical spiders were following their programs, scurrying back and forth, under the watchful eyes—all six of them—of their mother. Her pedipalps gleamed in the red background light.

"Be careful that he doesn't step on the little ones," Wesley said.

"Don't worry, I'm getting the hang of it."

He had designed the hand controls as backup to the electronic track, and to give a chosen few spiders a greater range, but with the grand opening now only fifteen hours away, he was second guessing himself; the operators weren't picking up the fine art of spider driving as quickly as he would have hoped.

The big spider missed crushing a baby by a hair's width; the little spider, coincidentally of course, then turned and ran for its mother.

"Shut him off," he ordered, getting to his feet.

"Sure, okay."

The spider slowed to a halt at the edge of the ride pathway, three of its eight legs suspended. At that moment, an empty ride pod swept by, and the air it displaced set the spider rocking.

He winced. "You do know how expensive these guys are, don't you?"

"Well, yes, but—"

"But nothing. Rice would have a coronary if one was hurt . . . I mean damaged."

"Gotcha," the operator said. "You won't clock this fella doing more than a mile an hour."

"That's the idea."

He watched then as the spider crawled off, almost in slow motion, with the operator following behind. At that speed, he thought, someone would think it had arachnid arthritis.

It was almost comical; if he'd had the energy, he might even have laughed.

What wasn't funny was the possibility of equipment damage. The big ones were a bargain at two hundred thousand each, but worth every cent of that. They could rear up on their hind legs; lower themselves to the ground in a squat, as though lying in wait; grasp small designated objects with their pedipalps; and—his favorite function—dispense silk via their spinnerets.

Which, unfortunately, they were unable to weave.

"Yet," he said aloud, correcting himself. He had in mind a number of refinements which might allow for that, but it would take a year or longer to incorporate the necessary design changes.

Nonetheless, even without being able to spin a web, the spiders were impressive. Their many pairs of eyes glowed threateningly . . . and came in a choice of red, yellow, or a bilious green. Their fangs opened and closed, allowing one of the shiny black widow models to perpetually feast on its unfortunate mate.

The eerily realistic tarantula utilized a mapping grid in its program memory to keep it from getting lost as it wandered throughout the Web. It was programmed to find, catch, and then drag a variety of victim insects, including a grasshopper and a wicked-looking scorpion, into its underground home.

The tarantula cost half a million.

Others were designed to climb the webs, and there was one in the second pavilion who could "parachute" using a strand of silk as a guide. Others were strictly robotic; the sensors in their abdomens detected an impulse from the electronic track, and they followed that impulse blindly, and without straying . . . much.

A daddy longlegs model had been sent back to the drawing board, to get, as the company line went, all of the bugs worked out.

The smaller species and infant spiders cost less to build, and had fewer functions, but even they were by no means cheap. If that spider baby *had* been crushed, it would have cost a minimum of sixty-five thousand dollars to replace.

Wesley wouldn't care to be the person who had to inform Sheldon Rice of its demise. The nearer it got to opening day, the more demanding and dictatorial Rice had become. He had gone on a firing spree a couple of weeks back that had everyone ducking for cover.

The order of the day? Cover your ass, or acronymically speaking, CYA.

Even Nancy Chan had been reduced to tears once or twice by Rice's tirades, and it was hardly a secret that she was directing significantly more than the company's "pub-

149

lic affairs."

Wesley was about the only employee Rice hadn't yelled at, a fact he attributed to Rice's awareness that he was near his breaking point. Eighteen-hour days and seven-day work weeks had challenged his endurance, and severely tried his patience.

Still, the end was in sight. When he finished here, he had only to adjust the wind-velocity in the Tunnel and he would have completed the final operations checks on Levels One *and* Two.

When he'd started twelve hours ago, it had seemed he would never get to this point.

And as for Level Three, there wasn't any rush. He estimated that it would be Friday before any of the guests had accrued enough points to qualify for admission to Level Three and the Games.

Besides, Level Three had only the Mercenaries to tend to, and there were just the six of them. Their sophisticated programming had been fine-tuned and perfected back in August, and the stun guns had cleared in January.

There was no reason that he couldn't handle the Level Three run-through in a single afternoon. He'd get one of the guys to come up and act as a target to make sure the robots' heat-sensing mechanism checked out; it wouldn't do to have them lock in on a chipmunk or jackrabbit or whatever other small animal roamed in these hills and run the poor thing to ground.

These days if you so much as gave a furry little creature a dirty look, you could count on animal rights activists showing up on your doorstep with their chants and placards.

Wesley liked animals as well as the next guy, but personally, if forced to choose between facing off an activist and outwitting a Mercenary, he'd take his chances with the robots. They were heartless, but at least they played fair.

Inspecting the Tunnel took forty-five minutes, the majority of which he spent in a totally aimless and therefore enjoyable argument about drag coefficients with the junior engineer.

The Tunnel was one of the simpler attractions. It was essentially a huge, deep, vertical tube through which incredibly powerful fans blew air at high speed. The guests were required to wear special winged jumpsuits, goggles, and padded headgear complete with two-way communication devices. After being given a rudimentary lesson on how to steer themselves, they would be instructed to jump down into the tunnel with their arms and legs spread.

It was quite a breathtaking drop at first, but the wind in their wings would lift them, allowing them to experience the closest thing to free flight that man could know within the pull of gravity.

Each flier found his or her own level, variable by body weight and the exposed surface area of the wings. Five feet from the bottom there were two tight mesh safety nets which would keep the fliers from getting too close to the air jets or, in the unlikely event of equipment failure, from plunging to the floor.

The only problem they'd had with the Tunnel was getting the volunteers who were testing it to come back out.

Flying, it seemed, was addictive.

At seven thirty he arrived at 3-C to enter the status reports on the work he'd done. Bell, who'd been hired to replace Perkins, was sitting at the central console with his feet up.

"Wesley," the engineer said, "I was just thinking about getting off my lazy ass and looking for you."

"Thinking about it, huh?" Wesley selected a terminal, grabbed a chair which he turned around backward, and sat down.

"Yeah." Bell frowned at the paper clip he'd apparently been straightening. "Needless to say, I decided against it. You know these things *never* can be restored to the original shape, as simple as it is."

Wesley laughed. He liked Bell and envied his irreverent attitude. "This is what the boss pays you overtime to think about?"

Bell considered and then nodded. "Pretty much. Any slave-driving son of a capitalist who'd expect a body to work more than eight hours a day doesn't deserve any deeper thinking, least as far as I'm concerned."

"Well, the worst is behind us." Wesley called up the file on the Web and scrolled it until he reached where he'd left off. "I don't know about anyone else, but as soon as I finish here, I'm going up and taking a nosedive into my bed."

"Sounds reasonable. Shit."

Wesley glanced up; the paper clip Bell had been manipulating had broken in two. He tossed the remains onto a small pile of similar pieces on the desk.

"So much for my theory on the tensile strength of distressed metals," Bell said.

"That reminds me," Wesley said, "speaking of tensile strength . . . did you see the latest report on the properties of the spider silk?"

Bell groaned. "Don't you ever stop?"

"No, really . . ."

The older man swung his feet off the desk, planted them resolutely, and stood up. He came around to Wesley's terminal, reached over his shoulder, and tapped the escape key.

"Hey!"

"You work too hard, kid." Bell logged off, using, to

Wesley's surprise, *his* access code.

"How did you—"

"Same way some of us old dogs got to *be* old dogs was by learning a couple of new tricks. You youngsters think you know all there is to know, but you forget there weren't any computers until *we* damn well made them."

"But my access code—"

"You can change it if you don't trust me," Bell said, and gave him a quizzical look. "But you don't trust anybody, do you?"

"That's not . . . ," he started, and then fell silent. In fact it was true.

Not that he didn't have justification for his mistrust; his own parents had appropriated money from the trust fund his maternal grandfather had established to pay for his education. He'd sued them when he'd found out, but of course by then the money was long gone, and the judgment in his favor was an empty victory.

Wesley frowned, remembering.

"Listen, I know it's none of my business," Bell said, "and I don't claim to know the whys and wherefores of how you came to feel that way, but it can't be a comfortable way to live."

The loner in him hated this and resented the intrusion and invasion of his privacy, but another side of him insisted on listening, hearing, or wanting to hear, something beyond the words.

"You don't know me from Adam," Bell said. "We've only been working together, what? Six, eight weeks now. But you can trust me. I've never put a knife in anyone's back and I'm proud to say I've never driven anybody that I know of to want to stick one in mine."

Wesley kept his eyes on the blank screen. He hadn't a lot of experience at this.

"I like you," Bell continued. "You got a good mind and a sense of humor, and you don't take yourself too awful seriously. But you've got to loosen up, Wes."

That he'd heard before.

"You've been working hard—"

"We all have," he interjected.

"But nobody's worked harder than you. You know what I think? I know you're tired, but I think that instead of you going up to bed, we ought to spiff ourselves up and go into McKenna's Creek and have a drink."

"I'm only twenty," Wesley said, and for once he wasn't really looking for an excuse. "And I look it. They won't serve me."

"Then I'll buy a couple of cold six-packs and we can serve ourselves."

He'd never acquired a taste for beer, but what the hell. "Okay," he said. "Why not?"

Chapter Twenty-one

McKenna's Creek

There was a tap at the door, and Sheriff Adam Young looked up to see Mason Duffy, head of the town council and all-purpose pain in the ass.

"Mason, what a pleasant surprise," Young said, and glanced skyward to see if a lightning bolt was coming to strike him dead for lying.

Mason curled his lip in a smile. "Can you spare us a minute?"

"Us?" He had a moment to wonder if Mason had gone off his medicine and was delusional again—the Duffys as a clan shared a tendency to hear voices now and then—when the door opened wider to reveal that Mason was not alone.

The man with him was none other than Sheldon Rice, who entered the office as if he owned it.

"You're Sheriff Young?"

No, he thought, feeling a mite ornery, I just like wearing the uniform. But he got to his feet, extended his hand, and said gruffly, "That I am. And you're Sheldon Rice."

Rice squinted as they shook. "Do I know you?"

"We met at a council meeting a few years ago, right

after you bought most of the mountain."

"Ah yes, of course. How could I forget?"

Young didn't believe that he had.

"You were worried," Rice went on, "about an increase in the crime rate."

"Among other things."

Rice smiled and looked around with a distinctly proprietary air. "This is the first opportunity I've had to see what the town did with my money. The civic improvements you fought so hard for. It's . . well, it's not bad, considering."

Considering?

"Although I would have gone for something a little less . . . rustic. Or rather, more modern."

Young wondered idly how arrogant Rice would look behind bars or having his picture taken while holding up a booking ID. He was midway into a nice little fantasy involving Rice in ankle chains sharing a cell with a biker named Bruno when he caught Mason's eyes.

"Mr. Rice was wondering, Adam, whether or not there've been any developments in the Hawell case."

"Developments in the case," he echoed. Hawell was a security guard from The Park who'd supposedly disappeared a couple of months back while on duty. As far as he'd been able to determine, the kid had simply gotten bored and had taken off. It had happened on payday, the guy was twenty-two, had a spotty employment record, and what the hell did they expect from a rent-a-cop earning six bucks an hour? Undying loyalty?

He'd advised one of Rice's minions of his conclusions, and had assumed it had been passed along.

There was, accordingly, no case to speak of.

Young glanced from Mason to Rice. "Actually," he said, "we seem to have come up dry."

"*But* you'll keep on looking," Mason added hurriedly. "Am I right?"

"Hmm."

Rice regarded him with a frown. "What I'm concerned about is that Hawell had a master access card with him when he left. In the wrong hands—"

"Change the codes," he suggested, rubbing absently at his right elbow; his arthritis was acting up.

Rice's expression hardened. "I don't think you understand the effort involved. Every gate and door on the property—and there are *thousands* of them—would have to be individually accessed by someone with the expertise to alter the codes."

So much for the superiority of computerized security systems. "Maybe you should've relied on old-fashioned locks and keys."

"Perhaps the lad destroyed the card," Mason suggested, "and we're worrying needlessly. I mean, it isn't as if national security is at stake—"

If Mason Duffy dropped dead this instant, Young would not have been surprised, considering the nasty look Rice gave him.

The councilman, having perceived this, fell abruptly silent. A moment later, he held up an index finger, as though he'd just recalled that he was expected elsewhere and was late. "Excuse me," Mason said, and scurried from the room.

As soon as the door closed, Rice turned to him. "Sheriff, there's something else I've been wanting to talk to you about."

"Oh?"

"It's that old mountain man."

"Ezra?"

"He's the one. Ezra."

"What about him?" Young reached across his desk and picked up a set of handcuffs that one of his five deputies had confiscated from a group of local teens during a traffic stop this afternoon.

"I want to know what you intend to do to keep him from harassing me."

157

"That depends." He noted that the cuffs were inscribed with an issue number which identified them as being county property. Great; now his own department was getting ripped off.

"Sheriff?"

Young looked up. "Sorry. My mind kind of drifts sometimes. What is it Ezra's doing?"

"Well, to begin with, he is forever climbing around the mountain—"

"On your property?"

"No, or maybe I should say, he's never been caught on the property."

"But you think he's trespassing."

"I imagine so. I definitely think he's the one behind the vandalism—"

"That doesn't sound like Ezra," Young said with a shake of his head. "I can see him showing up now and then, taking an interest. But as for destroying someone else's property . . . that's not his style. My guess would be that it's the kids who are doing that." The same smart-ass little bastards who were nervy enough to rip him off.

Rice didn't look at all convinced. "That remains to be seen. But even if he isn't the one defacing my property, I'd like him spoken to."

Young thought back to the conversation about Rice he'd had with Ezra a while back and found it ironic that now here was Rice, asking him to talk to Ezra. Who did they think he was, Western Union?

In fact, he never had gotten around to addressing the old man's concerns, but he refused to feel guilty about it. He had more pressing matters to attend to than delivering messages.

He was tempted to say just that, but curiosity got the better of him. "Uh huh. And what exactly would you have me tell Ezra?"

"Tell him to stay away. My security people have reported seeing him up there on the mountain, day *and*

158

night. Sometimes he just stands there, staring at them. He won't acknowledge a greeting, and never says a word. He just stares."

"Sounds pretty harmless."

"Spooky is the way they put it. He appears out of nowhere like a . . . a wraith, and disappears in the same fashion. It's disquieting. Frightening."

"He's an old man," Young said. "How frightening can he be?"

"I don't want my guests to be admiring the scenery and spot him instead."

"Maybe they'll think he's part of the show. From what I've heard, the whole idea behind your park is to scare the living shit out of the guests. What's one more little shock, eh?"

Rice's smile was as cold as his eyes. "Let me explain something to you, Sheriff."

Young was seldom in the mood to have anything explained to him by anyone, but he could tell the man had something eating at him, and so he gave a nod. Not that a man like Rice would need permission . . .

"In 1989, within weeks after I announced my plans for The Park, MGM Grand Incorporated held a press conference to reveal their intention to build a theme park in Las Vegas, at a cost in excess of a hundred million dollars. At about the same time, a developer in Arizona issued a statement to the effect that plans for an eighty-million-dollar park were being finalized."

"What does that—"

Rice held up a hand. "Bear with me. In November of that year, Six Flags Magic Mountain was touting the addition of the Viper, for which they were paying eight million dollars. Eight *million* dollars for one damn ride. Do you believe it?"

Young scratched his nose. "That's a lot of money."

"In January of 1990, Disney announced plans which they termed—and I'm quoting here—'the most aggressive expansion in the park's thirty-five year history.' The nineties would henceforth be referred to, modestly enough, as the Disney Decade."

"Ayuh."

"And that same month, within *days* as a matter of fact, it was announced that the Castlereagh District Council in Belfast, in Northern Ireland, was planning an amusement park, a *domed* park no less, with an equestrian center, a golf course, and essentially everything else but the kitchen sink."

Rice was talking fast and it was evident to Young that every detail the man recited had been etched with acid into his memory . . . but a scab had never formed. This was raw and bleeding, an open wound.

Apparently Rice realized that he was in danger of losing control; he took a deep breath, and wiped his forehead with an immaculate white handkerchief. "I have," he said evenly, "a great deal at risk."

"But he's an old man. . . ."

Rice went on as if he hadn't spoken. "The Park was always intended to be different from the others, to provide an intense, visceral experience unlike anything anyone else had to offer."

Young said nothing, steepling his hands and looking over his fingertips, watching as Rice paced and fretted.

"When people come to my park, I want them to forget that the outside world even exists. And for seven days, it won't. There will be no newspapers, no television, no telephones, no radio. No conference calls, no talk shows, no damn MTV. There won't be a six o'clock news, and most of all, no film at eleven. Nothing or no one will interfere with the world *I've* created."

It sounded claustrophobic.

"And there is no way," Rice continued in a whisper, "that I'd let anyone destroy the illusion."

He knew what was coming.

"And I promise you, Sheriff, I will destroy anyone who

tries."

Young stood in the doorway looking out on the night. A dense fog was hovering off the shore, as it had been all day. It was nearly the witching hour.

He would have a talk with Ezra, he decided, and warn him off.

Not tomorrow, though.

Tomorrow he figured to have his hands full with the opening of The Park.

Chapter Twenty-two

Ezra lowered himself gingerly into his grandmother's rocking chair and tried to will his old heart to stop aching. Ever since April, since that day up on the mountain, he'd been suffering from pains in his chest, and none of the remedies he'd brewed up had brought him even a moment of ease.

If his heart kept on hurting, he might have to go into town and see that old quack Chambers. Swallow his pride and ask for something stronger than the herb teas and elixirs he had sworn by until here lately.

He placed his hand over his heart, leaned his head back, and closed his eyes. He could hear his pulse whooshing in his ears, and knew it was faster than it ought to be. Faster but not as strong.

Do you expect to live forever?

Only a fool would answer yes and whatever else he had become since he'd drawn his first breath, Ezra wasn't a fool. He could understand how, after eighty-one years of beating, his heart had tired. *He* was tired.

A rest would be welcome if not for the pain.

His grandmother had died quietly in her sleep, a faint smile on her face. He had stood by silently as his mother had placed copper pennies on the old woman's eyes. At his mother's bequest, he had kissed his grandma good-bye, and even now, he could smell the scent of the lilac water she so favored.

In spite of the tightness in his chest, Ezra found that he was smiling, remembering.

Back then, McKenna's Creek had been no more than a wide spot in the dirt road. There'd been a store, a church, and the lumber mill, but little else. The miners who'd preceded Lucian McKenna to the area had found the earth to be barren of gold, and were long since gone, although they, as all men were wont to do, had left their mark behind.

As a boy, he'd spent days and weeks at a time roving the hills, and in his mind's eye, he could still see himself walking in the woods, and looking up to where patches of blue sky showed between the trees. Sunlight and shadow had played over his face. . . .

How peaceful life had been then.

He could almost feel the warmth of the sun caressing him now. . . .

His skin felt hot and dry, but, fanned by the ocean breeze, Ezra made no move to get out of the sun.

Even with his eyes closed, he could tell by the brightness that it had to be midday. Slowly, so that he would not be blinded by the light, he opened his eyes . . . and found himself to be seated on a wooden bench in The Park.

With mild astonishment, he looked around. How had he gotten here?

Twenty feet away, a path snaked its way up a slight incline, to the towering Death Spiral.

He had been witness to its construction, had watched as the black metal structure was erected, but he hadn't noticed before that the track itself seemed to writhe and undulate, as if alive.

163

And he hadn't heard the hiss of the sleek black cars as they sped along the track.

Ezra shaded his eyes as he got to his feet. His body felt odd, almost numb, but he staggered to the path and followed it to where the ride boarded.

All at once he became aware of people around him, saw their faces, heard their laughter but not their voices. They did not appear to see him. A couple holding hands passed on either side of him, their linked hands passing right through him, as if he—or they—weren't real.

He looked down at his feet. Through the soft soles of his deerskin moccasins, he could feel the pebbled surface of the path. He made no sound when he walked, but then, he never had.

The others, he saw, seemed to be floating an inch or two off the ground.

A dream, Ezra thought.

He walked on.

At the entrance to the Death Spiral, the attendant waved him through with a knowing grin, ushering him into one of the black cars.

"Have a nice ride," the attendant said, sounding garbled. Then he laughed, and Ezra saw that there were beetles in his mouth.

A dream, Ezra reminded himself, but even so, his dream-self shivered at the memory of the body in the woods, whose bones he'd later collected, which, along with a silver-and-blue plastic ID card, had been all that was left.

The ride began.

It was smooth and fast enough so that the wind whistled in his ears, but at the same time, he had a sense of moving in slow motion, of time suspended.

Ahead of him, two boys who looked to be about twelve threw their arms in the air as their car crested a rise and plunged almost straight down. Even though he was a fair distance behind, he could hear them yell.

At first, they were yelling from exuberance, and their cries were the lusty warbling of young males, feeling their oats, but with a suddenness that in itself was unnerving, the yells turned to screams—

Ezra reached the crest a moment behind them—their screams were still echoing in the air—and stared down to where their car hurtled toward the earth. The drop had to be hundreds and hundreds of feet, but instead of arcing in a right-angle turn which led into one of the many loops, the track dead-ended into the sheer rock face of the mountainside.

As he watched, the sleek black car gathered speed and slammed head-on into the mountain with the screech of twisting metal. The screaming came to an abrupt end as the boys struck the rock.

Blood splattered the granite a brilliant scarlet. . . .

Ezra had started downward. In those last few seconds, he saw that one boy's head had cracked open, revealing the pulpy matter of his brain, and the other's face had been flattened, forehead and nose and jaw forced back into his head, so that he did not even remotely resemble anything human.

Ezra felt strangely calm, awaiting his fate.

The scent of lilac welcomed him into the darkness and beyond into the light.

Chapter Twenty-three

The Park
June 15, 1992
Monday

His footsteps were muffled by the fog which only now had begun to dissipate, but Sheldon Rice wouldn't have heard them anyway, so absorbed was he in the moment. It was coming up on seven in the morning.

Two more hours and he would cut the ribbon, marking the official opening of The Park.

Finally, it had come down to minutes.

Today marked the culmination of years of planning, and while he had eggs in other baskets, The Park represented *the* major financial investment of Rice Enterprises, the crown jewel of his empire.

He had become wealthy developing land, buying depressed properties and razing them—the bleeding hearts never failed to point out that he'd turned people out of their homes and into the streets—to build high rises, office complexes, and obscenely expensive homes.

His first billion had been made almost before he was aware of it. Wealth begat more wealth, in the peculiar way of the financial world, and now he was—as his first wife Mary had put it so succinctly in divorce court—

filthy, stinking, disgustingly rich.

But he'd pooled a majority of his liquid assets into this place. If it failed he would not by any means be broke, but he'd probably slip beneath Trump in the net worth listings of the country's richest men.

That particular indignity, he could live without, considering that those in the know considered Trump's holdings to be artificially inflated . . . along with a few other things.

Worse, though, was the taint of failure that would follow him thereafter. Of all the deadly sins in the business world, none was as unforgivable as not realizing a profit.

Everyone in his echelon knew that he had more invested here than simply money. This was his baby. The Park meant more to him than any project he'd ever had; nothing less than his ego was invested.

More than one person had told him he was crazy to even consider such a thing.

His attorney had warned him against it. "An amusement park?" the attorney had said. "If you've got that much money to throw away, let's build retirement communities; the population is *aging*, not getting younger, as we both know too well. Or buy a film studio or something. At least then you could surround yourself—and me by the way—with good-looking ladies."

"Why?" his banker had asked. "Why an amusement park? It's not very liquid, any turn around would have to be considered long term, and worse still, you'll get zero in investment credits. I think you'd better stick with what made you rich in the first place."

His psychiatrist had been more blunt: "You think that'll help you stay young? You're going to die anyway, Sheldon, whether or not you construct a playland for yourself. So why don't you use the money for good? Donate it to charity. Build low-income housing. Fund a cancer research wing at a children's hospital."

167

His psychiatrist's grip on reality was far shakier than his own.

About the only person who'd approved was George, his longtime barber, who, despite many offers to relocate into one of his buildings, still worked in a tiny closet of a shop near Chinatown.

"Do it," George had said, wielding the straight razor with a light touch as he trimmed around the ears. "Life's too damn short for regrets, Mr. Rice. This isn't a damned dress rehearsal, you know."

He agreed.

Once, when he was a boy growing up back in Lawrence, Kansas, a carnival had come to town. He couldn't have been more than five or six at the time, but he remembered that day as clearly as if it were yesterday.

His mother had taken him on the ferris wheel, and just when they'd reached the top, the ride had stopped. His mother, perhaps fearing that he would be scared, had at first oohed and aahed, pointing out the landmarks of the town—not that there were many—and in general trying to keep him from looking down.

What else could he do *but* look down?

The strangest feeling had come over him, a kind of tingling, and with it, a sense of being apart from himself, as if he were seeing through someone else's eyes. He gripped the safety bar and leaned forward, ever so slightly, to look down into the workings of the ferris wheel.

The gondola—how he loved that word—began to rock, and his mother uttered a soft cry. "Sit back, Shelly, or you're gonna fall out."

He could not sit back, even to save his own life. He stared down at the people milling around below. He could feel the late afternoon breezes, smell the caramel popcorn and roasting peanuts, and—when he touched his tongue to the safety bar—taste the rust which he would later have a hard time washing from his hands.

It was wonderful while it lasted. When the ride resumed, his mother made something of a fuss, waving her arms and insisting in a strident voice that the operator stop the ferris wheel and let them off. His protests that he didn't *want* to get off had earned him a reprimand and a slap on the fanny.

For a few years afterward, he could close his eyes, envision the ferris wheel, and be rewarded by that delicious tingle. But by the time he was ten, the tingle—the *thrill*—was gone.

He'd never felt it since.

And no matter what his psychiatrist had said about unreasonable expectations, maybe that feeling he hadn't felt in nearly forty years would return.

It was worth a shot, anyway. As the old saying went, nothing ventured, nothing gained.

At eight thirty, he finished his tour of the grounds and arrived back at the fifteen-foot-high front gate. Two armed security guards stood on either side, and when they saw him coming toward them, they opened the gate manually to let him through.

The silver ribbon was stretched across the pathway which led from The Place to The Park. A neat bow had been tied at the midpoint, its ends flapping in the wind.

Already, the guests had begun to gather at the entrance, awaiting the designated hour. He saw Wesley and Nancy, who had the giant scissors he would use to cut the ribbon, and walked in their direction.

Chapter Twenty-four

Wesley had wanted to keep a low profile during the opening ceremonies—he really would have preferred to skip the whole thing—but Rice insisted that he be present. He'd protested, contending that he was needed in 3-C, but his boss had remained adamant.

"You've got to learn to accept credit when it's due," Rice had said. "You've done a magnificent job here, pulled it all together—"

"I didn't do it on my own."

"Don't be so modest. You're going to be at the ribbon cutting, and that's all there is to it. After today, no one will give a damn how much blood, sweat, and tears went into this place, so this is your one and only opportunity to take a bow."

So here he was, feeling as if he'd been steamrollered. His tie was choking him, and he suspected that he hadn't removed all of the straight pins from his new white shirt.

Add to that the vague headache which had homesteaded behind his eyes—the bright sunlight was murder—and this morning couldn't be over soon enough.

He did appreciate, however, that rather than the customary marching bands with their blaring, earsplitting brass sections, Nancy Chan had elected to employ several string quartets, who were playing classical music at a tolerable decibel level.

In fact, every aspect of the festivities was equally as tasteful and elegant.

Instead of releasing the requisite hundreds of thousands of balloons into the air, The Park would uncage a thousand snow white doves.

Instead of gaudy crepe paper streamers—invariably red, white, and blue—the trellised pathways were decorated with blue silk roses and silver satin banners. In the place of confetti were fragrant flower petals.

Several of his creations, including the prototype Guardian from the Graveyard and the newly operational Daddy Longlegs from the Web, were on hand to hint at what was in store beyond the gates. The spider was surrounded by at least a hundred wide-eyed kids.

An ice sculpture of the Glacier ride glistened in the sun, serving as a fountain for the champagne.

For those who found it too early to imbibe, there was a choice of iced coffee or tea, or sparkling fruit drinks. Waiters circulated through the crowd with trays of hors d'oeuvres, highlighted by incredibly expensive Russian caviar.

He watched a father stuff a rye cracker with a dab of caviar on it into his young child's mouth, who promptly shuddered, spit it out, and made a face. The father laughed while the poor kid looked as if she was ready to burst into tears.

Time for fun and games, boys and girls.

"Wesley?"

He turned toward Nancy, whose expression betrayed her own nervousness. "Lift-off, minus ten and counting," he said with a glance at his watch.

Nancy blinked. "Please don't confuse me . . . I'm

171

about ready for the rubber room as it is."

"Sorry." He looked over her shoulder to where Rice stood, surrounded by media types. "Would he notice, do you think, if I made myself scarce?"

"He'd notice, and so would I. You're supposed to have your picture taken with the kids from the Disadvantaged Youth Program—"

"What? I—"

"Don't even bother arguing, because it won't do any good." She consulted her clipboard. "I also have you down for an interview with *People* magazine. And our ad agency would like you to help them select a few sites to feature in our fall campaign."

"Isn't that your job?"

"Technically, yes, but you know this place better than anyone"—she grabbed a glass of champagne from a passing waiter—"and besides that, they're gonna want to scale the Death Spiral, and I'm afraid of heights."

"Are you? Then how is it you're always flying off somewhere in Rice's helicopter?"

Nancy wrinkled her nose. "All right, I lied. If you were a gentleman, you'd have taken my word for it."

"Well, take my word for this: I've got too much work to do to be giving interviews or any other bullshit. As soon as the ribbon's cut, I'm gone."

"Wesley—"

"No." The throbbing behind his eyes had gotten worse even thinking about ad campaigns. "If anything were to go wrong in 3-C while I was playing tour guide—"

"There you go again, always so dramatic. What on earth could possibly go wrong?"

Although he could think of any number of things, he simply shook his head. He'd never been superstitious, but he had the strangest feeling that saying the words out loud would be like issuing an invitation to disaster.

172

The ceremony began, finally. Wesley stood with his hands clasped behind his back, scanning the crowd—he was a little dazed by how many people there were—while ticking off the seconds in his mind.

He listened absently as a series of minor local dignitaries congratulated themselves for their foresight in allowing The Park to be built. A councilman—who had threatened time and again to rescind the building permits and shut them down—droned on about commitment, vision, and dedication.

"Greatness comes," the councilman said, "only to those who dare to meet the challenge. One of those who dared . . . is with us today. Ladies and Gentlemen . . . it is my pleasure, my honor, to introduce . . . Sheldon Rice."

Excitement rippled through the crowd in an audible wave as Rice stepped up to the dais.

"Good morning," he said, adjusting the microphone to his height. "In December of 1989, the ground was broken not far from where I'm standing today, and the quest to bring you the ultimate high-tech amusement park began. It's taken two and a half years, untold numbers of man-hours, and more money than even I can count, and let me tell you, I'm an old hand at counting money."

Appreciative laughter from the corporate sector.

"It also took a little bit of genius." Rice gripped the lectern with both hands and leaned forward intently. "When I say a little bit, I don't mean to suggest that Wesley Davison is less than a genius, but rather that I . . . you . . . *we* haven't seen anything yet."

Wesley frowned and lowered his eyes.

"The rides which you will enjoy today are but the first generation of innovation. In the years to come, The Park will be at the threshold of entertainment technology. The

173

term 'cutting edge' has lost some of its edge through overuse, but I can guarantee you, right here and now, that no one will surpass us, no one will render us obsolete. . . . From this day on, The Park will be the standard against which the others will be measured. . . . But they will never, ever measure up."

As rehearsed, the corporate sector broke into wild applause, and the guests joined in. For a moment, it seemed as if it would die out, but then a toddler who was sitting on her father's shoulders, clapped her tiny hands and chortled with such delight that it incited the others.

Wesley felt a hand on his back pushing him as Rice turned to motion him forward. He stumbled — his shoelace had come untied — and recovered to find himself center stage, all eyes upon him, as Rice led the applause.

Always cool in a crisis, he swallowed his jawbreaker. The rest was a blur.

"This'll only take a minute, I promise."

Wesley had yet to recover his composure, and he didn't trust his voice, so he let himself be led along to a grassy knoll where the five DYP kids and their chaperone were waiting, along with at least a dozen bored-looking guys with cameras who were clearly underwhelmed by this particular photo opportunity.

Nancy made short work of the introductions, to the extent that he wasn't clear on which name went with which face, and then they were herded into a tight semicircle with orders to smile.

"Wait a minute," one of the photographers said. "Davison should be in the middle."

"No, no," Wesley said, "I'd rather—" *drop off the face of the earth.*

174

The photographer stepped forward to jockey him into position. "Let's put you between the girls, okay? Here, let's stand a little closer together. . . . We're all friends here, right?"

"Put your arms around the young ladies," a second photographer said, and winked. "Pretty as they are, I'd get acquainted if I were you."

He looked at Celeste—or was it Betsy?—and smiled apologetically. The look he received in return was as cold as the iced champagne.

"Watch the hands, rich boy," the girl said under her breath.

If his head wasn't aching, if he wasn't being stabbed by straight pins every time he took a deep breath, if he wanted to be here in the first place, he might have chosen to ignore her remark.

"You think I like this?" he asked in an angry whisper. "I have better things to do with my time."

"I'll bet."

"Smile," someone said.

They did, and shutters clicked. The cameras with autowind whirred.

"The least you could do," he said through clenched teeth, "is pretend to be—"

"Grateful?"

Even though his arm was only just touching her, he could feel her back go rigid. "—having fun."

The shutters stopped clicking and the photographers drifted away, moving on to where Miss California was posing with members of the McKenna's Creek town council.

He found himself looking into the girl's hazel eyes. "It wouldn't hurt you to be polite," he added.

"And you can politely kiss my—"

"Celeste," the chaperone said, stepping in between

175

them, "I think we'd better go."

The girl lifted her chin. "Fine with me."

Wesley couldn't help noticing that her walk was almost as sassy as she was.

Chapter Twenty-five

Lawrence Kowalski did not think of himself as the kind of guy who was easily impressed, but he couldn't deny feeling a sense of awe when he entered a nondescript building and came upon the Spin.

The ride was enormous, and shaped like an atom. There looked to be at least a dozen tracks, all at different angles, around a central hub. Sleek black space capsules—he couldn't think what else to call them—apparently entered the lowest track and whizzed around the hub in a dizzying series of circles.

There were two of the capsules running, traveling at an amazing speed.

He got a rush just looking at them.

The ride attendant spotted him and waved him forward. "How are you today?" he asked, opening the capsule.

Lawrence found it hard to take his eyes off the ride. "How fast does it go?"

"That depends on how fast you want it to go." The attendant patted the top of the capsule fondly. "There are controls inside the pod."

The pod.

Lawrence nodded in the direction of the other pods. "How do you keep 'em from crashing into each other?"

"There are sensors mounted in each pod's nose cone which will override the manual controls and apply the brakes if you get too close. And you can't tell, but the inner two tracks there are designed as a kind of detour; the automatic pilot comes on-line to help the speed freaks find a route to bypass a slower pod. It's foolproof."

"That's incredible." He grinned. "Well, I guess I might as well go for it."

The attendant ushered him into the pod. "The controls are recessed in the far right armrest. When you want to stop, press the red button, and the pod will exit the loop and return to the base. Have fun," he said, and closed the door.

A blue light came on. "Please fasten your seat belt," a female voice said.

"Whatever you say, babe." The seat belts were similar to those used in race cars. The top part, an inverted V, was suspended overhead and, when pulled down, it connected with the left and right sections so that together they formed an X which held the rider snugly in place.

"Thank you," the voice said when he'd complied.

The seats themselves were incredibly comfortable, made of soft leather that molded to his body like a second skin. He ran an appreciative hand over the seat before turning his attention to the control panel.

The panel was pretty straightforward. There were three plastic buttons; green for go, yellow to slow, and red for stop. The speed was adjusted by a throttle similar to those in airplanes.

Lawrence touched the green button and the pod moved smoothly and soundlessly forward.

"Nice," he said. He increased the speed as the pod went into the first loop and sailed through it so quickly there was hardly time to realize that at the top of the revolution, he'd been nearly upside down.

The force of acceleration pushed him deeper into the seat, but he eased the throttle forward until it was at the midpoint. After taking a moment to acclimate himself, he increased it still.

"Approaching maximum speed," the voice said.

Around he went, turning this way and that, sometimes climbing straight up . . . and plunging straight down. He streaked by the other pods on a separate track, and waved even though he doubted they would see him.

All at once a display appeared on the windshield.

"Shit," he breathed, "they weren't kidding about this being high-tech."

There was a rate-of-flow indication, numbers giving the vertical velocity, and a bearing distance header indicator. The tachometer was nearly pegged, he noted, and quickly ran his eyes down a display of caution lights.

Nothing amiss. He pushed the throttle forward to its limit, and even as fast as he was going, he could feel the push of acceleration. Beyond the windshield, everything was a dark blur.

"Maximum speed," the voice said.

Lawrence closed his eyes and enjoyed the sensation of speed and motion. He could no longer tell up from down, but it didn't matter. He was having fun.

179

When he'd finally had enough, he pressed the yellow button, and then the red. The pod slowed as smoothly as it had accelerated, completing one last loop before exiting from the tracks. He heard compressed air being released—the brakes?—as the pod glided toward the base.

Lawrence released his seat belt.

"Caution! Caution! Do not unfasten your seat belt until the pod comes to a complete stop."

He ignored that, leaning forward to look out the windshield.

"Caution! Caution! Do not—"

"Hey, it's cool," he said, a little irritated. He wasn't some dumb-fuck twelve year old who didn't know his ass from—

The pod lurched suddenly, throwing him face first into the windshield. He saw a flash of light, felt something give in his nose, and then nearly passed out as the pain hit him. The bridge of his nose felt as if it were being crushed in a pair of vice grips.

"Shit!"

Blood began to drip from his nose, and he licked it off his upper lip. It tasted metallic and salty, and his stomach twisted. Not a good idea.

"Please wait until we have reached a full stop before exiting the ride pod," the voice said, ever helpful. "We hope you'll come back soon. . . ."

Lawrence covered his nose with both hands, gingerly feeling its contours, as the pod came to a stop. A second later, the door opened.

"Oh oh," the ride attendant said.

"Don't just stand there," Lawrence said, "I broke my nose."

A few minutes later, he was lying on a narrow bed

with an ice pack on his nose, waiting for the doctor to tell him what he already knew; he'd begun his vacation with one hell of a bang.

Chapter Twenty-six

Taylor McKenna held the X ray up to the light box and was relieved to see that the fracture, although it involved the ascending processes of the maxilla, did not extend into the nasal septum.

"Well," she said, turning to the patient who was watching her with dread, "reducing the fracture ought to be relatively simple."

"For who? You or me?" Lawrence Kowalski asked from beneath his ice pack.

"For both of us." She flicked off the light box, slipped the X ray back into its jacket, and went to the sink to wash her hands. "I'll have the nurse give you something to relax you, and then I'll set it after I've given you a local anesthetic."

"A needle, you mean."

It wasn't a question, but she nodded. "Altogether, it'll take maybe twenty minutes to set it, pack it, and splint it. Then you'll be on your way."

"My eyes are gonna be black?"

"Among other fashionable shades." She dried her hands

nd walked to the door to call Ilse.

"Doctor?"

"Yes?"

"This isn't gonna make me any uglier than I already
m, is it? I'm not gonna wind up with one of those
rooked beaks, am I?"

She smiled. "Not if I do it right."

Taylor lifted the depressed nasal bone anteriorly and
eld the stainless steel instrument with her left hand
vhile she applied pressure to the side of the nose so that
he nasal dorsum returned to midline. She felt and heard
he edges of the bone grating, and knew Mr. Kowalski
was hearing it too when he abruptly turned pale.

A rivulet of blood ran from his left nostril.

"You okay?" she asked.

He squeezed his eyes closed which she supposed meant
es.

She nodded at Ilse, who handed her the forceps and
he sterile nasal packing. She worked quickly but as
ently as she could.

Kowalski's eyes were watering, or perhaps he was cry-
ng, but he remained silent.

"The splint?"

Ilse handed her a foam-and-metal splint, which she
ositioned on his face experimentally to see if it needed
o be reshaped. It did. He had quite a bit of swelling
nd she bent and flexed the splint to allow for that.

When she was satisfied, she used white adhesive tape
o anchor the splint. He looked, she thought, as if he
ad a flattened white spider on his face.

"There you go," she said.

He opened one eye. "Is over?"

"Yes, and you're looking good. Just be careful not to

hit your face on any more rides."

"I won't." He sounded like he had a world-class head cold. "I'm gonna wear a seat belt in *bed* from now on."

Taylor switched ears with the phone, then tucked it between her chin and her shoulder as she searched through her desk for an incident form. "Did anyone see what exactly happened?"

"The attendant said the pod kind of jerked, as if it hit something on the track," Wesley Davison said.

"Did it hit something?"

"If it did, whatever it was is gone. I shut the ride down and went over every inch of the track, looking for a loose screw or whatever might have jarred the pod, but I didn't find anything."

She found the correct forms in the bottom drawer and tore one off the pad. "So what should I list Mr. Kowalski's accident as? Equipment failure—"

"It *didn't* fail."

"—or operator error?"

Wesley sighed. "Can you hold off for an hour or two while I see if I can hunt up the tape at the Video Monitoring Center? Wait until I get back to you?"

"Whatever you say—"

The office door was open, and Ilse leaned in. "We've got another one."

"Cherokee, honey, now stop your whimpering, and pull in that bottom lip before someone trips over it. The nice doctor isn't hurting you."

"I'm almost finished," Taylor said. She borrowed Ilse's bandage scissors and trimmed the steri-strips to fit the three year old's tiny finger.

"Where's Daddy?" Cherokee asked, tears running down her face.

"Out in the waiting room," the mother answered, and smiled apologetically, "breathing fire."

Daddy had indeed been ranting and raving nonstop, making it known at the top of his lungs that he hadn't scrimped and saved every spare nickel and dime for the past two years, and come all this way, only to have his baby maimed.

The maiming in question was a half-centimeter cut on the pad of her right index finger.

"Where are you from?" Taylor was curious as to what distance constituted "all this way." She found the box of special bandages they stocked for children, which were decorated with baby animals.

"Barstow."

"Isn't that—"

"It's about two hours and a light year from Los Angeles, and too damned close to Vegas."

Taylor smiled. She opened the sterile wrapper, removed the bandage, and showed it to Cherokee.

"Bunny," the child said.

"Ooh," said the mother, "and ducky."

Cherokee willingly held her finger out to be bandaged, and when it was, she brought it nearly up to her nose to admire in the cross-eyed manner young children sometimes have. "Pretty."

"Has she had her DPTs?" the nurse asked, referring to the diphtheria, pertussis, and tetanus vaccinations that were standard well-baby care.

The mother nodded; now Cherokee was letting her see the pink and blue animals. "That's nice, honey, but not in Mommy's eye."

Realizing that neither she nor Ilse had thought to ask earlier, Taylor said, "Did you happen to see what she cut

185

herself on?"

"No I didn't."

"How about your husband?"

The mother raised her eyebrows. "Do you want to ask him?"

Since his tirade had yet to end, and in fact seemed to be gaining steam, Taylor shook her head. "What about you, darling? How did you hurt yourself?"

Ilse looked up from taking Cherokee's pulse. "When I was bringing her back, she said a ghost bit her."

"She said that?"

"A ghosssss," Cherokee said, as she hiccupped and then shuddered.

"Poor baby," her mother said. "Daddy's been telling ghost stories again. . . ."

"What ride were you on?"

"Oh that one, you know, with all the skeletons. I told Homer, I said, 'Homer, this is too intense for Cherokee,' but when has he ever listened to me?"

Taylor doubted that anyone would be able to get a word in edgewise for him to listen to; the father was still going strong, now apparently blaming his daughter's accident on the Republicans.

"And he says, 'It's no scarier than those cartoons she watches on Saturday mornings.' Implying, of course, that if I was a better mother, I'd get up and find other ways to keep her entertained, as if I'm not entitled to sleep in the one day of the week I can."

"Men," Ilse said.

"Was she standing on the seat?" Taylor was trying to envision how the child had been cut.

"No, she was sitting on my lap."

"And you didn't see what happened?"

The woman shook her head.

"How about Daddy?"

186

"He was counting ribs or some such nonsense. Homer likes nothing better than to point out other people's mistakes. He's forever writing TV shows to rag on them about not being 'authentic'."

"Uh huh."

"When Cherokee started screaming, I thought she was just scared, but then I saw the blood. . . ."

"You're not wearing anything, a brooch or pin, anything sharp that she might have scratched her finger on?" Although the cut looked too precise for that; it reminded her of the incised appearance of Wesley's laceration a couple of months ago.

"My jewelry consists of this." The mother held up her left hand to reveal a plain gold wedding band. "Unless you want to count the magic decoder ring I got in a box of Cracker Jack."

"What about your husband? Maybe he's wearing a belt buckle or . . . or something," Taylor finished lamely, running out of ideas.

"Not that comes to mind."

They both looked at Cherokee, who was allowing Ilse to take her temperature, and watching the red LED display as if hypnotized. Except for the bandage and a slight puffiness around her eyes from crying, there were no signs of her earlier trauma.

"The only thing I can think of," the mother said, "is that maybe she cut herself *before* we got on the ride, and didn't cry until she saw the blood."

"I don't know. . . ."

"Once when I was washing dishes, I cut myself pretty bad, but the knife was so razor sharp that I didn't even feel it slicing into me."

"But what would be that sharp out by the ride?" Taylor asked. "Or on it?"

"The ghossss," Cherokee said, her clear blue eyes

187

opened wide. When she spoke, the thermometer dropped into her lap, and a second later, the monitor beeped. "All done," the child announced.

"I guess we are," Taylor agreed.

She gave Cherokee a Tootsie Pop after Mommy okayed it, and watched as they left the Medical Aid Center, the little girl skipping between her parents. Each held a hand, and at every fifth step or so, they gently lifted the child off her feet and let her swing free.

Even at a distance, she could hear Cherokee's delighted giggles.

"Now that was a cutie," Ilse said, coming up to stand beside her.

"Adorable."

"Although her father could use a high colonic, he's so full of shit."

Taylor shrugged. "He loves his little girl."

She watched until they disappeared from sight around a bend in the pathway, then went back to her office to call 3-C and inform them of the incident. They'd need to send someone to check out the ride.

Most certainly it hadn't been a ghost that had injured Cherokee, but whatever it was, Taylor didn't want to see another child—or anyone else—get hurt.

Chapter Twenty-seven

"Hey, get the lead out, wuss."

Nick broke into a trot, following Max toward the walkway which would take them up to Level Two, and something called the Glide.

If he'd known this morning that Miss Fremont was going to pair him up with Max, he would have feigned an epileptic seizure or hysterical blindness, and stayed in bed. It was not yet noon, and he had practically worn out his sneakers chasing after Max, who ping-ponged from one ride to another like a man possessed.

"Would you hurry?"

Nick could only nod; he was out of breath. Luckily, he'd reached the walkway, and he stepped on, grabbing the handrails to keep from falling on his face.

Max stood with his arms folded across his chest and facing backward, so that he saw where they'd been and not where they were going. Max was also facing him.

Watching him.

Nick understood very clearly that he was in the midst

of a balancing act. He'd met guys like Max before, usually, thank God, in passing. With these guys, there was only black and white; you were either with them or you were against them.

They didn't believe in the middle ground, and if they thought about it at all, they were certain to conclude that anyone proclaiming to be neutral was, in fact, a coward. In their steely eyes, a coward deserved whatever he got, perhaps more so than a true enemy.

What he had going for him, Nick thought, was his age. There would be little glory for Max, who was built like a tank, in pounding a skinny twelve year old into the ground. He was too insignificant to be an enemy.

What he had going against him was the probability that Max *liked* knocking people around, and needed only the most minimal of reasons to do so.

As a rule, Nick was good at avoiding fights. Basically, he ran. It was simple and instinctive, and while the bully had an instinct to chase, most of the time there was a lapse as the thought "get the mother-fucker" found its way along unused synapses to a poorly developed brain.

Bullies were often clumsy, too. An infuriated bully might overload his brain's circuits—not hard to do—and trip over his own big feet. If this occurred, it was imperative not to laugh, because clumsiness had a tendency to evaporate at such moments.

Still, if he could avoid it, he'd rather not wind up on Max's shit-list. This place offered abundant opportunities for anyone so inclined to express himself by giving someone a little shove into the machinery.

The walkway, for example, was a prime location to commit mayhem. Nick tightened his grip on the handrails.

Max smiled.

190

The Glide differed from other rides they'd been on first in the design of its pod. Rather than sitting side by side, the maximum two riders sat one in front of the other, bobsled style.

"I'll get in back," they said at the same time.

"I will," Max said and, without waiting, stepped into the gunmetal blue pod.

Nick got in and the attendant lowered the gull-wing door, which locked with a substantial click.

The sound reverberated in Nick's mind.

"Here we go," Max said.

Nick tried to turn around, but the padded safety bar that had come down of its own volition limited his movements. "Maybe," he called over his shoulder, "we should take it nice and—"

"Let's see what this baby can do," Max said.

And they were off.

The ride had been aptly named; it *was* a glide. The pod seemed almost to float as it passed through the threshold and entered the darkness of the building.

It was pitch black inside, except for an occasional flash of laser light. The lasers weren't bright enough or frequent enough to actually see by, and the effect, Nick suspected, was intentionally disorienting.

"Whoa!" Max yelled as they went into a turn that had them at a ninety-degree angle and doing what felt like at least seventy miles an hour.

And they were still accelerating.

Nick dearly loved the sensation of speed, and he gave himself up to it, imagining that he was driving a Ferrari on the salt flats in Utah. He could picture the miles of barren flatland ahead and the dust whirling up behind

191

him. He could taste its gritty substance, and feel the steering wheel vibrate in his hands.

In his mind's eye, the Ferrari began a sideways skid, the tires kicking up thick plumes of dust, the body shimmying as he struggled to regain control. Sweat beaded on his forehead and his racing goggles fogged as the car became airborne and began an end-over-end roll. . . .

Around they went in a clockwise turn that descended as though into a bottomless pit. In the darkness, with only the sound of the wind rushing by, it was easy to lose track of time, and to forget that there was any other world than this.

It was a forgetfulness he welcomed, because otherwise there was Amy. . . .

Chapter Twenty-eight

Frank Hightower stepped from the brightness of the day into the honeycombed interior structure of the Glacier. He used his security ID card to gain entrance to the maintenance corridor, and headed for the Operations Center.

There were blue lights at twenty-foot intervals along the corridor, but the walls had been painted a mat black, and the dark background seemed to absorb what little illumination there was.

Hightower could hear, faintly, the screams of the guests from the other side of the walls. Their screams and the echo of his own footsteps followed him as he wound his way through the maze.

He paused once, thinking that he'd heard someone coming up behind him, but when no one came into view, he shook his head and continued on.

Something about this place made him jumpy; he was forever hearing voices and sounds which he couldn't quite identify.

He reached the spiral staircase and, with a hand on his holstered gun, he hurried up. The metal railing was cold to the touch—they didn't call this ride Glacier for nothing—and when he reached the top, he realized it was also wet. Wet and sticky.

Was there a leak? He'd have to call maintenance to come and take a look.

Meanwhile, he wiped his hand on his pants.

The door to the Operations Center was open—a violation of company policy—and he rapped it sharply with his knuckles as he entered. "Security," he said.

The two Operations engineers did not bother to turn. They were standing in front of the one-way observation window, which provided a bird's-eye view of the ride, or most of it, anyway. Whatever they were looking at had their full attention.

Hightower joined them, hooking his thumbs in his belt and rocking on his heels. At first everything appeared normal to him, but after a moment he realized that the pods were stationary. Nothing was moving.

The Glacier was the amusement park's premier water ride, bigger than the others three times over, with the pavilion encompassing in excess of two acres. Canals had been carved through simulated ice which was overlaid with the real thing, and the pods floated on rushing water through a hundred twists and turns.

There were icicles like stalactites hanging from above, jagged-edged miniature icebergs, and waterfalls of varying heights and configurations. There were crevasses and ice caverns, and even a blizzard—courtesy of a snow machine—near the end of the ride.

The Glacier was sparkling white and icy blue, dazzling to the eyes, if otherwise chilling.

The ride boarded on an upper level, and depended

on gravity to propel the pods downstream, assisted by air jets along the canals which kept the pods on an even course. Gravity never failed, but the air jets apparently had, and dozens of metal safety gates had sprung up from the canal bottom.

The pods, trapped between the gates, were either turning circles in the whirlpools, or slamming back and forth between the gates and the side of the canal. The guests were getting more of a ride than they'd bargained for.

Hightower glanced at the engineer next to him. "Aren't you gonna do something?"

The engineer snorted. "Like what? Our control board is frozen, you should pardon the expression."

He frowned. "Did you notify 3-C?"

"Davison's on his way, but I don't know what he can do, the frigging controls are jammed or—"

The other engineer reached up and grabbed an overhead microphone. "Please stay seated," he said into it. "Do not attempt to exit the ride. We are experiencing a minor technical problem. Please stay seated, and the ride will resume shortly."

Hightower watched a pod with a teenage girl and a young boy in it spin, bump, and spin. It made him dizzy and more than a little nauseated.

"We could drain the water," the second engineer said, "and get everyone out of there."

"Drain it, and it'll be out of service for six to eight hours—"

"Yes, but we'll never be able to rescue them otherwise. That water is near freezing, and there's probably ice on the canal floor . . . some fool steps out of a pod into the canal and he's likely to slip and break his neck."

"You want to take responsibility for six hours of

downtime? If you do, fine, let's get to it, but otherwise, count me out."

Hightower's breath fogged the glass. The boy he'd noticed had unfastened his safety belt and was standing up, causing the pod to sway. "Hey, the natives are getting restless. . . ."

"Please stay seated," the second engineer said, a hint of panic in his voice.

At that moment, Davison *and* Sheldon Rice entered the room. Without a word, Davison went to the control board and sat down, his fingers flying over the keyboard.

Rice, whose face was thundercloud dark, came to the window and stared out at the ride. The veins in his neck were bulging, and his fists were clenched.

Hightower tried to fade into the woodwork, moving out of Rice's line of sight.

"What," Rice said, "is going on here?"

The engineers looked at each other; neither appeared eager to answer. The one holding the microphone took his thumb off the transmit button.

". . . is going on here?"

". . . going on here?"

". . . on here?"

". . . here?" echoed through the pavilion.

Rice glared at them. "Imbeciles. I've hired imbeciles. This"—he hit the glass with the palm of his hand—"is not acceptable, do you hear me? Not acceptable at all."

"We—"

"Do you have any idea, any clue at all, as to what kind of an effect an incident such as this might have on the guests?"

Looking at his boss, Hightower found it hard to believe that this was the same man who'd been smiling and making happy talk at the Grand Opening only a few hours ago. Of course, what with the *other* accidents, the man was bound to be feeling a tad uptight.

"I want an explanation—" Rice was saying.

Davison got up abruptly from the control board. "I've located a malfunction in the relay panel."

"You"—Rice pointed at him—"go along, in case it's him."

Hightower glanced at Rice, then hurried after Davison. They clattered down the stairs and ran along the corridor, the kid leading the way through a maze of turns without a moment's hesitation.

A couple of minutes later, they arrived at the power plant.

The relay panels were secured with simple sliding bolts. Davison threw the bolt to the third panel from the left and swung the door open, and though the door blocked Hightower's vision, he could tell from Davison's sudden stillness that the kid hadn't expected to see whatever he was seeing.

"What is it?" He hadn't planned to whisper, but it came out that way. He cleared his throat, and tried to speak louder. "What's wrong?"

Something dropped onto the floor from the panel and crawled away.

Crawled away? Hightower blinked and shook his head as two more bugs—they had to be bugs—followed the first, disappearing behind an air compressor.

Then Davison reached into the relay box and swept at least fifty more onto the floor.

Hightower realized that from force of habit he had drawn his .38 Special, and, feeling foolish at the prospect of shooting at bugs, he reholstered it. "How the hell did they get in there?"

"I don't know," Davison said tersely. When the bugs had scattered, he stepped closer to the panel and started fiddling.

After a minute or two, there was a click and a humming sound. The lights flickered, dimmed even further, and finally brightened. The air compressors throbbed to noisy life.

"We're up again," Davison yelled.

Back at the Operations Center, Hightower found himself watching Rice's face as Davison related what he'd found. The man was not a happy camper.

"*He* did this," Rice said.

Davison frowned. "I don't see how he could have. This is a secure building—"

"That hasn't stopped him before."

Hightower realized, belatedly, that they were talking about the old coot up on the mountain. What was his name? Some kind of biblical name . . . Ezra, that was it.

That crazy old man had been the focus of at least ten security alerts in the past year, all of which instructed anyone who caught him on the premises to "take measures" to detain him, and to notify Rice immediately.

But no one had ever been able to catch him, despite the fact that a couple of the guys—including Hawell before he'd made himself scarce—had gotten it into their heads that there might be a bounty of sorts for bringing Ezra in. Funny, how he'd forgotten all about that petty little detail until just this second. . . .

"—troubleshoot the system before anything else happens," Davison said.

The look in Rice's eyes was of barely controlled rage.

"If someone is deliberately sabotaging the rides, I want them stopped. Do you understand?"

"I'll see to it," was all Davison said.

Hightower shook his head. Since his first day at The Park, he'd been hearing about Wesley Davison being such a whiz kid, and maybe in electronics and computers he was, but this was another matter entirely, and anyone with half a brain knew you didn't send a boy to do a man's job.

Hunting down a saboteur required a different kind of expertise; his kind.

Chapter Twenty-nine

"Isn't this fun?" Betsy said.

Celeste gave one of her split-second fake smiles. "Just get in, will you?"

The attendant opened the pod, took Betsy's hand, and steadied her as she stepped inside. "Welcome to the Nebula," he said, turning to Celeste and looking her up and down. "I hope you like the ride."

She made a point of bypassing his outstretched hand — which was probably sweaty and disgusting — and ducked into the pod.

"Are you ladies having a good time?" he persisted, his tone insinuating.

"We will be, as soon as you shut the damned door." Beside her, Betsy made a sound of disapproval, which she ignored. Instead she gave him a hard look, a Boston look that said, "Don't mess with me unless your life insurance is paid up."

He got the message, and had sense enough to slide the door shut.

"You didn't have to be rude," Betsy said.

"No? I thought I did." The pod took off slowly, winding up along a series of switchbacks toward the so-called launch platform.

"The guy was just trying to be friendly."

"I don't *need* any more friends." She fastened her seat belt and glanced at Betsy. "But I suppose, coming from New Mexico, you have all kinds of experience dealing with jerk-offs."

Betsy, already pink from the sun, blushed. "I didn't say that."

"Well then, take it from me, some guys you gotta cut off at the neck"—she drew a finger across her own throat—"or you'll never be rid of them."

"If you say so."

"I do." The pod hovered above the launch platform, and Celeste felt it vibrate momentarily before it made a quarter turn and plunged suddenly into the blackness.

Beside her, Betsy screamed.

"Why don't you and Betsy team up for the evening," Miss Fremont had suggested.

At six o'clock, Celeste had taken Joey—her partner for the day—to meet Miss Fremont at the front gate, as planned, so that the boy could have a nap.

Joey protested, claiming he wasn't tired, but she could tell by the way his eyelids drooped that nine hours of running around The Park had wiped the kid out. In fact, the last time through the Water Devil, she caught him drifting off to sleep.

There was no way Joey would last till closing at midnight, but she intended to party until the clock struck twelve. And she preferred to party alone.

201

Miss Fremont had other ideas. "The two of you girls can get better acquainted."

Celeste could think of few things she'd like less. But she said, "Sure, if I see her . . ."

As luck would have it, Betsy chose that exact moment to show up, looking a little disheveled—wisps of red hair had escaped her thick French braid and her mascara was smudged beneath her eyes—but seemingly filled with enthusiasm and energy.

Knowing there was no way out of it, Celeste had accepted her fate.

The pod swayed and rocked through a figure eight among a cluster of miniature stars, then entered an asteroid belt where, after a few near misses, they were struck a glancing blow by a huge pockmarked asteroid, which set them spinning in place.

"Shit," Celeste said, bracing herself against the padded interior.

Although they both were belted in, Betsy came sliding across the seat, bumping into her before being whipped back in the other direction as the pod slammed into an even bigger asteroid.

"Help," Betsy gasped between alternately laughing and screaming.

"This is too real," Celeste said. The pod was now moving sideways—they couldn't see where they were going—and shimmying to beat the devil, as if it were about to break into pieces.

A sudden flare of red light illuminated the windscreen, and then a blast of air set them spinning violently counterclockwise.

"It's a sun exploding," Betsy said.

Celeste closed her eyes, but the jostling felt worse

that way, and when she opened them again she saw they were heading straight toward a ringed planet. To her, the rings resembled the whirling blade of a circular saw, ready to cut right through them. A heartbeat before impact, the pod was wrenched upward.

"Do you believe this?"

She shook her head but didn't answer, concentrating instead on trying to identify and prepare for the dangers ahead. There were dozens of planets, countless star-suns, and the multi-hued gas and dust clouds which gave the ride its name. In the distance, she could see spiral galaxies being sucked into a black hole.

The pod veered toward a grouping of stars which gave off bright, intermittent light, but then shot up again into a vertical loop.

For the first time, Celeste screamed.

Betsy joined her.

At the bottom of the loop, the pod made a hard right turn, shimmied, shuddered, and then reversed direction, so that they were climbing backward—

—and at the top of the loop, with them suspended upside down, the pod came to a grinding halt.

Celeste felt the blood rush to her head, and felt the pull of gravity on her body. The seat belt was digging into her shoulders, across her abdomen, and between her legs. And she was hanging free; there were at least three inches of space between her and the seat.

"Celeste?"

"Ssh!" There were creaks and groans coming from the pod, and she tried to remember how the damned thing was secured to the track.

If it gave they would fall. . . .

"What is it?" Betsy persisted. "What's happened? Is this part of the ride?"

"I don't think so."

"If it is, it isn't funny."

"Stay still." Maybe if they didn't move — didn't breathe, didn't blink, didn't cross their eyes — the pod would hold.

The creaks and groans continued, accented by a few metallic pings which she imagined were the track breaking apart. Through the windscreen, she could see flashes of laser light, and little else.

"Can we get down?"

"I don't know." The pressure of the belt buckle on her abdomen was becoming painful, and now her pulse was roaring in her ears.

"They must know . . . we're up here?"

"Yeah, sure."

"And they'll do something?"

"Sooner or later."

"Oh God, Celeste, I think I'm gonna pass out," Betsy said, and the tone of her voice left little doubt that she meant it.

"Hold on, okay?" Celeste shifted her body, drawing her knees to her chest. Relying on the shoulder straps to hold, she unclasped the leg bindings, did a kind of somersault, and then swung down until her feet were touching the ceiling of the pod.

Slowly, she released the top of the buckle, and gently shifted her weight to the ceiling, holding her breath until she saw that the change of position hadn't pulled the pod loose from whatever was holding it on the track. For a moment she stood perfectly still, her heart racing, while a wave of dizziness passed over her.

Then she positioned herself to Betsy's right, wedging herself carefully between Betsy and the side of the pod. "Okay, you can do this."

"I'm scared."

"Me too." It crossed her mind that if the ride were to suddenly resume, she'd be tossed around the pod like clothes in a dryer. "But what else can we do?"

A few minutes later they were sitting on the ceiling of the pod, the straps of their seat belts hanging down between them. The air was noticeably warmer, and the windscreen had fogged over so they couldn't see out.

Betsy's face was wet with tears, but she appeared oblivious to the fact. "What do we do if the ride starts up again?"

"Roll with it," Celeste said grimly.

Chapter Thirty

In the Video Monitoring Center, Wesley went into one of the two private booths, sat down, and stared at a blank screen, waiting for the supervisor to bring him the tapes from today's incidents. Even though he knew that being angry wasn't helping matters, he fumed, drumming his fingers on the counter, and fighting the urge to throw something or yell at someone, anyone.

Thirty seconds passed, a minute. Finally the door opened and one of the gofers handed him a cassette without saying a word.

He fed it into the VCR, hit the play button, and then he was viewing, according to the legend, Graveyard camera number 163.

It was only about fifty feet into the ride, near where a skeletal hand was trying to dig its owner out of a grave. Two of his buddies who'd already escaped their supposed final resting places were standing by, offering encouragement.

"A few more inches," one of them said, in a garbled sepulchral tone.

Wesley had asked for a loop covering two minutes prior to each incident and ending two minutes after, so he had to wait a bit. But his patience was rewarded as the pod containing Homer and Gretchen Goodenough, with their daughter Cherokee, came into view. The video cameras were high resolution, and he could make out the details of the father's plaid shirt as clearly as if the man had been standing within arm's reach. These particular cameras were also equipped with sound.

"How can they talk?" the man was saying, "They don't have tongues. Tongues are soft tissue and soft tissue decomposes."

"It's make-believe," his wife said. "If you can believe they're standing there, then you gotta believe they can speak."

Homer frowned, his skepticism plain.

It was the little girl Wesley was interested in. She was sitting on her mother's lap, and seemed uncomfortable, he thought, as if she hadn't quite decided whether she liked this or not.

One of the onlookers glanced over, as programmed, and lurched in the direction of the pod as if hoping to catch a ride.

Wesley noted with satisfaction that the father flinched, the mother gasped, and the child—this was interesting—reached out with her hand, much as he had done with the Guardian.

And then she screamed.

Wesley hit the rewind and played it again in slow motion. When he reached the scream, he rewound it a second time. In the video equivalent of advancing it frame by frame, he watched the skeleton jerkily clutch at the air near the pod, saw the little girl's hand reach out, and almost instantly pull back.

Her expression at that moment was of absolute terror. She closed her hand into a fist, so it was impossible to see her injured finger, but he was certain that she hadn't been bleeding when she extended it.

The only thing was, there were a full six inches between her fingers and those of the skeleton.

They'd never made contact.

So how, he wondered, had the child been cut?

The tape from the Spin offered a more straightforward event, enhanced by a camera angle which allowed him to see directly into the pod.

The guest, one Lawrence Kowalski, had unfastened his safety belt prior to the conclusion of the ride. For reasons they'd been unable to determine despite an inch-by-inch examination of the track and the brake mechanism, the pod had suddenly lurched, throwing Kowalski face first into the windscreen, and breaking his nose.

"Shit!" Kowalski swore.

"Damn," Wesley said, watching in slow motion as blood spurted. It looked incredibly painful.

The Park's legal department was denying responsibility, contending that Kowalski would not have been injured if he hadn't unfastened his seat belt, but Wesley didn't care to lay blame.

He wanted to know what had happened, and why.

The tape from the Glacier had been compiled from thirty separate cameras, and was MOS — without

208

sound—because the rushing water tended to drown out voices. Even so, he could tell that a majority of the people on the ride weren't too thrilled at the malfunction; it didn't take a lot of experience as a lip-reader to make out some of what was being said. Or gestured.

He didn't really expect to learn anything new from watching this—the cause of the malfunction had been quite evident—but he had a compulsion to examine every aspect of each incident.

It was important to him to impose order on what had happened today, and the only way he knew how to do that was by an exhaustive review of the facts. Only by identifying the known could he isolate the unknown.

He watched the tape to the end, twenty-odd minutes worth of tedium, and learned nothing of value.

Wesley pushed the eject button on the VCR and took out the tape. He was searching for a pen so that he could label it, when the door behind him opened. It was Koch, one of the night shift engineers.

"Wes," Koch said, "we've got a shutdown on the Nebula ride."

"What are you talking about? I didn't order—"

"It just came to an abrupt halt. There was no warning. I talked to the operator and he's tried to restart it, with no luck."

"How many pods?"

"Only eight, and six of those have been evacuated, but I gather there are two pods which are upside down in the quasar loop."

"Shit, not the loop." He tossed the tape cartridge on the counter and followed Koch out the door.

The Nebula was one of the fully enclosed rides, and

the interior of the building had been painted a flat, nonreflective black as background to the special effects astronomical bodies. Even with the blue maintenance lights on, it was dark inside.

Wesley put on what looked like a miner's hat, equipped with its own light, and strapped a forty-pound tool belt around his hips.

Koch had been replaced by Davenport, who was fifteen years younger and considerably lighter on his feet. Since they would have to climb through the ride infrastructure to reach the two pods, agility and limberness were considerations.

The preferred course of action was to release the braking mechanism located beneath the pod, which would allow it to continue forward out of the loop into a turnabout. The backup braking system could be engaged manually, by the rider, and all would be fine.

If one or both of the pods were in the wrong position in the turnabout, however, the pod would fall backward instead of forward, and the manual brake would be useless. In that instance, they would have to remove the riders from the pod and—using safety harnesses—help them individually to the building floor.

In the interest of time, they'd decided to work independently, each taking one pod.

Davenport handed him two harnesses. "Good luck."

"Same to you."

Wesley knew the Nebula like the back of his hand, and he climbed it quickly, his movements sure and automatic. When he was about fifty feet up, he saw the two pods, and headed for the one higher in the turnabout, in the more precarious plight.

When he directed his helmet lamp toward the windscreen, he saw two faces peering out at him. They had apparently released their seat belts so that they weren't hanging upside down.

Good, he thought, that shows initiative.

He crossed a narrow catwalk to a set of metal rungs which he could use as a ladder to reach them. He determined that the pod was unretrievable at present, and unhooked his belt, draping it over one of the camera posts. Just in case anyone was watching, and to let off a little tension, he waved into the lens.

With only the harnesses to carry, it would take only a few seconds to reach the pod.

Both riders were female, and when he got closer, he recognized them from this morning. The sassy one, Celeste, was mouthing something he couldn't understand at first. Then he realized she was telling him that they couldn't open the door.

Which they couldn't; the pod had been designed to prevent some fool opening the door in midride and falling out.

He signaled it was okay, then slid back the control plate to the right of the door. For a second he had to think to recall the access code and override command, but it came to him and he entered it in.

The lock disengaged.

He opened the door only partway so that neither rider could jump out at him in her eagerness to be rescued. "Hi," he said.

"Hi?" Celeste turned to her friend. "The man said 'hi'."

The second girl, whose name he couldn't recall, began to laugh helplessly. He saw that she was trembling, and her face was streaked with tears. She was, he

211

thought, on the verge of hysteria.

"Listen," Celeste said, "if you've come to save us, do it. If you were just in the neighborhood and thought you'd drop by, you'll have to excuse us."

That made the redhead laugh harder.

Wesley forced a smile. "Which one of you wants to go first?"

"She'd better, before this turns into a water ride. Betsy, you go first, okay?"

Betsy tried to compose herself, but couldn't, so she kind of shrugged and nodded and shook her head, which he took to mean yes.

Wesley handed her one of the harnesses. "I'm Wes, by the way."

"Ask him," Betsy gasped.

"Ssh, now."

He gave the second harness to Celeste. "It'll take me about ten minutes to get her down and come back for you. And I'll have to close the door."

"No problem," Celeste said.

Betsy nudged her. "Go on and ask him."

"Later."

Wes reached and gave a yank on the buckles of Betsy's harness to make certain they would hold, which made her giggle more. "Ask me what?"

Celeste shook her head, but Betsy, wiping tears from under her eyes, said, "We want to know where your cape is, Superman."

The trip down was uneventful, although it took longer than he had supposed. Betsy proved to be extremely co-operative, but she was understandably hesitant in letting go of one rung until she was convinced of the stability

212

of another.

It was very much a stop-and-stop process.

"I'm sorry," she said when they were approximately half the way down.

"You're doing fine."

"I mean, that crack about the cape. I didn't mean to be rude."

He could feel her trembling, and found it odd that she'd chosen this moment to offer an apology, unless maybe she was afraid of falling with that on her conscience. "No problem."

"It's just we couldn't imagine anyone coming up there to get us."

Wesley guided her hand to the next rung. "Don't give it a second thought."

"You're brave, and so is Celeste, letting me come down first. I could never"—her voice broke—"*never* wait up there all by myself."

"Then we'd better hurry so I can get back up to her."

If he'd been concerned that Celeste would be anxious because of the length of time he'd been gone, it was for no cause. When he opened the door, he found her sitting cross-legged on the cushioned roof of the pod.

"I assume Betsy made it down?"

Wesley nodded. "Now it's your turn."

"This"—she pulled at the harness strap—"is one ugly piece of gear. What is it for, anyway? You don't have a guy wire."

"So I can hold on to you."

"Right, and if I start to fall, you're going to hold me up? Or we'll fall together?"

"Never mind. Let me check your buckles." He yanked

213

at them, his fingers brushing against the smooth bare skin of her shoulder. He pulled back as if burned, even though—or because—she was as cool to the touch as satin.

She didn't seem to notice.

"Okay, now, I'll be standing out here and you back out into my arms. I'll tell you where to place your hands and feet."

Celeste laughed. "Where have I heard that before?" But she did as he asked, and in very quick order, she was encircled by his arms.

Wesley was startled at how good it felt.

He took a deep breath to clear his mind, and then took her right hand in his, guiding it to the nearest support beam.

Somehow, he got them down, moving from the upright to the rungs to the catwalk. When they were four feet from the ground he jumped down and reached up for her.

When he set her down, she kind of leaned against him for a moment before stepping back, and when he looked into her eyes he saw that she had been frightened all along. . . .

"I was wrong," she said, "about you needing a cape."

Then she was gone.

Chapter Thirty-one

June 16, 1992
Tuesday

Wesley directed the beam of his flashlight along the thick gray cable that connected the Nebula control panel with the emergency braking system. The cable, intertwined with coaxial and electric lines, snaked through the crawlspace above the Operations Center and into the adjacent Special Effects studio.

There was hardly space to move, but he inched forward on his belly, brushing aside an occasional cobweb and raising fine particles of dust which danced in the light.

"Find anything?" a muffled voice called from below.

"Not yet." He hit his elbow on a corner of the air-conditioning duct and swore softly. Then he steadied the flashlight, and squinted as he concentrated on tracing every inch of cable.

The break had to be here somewhere, *had* to be, for the simple reason that there was nowhere else it could be. They'd spent the past six hours looking, and had found nothing. . . .

Not trusting his eyes, he reached out and ran his fingers along the cable. He wriggled forward still, and had to keep his head down to avoid the pneumatic lines which were strung above.

"Thank God you're not claustrophobic."

This time the voice sounded clear, as if the speaker were in the crawlspace with him. Instinctively, he raised up and nearly put his eye out on the protruding edge of a copper coupling. "Shit. What—"

"Over here."

Koch had apparently taken out a ceiling panel, climbed up on a desk or something, and was peering at him owlishly from an arm's length away. He looked disconcertingly like a disembodied head.

Wesley sighed as he tucked the coupling behind the pneumatic line. "Next time warn me when you're gonna scare the life out of me, okay?"

Koch reached in and squashed a plump brown spider between his thumb and forefinger. "You mean it's possible to scare our fearless leader?"

"That scares me," he said, indicating the spider's remains, which Koch wiped on the insulation. "What do you want?"

"Would you look at all of them," Koch said, and whistled in amazement. "And I just killed their daddy. Or was it their mama?"

Wesley frowned. "All of—"

"But that's neither here nor there . . . it's after two a.m., Chief, and the Indians are getting restless."

Maybe he was more tired than he thought. "What

216

are you talking about?"

"Overtime. Is it all right with you if I send the ride operators home? They're supposed to be off the clock at midnight."

For a moment, his mind refused to work. He opened his mouth and nothing came out, despite Koch's encouraging nod. Instead he stared at the knuckles of his right hand, which he'd skinned at some point during the evening. Specks of dried blood and raw abraded flesh, streaked with dirt. Glistening particles of fiberglass had worked their way into his skin, and itched maddeningly.

"What am I doing here?" he asked under his breath.

"Excuse?"

Wesley flexed his hand, feeling oddly removed from his physical self. Exhaustion, probably; he'd been up since dawn. "Tell them to go home," he said. "And you go home too."

"But—"

"I'm almost done here." There were six to eight feet of cable left to examine, ten-minute job, max. If he located the problem, fine, but if not, he'd reached the limits of his endurance, and continuing to work would be counterproductive.

"If you're sure. . . ."

He nodded, careful this time not to hit his head. "I'll lock up when I leave."

"Right." Koch's head disappeared momentarily and then popped back up. "Oh, and Rice wants to talk to you when you're finished."

Icing on the cake, he thought, and resumed his examination of the cables.

Shortly thereafter, he found what he'd been looking for; a section of the cable had been cut approximately two inches beyond the junction of the ceiling and a interior wall of the Special Effects studio. The straight edges of the cable left little doubt it had been a deliberate act.

The hallway was dark and silent when he left Special Effects half an hour later. He flicked a series of switches, but to no avail. "Damn it, Koch, you could've left the lights on."

The batteries in his flashlight were drained from hours of constant use, and it barely provided enough light to see a few feet ahead. As deep within the bowels of the building as he was, it would take him five minutes or so to reach an exit.

He could waste time searching through desk drawers looking for fresh batteries, or he could get his butt out of here. . . .

A simple choice.

Wesley started walking, trusting his memory to find the way. He ran one hand along the wall as a way of anchoring himself and to keep the dark from disorienting him. He kept the faint beam of the flashlight directed at the floor.

There was some kind of grit underfoot, as though someone had spilled salt or tracked in sand, and it made a whispery sound beneath his sneakers. Obviously the janitorial crew hadn't made it to this building—

From behind, very distinctly, he heard footsteps coming in his direction.

He turned so fast he almost slipped. "Koch?"

There was no answer. His hand tightened around the flashlight as he brought it up to shine ineffectually down the hallway. Did he see or just imagine a shape looming in the dark?

"Hello?"

The footsteps slowed, stopped, and he heard what had to be the rasp of a leather-soled shoe grinding the sand—or whatever—beneath it. Then the footsteps resumed.

Wesley remained still. His eyes had adjusted to the lack of light and he could almost make out in the different textures of darkness, the silhouette of a man.

All at once, a light flashed in his face and he raised his arm to keep it from blinding him.

"That you Mr. Davison?"

"Who's there?"

"Security."

The guard came close enough for Wesley to recognize the face, but he couldn't recall the man's name. "Security, and you are?"

"Hightower, Frank Hightower. I hope I didn't frighten you by not answering just now, but you might've been an intruder."

Wesley realized he'd been holding the flashlight as he would a weapon, and, uncomfortable with that thought, he switched it from his right hand to the left. "That's all right; you were doing your job."

"I didn't know anyone was in the building," Hightower continued. Reflected light shone off his badge. "It's probably not a good idea to be wandering around in the middle of the night."

"No, I guess not. If it happens again, I'll be sure to have someone notify Security—"

The guard nodded. "There you go. I mean, it's spooky in here to begin with, and you hear somebody prowling around, well . . . someone could get hurt."

Which translated meant someone could get shot.

"Anyway . . . I'll walk you out if you're through for the night."

"I am," Wesley said, and then corrected himself, "or at least, I'm through here."

Chapter Thirty-two

Alerted by the desk that Wesley was on his way up, Nancy Chan was standing by the door when the chimes sounded—a brief movement from Beethoven's "Ode to Freedom"—and had opened it well before the last note was played.

"God, Wesley, you're a mess," she said, ushering him in. He had cobwebs in his hair, dirt on his face, and his clothes looked as though he'd rolled around in a pigsty or worse. "What happened to you?"

He smiled halfheartedly. "I've taken a new position as a human roto-rooter. Actually, I've been crawling through air ducts and—"

"Whatever for?"

"Looking for this." He held out a length of gray cable to her. "See?"

Nancy took it, frowning. There were eight wires, each protected by a different colored plastic insulation, encased within the gray cable. She touched a fingertip to the exposed copper tips, which she quickly discovered, were sharp. A tiny drop of dark red blood welled, and she touched her tongue to it. "What about it?"

"You see how clean the cuts through the cable and insulation are? They're too straight edged for this to be accidental."

"Which means . . ."

"Someone is tampering with the rides." Wesley ran a hand through his already mussed hair, then reached and took back the cable. "Which means Rice was right all along. Is he available?"

"He asked that you wait in the study. He had to take a conference call from Zurich." She led the way, then paused at the study door. "You have heard of delegating, haven't you?"

"What?"

"Couldn't someone else have crawled through the ducts?" She picked a strand of spider web out of his hair with one hand while opening the door with the other.

"I'm smaller than they are; I was the only one who'd fit."

"Gain weight," she advised.

Sheldon appeared ten minutes later, and Nancy knew by the worry lines in his forehead that he was not pleased with whatever had transpired in Switzerland. She frowned to show her empathy, but his glance at her was dismissive. "Coffee," he said.

Feeling absurdly like a parlor maid, she went to the sideboard, but the silver carafe was empty. She grabbed it and stormed from the room, heading for the kitchen, which was all the way on the other side of the penthouse. Her heels kept getting stuck in the deep-pile carpet, and after the second time she turned an ankle, she kicked the damn things off, hoping that one would fly across the room and break something valuable, or if she were truly lucky, irreplaceable.

Neither did.

But that was the way her luck had been going.

The kitchen door was equipped with an electronic eye, and the door swished open as she approached it, denying her the opportunity to kick it open and have it slam into the wall.

"Bastard," she said.

Nancy put the carafe down on the spotless Italian marble countertop, braced her hands on either side of it, and took several deep breaths. Calm down, she told herself, but the truth was, she didn't want to be calm. She needed to express her feelings, even if it was only to herself.

What was she *doing* here? And who was this person she had become?

Not Nancy Chan. When she looked into the mirror she didn't recognize herself anymore. The elegance that she'd coveted had somehow transformed her into just one more of Rice's women.

Mary, Debra, Susannah, and now Nancy.

Except he had married them, and he apparently had no intention of marrying her.

Was it because she was Chinese? That didn't make sense, because if anything, Rice had diluted her ethnicity until she had no race. He bought her expensive clothes from European designers, which she wore over provocative French lingerie that would have shamed her ancestors. Her shoes were handmade for her in Italy, and the car he'd given her—a Jaguar XJE—was British in spirit if not by corporate ownership.

These days, her hair was styled by a moody young man from Brazil who never seemed to take his eyes off his own reflection. Her perfume—which she thought too musky but Sheldon adored—had been purchased in Damascus, of all places. The heavy gold chain around her throat had been made in Thailand.

Nowhere in any of this was the Nancy Chan who'd learned to read and write at a wobbly table in the corner of the kitchen with her cousins while her mother and father and aunts and uncles ran the family's restaurant. This Nancy Chan never went to bed with the smell of ginger in her hair, nor was she the child who dressed up in her mother's silk dresses.

This Nancy Chan was unfamiliar to her. Sheldon had changed her, albeit with her consent at first, although as far as he was concerned, consent didn't begin to enter into it; her willingness to be transformed was a given. He had changed her into his image of what she should be.

As a third-generation Chinese American and perhaps more acutely as a journalist, she had known, of course, that the concept of a melting pot was a fondly held myth with little connection to reality. Those in power—primarily rich white males—tolerated the myth as long as those representing the minorities were *like* them beneath the skin.

Be black if you must, but live in a restored brownstone and forget the old neighborhood loyalties. Be Hispanic if you've no other choice, but dress in thousand-dollar suits and graduate magna cum laude from Harvard. Be oriental if that is your heritage, but drink French wines and vacation abroad.

Be female if misfortune dictates, but develop a tough

skin so that when the time comes for the knife, you won't feel it cutting through you, and won't resort to anything as unseemly as crying.

Be different, but be the same; *that* was the message from the power elite.

Like a chameleon, she had taken on the coloration of Sheldon's world, and had given up her own. She had bought into all of this, embraced it with eager arms, and had succeeded too well at acclimation, because now when she would welcome tears, they would not come. Her eyes were so dry they stung.

"But you let him make you this way," she said fiercely to herself. "And you can make him stop."

She stared for a long time at her distorted reflection in the mirrored surface of the carafe. Gradually it came to her what she might do, what she *could* do.

Then, calmly, she set about making fresh coffee.

"—no question that it's tampering," Sheldon was saying when she entered the study with the carafe and clean cups on a black tray.

"Not in my mind." Wesley looked as though he was trying to stifle a yawn. "We held extensive run-throughs on all of the rides last week, and there's no way that we would have missed something as obvious as this. In fact, the Nebula would have been non-operational."

Nancy poured coffee and took cups to both of them, giving Wesley his first and then coming back to sit down next to him. She crossed one leg over the other so that Sheldon would be certain to notice her nyloned foot, and pointedly ignored his frown.

"Someone," Sheldon said, "came onto the grounds, evaded Security, entered a restricted area, and cut the

225

wires with the intention of disrupting the ride."

"Yes."

"How is that possible?"

For a moment, neither spoke.

"Could it be," Nancy ventured, "someone who works here?"

"An employee? I can't believe that. Why would anyone risk their job by doing a stupid and dangerous thing like that? Besides, everyone who works here knows we have cameras all over the place."

"The cameras didn't record whoever did this," Wesley said, turning the cable over in his hands. "Or who threw a circuit breaker in the Glacier. Or who jammed the brakes on the Spin. Or—"

"What's this?" she said, interrupting. She leaned forward and picked up a small metal ball off the coffee table. She tossed it in the air, caught it, and closed her fingers around it.

"It's a ball bearing," Wesley said. "I found it this morning, rolling in the bottom comb of the moving walkway."

"Okay, so what's a comb?"

"Never mind that now." Sheldon made no effort to disguise his irritation with her. "It's not important."

But she refused to be dismissed. "Here," she said, tossing it to Wesley. "Just don't mistake it for one of those jawbreakers you're always chewing."

Wesley ducked his head and smiled.

"Nancy?"

She looked at Sheldon.

"Are you quite through? This is an important matter we're discussing. People have been injured."

"Not the right people, I assume."

It wasn't often that she'd seen him really steamed, but

his anger was unmistakable: those frigid blue eyes of his narrowed, and his thin upper lip became even thinner. She wondered if any of his wives had ever told him how unattractive he was when riled.

Sheldon Rice, though, wasn't one to let emotion get the better of him. He stared at her hard for thirty seconds or so and then it was as if she'd fallen off the face of the earth.

"You understand that this can't continue."

There was a quality to his voice that sent a shiver up her spine, and she felt an icy chill as adrenaline entered her bloodstream.

"We must adopt a siege mentality," he went on in the same tone. "Everyone is suspect. We must tighten our security measures, increase our vigilance. . . ."

Nancy met Wesley's eyes; he frowned and shook his head slightly.

"We've been fortunate that no one has been seriously injured thus far, but we must prepare ourselves for the worst."

"Sir?"

"There are forces at work here, forces against us, trying to shut us down, to ruin us, to ruin me. I won't let that happen!"

"Sheldon," she said, "aren't you making too much of this? I mean . . . Magic Mountain had to shut Viper down the week after it opened, because something was wrong with the pull chain, but . . . no one was ruined."

He ignored her. "And that damned sheriff, always finding excuses not to do his job . . . something will have to be done about him. As for Ezra . . ."

"I don't think that he could be the one behind all of this," Wesley said. "He's just an old man who lives in the mountains."

227

"Is he?"

"It would take someone with an engineering background, I think, to have done these things. It's pretty high-tech stuff for an old man."

All at once, Nancy was intrigued; who could it be doing the tampering? "A guest?"

"It's possible," Wesley allowed.

"But why?"

"People set fires to watch them burn—"

"It doesn't matter why," Sheldon said flatly.

Wesley sighed. "Some people are their own worst enemies—"

"No"—Sheldon's smile was cold—"I am."

Chapter Thirty-three

Max was both pleased and pissed.

Pleased because Miss Fremont had left shortly before 9:00 a.m. to take the shuttle into town. There were, she said, several important phone calls that she had to make. Only emergency calls were allowed in or out of The Park, but in any case, the long-distance service had been mysteriously disrupted.

What it meant was that they were on their own for the morning. Miss Fremont had no sooner left than everyone scattered to the wind, like roaches scurrying for cover when the lights come on.

That pissed him off; he and Nick had made plans for today.

So much for loyalty.

He saw Joey a few minutes later in the lobby, gazing with open-mouthed wonder at the crystal chandeliers. He called to the kid a couple of times, but got no response. Either he was deaf, Max thought, or too dumb to recognize his own name.

Nick, ungrateful little bastard that he was, he located outside.

There was a cop car parked near the lobby entrance and Nick was standing by the driver's door, leaning over, his hands casually in his pockets, and looking inside. There was a peculiar expression on the kid's face that Max hadn't seen before, a kind of hunger.

"You're gonna need a cop to save your sorry ass," Max said, coming up to him.

"What'd I do?"

Judging by the bewildered expression on his face, the kid didn't have a clue. "You know, it's hard to believe that someone as smart as you are could be so stupid."

"What? What are you talking about?"

"We're supposed to ride the Death Spiral, remember? We had an arrangement." He rested a hand on the roof of the car, which was warm from the morning sun, and drummed his fingers impatiently. "What were you doing standing here, anyway?"

"Me? I was just having a look."

"Checking to see if the keys were in it, huh?"

Nick smiled but shook his head. "Not exactly. I was curious how many bands he had on his radio. You know, the police band, county communications, CB, and maybe a couple of alternatives to keep the real sensitive stuff off the usual channels that anyone can pick up with a police scanner. That kind of thing."

"You know about stuff like that?"

"Some of it." He rapped a knuckle against the glass. "I think he's patched into the highway patrol, too."

Max felt a grudging respect for the younger boy's knowledge, but reminded himself that he was pissed off at him, too. So he scowled. "How is it you know so much, anyway, hot shot?"

Nick shrugged. "I've had a few rides in the cage."

"Yeah, well, who hasn't? By the time I was twelve, I'd scratched my initials into half of the patrol cars in town, and—"

"We'd better go," Nick interrupted, and gestured toward the hotel.

Sure enough, a cop was crossing the lobby, heading their way. Out of habit, Max sized him up, determining that they were about the same height—maybe the cop had an inch on him—and of the two of them, Max noted with satisfaction that he was the one more solidly built.

Plus, the dude had to be fifty, sixty years old, a real senior citizen.

Still, the cop had an air about him, that even at a distance gave Max pause. This was someone who could handle himself.

"Come on," Nick said. "He sees us."

"So what? We're not boosting the car or anything. It's a free world." But he allowed Nick to lead him away, and even broke into a half run.

"That was close," the younger boy said when they were out of sight.

"Shit, you'd think you had a guilty conscience or something." A thought occurred to him. "Hey, did you ever steal a cop car?"

"No."

"But you wanted to, right?" Max started to laugh, thinking how crazy an idea that was, as if a little kid like Nick would—or could—do such a thing.

"I thought about it," Nick said.

"So what stopped you? Had to take your nap? Or was it time for milk and cookies?"

This time, though, the kid hung tough, refusing to be drawn into anything. "You'd be surprised," he said.

231

The exterior track of the Death Spiral seemed to take up the sky, and Max whistled through his teeth as they approached. "Wicked," he said. "That's what I call a monster ride!"

"It is impressive," Nick agreed.

Max quickened his pace, eager to meet the challenge. He didn't realize he'd left Nick in his dust until he reached the entrance.

"You're going on the Spiral alone?" the ride attendant asked.

"No, I . . . where is that dork?" He turned and motioned for Nick to hurry and catch up. As he waited, he patted the outside of his jeans pocket, verifying that the ball bearings were safely tucked away.

Nick was out of breath when he finally got there. He leaned over, hands on his knees, and gasped for air. "Why," he wheezed a moment later, "did they build this place on a mountain?"

"Because it's here." Max gave him a little shove toward the coaster-style pod. "Get in, will you?"

The ride attendant, an ugly dude who had hair growing out of his ears, frowned and put a hand on Nick's shoulder. "Maybe he should sit this one out. This is the wildest ride in The Park, and he doesn't look so good."

"Yeah, well, I guess you haven't looked in a mirror lately, or you wouldn't talk. Come on, Cole, get your ass in and let's go!"

Nick complied.

"Remember," the attendant said as he slid the door shut, "I warned you."

And they were off, slowly at first, climbing upward to the first spectacular height. There was time to enjoy the view; the whitecapped waves, the swell of the sea, and the mountains to the north, east, and south.

He thought he saw an old man, standing on a cliff above the amusement park, but as he turned to point him out to Nick, the pod reached the first summit, and then there was no time to think of anything at all.

The force of acceleration pushed him so hard into the cushioned seat that he suspected that even without a safety harness, he wouldn't have moved a muscle. The ride twisted and turned, rose in a rush and fell even faster, made heart-stopping loops and sudden drops that seemed to go straight down.

It wasn't easy, but Max wormed his hand into his pocket and brought out three of the bearings.

Nick grabbed his wrist. "Are you crazy?" Nick screamed. "You're not going to—"

Max yanked his arm free and then extended it out over the side of the pod. "Bombs away," he yelled, and let one of the bearings fall. As fast as they were going, there was no way to know where—or on whom—it had landed.

On the ride went, faster and faster, the wind roaring in his ears. The world beyond was little more than a blur, now blue, now white, now green. Flickers of light and shadow, back and forth, changing almost too quickly for his mind to register.

He dropped a second bearing.

Then, after the steepest loop yet, the track entered the dark part of the ride.

Although he'd known this was coming, he wasn't prepared for the shock of complete blackness, of losing even momentarily a sense of where he was. It was impossible to tell up from down without some reference point, and it was easier to just close his eyes and let it propel him through space.

This was better than he'd hoped it would be. As dizzy

as he was, as disoriented as he felt, he intended to tell the attendant with the hairy ears to let them ride through a second time. Maybe a third.

Which reminded him. He reached out to release the third ball bearing, and heard rather than felt a sharp crack. Then pain began to pulse its way up his left arm, which soon felt as though someone had cut it open and laid smoldering embers along the bone.

"Sit down, Max, and put your head between your knees," Nick said a few minutes later. They'd gotten off the ride and were waiting for an electric cart to take them to a doctor.

"My arm's broken. It ain't got nothing to do with my head."

"The hell it doesn't. You're gonna pass out if you don't do as I say. Here."

Max felt Nick's fingers on the back of his head, felt them pushing down.

"Resist," Nick ordered. "Try to raise your head while I'm holding it down."

It should've been a piece of cake—he was bigger and stronger—but somehow he found himself struggling to raise his head as much as an inch or two. Surprisingly, after a minute or two, the woozy, lost-in-space feeling started to go away.

"Works, doesn't it? It increases the flow of blood to the brain."

"Where'd you learn—"

"An emergency room nurse taught me. She said it would keep someone from passing out if . . . if . . . if there weren't any ammonia ampules handy."

Max heard something change in the younger boy's voice, but before he could ask, the electric cart arrived.

and he was being lifted onto the back.

"Nick?" He looked around, but Nick was nowhere in sight. He sighed. "Great. I knew I should've put a leash on the runt."

Chapter Thirty-four

"Cherokee! Come back here, you little devil," Gret chen Goodenough called after her daughter. "Mama i too tired to be chasing you."

Cherokee, though, merely giggled and, as she'd been doing for the last five minutes, continued to run on She soon disappeared around the curved side of th building which housed the Final Flight.

Where did the child get her energy? Even allowin for the fact that Cherokee was only three and thus ha a surplus, there were plenty of times when she seeme wound so tight that she'd never slow down.

They ate and drank pretty much the same things, s it probably wasn't a matter of nutrition. And heave knew it wasn't hereditary; she'd never met an easy chai she didn't like, and as for Homer, the only exercise tha man ever got was from jumping to conclusions.

Whatever the cause, Gretchen decided to change he method of pursuit, and leaned against the wall to wai for her daughter's plump little legs to bring her full circle. Then she'd cut her off at the pass.

Darn Homer anyway, going on that gruesome ride and leaving her to tend to Cherokee on her own. He knew her feet were blistered from yesterday's marathon session. And why would anyone want to experience a simulated plane crash in the first place?

"That's why," he'd said when she'd asked him. "I sure as hell don't want to ever be on the real thing, but this way I can have my curiosity satisfied."

Homer was a curious person, all right, and never gave a thought to what curiosity had done to the cat. But as far as she was concerned, only a ghoul would wonder about a thing such as how it must feel to know the plane is going down, and that your life is coming to a spectacular end. As it was, she often had to put her hands over her ears when he would read to her from the newspaper about how the bodies of air-crash victims were broken into such little pieces that they could be picked up with tweezers. . . .

Gretchen shuddered. "Thank you kindly, Homer T. Goodenough, for ruining my peace of mind."

She *had* put her foot down as to him taking Cherokee on the ride. Only a man would be foolish enough to suggest it in the first place, that being one and the same man who'd later turn over in bed and go back to sleep while she got up to comfort their child at three in the morning when the nightmares came.

Sometimes she thought the animals had it right; the purpose of the male animal was to sire the young, and after that, it was "see you next year."

Her sister had a knack for finding men like that, what with each of her four kids having a different daddy. Either that, or they had some way of rooting her out, like pigs after truffles—

"Ma'am?" a voice said, breaking her train of thought, and she turned.

A boy of twelve or thirteen had Cherokee by the hand, and was looking at her with the most sorrowful blue eyes she'd ever seen.

"Is this your little girl?"

"Oh, bless your heart," she said, and reached to pick up her daughter. "Cherokee, I swear, sometimes you give me fits."

"Where's Daddy?" Cherokee asked.

"Inside going pee-pee." She really hated having to lie, but she dare not reveal that Daddy had gone on a ride without his darling daughter. . . . Cherokee would throw a tantrum loud enough to wake the dead.

The boy, who'd been standing quietly by, reached to tuck a strand of Cherokee's hair behind her ear. "I'm glad she wasn't really lost. Running around the way she was, she might've gotten hurt."

"Hurt" was one of those words which never failed to catch Cherokee's attention, and she frowned, holding up her bandaged finger. "Ouch," she said. Like her father, she knew how to milk a situation.

"Now Cherokee, your finger is just fine. The doctor made it all better." To the boy, she added, "She got a teeny-weeny cut on one of the rides."

"Poor baby." His voice sounded tender, and Cherokee smiled in response.

"So . . . are you on your own today?" Gretchen asked. She took her daughter's hand and brought it up to her mouth to kiss the "ouch." "Or did you decide to sit this r-i-d-e out? My husband's in there."

His eyes followed hers, and he shook his head. "I'm supposed to fly back to Iowa on Sunday, and I don't even want to think about that kind of stuff."

"I'm with you." She shifted Cherokee to her hip, then

238

saw a shaded bench, and started for it. She wasn't much surprised when the boy tagged along after them; he had a lonely look about him, as if he were sorely in need of a home. And ever since she was knee-high to a grasshopper, there was something about her that had always attracted strays. That included Homer, who'd been good for nothing when the army kicked him out. . . .

"Thank heavens we're driving," she said, hoping to signal her willingness to have him along.

"Where to?"

"Barstow, down in Southern California."

"I've been there."

"No fooling?" She sat down with Cherokee on her lap and extended her hand. "I'm Gretchen Goodenough, by the way, and of course you've met Cherokee."

"My name's Nicholas Cole." He sat beside them. "I was in Barstow, a year ago in January, I think."

"Well, then, you haven't seen the real Barstow, when it's a hundred and ten in the shade."

"Not that time, but I've been through in the summer a time or two. Once I remember we drove by a car that had overheated and caught on fire."

"It happens." In fact, one of the ways she amused herself on the drive to Vegas was by counting the scorched spots on the side of the road. "You're from Iowa, you said? You must do a lot of traveling."

"I'm not really *from* Iowa—"

Cherokee, now that she had temporarily tired herself out, was trying to curl up in her mother's lap and sleep, but was having a hard time fitting now that she'd grown so, and kicked Nicholas in the leg by accident.

"Ow," he said.

"Sorry. Take her shoes off, would you? That way if she kicks again, it won't leave a bruise."

Nicholas slipped the tiny Reeboks off as if he did it

239

every day, and cupped her stockinged feet in his hands to keep them warm. He smiled as he ran a thumb across the baby's instep and her toes curled.

"You must have younger brothers and sisters," Gretchen said, "to be so natural with kids."

"I had a sister," he said, and averted his eyes.

She saw that his throat was working, the way people's throats did when they were trying not to cry, and realized that she'd done it this time. Maybe she should ask him to reach down and take her shoes off, so she could fit her foot in her mouth.

The dilemma now, as she saw it, was whether to pretend she hadn't noticed his distress, or to simply apologize for upsetting him. She didn't believe that is was necessarily always better to talk problems out—the few friends she had who'd gone through therapy seemed to be miserable a lot of the time, always analyzing every blasted thing to death—but for some reason, she had the feeling that this kid was aching deep inside to talk.

Gretchen waited until he looked back at her, and then gave him an apologetic smile. "I'm sorry . . . did something happen to your sister, Nicholas?"

For a moment, she thought he wouldn't respond; she could *feel* the waves of tension coming off him, as though he were preparing himself to run. But then he looked down at his hands still holding Cherokee's feet and a bit of that anxiety was somehow released.

"She died," he said. "Last September. Her name was Amy."

"That's so sad. How old was she when . . . if you don't mind me asking."

"Three."

No wonder he'd taken to Cherokee. Gretchen placed her hand over his and gave it a squeeze. "I won't pretend to know how you must be feeling, and to be hon-

240

est, I can't bear the thought of even trying to, but I am sorry for your loss, you and your parents."

At that, he stiffened. "They didn't care."

The first thought she had was to say, "You don't mean that," which would have been a mistake, judging by the look on the boy's face. He did mean it, and in spades. Gretchen got the impression, too, that he'd been challenged on that point before and was bracing himself to hear again it from her.

Instead, she squeezed his hand again. "Then Amy was very lucky to have you for a brother."

He looked up so quickly that whiplash was a distinct possibility. In a second, his sad blue eyes had filled with tears.

Without a word, Gretchen reached and pulled the boy to her, so that his head rested on her shoulder, and then stroked his hair as he cried.

"Hush," she said, "It'll be all right."

Chapter Thirty-five

Jesus supposed that it had been wrong of him to run, but when he'd turned and seen the *policía* walking toward him, he had been truly frightened. Was the *agente* here to take him back to Tijuana? The man had not been wearing the uniform of the *inmigración,* but that did not prove he was not from the Border Patrol. . . .

So Jesus ran, and as he did, he realized that he had made a bad mistake by not having searched for a place to hide—like under a porch as he had in San Diego—when he'd first arrived here. And although he very much wanted to enjoy the rides, he knew that he did not dare to waste another day without finding a secret place, or many secret places, where he could run to.

He would not draw an easy breath until he had done so; it was nothing less than a matter of survival, and only a fool would leave his fate to luck.

Jesus wandered along the pathways, his eyes searching the underbrush, looking for even the smallest space which he could tuck himself into. But the trees and bushes were well tended, and after many hours searching, he'd found nothing on the First Level of The Park except for the entrance to a ground squirrel's den.

He thought of hiding up in a tree, but there were few things he could imagine that would be worse than having to climb a tree while someone chased him. He wasn't a good climber, and he could almost feel a hand closing around his ankle and pulling him down. Or in his hurry to escape, he might lose his grip and fall. . . .

No, a tree would not do.

There were many buildings in The Park, but when he worked up the courage to try a door, he found it locked. There were air vents along the sides of the buildings that perhaps he could squirm through, but they were protected with sturdy wire mesh.

He struggled for a moment with the temptation of trying to kick the mesh out, and had even lifted his foot, ready to try, when he heard a voice in his head say that he would be dishonoring his family by destroying what did not belong to him.

"A hiding place found by dishonor would not be safe," the voice said.

He considered, finally the rest rooms, of which there were many, all over the place. But a quick check of the closest one convinced him that, unless he were to stand on the toilet seat, his feet would be visible beneath the metal partitions. He did not think he would remain hidden for long, and he might end up trapped, since there was only one exit.

Discouraged, Jesus went to the sink and pooled water in his hands to splash on his face. Then he drank from the faucet, letting it soothe his dry throat.

When he met his own eyes in the mirror, it was despair that he saw. This place was too new, too well cared for, and there were too many people. Besides the other guests, there were attendants on all of the rides, uniformed workmen, and the gardeners, who, though many were his countrymen, looked at him with suspicion.

There were also the private *policía* who spoke to each other in urgent whispers using hand-held radios, and today they seemed to be everywhere.

What chance did he have?

Worse yet, he feared that Señorita Fremont would find out that he was not Joey Castellano and be angered by his deception. Would she believe the truth, that he had not intended to lie?

The señorita had been very kind to him, buying him clothes and bringing him here, letting him fill his stomach and sleep in a room he had all to himself, but if she thought he lied, what then?

He had to find a place where he would be safe, even if it took all day.

The sun was low in the sky, casting its rays across the ocean, turning the water to gold.

Jesus went to sit on a large flat rock near the top of a hill and beneath a tree whose tiny white blossoms scented the air. He stared at the golden waves and listened to the sea gulls cry as they swooped overhead.

There were, he thought, very many gulls, and they were ill behaved, crashing into each other as they circled above a dark patch in one of the flower beds.

Back in Tijuana, the gulls could be found at the dump, where they and the bad-luck crows feasted on maggots bred by the millions of flies that, when disturbed, rose in a buzzing cloud that threatened to block out the sun. . . .

Jesus frowned and got up slowly. He made his way closer to where several of the bigger gulls were perched, flapping their wings and shrieking. He guessed that they had found something to eat, but the flurry of wings made it difficult to make out just what they were after.

A shadow passed over the flower bed, and when he glanced up, he saw that the numbers of gulls were twice what they had been. Feathers drifted in the air.

He waved his arms and whistled, thinking to frighten them, but the birds stood their ground. One even made as if to peck at him, then turned its head to look at him through one red-rimmed eye.

Jesus had nothing to throw. He did not wish to back away from them—would they fly at him if he retreated?—but how else would he find the necessary stones?

Cautiously, he turned, scanning the surrounding area for a weapon, and realized that there was a group of pine trees nearby. The pine cones were big enough and heavy enough to serve his purpose.

He ran toward the trees, shielding his head with an arm to protect himself if the birds attacked.

The gulls did not stir from their feast.

The trees were lush and green, with sharp-tipped needles. Dozens of pale yellow cones littered the ground beneath the branches, and Jesus dropped to his knees to collect them, stuffing them into the pockets of his shirt and jeans. The fragrant pine resin made his hands sticky and dirt clung to his skin.

But as he prepared to stand, his eyes fell upon what appeared to be a small clearing in the middle of the trees. Several large boulders were piled like a fire ring in the center—

Que es esto? What is this?

The shrieks of the gulls regained his attention, and he scrambled to his feet. A branch whipped across his cheek and along the side of his neck. It felt as though he'd been stung by a wasp.

He threw the first pine cone from twenty feet away, but it sailed harmlessly over the birds' heads. A second caught one gull on an outstretched wing. The gull lifted off, flapping its wings furiously, before taking several hopping steps toward him.

"Bastardo," he swore under his breath. This time he took better aim and threw as many cones as he could hold in his hand.

All at once, the gulls took wing in a frenzy of beating wings. Those circling overhead looked ready to take their place, but he flung another handful of cones skyward and not one tried to land.

Jesus knew very well that the gulls would return, but sought to satisfy his curiosity as to what had brought them here. Still waving his arms, he neared the dark area in the flower bed.

Thousands of shiny black insects, most crushed or half-eaten, had been trampled into the soft dark soil. Those not dead were mortally wounded, their green insides torn from the protection of their bodies.

He could hardly believe his eyes. He looked around, but the people passing by seemed unaware of anything other than where they were going. A girl who appeared to be about his age was the only one who even glanced at the birds, but she looked away, uninterested.

Jesus backed off. He did not want to see any more.

The gulls returned.

Within the ring of boulders hidden by the pine trees,

he found the entrance to an underground passageway. Daylight was fading. After a moment of hesitation, he dropped down into the passageway, which widened to form a cave before branching off in two tunnels.

He sat on his heels, letting his eyes become accustomed to the dark. The curved earthen wall of the cave was cool against his back, and the air was musty, which made him sneeze. He rubbed at his nose absently, then remembered that his hands weren't clean.

He heard a soft scurrying sound, and forced himself to remain still while he listened, trying to discover which direction it had come from. But the sound did not repeat, and after telling himself that it was only one of the ground squirrels, he set off into the first of the tunnels.

It quickly grew even darker. . : .

Chapter Thirty-six

"I'm sorry," a prim and slightly nasal female voice said, "but Mr. Rice isn't available at present."

"Would you ask him to return my—" Taylor McKenna heard a click and then the dial tone, and realized that she'd been cut off. Again.

She'd been trying to reach Sheldon Rice since early afternoon, but thus far had been unable to get past the secretary, who apparently had taken an oath of secrecy as to where her boss might be found. And who seemed as if she were allergic to taking messages.

Taylor let the receiver drop gently into the cradle as an alternative to throwing it across the room. She sat back in the chair and rubbed her temples, hoping to stave off the return of her headache. As many aspirin as she'd taken today, the level of salicylic acid in her blood was probably near toxic.

"Dr. McKenna?"

Ilse stood in the doorway, her arms full of supplies

she'd had to get from the storeroom to replenish the shelves and drawers. The uniform that had been a spotless white this morning was now stained with Betadine and blood.

"Yes?"

"Dr. Bork is here."

After a month of promises, Rice had finally come through with a relief doctor to cover the Medical Aid Center from nine p.m. until closing at twelve, after which he would be on call for the guests throughout the night. Taylor glanced at her watch; Bork was fifteen minutes late.

"Off to a great start," she said.

Elvin Bork, M. D., sixtyish and with the rosy-cheeked complexion of a chronic alcoholic, had a curious way of taking report; he stared at the ceiling and hummed continuously.

"You might get a call on this," she tapped the chart. "The patient is Maxwell Brown, a sixteen-year-old male, who sustained a fractured left radius with minimal displacement. I reduced the fracture, gave him a fiberglass cast, a sling, and Tylenol number 3, one or two tablets q four hours, prn for the pain."

A variance in Bork's humming seemed to indicate he was listening.

"He's a big strapping kid, but the way he was carrying on, you'd think no one had ever broken an arm before. I have a feeling, too, that he's going to be wanting something stronger than Tylenol before the night's over." She held out the chart so that Bork could review it if he wished, but he merely hummed.

"Another one you might hear from is Walter Brumfield, thirty years old, who tripped and landed face first

249

on the walkway from Level One to Level Two. He has a swollen lower lip and an abrasion on the tip of his nose, neither of which will take more than a few days to heal, *but* he also sustained a nasty hematoma on the back of his head. His skull series was negative."

Bork sighed.

"I've instructed his roommate to watch for signs of concussion." She paused. "Brumfield hasn't a clue as to how he managed to bump his head."

The humming deepened in tone, became more involved and rather baroque.

"Dr. Bork?"

He finished his little song before looking at her, his eyebrows raised questioningly.

"I can tell you've got other things on your mind, but if I could have your attention, your *full* attention, for a moment or two, we could get this over with. Okay?"

"Why, of course."

Uncertain as to the length of his attention span, she hurried through the rest of the patients:

The maintenance worker who'd gotten second-degree burns on the palms of his hands when he'd grabbed an ungrounded wire.

An elderly woman who'd come close to choking to death on her false teeth after they were dislodged when the Vortex pod she was riding in came, without warning, to a sudden, bone-jarring stop.

Six-year-old twins boys who, without adult supervision and sans safety belts, were standing on the seat of their water pod when it entered the Four Rivers junction of the Water Devil ride, where it nearly capsized. They were battered nearly senseless by the time they made it through the white-water rapids. That neither boy had been seriously injured was a testament to the remarkable resilience of children.

The Guardian of the Graveyard had claimed another victim, a nine-year-old girl whose waist-length hair had somehow gotten tangled in its bony hand. The child became hysterical when no one could get the skeleton to let go — someone had to cut her free — and both she *and* her rather high-strung mother had required sedation.

All in all, they had seen twenty-three patients during the course of the day, a number that struck Taylor as being unacceptably high. Given that most of the injuries had occurred on the rides, she felt it only prudent to suggest to Sheldon Rice that something might be amiss . . . but Rice was nowhere to be found.

If she didn't reach him by tomorrow noon and get a satisfactory response to her concerns, she would have no choice but to call the Department of Public Health and Safety.

Despite the rigors of the day, after leaving The Park Taylor was reluctant to go home to the silence of an empty house, and she drove into McKenna's Creek instead. Most of the town's businesses would be closed and dark for the night, but maybe she'd stop at the Nugget Bar for a glass of white wine.

She rolled the car window down and breathed the fragrant air. She'd missed the salty tang of the ocean breezes mixed with the scent of pine and fir trees. Wisps of fog curled along the asphalt, and changed shape in the light from her low beams.

Like ghosts.

Out at sea, a foghorn wailed its warning.

Taylor found herself pulling into the small parking lot in front of the sheriff's office, and although she hadn't

251

consciously planned to come here, she realized it had been her intention all along.

Sheriff Young would never admit it, but he suffered from insomnia, and could be found at work both night and day. The lights were on and his patrol car was in the lot. When she passed it, she placed her hand on the hood; it was warm and the engine was pinging.

The outer office was deserted, but as the door closed behind her she heard a chair squeak and then footsteps.

"Sheriff Young?"

Young appeared in the doorway. "Taylor, what a pleasant surprise."

"Do you have a minute?"

"For a taxpayer? Always. Come on in. . . ."

She followed him into his office, which looked exactly as it had the last time she'd been here, six months after her father died. Papers were stacked on the desk, the filing cabinets were full to bursting, and the bookshelves were crammed with legal texts and what had to be thirty years of editions of the California Penal Code.

"Have a seat. Would you like a cup of coffee? I just sent Mary Beth over to the Nugget to get a couple of sweet rolls—nothing quite like an apple Danish with hot fresh coffee—or I think I've got some cookies in a drawer here somewhere."

Since she was five years old, the sheriff had been offering her cookies. Probably the same cookies, she thought and smiled. "No, I'm fine."

"You sure?" He ran a hand through his salt-and-pepper hair. "All right then. I guess I don't have to ask why you're here."

It seemed to her that in the back of her mind she could hear the echoes of the countless arguments they'd had, she imploring him to do more, and he insisting that there was nothing else that could be done . . . and even if there were, that it wouldn't change anything. It wouldn't bring her father back.

Taylor felt a familiar tightness in her throat, and she had to wait a few seconds before trusting herself to speak. "You haven't found anything new? You still don't know who was behind the harassment?"

The sheriff shook his head. "No, and what with all the time that's passed, I doubt if I ever will."

"But you won't stop trying."

"Well now, I don't know what good it's going to do to keep on—"

"What harm will it do?"

"That's not the point, but since you asked, I'll tell you; if you keep worrying at this like a dog gnawing at a tick, you might end up drawing blood."

"I'm not afraid—"

"No, I don't believe you are. I have to tell you, though, that I think it's way past the time when you should be getting on with your life. It's been a while now since your dad died, and the only one being hurt by this is you. Sometimes you gotta let go."

"My father is dead. He didn't have to die. I want to find whoever is responsible. It's as simple as that."

"Taylor, you don't know that anyone—"

"I'm a doctor. I know what I know. Those damned phone calls at all hours of the day and night, the letters and the pranks . . . the hostility as good as killed him."

He stood and came around the desk to stand beside her, one hand resting on her shoulder. "Listen to me for a minute, would you?"

"Whoever did those things," she said, "is guilty of murder."

The sheriff reached and tilted her chin up so that she was looking in his eyes. "Taylor honey, I've known you all of your life. I used to walk the floor with you when you

253

had the colic and your daddy was too tired to hold his head up. He was a good friend. And you have to believe me when I tell you that if there'd been even the slightest evidence that someone had intentionally caused your father's death, I would have tracked that person down."

"But—"

"Now listen. I did all the things I knew to do. I had the phone company get the records for your father's line, and all of the calls originated from a pay phone, the one out by the Wayside Inn."

Taylor frowned. That particular phone was hidden from view, tucked around the corner of what had been the inn's companion restaurant. She got up from the chair and crossed to a window, pausing to look out on the night.

"What I mean to say," the sheriff continued, "is that any one of us could have made those calls."

"And the letters?"

"Typed on an old portable Smith Corona, but unless there's a machine to compare with, knowing that don't amount to a hill of beans, evidence-wise."

She knew the answer, but she had to ask anyway. "What about fingerprints? Did you examine the letters for fingerprints?"

"By the time your dad came to me, the only fingerprints left were his. He'd folded and unfolded the damn letters so many times, they like to fell apart."

It hurt her to think he hadn't called her before it got to that stage, but he was always saying how he didn't want to disturb her while she was doctoring.

She turned to face him. "I'll never know, will I?"

"Honestly? I doubt it. One of the first lessons I learned as a cop was that there are some questions that don't have answers."

Why then did she feel as if she'd failed her father?

Chapter Thirty-seven

"Homer? Are you going out?"

Homer Goodenough shook his head in wonder. "How do you do it? I'm wearing a jacket, I've got a hand on the doorknob, and from this, you conclude I'm going out."

"Homer."

He hated the way Gretchen could make his name sound like a reprimand. "What?" He bit hard on the t to show his impatience.

"I thought the two of us were going to have a quiet evening. Cherokee's finally asleep and—"

"I need to get out." He jingled the change in his pocket. "You know I go a little stir-crazy when I'm cooped up all day."

"But you haven't been—"

"I *feel* like I have." As far as he was concerned, that was what mattered. "I'm just gonna take a walk, look around, get some fresh air."

Gretchen regarded him with hurt eyes. "Maybe I could

get someone to watch Cherokee and we both could go?"

"This isn't Barstow, babe. These people aren't our neighbors. You can't ask some stranger to watch over the kid." Homer knew he was acting like a total crud, but as much as he cared for Cherokee and Gretchen, there were only so many hours of playing the loving husband and father that he could take.

Besides, he had places to go and things to do. . . .

"Okay, then." Her voice was higher pitched than normal. "Have fun."

"I won't be—"

"Hey, it doesn't matter. You want to get some air? Get *lots* of air."

"Gretchen, I—"

"And don't worry, I won't be waiting up for you." She pulled her bathrobe tighter around her. "It'll be like old times, right? I'll see you when I see you."

Before he could respond, she turned and went into the bathroom, not quite slamming the door, but closing it emphatically enough to make her point. A second later he heard the lock engage.

"Women," he said, and left the suite.

The air was fresher without other people breathing it, Homer believed, richer in oxygen and kinder to the lungs. It smelled better, too, untainted by perfumes or after-shave or deodorant, although he supposed the latter was a kind of trade-off.

One of the reasons he chose to live in Barstow—besides its proximity to certain military facilities—was the lack of competition for the available air. In Barstow, when he began to get light-headed from breathing everyone's exhalations, he could hop in the truck, drive for ten minutes, and be as alone as a man could get in California.

This place was fairly remote, and the come-on about there never being a line was true so far, but there still were too many people fouling the air.

It bothered him, too, the way he was trapped here, deprived of his wheels. A fucking valet had parked his Ford down in an underground parking lot, and wasn't even going to give him back his keys until the valet got a good look at his expression and decided that some rules were meant to be broken.

Besides, the guy must have figured that there was no way anyone could get through the metal-link gates unless they were driving a tank.

Or were motivated.

He visualized hooking the winch on the truck's reinforced front bumper to the gate and yanking it off, and smiled. These guys didn't know jack-shit about security; if he really wanted out, they couldn't stop him, any more than they could stop him from getting in.

If the army had taught him only one thing, it was that there were no totally secured buildings, period. Even if they pulled a Chernobyl and buried the buildings under tons of concrete, there were ways of getting in.

Homer slipped through the maintenance door of the Final Flight pavilion, and stood for a moment, listening. Not for an alarm—he doubted the place was rigged, and even if it was, the alarm would be silent—but rather for voices.

Cleaning crews were probably responsible for more interrupted burglaries than the police or security services, and although all he was here to steal were ideas—and they could hardly shake him down for those—he'd just as soon not be caught in the act.

He didn't hear a sound.

257

When he'd been on the Final Flight this afternoon, he'd been impressed in spite of himself. He had only a little experience with flight simulators, but figured he knew enough to tell that this one was at least as good as those the fly-boys used.

What really intrigued him was the hologram stewardess, who sashayed up and down the aisle offering drinks from her cart. She looked so real that when she accidentally knocked over a holographic glass of vodka and orange juice, he had jumped, expecting to be splashed.

A few minutes into the ride, the copilot made an appearance, and Homer had marveled at how closely his movements matched the motion of the plane, once reaching out to brace himself by placing his see-through hand on the solid cabin wall.

Whoever orchestrated the holograms with the simulator had done a masterly job. The special effects far exceeded what Disney had been able to come up with in the Haunted Mansion. . . .

Homer meant to find out where the projectors were located, how many there were of them, and most importantly, how it was that the holograms had such a wide range of motion. Then he intended to sell the information to anyone who would pay his price.

Thanks to the army's stinking dishonorable discharge, he couldn't get rich selling out his country like the Walkers, so he'd have to wing it, and free-lance for awhile as an industrial spy.

Of course there would be others trying to do the same thing and get the same information, but they would be limited by having only minimal access to the ride. Any bozo could do as much, but *he*, through the wonders of the old standby B & E—breaking and entering—would have all night to go over the simulator.

The Final Flight's secrets would not remain secret for long.

He switched on his flashlight and was pleased at the way the handkerchief he'd wrapped around the lens softened the light. Instead of a beam, it glowed, providing enough light to see by, but not so much that someone entering the pavilion could use it to home in on its source. which meant that he'd probably hear them before they saw him.

Homer walked slowly, allowing himself time to fix the layout in his mind, in case he needed to make a hasty exit. There were a few obstacles to avoid, especially the black cable that connected the simulator to the control booth, and a forklift loaded with what appeared to be, and on closer inspection were, sandbags.

What did they need sandbags for? Puzzled, he jabbed a forefinger at one, but when after a moment of thought he couldn't come up with a logical reason for their presence, he shrugged and continued on.

He noticed a set of metal stairs that led up to the nose cone, and detoured toward them. He didn't imagine that there would be much of interest outside the simulator, but there was no harm in being thorough. And who knew? Perhaps one of the holographic crew originated from a projector in the cockpit.

But as he reached the top of the stairs, he paused. The hair on his arms was standing on end, as though the air were charged with static electricity. . . .

But then, there were so many electronic devices around and the air in the pavilion rivaled that found in the desert for dryness, so why wouldn't there be a little errant electricity?

Ignoring the cautious words his brain was whispering at him, Homer stepped onto the platform and moved toward the simulator's nose cone. If he propped himself against the curved surface of the nose cone, he should be in the perfect position to look into the cockpit.

From somewhere distant, he heard an odd series of clicks, followed by a low-throated hum. He glanced at both the main and side entrances, but saw no one.

He took a wide stance, his legs apart, and leaned forward until he was resting most of his weight on the nose cone. Pressing his face close to the glass windshield, he raised the flashlight and adjusted the handkerchief so that a thin beam of light shone into the cockpit.

No one inside.

The hair on the backs of his hands and fingers was bristling. He rubbed his free hand against his jaw and smelled ozone. . . .

Chapter Thirty-eight

After trying everything he could think of to stop what he'd started, Hightower stood in the shadows of the Final Flight Control Center, and watched helplessly as a man was crushed to death.

Heart pounding, his face slick with sweat, he closed his eyes when it got too intense, and was thankful for the soundproofing that kept him from having to hear what had to be bloodcurdling screams.

If only he hadn't hit that damn button on the control panel.

If only there had been a way to abort.

He *had* tried, feverishly flipping switches and turning dials, but the markings on the panel were too cryptic for him to decipher—what did D-2 or H-7 mean?—and he hadn't found a way to stop R-16 from squeezing the guy's innards up his gullet and out his nose.

Hightower winced and had to swallow to keep from heaving. The plan he'd begun formulating even as he realized what he'd done would only work if there was not a single sign that anyone other than the deceased had been in the building. . . .

A pool of vomit on the floor would be a dead giveaway.

He considered and quickly rejected telling the truth. Rice would want to know why he hadn't apprehended the intruder the moment the guy had set foot inside. Why, Rice would ask, had he waited? By waiting, hadn't he given the intruder a chance to damage, sabotage, or destroy Park property?

And hadn't he pretty much ignored a direct order to take anyone found on the premises without authorization into custody immediately?

Yes, he had. He had because, after fourteen straight hours on duty, he'd sought a dark and quiet place to catch a few winks. When he woke and realized that someone was wandering around, he should have radioed for backup, but, wanting to avoid the embarrassment of having been sleeping on the job, a cardinal sin for a security guard, and so he'd waited.

While waiting for the circulation to return to his sleep-numbed arm, he'd accidentally hit R-16, a small square button that looked no different from any other on the panel, but which proved to be brutally lethal.

Still, what was done was done, and nothing could change that. He was sorry it had happened, but for now he needed to focus on damage control, to keep a bad situation from getting worse.

At least, he thought, his security training had taught him how to cover his ass.

Averting his eyes from the observation window, Hightower set to work.

Chapter Thirty-nine

Loretta Billingsley stood in front of the printer, watching as the last of the day's status sheets spewed out. It was almost hypnotic, seeing page after page print out at precise intervals, filling the paper tray slowly but ever so surely.

Or perhaps it was the lateness of the hour that was leaving her feeling dazed. She definitely was not used to being up at this hour, having worked all of her adult life from eight to five.

Still, when Mr. Rice had called her in the San Francisco office this morning—or was it yesterday now?—he'd made it very clear that he needed her as he seldom had before. All hell was breaking loose—something to do with the rides, she thought—and under the circumstances, he'd implied, sacrifices must be made.

What else could she have done? She'd rushed home to pack a bag and then hurried back to the office to catch the company helicopter he'd sent for her. And certainly she knew that he had in fact dispatched the helicopter before he'd even spoken to her, but that only reinforced her belief that he knew he could rely on her and count on her regardless of the circumstance.

As many years as she'd worked for the man, there could be no doubt of that. And to those who said that he merely took advantage of her, the way he took advantage of everyone, she said "pshaw." They obviously had no idea what loyalty to one's boss entailed.

If an occasional sacrifice was necessary, then it was up to her to rise and meet the challenge. Any inconvenience that might occur in her personal life was far outweighed by the satisfaction she received from a job well done.

Oh, she could imagine what Emily would have to say about that. "Satisfaction is one thing, and appreciation is quite another. He might say thank you once in a while. Or give you an extra day off with pay."

Emily, who worked for a divorce lawyer, was forever getting days off with pay, but Loretta had a suspicion it was not out of the goodness of her boss's heart, but rather a way to get her out of the office so that he could dilly-dally with a female client or two.

As far as *she* was concerned, the old joke about what did you have if you ran a bus full of fifty lawyers off a hundred-foot cliff—the answer: a damned good start—had never been more true, and she'd rather work for an ungrateful boss than a hypocrite.

Regardless, what mattered to her more than days off or being told thank you was the knowledge that she was the one Sheldon Rice always turned to when he found himself in a fix. Even, as in this case, a fix of his own design.

She could have told him that Nancy Chan was not for him, any more than any of the others had been, although at least she was a change from the usual "accessory blond" men of his stature seemed to collect.

Always circumspect, he would never come right out and

admit that things were bad between them. What he had said was that Nancy had been working too hard lately, and that exhaustion had made her quote, ineffective, unquote.

Reading between the lines, Loretta knew that the clock was ticking off the last hours of this relationship. What ineffective really meant was that Nancy Chan would no longer do what he told her to do.

Exhaustion did indeed translate into tired, but past experience would suggest that it was Sheldon who was tired . . . of Nancy.

Men were so transparent sometimes.

The printer finally produced the last status sheet and she collected them, tapping the edges of the papers on the counter until she had a neat stack, then turned off the machine and left the small office.

At a quarter to one, Loretta finished reviewing the paperwork. She took the top sheet, folded it and sealed it in an envelope, then headed for the elevator.

Her intention was to drop the envelope into the night slot outside Mr. Rice's office on the fourteenth floor so that he would have access to the status information in the morning, but when she saw that the lights were on inside, she went ahead and knocked on the door. It hadn't been closed tightly, and it swung slowly open.

"What is it?"

She heard his voice but didn't see him. She took a cautious step into the room. "Mr. Rice?"

"Loretta, come in, I'll be right with you."

She still didn't see him, and as she walked toward the desk, she found herself peeking back over her shoulder, half expecting to see Mr. Rice coming up behind her. But just as she reached the desk, a panel in the wall six feet away slid open.

Sheldon Rice came out of the darkness, dressed entirely in black.

"Oh my," she said, her hand flying to her throat in shock. "You scared me half to death."

"Did I? Sorry."

The panel closed abruptly, and once it had, Loretta could not tell that section of the wall from any other. "Very impressive," she said, and held out the envelope to him. "A secret passage."

He looked at her as if he had no idea what she was referring to, and she realized that it had been inappropriate of her to comment on what she'd seen. She felt herself begin to color, and lowered her eyes as he took the envelope from her hand.

"These are the updated status reports?"

"Yes, Mr. Rice."

He ripped the envelope open, pulled out and unfolded the sheet. "Hmm. Interesting."

Loretta felt a twinge of nausea—lack of sleep always made her dyspeptic—and she leaned forward so that she could discreetly hold onto a corner of the desk. She noticed that the stack of messages she'd been accumulating for him all afternoon were still paper-clipped together, which told her that he hadn't as much as looked at them. "I'm sorry, Mr. Rice, but did you—"

"It seems," he interrupted, "we'll be on Level Three before the weekend after all. Excellent, excellent. Make a note, will you, to inform Wesley?"

"Of course, Mr. Rice."

"And by the way, you might also draft a note to the gardener that they're overwatering the oleander, and the ficus near the lobby entrance seems stressed . . . perhaps it should be transplanted . . . somewhere."

Loretta Billingsley could have sworn on a stack of Bibles that her employer wouldn't know a ficus if it came up and bit him, but then she remembered reading once that, when highly stressed, the human mind often sought refuge in meaningless details.

"Yes sir," she said, "of course."

Chapter Forty

June 17, 1992
Wednesday

When the call came at 3:17 in the morning, Wesley had not yet fallen asleep. He sat up, grabbed the phone, and identified himself, then listened with a growing sense of dread to the security supervisor's account of what a subordinate had found.

"Shit," he said when the supervisor fell silent. "I'll be right there."

"Hurry," the man suggested, and the line went dead.

Wesley hung up the phone and got out of bed to dress, thinking his way through a course of action. Security said they'd already called Rice, and the sheriff, and presumably an ambulance, although from what the supervisor told him, it sounded as if it was too late for the last of these to be of any help.

Awareness hit him then: A man had died. Or rather, a

man had been killed.

The feeling was very much like having ice water thrown in his face, and he took a deep, shuddering breath. Was he responsible in some way?

He wouldn't know until he got to the Final Flight ride and looked for himself.

The fog covered the mountain, and even as often as he'd walked these paths, he had the odd impression of being in a place he didn't know. Twice he went the wrong way and had to retrace his steps.

Finally, though, he spotted the blue emergency lights on the security vehicle, and set out running in that direction. The sound of his breathing seemed magnified in the close air, but he heard, too, an echo of the voices from above.

"Dead," a voice said, "no, he's dead." Again and again, the same thing: "Dead, no, he's dead."

Or maybe the echo was in his mind.

There were two men standing outside the Final Flight pavilion, both in the dark blue Park security uniform. The younger of the two put a hand on his holstered gun as Wesley approached.

Kind of jumpy, Wesley thought. But he didn't blame him for that. This entire situation was the stuff of nightmares, as far as he was concerned.

"Mr. Davison," the older man said. "I'm Beechum and this is Hightower. He found the . . . deceased."

"You're sure he's dead?"

Hightower nodded vigorously. "They don't come any deader, I can promise you."

"You want to go in?" Beechum asked.

There was nothing he wanted less than to go look at a dead man, but there didn't seem to be a viable alternative, so he nodded.

"I'll stay out here," Hightower said, making no attempt to disguise his relief, "and wait for Mr. Rice."

The Final Flight was in essence a flight simulator on a grand scale. Instead of including merely the cockpit, as did the simulators used to train pilots, this ride had nine rows of two seats each—the rough equivalent of a first class section—and, including the three seats in the cabin, could accommodate twenty-one guests at a time.

As with training simulators, the fuselage was surrounded by hydraulic equipment which approximated most angles of real flight. It could realistically imitate air disturbance, for example, as well as make reasonable facsimiles of wide banking turns, climbs, dives, and, most spectacularly, a barrel roll.

This last maneuver was facilitated by a rotator which attached to the fake nose cone and the abbreviated tail section. The rotator, despite its impressive size and power, was very much like an oversize rotisserie, with the plane functioning as the spit.

Wesley had always thought of it thusly, but the analogy was an unfortunate one; the man whose body was suspended some fifteen feet in the air had been caught between the rotator arm and the nose cone.

The crushing force of the rotator had resulted in the displacement of a great deal of blood. The windshield on the flight deck was nearly covered with it, and so were the first two passenger windows on the boarding side. Blood had also dripped from the plane onto the hydraulic lifters below, lubricating the gears.

The boarding door was open, but the interior of the plane was dark.

"My Lord," Wesley said.

"A mess, isn't it?" Beechum took several steps closer, craning his neck to look up. "Why the hell do you figure he went up there, anyway?"

"I don't know." He had to stop for a moment and take a few deep breaths. "Is he . . . was he one of the mainte-

270

nance crew?"

"Maintenance? I don't think so. I know most of the guys, and he doesn't look familiar," Beechum said.

Wesley didn't see how anyone could look familiar in that state. But if the man was a Park employee, he was out of uniform, dressed in a bomber jacket, a white T-shirt, faded jeans, and what were probably steel-toed black boots. Moreover, it was doubtful that an employee who knew how the ride operated would be fool enough to allow himself to be skewered that way.

Then again, he was facing the cockpit, away from the rotator; perhaps he hadn't known he was in danger until it was too late to escape.

The question remained, though, what he was doing here in the first place. The pavilions were all autolocked at 1:00 a.m., and only those with approved access codes should be able to get in.

The cleaning and maintenance crews worked from 5:00 a.m. until opening at 9:00. Both crews were required to wear the standard jumpsuit uniforms. And, as a rule, they worked in groups of three or four.

Ride operators were actually at the bottom of the command chain. As far as he knew, no operator had been granted anything beyond the basic access code, which would not override the autolock.

So . . . who was this guy?

"Who is this guy?" a voice from behind asked, and Wesley turned to see Sheldon Rice.

"I don't know," Wesley said. "I haven't gotten close enough to see his face."

"Or an ID," Beechum added.

"Well, then, let's take a look." Rice started up the gangway.

Wesley followed. "Maybe we should wait for the police. We shouldn't be touching anything."

"I have no intention of touching anything," Rice said without missing a step. "But if someone has the nerve to be killed on my property, I'm damned well going to see who it is."

They went into the plane and Rice started up the darkened aisle toward the cockpit, while Wesley lagged behind to turn on the cabin lights. while he was at it, he requested the computer to display a twenty-four hour log, and it verified that the last entry until his own had been shortly before 1:00 a.m.

"Damn," he heard Rice say.

He sighed, knowing that whatever was waiting for him wasn't going to be pleasant, and then headed resolutely up the aisle.

The first thing he noticed in the cockpit was that all of the instrument panels were functional and lit. The second was that the windshield was filmed with a coat of blood. The third was that even through the blood, he could make out the dead man's face.

He sank down into the co-pilot's seat.

Rice was still standing, although his head was bowed. Whether that was from respect or to keep from striking his head on the cabin roof was debatable, but the smart money, Wesley thought, was on the latter.

"I thought it was an old wives' tale," Rice said in a peculiarly dreamy tone of voice.

"What?"

"That someone's face could be frozen in agony."

Rice's own face, Wesley thought, had an avid look, as though he were fascinated instead of repulsed. "Well, you were wrong."

The dead man had died with his mouth open, his eyes bulging, and his features distorted. Blood from his nose covered the lower half of his face, but even the half that wasn't bloodied was suffused with red.

It was the rotator, Wesley thought, that had forced the blood flow up into the head. There were dark trickles of blood coming from both ears.

"Yes," Rice said belatedly, "I was wrong."

272

Sheriff Young arrived fifteen minutes later, and in spite of the lateness of the hour, there was nothing slow about the way that he took charge. A deputy had accompanied him, and Young immediately sent him to seal all doors but the main one, securing the pavilion.

He instructed Beechum to call the gate and order the guard there to allow only emergency vehicles in or out. He called his own department for reinforcements, and then brought in a large canvas bag which he apparently kept in the trunk of his patrol car.

In a scant thirty minutes, the scene had been cordoned off, photographed, measured, and drawn. Then Young put on a pair of latex gloves, and, using a cherry picker to keep from disturbing a deputy who was taking samples of the blood on the stairs, had himself boosted up so that he was level with the dead man. Young searched his pockets for identification, and came up empty.

Wesley sat at the foot of the ramp and watched, grateful that nothing was required of him for now. Every time he closed his eyes, he saw that agonized face, and he couldn't stop himself from imagining what it must have felt like to be crushed to death.

His respite didn't last long. A short while later, after they'd dusted the control panel for fingerprints, they asked him to retract the rotator so that they could remove the body.

When the body slipped free, it made a noise almost like that of a bellows drawing air.

It made his flesh crawl.

For what seemed like forever, the only sound in the pavilion was that of the metal zipper on the body bag being closed. It had a finality to it, and that, Wesley supposed, was fitting.

Rice, who'd been acting almost as if he were a disinterested bystander, cleared his throat. "Do you know this man, Sheriff Young?"

Young frowned. "It's hard to tell, with his face the way it is, but I don't think so. You're sure he's not one of yours?"

"If he is, he's not wearing his ID badge."

"Which means, you don't know either," Young interpreted. "Whoever did this to him—and from what y'all have told me, someone had to have been at the controls—might have made off with the badge."

"He doesn't look familiar to me," Hightower said quickly, putting, Wesley supposed, his two cents worth in. "And I know most of the employees."

Young motioned for the ambulance crew to take the body out. "A guest then?"

"Dear God," Rice said, "I hope not."

At Rice's urging, Young finally allowed the janitors to begin cleaning up the mess at 6:00 a.m., and they left the Final Flight pavilion, heading for the hotel. Hightower was being driven into town to give his statement, while Beechum went off duty to catch some sleep before his normal shift began.

Wesley sat in the back of Rice's limo—trust Rice to have come even that short a distance in style—and held his head in his hands. There was a dull ache between his eyes, and he found it difficult to concentrate on the discussion, as important as it was.

". . . the other part of the equation," Young was saying, "is who did that to him? And why?"

Chapter Forty-one

Even four days into the trip, Dinah had yet to adapt her inner clock to West Coast time, and by 6:00 a.m., she'd already been awake for an hour. At first, she'd tried to go back to sleep, knowing how exhausted she was sure to be later, but after tossing and turning and trying every mental trick she knew to hypnotize herself into dozing off, she accepted the inevitable and got out of bed.

The problem was, there was nothing constructive to do once she was up and dressed. Even forced idleness begat guilt; the paperwork that she should be doing was stacked on her desk thousands of miles away, where, unattended, it would be fruitful and multiply.

Of course, pursuing the other aspect of her job as counselor could fill the paperwork void, but somehow she doubted the kids would be amused if she woke them up to ask if they were having a good time.

Feeling antsy, she went into the spacious living room and over to the minibar, selected a bottle of apple juice from the refrigerator, then went to the window to watch the sunrise. Or in this case, since the window faced northwest, to watch the retreat of the night.

If she had a phone available, she could call Boston to check in with Peter again; when she'd spoken to him yesterday he was up to his ears making the travel arrangements for next month's disadvantaged youth program. And, she fervently hoped, hiring a chaperone with no living relatives and no possible excuse to cancel at the last minute.

Not that she wasn't enjoying herself, because she was, if for no otner reason than it was nice to be able to witness for herself the transformation taking place in these kids.

Celeste was beginning to soften a bit around the edges, although in her quixotic way, it was impossible to predict from one minute to the next which side of her she would choose to let anyone see. She could be smiling one minute and sullen the next, very much the classic Dr. Jekyll and Mr. Hyde personality.

But a lot of teenagers were that way, Dinah thought, and she took it as a positive sign. Better the peaks and valleys than what a psychiatrist would probably term "a flattening of affect."

Still, Celeste was a young girl at enormous risk. At fourteen, she was in her peak earning years as a prostitute, and although Dinah kept getting vague hints from her that she was ready to give up the life, her "manager" was unlikely to let her quit.

And if she wanted out, she'd have to do more than hint; the program Dinah had in mind for her would require her to stand up in peer counseling sessions, admit to her problems, admit she couldn't handle them on her own, and *ask* the others for help.

For Celeste, who never needed anyone's help, that last requirement was a killer.

It saddened Dinah that the girl had such limited expectations for herself; her goal was to get a job dancing at the Top Hat where her friend worked.

What kind of a life had Celeste lived, that she actually believed that stripping was a step up in the world, something to be coveted, a goal to be sought?

It broke Dinah's heart. She imagined Celeste balanced on a precipice, from which to fall meant certain, if not necessarily fast, death.

Betsy, on the other hand, appeared to be blossoming before her eyes. As quiet as Celeste was tempestuous, she'd begun to spread her wings. Dinah didn't know a whole lot about the girl's circumstances; the file she'd requested from the program intermediary in New Mexico had been mysteriously lost in transit not once but *twice*. Even without knowing Betsy's background, Dinah thought the Parker family would have a few surprises in store for them when she went home at the end of the week.

As for Max . . . well, Max hadn't changed much on the surface. In her professional opinion as a social worker, he was masking a deeply ingrained inferiority complex with the bully persona he portrayed, but she had a feeling that he was all bluff. In fact, Ann Brennan had told Dinah that while Max hadn't been her first choice for the DY program—or even one of the top five candidates—her mind had been changed when she ran into him at a hospital where he was bringing a gift to an injured friend. So impressed was she by his thoughtfulness, she'd decided right then and there to reward him by sending him on this trip.

"It was so obvious," Ann Brennan had told her, "from the look on Max's face that he never expected to run into me in Kevin's room. If I hadn't been there to see for myself, I'd never have known—or believed—that he was capable of such a sweet and caring gesture."

If Celeste was a tough cookie, Dinah thought, then Max had to be a Tootsie Roll . . . hard on the outside, but with a soft interior. And while she personally hadn't witnessed that aspect of his character, she respected Ann Brennan's judgment.

She found it ironic that he'd been awarded this trip because of a friend's broken arm, and now would be going home with one of his own.

Life could be funny sometimes.

With Joey, or whatever the child's real name was, the results were less ambiguous. The boy had gained at least five pounds, and his eyes had lost the cloudy look she'd always associated with hopelessness. It was because she didn't wish to be the cause of that look returning that she had decided not to actively pursue the matter of who on earth he really was.

The real Joey Castellano, Peter had informed her yesterday, had shown up for his trip a day late because the grandmother who was raising him spoke little English, and with a third party interpreting, something apparently had gotten lost in the translation.

The real Joey Castellano had been rescheduled for the August outing, and everyone apparently was happy, although Dinah wondered why, as far as they'd been able to determine, there'd been no inquiries to the San Diego Police Department about a lost or missing child.

What it meant, she suspected, was that the poor kid very likely had no family *to* miss him.

Nick, on the other hand, had family who had essentially thrown him away. She'd finally had an opportunity to read his case history from Iowa, and it had come close to making her physically ill —

Dinah blinked, distracted from her musings by the sight of three police cars, an ambulance, and a black limousine coming down from the amusement park grounds. The ambulance and two of the patrol cars continued on toward the main gate, while the third followed the limousine into the hotel's circular drive.

"What in heaven's name . . . ?"

Chapter Forty-two

Nicholas wanted to put his fingers in his ears and shut out Max's constant droning, but there wasn't a doubt in his mind that if he did, broken arm or not, Max would box his elbows, driving his fingers *into* his ears, where they would penetrate the pulpy gray matter of his brain, and then he would fall, twitching, to the ground.

And die.

"You know she doesn't expect us to fucking starve to death," Max said for the millionth time. "Did she, like, say that?"

"Like, no, she didn't," Betsy said. As a girl, she could get away with mocking. "What she did say was that there was something she wanted to look into, and she wouldn't be long."

"That was hours ago. You really think she expects us to wait?"

"I don't know what she expects, but we're going to wait for her to get back." Betsy reached over to Joey, who was sitting beside her on the couch, and patted his knee. "We can wait, can't we?"

"Sí."

"Sí señorita," Max mimicked. "You know the kid'll agree with anything you say. Besides, I know his gig, he's probably got food stuffed under his mattress. Don't you, hombre?"

"What's it to you if he does? If you're hungry, go ahead and *have* breakfast. No one's stopping you."

"I thought we agreed last night that all five of us would go together this morning—"

"I don't think it matters," Nick interrupted. He couldn't see making an issue out of it, considering that none of them were great friends. "Celeste's not here anyway, so there is no 'five of us'."

"You"—Max pointed and made a sucking sound through his teeth—"had better shut up if you're gonna take her side."

He raised his hands to surrender. "Consider me shut up. . . ."

Betsy sighed. "Don't you ever get tired of pushing people around?"

"Not when it's push or be pushed," Max said.

"Well, you're not pushing me around, so forget it. I've got six brothers and I know a thing or two about holding my own."

Nick could not recall ever seeing a woman with a more stubborn look on her face. He glanced from Betsy to Max, and was surprised to see that Max was taking it well, kind of smiling and nodding as if to say, "you win some, you lose some."

Max motioned for Nick to follow him. "Have it your way. Just don't come down later, expecting to sit with us, babe. You had your chance."

"Break my heart."

"Hijo de puta," the little kid said.

Nick had picked up a word or two of Spanish traveling, as he had, through the Southwest, and he almost choked trying to keep from laughing. Both what Joey had said and the way he'd said it—making no effort to hide the disdain in his voice—caught him off guard.

Although it was unfair, he thought, to put the blame on Max's mother, just as it would be unfair to blame *him* for his parents' sins—

"What was that?" Max asked. "What did he say?"

"Beats me," Nick lied.

"So," Max said while they were waiting for the elevator. "What do you think?"

"About what?"

"Betsy."

Not knowing what was expected of him, Nick frowned. "What about her?"

"She likes me. I could see it in her eyes."

Nick shrugged. "There's no accounting for taste," his mouth said before his brain could stop it.

"Lucky for you, I'm in a good mood this morning," Max said conversationally, "or I'd make you eat your words, one letter at a time."

Both of the hotel restaurants were crowded, and at each, the hostess had a list of people waiting for tables. "It will be at least twenty minutes," the second hostess said. "It looks like everyone decided to have breakfast at the same time."

"That figures," Max said. "I knew we should've come earlier. Well, what do you say we go upstairs and order from room service?"

But Nick had spotted a familiar face. "Wait a minute, will you? I'll be right back."

"Hey!"

He ignored Max and set off, winding his way through the tables and to a booth at the back of the dining area. Once there, though, he realized that he might be imposing, and he was ready to make a U-turn and disappear when Gretchen Goodenough looked up from her coffee.

"Nick," she said, and smiled.

"Hi."

"Cherokee, honey, look who's here."

Cherokee had what was probably oatmeal smeared over most of her face and after folding a piece of bacon and stuffing it into her mouth, she gave him a chipmunk grin and said around it, "Where's Daddy?"

Gretchen frowned, watching her daughter. "So much for table manners. It's enough to make you lose your appetite sometimes."

"Kids will be kids."

"I guess. You want to join us?"

"Actually, I'm not alone." Nick looked over his shoulder, expecting to see Max, but didn't. "Then again, maybe I am."

"Come on then, have a seat."

"Your husband won't mind?"

"It's just the two of us this morning," she said, scooting over to make room, "since Homer is off doing who-knows-what-with who-knows-who."

Nick sat down. "Sorry?"

"Daddy's bye-bye," Cherokee said.

"You might try to get at least some of that milk in your mouth, Cherokee." Gretchen mopped up a puddle on the table. "Homer got a wild notion to go out for a walk last night, and I haven't seen him since."

"Aren't you worried?"

"Not yet." She picked up two packets of sweetener and shook them, ripped off the tops, and poured the contents into her coffee. "Homer is a good ole boy, you understand, and he doesn't feel he should have to account for his time to anyone. He hates the thought of being reined in by the little woman."

"That seems kind of. . . ." Nick searched for a polite way to phrase what he was thinking.

Gretchen read his mind: "Childish."

"Well, yeah. I mean, Cherokee is the kid in your family; he ought to act more grown up."

"You won't hear any argument from me. Anyway, he's pulled this trick before and I'm sure he'll do it again. It burns my ass, though, him taking off and leaving me high and dry on our vacation."

"Maybe you should try to find him."

"You don't know my Homer. Unless he's ready to be found, there's no point in looking. He'll show up when he's good and ready."

"You don't think something might have happened to him?" Nick wasn't sure why, but he had a bad feeling about all of this.

"Could be, but if his fat's in the fire, he lit the match himself."

"You could call the police," Nick persisted, and then sat back, astonished to hear those words coming from him. In his experience, the police were always too late and when they did show up, there was nothing they could do.

Nothing they could do.

Nothing they could do.

"Nick," Gretchen said, waving a hand before his eyes, "are you in there?"

It felt as though he were swimming in quicksand, and couldn't get out. His arms and legs were leaden, too heavy to even move, and the room had suddenly gone quiet, as if a vacuum had formed.

"What is it?" Gretchen, sounding far away, touched his arm, gave it a shake. "Are you all right? You look like you've seen a ghost."

"A ghosss," Cherokee echoed.

"Amy," Nick said.

"Your sister? What about her? Nick?"

"Is this your sister?" the cop asked.

Nick could only nod. He held her close to him, her head tucked beneath his chin and breathed the clean scent of her hair, which smelled of baby shampoo and bubble gum.

"You'd better let me take her," the state cop said.

Nick shut his eyes. His chest ached so badly that he thought he would die.

The local cop who'd gotten there first came over and drew the state cop aside. "Let him be."

"But the little girl is dead."

Did they think he couldn't hear them?

"Right. And if there's nothing we can do for either of them, he might as well hold her until the ambulance gets here."

"But she's —"

"Leave them alone."

Both cops walked away.

Nick sat on the bench, holding Amy. He smoothed her hair and kissed her, rocked back and forth and cried.

A long time later but far too soon, a red-and-white ambulance pulled into the rest stop. Two men got out and after consulting the cops, came over to the picnic table where he sat.

Neither spoke for a minute or so, and Nick kicked at the blood-stains in the dirt, trying to cover them.

"What's your sister's name?" the heavyset man asked.

His throat seemed to close on itself, and he had to work at getting it clear. "Amy," he said.

"That's a nice name. What's yours?"

"Nicholas."

"Nicholas. You know, don't you, Nicholas, that there's nothing that can be done for Amy?"

"She's sleeping."

The man sighed and patted his knee. "Can I take her for you?"

His arms did not want to let go.

"Let me have her, son. I promise I'll be very gentle with her."

"She doesn't like dark places," he said.

"We'll leave the light on. She won't be afraid, Nicholas. Not any-more."

Somehow, he let go, and then she was lifted out of his arms. He looked down at his shirt, which was still wet with blood, and at his empty hands. Blood was caked under his fingernails.

The heavyset man carried Amy off.

Nicholas couldn't watch.

"Do you know what happened here?" he heard somebody ask. "Who did that?"

He had been warm as long as his arms were full, but now he began to shiver. He sat forward and pulled the wet shirt away from his skin, thinking that it would dry quicker that way.

The local cop came to sit on the other side of the picnic table. "Can you tell me what happened?"

"Nick?" Gretchen was saying, "are you okay?"

He gripped the edge of the table, forcing himself to be here, now. He felt himself sweating, and raised a shaky hand to wipe it from his brow. Then he raised his eyes to meet hers. "I'll be fine," he said.

Chapter Forty-three

Betsy inserted four quarters into the stamp machine and it spit out a small glassine envelope with three thirty-cent stamps inside. They were, she was disappointed to see, just the ordinary flag issue; it would have been nice if they were the ones with "Love" on them.

She crossed the hotel lobby and found a quiet place to sit down, wanting to review the letter one last time before she dropped it in the mail slot.

"Dear Steve," the letter began, and in some ways that had been the hardest thing to write. Addressing him as Mr. Torrance sounded too distant, given that he'd admitted his feelings for her, and yet considering what she had to say, it probably was the proper salutation. Even so, she couldn't bear the thought that he would be hurt by her formality, and so she'd chosen to be more intimate.

Dear Steve;
    I am sorry bat I haven't written sooner. I intended to, but I've been so busy, having the best time. You were right to insist that I come, and right, too, that I

owed it to myself to experience life a little.

I guess I always knew there was more out there in the "real world" than I could ever find in Mountainair, but I was scared to go looking. I was scared to be alone, away from people who cared for me. Until now.

Getting to know these kids who are truly disadvantaged has made me ashamed of how timid I am, and how I've always wanted to play it safe, letting others take the risks. And I see, now, that you were right, and I shouldn't squander an opportunity.

I've decided to go to college and become a veterinarian. My secret dream.

In my heart, I want you to be part of that life, but you can't. You have to do what's right for you, and I have to do what's right for me.

I feel as if I owe you so much that I can never hope to repay you. You opened my eyes and my heart, and I will . . .

love you forever,
Betsy

Betsy refolded the rose-scented paper and tucked it back into the envelope. She licked the flap and sealed it, taking care that the glue held. The last thing either one of them needed was for the school secretary — to whom an improperly sealed envelope was an invitation — to find a loose corner and take a peek inside.

Word would spread throughout Mountainair like wildfire, and forever after, the town would believe that it wasn't college she'd gone off to, but a home for unwed mothers. No matter to them that all Steve had ever done was kiss her hand.

Betsy sighed, got up, and walked over to the registration desk where the mail drop was located, where she stood behind a woman who was feeding postcard after postcard through the slot. When her turn came, she hesitated, then let the envelope fall from her fingers.

287

The ride attendant at White Water offered a hand to balance her as she stepped into the pod, but she smiled and shook her head. She very much liked the sense of self-assuredness that she felt.

"Enjoy the ride," the attendant said.

"Thanks." She adjusted the seat belt as the pod exited the boarding area and began drifting languidly along the canal. Tilting her head back, she stared up at the sky, enjoying the sun's warmth on her face.

Had she ever seen a sky as blue as this? Had the air ever caressed her as gently as it did now?

She remembered a day almost as beautiful. She'd been at the school library doing research for a term paper for her history class. Sitting at one of the old wood tables, her books spread out all over, she'd taken a moment to admire the sunlight slanting through the louvered windows. Outside, the sky seemed close enough to touch. . . .

Mr. Torrance had come in, as he often did when she stayed after school to study, asking her how her work was coming, and offering to help if he could.

"You can stay as late as you want," he'd say, and give her a big smile. "I have to work for a few more hours myself, and I'd welcome the company."

Later he'd told her that he often had sought her out the way a man would seek to fill his lungs with fresh air, the better to breathe.

She found it odd, now, to realize how many of her memories of school and studying were entwined with those of Steve.

But all of that was in the past.

Betsy reached over the side of the pod and trailed her fingers through the cool water, then cupped her hand and brought it quickly to her throat so that water splashed along her neck. Droplets ran down and wet her white cotton blouse, making it adhere to her damp skin.

She closed her eyes and let the sway of the water bring her ease.

A cloud must have drifted in front of the sun, Betsy thought drowsily, feeling a sudden chill. She opened her eyes and discovered that she had entered the caverns where the white water awaited.

And although she couldn't yet *see* the white water, she could hear it, the roar of rushing water as it churned and foamed, punctuated by the laughter and screams of those ahead of her. She grabbed onto the recessed handholds and braced herself, but even as she did so, the ride came to an abrupt halt.

"Not again," she said, and looked back over her shoulder to commiserate with her fellow riders, but the pod behind her was empty.

"Please remain seated," a voice said, echoing through the cavern. "White Water has developed a minor technical problem."

Betsy frowned. Perhaps six feet ahead and off to the right she saw a narrow pathway that ran alongside the canal. The path disappeared around a corner, but she could see the glowing red T of what had to be an exit sign.

Why not get out of the pod and exit the ride? She would get wet, but it really was only a couple of steps to the pathway.

After her experiences getting stuck on the Nebula and Glacier, she thought it better to get wet than spend a half hour — or longer — waiting for them to fix the ride.

"Please remain seated. White Water has developed . . ." The voice warbled and fell silent, which wasn't exactly a confidence booster.

Betsy unbuckled her seat belt and stood up in the pod, then sat down again to take off her shoes. She tied the laces together and draped the shoes across her shoulder, then moved carefully to the side of the pod. Turning around, she stepped backward out of the pod, holding onto its side while she made sure her footing was steady.

The water came to just below her knee.

The canal bottom sloped down, and her right foot slid a

couple of inches until her leg was resting against the side of the pod.

This might not be as simple as she'd thought.

Betsy swung her left leg out of the pod, and the awkwardness of the motion made her slip forward still, so that her right foot was underneath the hull. When she tried to straighten up, she felt something snag on the cuff of her jeans.

"Darn." She reached into the water under the hull to try and pull free, but her arm wasn't long enough. She steadied herself and tried to kick back with her leg, but the resistance of the water and whatever had caught on her jeans combined to render the move ineffectual.

"Now what?" She looked toward the next pod, hoping that someone would appear there as if by magic, and help her out of this fix.

No such luck.

Betsy considered for a moment and then lowered her body further into the water, thinking that perhaps she could unhook her jeans by letting her leg go farther still beneath the pod's hull, but as the water rose to waist level, the pod lurched forward and —

— her hands slipped off the side.

She fell backward into the water, which rushed into her nose and mouth. She gasped, swallowing some of it, then fought her way to the surface and, sputtering, tried to grab onto the pod.

But the ride had resumed, and it only took her a second to realize that she was being dragged behind, the pod's wake splashing in her face.

"Help!"

The pod made a sweeping turn and even with her head partly underwater, she could hear the fury of the rapids increase as the distance between them lessened. If she didn't get free before the pod entered the white water, Betsy knew that she would drown.

Choking on the water being forced into her mouth, her sinuses stinging from the chlorine up her nose, she had to use

290

both hands to unbutton her jeans. The zipper jammed halfway down, and she fumbled desperately with it, unable for the moment to find the metal pull tab.

The pod rocked to one side, and she was completely submerged for what seemed to be forever. She could see through the blue water to where it foamed white, and saw that the bottom of the canal curved down. The water there would be deeper. . . .

Fighting a sense of panic, Betsy grabbed either side of her jeans and yanked them apart. The zipper held briefly but then she felt it give.

Her head cleared the water and she coughed violently before drawing a convulsive breath. The temptation was to stop struggling and just breathe, but she didn't dare succumb to it. Instead she twisted her body furiously, trying to wriggle out of her jeans.

The water's roar thundered in her ears.

She kicked with her legs and felt the wet denim slide away from her skin until only her right foot was caught in the tangle of fabric. She straightened her foot like a ballerina on pointe and—

—floated free. The pod continued on without her, disappearing into the rapids.

Her lungs aching, her arms and legs heavy with exhaustion, she made her way toward the side of the canal as another empty pod moved by, narrowly missing her.

Somehow she found the strength to crawl out of the water, and then the blackness came.

Chapter Forty-four

Sheldon Rice steepled his hands and looked over his fingertips at Sheriff Young. He was trying to gauge how best to deal with the man, who appeared to be determined to make an unfortunate situation even more difficult by his stubborn adherence to following "the book."

The very last thing he needed was the presence of the police on the grounds, and yet he knew that he could not demand that they leave. He had tried all morning long to arrive at a mutually satisfactory compromise, in which all aspects of the investigation were to be conducted in town—out of sight of the guests—but Young had refused to make any such deal.

There was, apparently, some advantage to be gained by staying near the so-called death site. Perhaps the sheriff believed that the murderer would return to the scene of the crime.

If the murderer was a fool he might, Sheldon thought. But what were the chances, really? And was it worth the inconvenience to himself and his staff?

Not from his perspective.

He cleared his throat. "Shouldn't you be witnessing the autopsy or something?"

Young glanced up from the printout of the guest registry. "It won't be done until tomorrow. Doc Chambers is up county, delivering a baby."

"I see. Life having, of course, priority over death. Very commendable."

The sheriff smiled faintly. "Do you mind if I ask you a question?"

"Can I stop you?" There'd been hundreds of questions thus far.

"Does being arrogant come naturally to you, or do you have to work at it?"

Across the room at his desk, Wesley coughed.

"I'll pretend I didn't hear that," Rice said. His face felt stiff from anger, but he would not give Young the satisfaction of knowing he had drawn blood.

"And if I ask you again?"

It was evident that Young hadn't the sense to know when to back off. Perhaps he ought to bring that to the attention of the town council members, in particular those who owed him allegiance. Too bad that sheriff was an elective office or he could settle it today.

But it would have to wait. For now, he wanted to avoid any further confrontation.

"You'll have to excuse me if I'm a little short-tempered," he said. "I'm not used to having people killed by my rides."

"Not *by* the ride. The man who died was killed by someone, not some *thing*."

This was becoming tiresome; it was too minor a point to argue. He got up and walked to the window to look out at The Park, keeping his back to the sheriff as a rebuke.

"Mr. Rice," Wesley said, "I've reviewed all of the tapes."

Rice saw that Sheriff Young had turned to listen, and felt a flash of irritation at how his privacy was being invaded. Although this was Wesley's office, so he supposed it really was Wesley's privacy.

293

He frowned at the erratic nature of his thoughts and made an effort to channel them. "And what did you find?"

"Nothing."

Rice closed his eyes momentarily. When he opened them, the sheriff had crossed the room to join them, his thumbs hooked in his belt.

"How can there be nothing?" Young asked. "I thought you had cameras everywhere."

"We do," Wesley said, "but after The Park closes at midnight, as an economic measure, they're programmed to tape only at certain locations and at random intervals. As it happens, the Final Flight cameras were not in the loop last night for recording. But neither were about a third of the other rides."

Young shook his head. "All that high-tech surveillance and it comes up with a big fat zero."

Rice placed a hand on Wesley's shoulder. "Good work, though."

"It's what you pay me for."

"The thing is," Wesley went on, "the more I think about it, the more I get the feeling that I should know who he is, that I've seen him before."

By 2:00 p.m., Rice had exceeded the limits of his patience, and he excused himself by pleading a headache that required aspirin. But instead of going to the executive lounge, where there was a medicine cabinet, he slipped off down the hall to his own private office.

He had to enter his damned access code twice, but once inside he was rewarded by absolute silence and the luxury of being unobserved.

"Thank God," he said, and sat on the couch. He would very much have liked to lie down, to stretch out and put up his feet, perhaps have a nap, but he knew that too long an absence would set Young on his trail.

If he fell asleep now, it would be hours before he awoke.

Besides, he needed to decide what to do about Nancy,

whose attitude had become all but intolerable in the last few days. Something would have to be done to rectify that. He didn't really care whether she stayed or went, as long as peace was restored.

What bothered him most was the inconvenience of having to replace her, professionally at least. She'd done a good job with the media, developing an excellent rapport. Hardly a day went by without a positive mention or two in the press. . . .

Maybe he should postpone their parting until after the present difficulties had subsided. Her expertise might come in handy, considering the sensitive nature of this turn of events. She might be skilled enough to avoid the kind of public relations debacle that Universal Studio's movie theme park in Florida had suffered when their opening day was marred by malfunction after malfunction.

The guests had vented their frustrations on national TV, complaining of long lines and inoperative rides. Rice could well imagine vacation plans being changed across the country even as Brokaw smiled dryly and thanked his correspondent for the report.

Yes, he thought, it would be prudent to let Nancy deal with the current crisis before confronting the more personal problems between them.

And there were the Games to consider. Dead man or not, he intended that they go on.

Which reminded him. He crossed to the desk, picked up the phone, and dialed. "Loretta," he said when she answered, "Did you have the invitations sent?"

"Yes sir."

"Good. And there were how many who had scores over two thousand?"

He could hear her shuffling through papers. "Six, seven, eight . . . there are eight of them."

"Excellent." With six Mercenaries and himself, it would be seven against eight. "As soon as you get confirmations, I want you to see that they're issued new ID badges, with their photographs on them."

"Of course, sir."

"I don't want any last-minute substitutions."

"No, sir."

"There are rules," he said, and thought, why am I telling her?

"Is there anything else, Mr. Rice?"

"That ought to do it. Oh, wait. Have you seen Miss Chan this afternoon?"

"I'm afraid not. Shall I look for her and ask her to call you?"

"That won't be necessary." There would be no news released until it became unavoidable. "I'll be in touch later," he said, and hung up.

"Mr. Rice," Wesley said when he walked in the door, "I think I know who the man is. Or was."

He stopped in midstride, and felt the blood drain from his face. "How did you . . ." He looked at Sheriff Young, who had the phone to his ear, but appeared to be listening to them instead.

The sheriff had said earlier that identification by fingerprints was an uncertain proposition, since many people went through their entire lives without being printed. And even if the deceased's prints were on record, it still might take days, regardless of the sophisticated computerized ID system now in use.

He had been counting on that delay.

"I *thought* I'd seen him before, but I couldn't put my finger on where or when, and then it came to me."

"Yes?"

"He was in those tapes from Monday."

Sheldon Rice shook his head. "What tapes are you talking about?"

"Remember the little girl who cut her finger?"

It took an effort to keep from showing his exasperation. One minute the talk was of dead men, and the next of little girls? "I assume there is a point to this?"

"What I'm saying, Mr. Rice, is the man who was killed is

296

the same one in the tape. He's the little girl's father. I looked up the name. Homer Goodenough."

"Ah . . . I see."

"And he is a registered guest, with his wife and daughter."

Rice winced. A guest. Why couldn't it have been a local?

On the phone, Young was spelling Goodenough: "Right, like good enough, only it's one word. No, the g-h is silent. Good-en-now. First name, Homer."

"His wife hasn't reported him missing?" Rice asked, feeling cross. "It's been twelve hours, for crying out loud."

Wesley frowned. "That is odd, but—"

"Hell, maybe she did it," Rice said facetiously. "That would explain a lot."

Young hung up the phone. "Except how she came to figure out how to do it."

"Beginner's luck," he replied, and felt a surge of anger at the man for having the gall to go and get himself killed, and in such a spectacular fashion. Already he could envision the stories that would result.

The media would swarm like locusts.

"We'll have to inform Mrs. Goodenough," the sheriff said. "Take her into town to identify the body."

"Yes, of course." Although he was seething inside, Rice had to present a calm front. "Wesley, call Dr. McKenna, and ask her if she'll accompany us. If the wife becomes hysterical, she may require sedation."

If the gods were kind, perhaps she could be sedated well into next week, and the story of her husband's death would fall by the wayside. . . .

297

Chapter Forty-five

Jesus was on his own again this afternoon.

He did not mind being on his own; it was what he was accustomed to. So he set out with the intention to explore more thoroughly the underground tunnels he had found yesterday.

First, though, he needed to be able to see in the darkness. His night vision was good, but deep in the tunnel it was blacker than any night. He needed a flashlight.

Once, with Betsy, he had gone into a small shop that sold hats and sunglasses, as well as many other things which Betsy had called trinkets. There he had seen a flashlight on a chain.

It wasn't very big, about the length of his hand, and the light which it provided would only show him what lay a few feet ahead, but it was safer than using matches to find his way. And a clasp at the end of the chain opened—for keys, Betsy had said—so he could attach it to his belt loop. That way, if he fell or somehow dropped it, it would not be lost.

And neither would he.

The Park looked different today, he thought. The sun had been softened by the presence of puffy white clouds high in the sky, and there seemed almost to be a bluish haze. Although it was several hours to sunset, the sky hinted at the coming of night.

In Tijuana, a sky like this one often foretold a storm, but here they were high up on the mountain and he could see far out to the sea. If there was a storm out there waiting, it was a long way off.

And anyway, if the rain came, it came. There was nothing he or anyone else could do that would stop it. The rain clouds did not bow to the wishes of man.

One day, when he was grown, neither would he.

It took him awhile but he finally found the little trinket shop. He passed among shelves full of tiny glass animals, hats and bonnets, ceramic mugs, and brightly painted pins, heading for a rack in a corner.

There were ten or so of the flashlights, and Jesus checked them one by one, flashing the beam into the palm of his hand, looking for whichever had the brightest light. They were of many colors, he hoped that the gold one would prove to be the best, but after many tests it was the pink flashlight that was the strongest.

He returned the gold one to the rack and carried the pink up to the register. As he reached to place it on the counter, he noticed a big glass box on a shelf behind the counter, with a very bright light inside. On the bottom of the glass box were hundreds, *hundreds* of tiny plastic skeletons and spiders.

"*Que es* . . . what is that?" he asked, and pointed.

The clerk turned to see. "These?" He tapped the glass box. "Yes."

The clerk lifted the top of the box, reached in, and grabbed a handful. "These are those things that glow in the dark."

Jesus accepted a skeleton, turning it over several times to see if he could discover how it worked. There was no switch on it; it seemed to be solid plastic, yellow-white in color. "How does it work?"

"You got me there. All I know is it does." The clerk placed a spider in one hand, covered it tightly with the other, and then motioned to Jesus to peek through a gap in his fingers.

The spider glowed a pale green, and Jesus drew back in amazement. He shaped his hands around a skeleton and brought his face near. It, too, glowed. "How much does it cost?"

"Fifty cents each."

The señorita had told them that they could buy what they needed from the shops "up to a limit." The others had been buying gifts for family and friends, but until today, he had resisted the temptation.

Today he had a good reason to buy; the spiders and skeletons which glowed in the dark would make good markers in the tunnel.

Jesus unclipped his *disco de identificacion* and slid it across the counter to the clerk. "How many of these can I have . . . up to a limit?"

"Well, let's see." The clerk ran a wandlike device which emitted a red light across the back of his magic card, then punched in some numbers on the register. "Holy cow, you've got a little account built up. A hundred and fifty dollars."

"And if I buy the flashlight, how much will be left?"

"This?" The clerk picked up the pink flashlight. "It's only four bucks. Even with tax, that leaves you with more than a hundred and forty-five green ones."

Jesus did not know what green ones were, but he persisted. "How many of these spiders and skeletons will that buy?"

"A lot," the clerk said. "A lot."

"I will take them."

The clerk's eyes opened wider. "What in the world are you gonna do with them?"

Jesus only smiled.

It had taken some time for the clerk to figure how many skeletons and spiders to give him, allowing for the tax. He'd also had to count them out, first into piles of ten, and then into hundreds.

They filled a blue-and-silver shopping bag which closed

with a drawstring. Jesus wound the drawstring around his hand, and draped the bag over his shoulder. He tucked the receipt into his pocket, and attached the pink flashlight to a loop on his jeans.

Thus prepared, he headed for the tunnel. The sky was noticeably darker, and the sea gulls which had been riding on the wind earlier were not in sight. Their cries, though, echoed in the stillness.

He wondered if they had found another feast.

Back at the tunnel entrance, secreted between a group of rocks as big as he was, Jesus glanced around him to make certain he was not being watched — the branches of the trees surrounding the area were a good but imperfect shield — and then disappeared into the opening.

Chapter Forty-six

Taylor McKenna stood behind and to the side of Gretchen Goodenough, who had asked for a moment to compose herself before Sheriff Young lifted the drape and exposed the face of the man assumed to be her husband.

Mrs. Goodenough took several deep breaths, squared her shoulders, and then nodded.

Young took hold of the drape with both hands and brought it down to clavicle level.

"Shit, Homer," the woman said in a hoarse whisper. "How could you go and do this?"

Out of the corner of her eye, Taylor noticed that Sheldon Rice was perspiring heavily and had turned a nasty shade of gray. It concerned her; he had been acting strangely on the way into town, lapsing into a moody silence the moment they'd left The Park grounds. But even more unsettling was the impression he gave that, rather than feeling remorse at the man's death, he somehow blamed the victim for what had befallen him.

She noted, too, that the muscles of his face were visibly lax, so that the skin sagged; he had the look of someone who was clinically depressed. He was also puffy around the eyes, which were as red-rimmed as those of a habitual drinker.

Not a healthy man, she thought, wondering if she should suggest he consult his own physician. She knew he was under a great deal of stress. . . .

She glanced again at Gretchen Goodenough, who had reached out and placed the back of her hand against her husband's cheek. A second later, she began to shake, as if the chill of death had touched back.

Taylor stepped forward and put an arm around her, while Sheriff Young replaced the drape and quickly came from the head of the table to do the same. Wesley Davison, who'd been standing with his back against the far wall, took a few steps toward them as though to offer his assistance.

Only Rice remained where he was.

She and the sheriff escorted Mrs. Goodenough from the morgue and into the office. They sat her down, and Taylor cracked an ammonia ampule, then waved it under the woman's nose to keep her from passing out. Young brought a paper cup of water, holding it with her as she drank.

"I'm sorry," Mrs. Goodenough said.

Taylor sat beside her. "There's nothing to be sorry for."

"I didn't expect him to be so . . . cold," she said, and shuddered. "Poor Homer."

As a physician, Taylor was more or less used to death, but she'd never gotten used to dealing with the aftermath. The deceased's troubles ended with the cessation of a heartbeat, but for those who survived a loved one's passing, the problems had only begun.

Gretchen Goodenough had a tough road ahead of her, particularly having been left with a young child to raise on her own.

"I have to tell you, your husband didn't have a wallet or anything else on him when he was found," Sheriff Young said matter-of-factly, "so if you need to be notifying anyone about missing credit cards or whatever, Mary Beth will be glad to help you with that."

Mrs. Goodenough shook her head. "Homer didn't believe in owing money. We only had the one credit account for gasoline, and we kept that card in the truck. Oh lord, the truck.

303

You didn't find his keys?"

"No, ma'am."

"Damn. I don't *have* a key to the truck. It was his baby, he wouldn't even let me drive it. Said I wasn't strong enough to push the clutch all the way to the floor and that I'd strip the gears."

"We can get a locksmith up from the city to take care of that in a day or two," Young said, and smiled as if to reassure her. "Now. What about cash? Did Homer have money on him?"

It struck Taylor as an insensitive question to be asking a newly bereaved widow, but Mrs. Goodenough appeared to take it all in stride. Focusing on details was one way to keep from being overwhelmed by emotion.

"I doubt he had more than twenty dollars and pocket change," Mrs. Goodenough said. "We brought a cashier's check for the week, and that was it. Well, I have a few dollars tucked away . . . but if he was . . . if someone did that to rob him, they didn't get much."

Taylor knew by Young's eyes that he would not be in the least surprised that a man might be killed over twenty dollars.

"You said that Mr. Goodenough had gone for a walk last night?"

"Yes."

"Was there a reason, or was he just out for a breath of air?"

She was silent for a moment, and then shook her head. "Homer is . . . was the type of a man who tends to feel pent up quick. He wouldn't need a reason. I think he probably just wanted to take a look around."

"I see."

"And," she said, "he fancied himself something of an expert on security and the like. . . ."

In the doorway, Sheldon Rice became noticeably still. Wesley, who'd been staring blankly at the floor, looked up with a frown.

"What did your husband do for a living?" the sheriff asked.

"Well, he is . . . was unemployed, but before he got kicked out of the army he was an MP—"

"How"—Rice interrupted, his face grayer still—"could you

304

afford to come to The Park?"

Taylor noted that Mrs. Goodenough's hands were trembling and was about to suggest that further questioning be delayed when the young widow spoke:

"I don't honestly know where the money came from. I mean, I make good tips at the IHOP—it's on West Main and we get a lot of the turnaround business—but even so it seems most months there's hardly enough to make ends meet, much less set any aside. And then Homer up and announces he's come into some cash. An inheritance, he said."

"An inheritance." Rice didn't bother to hide his skepticism.

"Knowing Homer, he probably snuck off to Vegas with the cookie jar money, and then didn't want to admit he'd been gambling." Gretchen Goodenough smiled faintly, ever tolerant of her man's failings. "I figured it was better for both of us if I didn't know."

And then, finally, she began to cry.

Taylor helped Wesley take Gretchen Goodenough out to the limousine, then returned to the sheriff's office for her medical bag. The door was standing open, but she could hear a heated argument, and rather than going in, she stood outside and listened.

"—has to be done," Rice was saying. "You have to do something about that old mountain man."

"It's not as simple, Mr. Rice, as picking up a phone." Sheriff Young's exasperation was evident. "I don't think you understand—"

"You are the one who doesn't understand. I've asked you time and again to talk to him—"

"The man lives way up in the mountains, way the hell off the main road—"

"—threaten him if you have to—"

Young raised his voice. "You can't even reach his place by four-wheel drive; the road tapers down to a footpath, and it's about a three-mile hike—"

"—or arrest him, I don't give a damn."

"Now just hold your horses, there. The man's gotta be eighty years old—"

"Do I look as though I care? I don't. He's been harassing me since day one, and I've had it, do you hear me? I've had it."

Taylor frowned. It could only be Ezra they were talking about.

Ezra, she thought, who didn't have a telephone. Who would have *had* to use a pay phone . . . an old eccentric who planted pine seedlings to "put the blue back in the sky" and who seemed sometimes to appear—and disappear—into thin air.

Ezra.

Had it been Ezra all along?

She'd left her car at The Park, so she went with the others in the limousine. No one appeared to be up to making conversation, and she welcomed the opportunity to think through her options.

Young had told Rice that he would go out to Ezra's place first thing in the morning, and bring him in for questioning. "I'm not about to go stumbling all over the mountain in the dark and break a leg . . . or my fool neck."

"Then I'll send my own men," Rice had threatened.

"Yeah, well, they might be able to find their asses if they used both hands, but if you send your rent-a-cops into those mountains at night, I can guarantee you, they'll have to be airlifted out."

Rice had backed off, but that didn't mean she had to. She'd grown up climbing in the hills, and while it had been a few years since she'd done any hiking, she thought she could find her way, day or night.

It was time to talk to the old man in the hills.

Chapter Forty-seven

Max had not had a good day.

His broken arm continued to ache something fierce, and then this afternoon he'd gone and caught his right hand on the safety bar on the Annihilator, dislocating his little finger as pretty as you please.

The finger hadn't hurt much to begin with, kind of a dull throb, but it was very odd to see it sticking off at an angle, and he couldn't bend or move it. He'd gone on over to the Medical Aid Center, where the nurse informed him that the doctor had been called away on an emergency.

"What do you think this is?" he'd asked. "You think maybe it got stuck that way while I was holding my pinkie out, drinking tea? It hurts, man."

The nurse suggested that he wait for the night shift doctor to come on duty at nine o'clock, but right then he was more annoyed than in pain, so he'd waved her off and had come back to the suite.

Not used to being on the receiving end of pain, he was getting acquainted with it in a hurry. He sincerely hoped that the four aspirin he'd swallowed would take the edge off it. . . .

He made a makeshift ice pack by wrapping ice in a wash-cloth, but it kept slipping off the back of his hand, and after the millionth time, he got pissed and threw it across the room. Ice cubes rained on the carpet, and the washcloth slid wetly down the wall.

No one stirred. Apparently they all were asleep, except for Betsy, who had yet to return, although the rides had shut down ten minutes ago.

So much for sympathy, he thought.

All in all, it had been one shitty evening. The only high point was the black-bordered invitation he'd received to something called the Games, and even that had been tarnished by the fact that the others had been invited, too.

With his luck, it would turn out to be kid games, and they'd be pinning the tail on any jackass who was fool enough to fall for it. . . .

The front door opened and he turned as Betsy came in.

"Out a little late, aren't we?" he asked, and then realized she looked as though she'd gone to summer camp in Beirut; one leg of her jeans was torn up to the knee, and her blouse had what appeared to be rust stains down the front. Plus she was barefoot.

"What happened to you?"

"Nothing I want to talk about." Her blue eyes were grimly determined.

He knew the feeling. "Forget I asked."

She ran a hand through her tousled hair—which didn't help—and then sighed. "Sorry, I didn't mean to be rude. Are you staying up?"

"What's it to you if I am?"

She sighed again. "Everything's a battle with you, isn't it, Max? *Are* you staying up?"

"Maybe."

"Yes or no."

"All right, yes."

"Good." Betsy went to her room and came out a moment

308

later with one of those miniature TV-VCR devices and two black video cases. "My graduation gift. Want to watch a movie with me?"

Max sneered. "What movie? *Mary Poppins?* Or what's that other one . . . *The Sound of Music?* The sound of barfing, is more like it."

"Actually, I brought the original black-and-white version of *The Invasion of the Body Snatchers* and the first *Halloween.*"

"No shit?" It didn't figure that little Suzy Sunshine would be a horror freak, but what the hell. "Just don't be screaming and grabbing me—"

"You wish."

"—because you might break this sucker right off." He held up his injured hand.

Betsy, though, didn't even blink. "What did you do now?" she asked, coming over to see.

"I hit a guy." He knew girls who got off on guys fighting, and although Betsy didn't seem the type, it sounded better than the truth.

She took his hand and ran her thumb along the side of it. "The finger's dislocated," she said, looking up into his eyes.

"No fooling."

"If you want me to, I can put it back in place."

He tried to withdraw his hand, but she was holding on tight. "Not on your life."

"No, really. My brothers are always dislocating fingers and thumbs. You have to give it a good yank, but most of the time, the bone just pops back in."

"Most of the time?"

"Don't be such a baby. I can do it. It's better than trying to sleep with it that way; if you roll over on it or something, it could break."

"I don't know," he said. "Are you sure you know how to do it?"

Betsy sighed. "Yes, I'm sure."

"It'll hurt, though."

"Doesn't it hurt now?"

There was no arguing that. "Have at it," he said.

They sat facing each other on one of the couches. She had started the tape of *Halloween* and he'd never found the eerie music more appropriate. The flicker of the tiny TV was their only light.

She held his hand in both of hers, gripping tightly at his wrist with her left hand, and holding onto his baby finger with her right.

"You can close your eyes," she said, "if you want. It looks kind of . . . icky."

"I want to watch." He wasn't sure he did, but not to would mean he was squeamish, and that wasn't how he wanted to think of himself.

"All right. Ready?"

He nodded.

Betsy tightened her grip on his wrist, and then yanked and straightened his finger so quickly he barely had time to react. He did not cry out.

It hurt, there was no doubt about it, especially since he could sort of *feel* the bones moving around, but almost simultaneously the throbbing ache he'd been putting up with all evening began to subside.

"Better?"

"Ah . . . ask me in a minute," he said.

"In the morning you should tape your little and ring fingers together so you don't displace it again." She smiled ruefully. "I hear it hurts worse the second time."

"Thanks for the warning. And"—he touched his finger gingerly—"for the repair job."

"Any time."

Chapter Forty-eight

The elevator door slid open and the noise of Sub-Level Two greeted him; Wesley could feel its vibrations in his bones. Even at this late hour, the generators, compressors, and turbines were operating, albeit at fifty percent of their capacity.

He grabbed a hard hat and started down a deserted corridor toward the engineering office. As he walked, his eyes scanned pressure gauges, usage registers, and capacitor voltage indicators. He noted a yellow caution light on an air intake nozzle and made a mental note to have it checked out.

At the office he paused to enter his access code into the computer, but before he finished, the door opened and Bell nearly ran him over.

Wesley grabbed Bell's arm. "What are you doing down here?" he yelled, trying in vain to make himself heard over the din.

Bell shook his head, pulled free, and disappeared around a corner.

311

Wesley stared after Bell for a second, then stepped into the office. The door closed automatically and the roar of machinery faded to a low-pitched hum.

None of the duty engineers were in the office, a direct violation of company policy.

"Damn it." Wesley tossed his hard hat into a corner of the room and crossed to the control panel. A triple-paned glass wall allowed him a view of the belly of the beast. The night crew seemed to be making themselves scarce; he didn't see a soul.

He turned his attention to the telemetry, eyes moving from screen to screen, absorbing data. Nothing appeared to be amiss — the readings were within normal limits — and yet he had a nagging sense that something was desperately wrong, perhaps fatally wrong.

Wesley frowned. He grabbed a chair and pushed it over to the master computer terminal, where he sat down. "Talk to me," he said, entering his super-user code.

The computer complied, its yellow-on-black screen listing incident after incident of ride malfunction. There were many more of them than he'd anticipated. Many, many more.

Were the incidents, as he'd begun to suspect, the result of some kind of intermittent magnetic disturbance? All of the rides were computerized, and the presence of a strong magnetic field would disrupt their programming.

Or, even more likely, destroy it.

Thank God it hadn't come to that.

He forced himself to concentrate as he scrolled, looking for answers, but none were forthcoming. Finally, losing patience, he requested a printout. He rubbed at his eyes, which felt hot and gritty, as he waited.

It took a few seconds before he realized that the printer was not, in fact, spewing out pages. He lowered his hand and peered somewhat blurrily at the screen.

I/O Error it read.

"Bullshit." He reentered the command.

I/O Error.

Irrational as it was, Wesley gave the computer a whack. "Do as I say, you useless pile of microchips."

Unmoved, the computer continued to insist that he—he who had programmed it—had made an input/output error by asking for a printout of the ride malfunctions. He'd positioned his hands at the keyboard to ask again when it occurred to him that someone might have gone to the trouble of altering his program to keep him from doing just that.

He sat back, chewing at his lower lip as he considered the possibilities.

Bell, he thought, could have done it, given that he'd shown himself capable of breaking Wesley's code, and he was in the vicinity. But why would Bell stop at denying access to a printout? Why not erase the file entirely?

True, he'd put a "protect" on the malfunction file, but it was a fairly simple procedure to bypass.

Except . . . if Wesley had found the file erased he would assume tampering. No doubt that would alarm him enough to spur him to use a more sophisticated system of protection. If he put his mind to it, he could weave an impenetrable web of hidden commands and countercommands that no one could circumvent.

Which led him to believe that Bell's purpose was merely to delay him in accumulating information, and thus buy time.

But for what?

He didn't know. He reached and hit the "home" button, watched the screen blink to the start of the file. After a moment's reflection, he sat forward and began to do what he should have done in the first place.

He was tired of playing games.

Back in 3-C, he locked himself in his office and quickly connected a tape recorder to his phone. Although it was late, he doubted that anyone was getting much sleep tonight, and he punched out the number to the penthouse.

"Mr. Rice?" he said, and hit the record button.

"Yes, what is it?"

"I know we discussed this earlier, but I'd like to suggest—again—that we shut down the rides for twenty-four hours so that I can determine what's causing the problems—"

"It can't be done." Rice's voice was measured, his tone even. "And it shouldn't be."

"I disagree."

"Well, you're entitled to your opinion, but what you're suggesting—"

"—is the only logical course."

Rice laughed but didn't sound amused. "What you're suggesting is rather extreme, like amputating an arm to cure a hangnail."

"A man is dead, Mr. Rice."

Silence.

"I don't think anything we might do to prevent someone else from being hurt can be considered extreme." Wesley tightened his grip on the phone. "If we do nothing, it could come back to haunt us."

"Now you're being melodramatic. Mr. Goodenough's death was unfortunate, but I believe that a thorough investigation into the matter will reveal that he somehow precipitated his own . . . demise."

"Even if that's the, case—"

"I appreciate your concern, Wesley, and your candor, but a bell cannot be unrung. If we close down the rides now, the damage to The Park's image will be forever tarnished. I can't allow that. I *won't* allow it."

Wesley, though not surprised by Rice's attitude, was disappointed. "If that's your final word . . ."

"It is."

"I just hope, Mr. Rice, that you don't live to regret not ringing the bell."

Chapter Forty-nine

After stopping at home to change clothes and pick up a camping lantern from the garage, Taylor headed for the mountain. She drove slowly, getting used to the switchbacks in the road as it climbed upward. A couple of times cars came up behind her, and she pulled off onto the shoulder to let them pass. Each time she expected it to be Sheriff Young—he might not have felt it necessary to tell Rice his true intentions—but so far her luck was holding.

Half an hour later, she came upon the dirt road which led into Ezra's property. He hadn't kept it up well, and she drove slower still, no more than five miles per hour, to avoid the deeper ruts and potholes. Grass grew in the center strip, and it brushed the undercarriage of the car.

It seemed to take forever to get to the shed where Ezra's pickup was parked. She angled her car behind his, blocking him in.

Now for the hard part. She got out and turned on the lantern. It was at least another three or four miles to the cabin, along a narrow dirt pathway that hugged the side of a hill.

Something rustled in the trees, and she flashed the lantern in that direction. Yellow eyes glowed in the light. An owl, she hoped.

With a final glance down the dirt road where she'd come from, she started up the path.

The first fifteen minutes went easily compared to the second fifteen, which were a breeze compared to the third. The path not only got narrower, it headed more steeply uphill. She had to stop every now and then to catch her breath.

She couldn't imagine what would possess someone to live so far from the road. How did he get his supplies to the cabin? He had to eat, didn't he?

He wasn't a young man; presumably he suffered from the maladies of old age. Arthritis, perhaps, or the brittle bones of osteoporosis. Even living a vigorous life, he probably would have developed at least the beginning of arteriosclerosis. How could a man his age lug a week's groceries up this blasted hill?

She had only the lantern, which didn't weigh more than a pound or two, but it had begun to feel more like a ton. If it wasn't so dark, she'd be tempted to chuck it. Maybe she would anyway; the battery was growing weak.

The cabin was not yet in sight.

"Damn it, Ezra," she said. She leaned against an outcrop of what she thought were rocks but proved to be tree roots, dislodging the loose dirt above. It cascaded onto her, a good deal of it finding its way down the collar of her shirt. She pulled the shirt free of her jeans, hoping the dirt would fall out, but she was sweating, and most of it stuck to her skin.

It occurred to her that there were often tiny beetles in the dirt up here, and that made her itch.

"Don't think about it," she chastised herself.

Some creature of the night chose that moment to crash through the bushes somewhere up above her, startling her so that she nearly fell off the path. Only by flinging herself face first against the embankment did she escape falling, but in the process, she got a mouthful of dirt.

A good trade-off, she thought, spitting it out.

Taylor finally reached the crest of the trail. It widened and led into the flat wooded acre where Ezra had built his cabin.

Somewhere.

She pressed the button on her watch and its face glowed. Nearly 1:00 a.m. The man was known to be an early riser, so it wasn't surprising that there'd be no light coming from the cabin windows. And he wouldn't have a fire going, not in June.

The lantern's glow didn't reach more than five or six feet ahead of her, so she had to rely on her childhood memory as to where the cabin was. Not quite in the center of the woods, she recalled.

She hadn't gone more than a hundred yards when something grabbed at her right foot and she fell down, hard, wrenching her ankle. She stifled a scream—who other than Ezra would hear her?—and scrambled to her knees, ready to run, or try to.

But a glance behind her showed that it was only another tree root.

She sat on the ground and ran practiced fingers over her ankle, which had already begun to swell. It didn't appear to be broken, but a bad sprain sometimes was even worse than a break.

After she caught her breath and her heart rate had returned to normal, she tried to stand, testing the ankle to see if it would bear her weight.

"Oh!" Pain shot up her leg, and she balanced on her left foot and the toe of her right. "Damn."

She would have to hop to the cabin. And she could forget about walking out; Ezra would have to put her up for the night.

She stared into the dark growth of trees. Where the hell *was* the cabin?

By the time she found it, sweat was running down her back and her hair was plastered to her head. Her ankle was so tender that it hurt even to rest her foot on the ground, much less stand.

She sat down gratefully on the wood porch, and wiped her face on her shirttail.

It was odd, she thought, that Ezra hadn't come out to investigate the noise; she'd made enough of a commotion to rouse the heaviest sleeper.

Maybe he wasn't even here.

She rapped her knuckles on the wooden porch as hard as she could. "Ezra? Ezra, it's Taylor McKenna."

There was no response.

"Damn." She stood on her left foot and, using the edge of the porch for support, hopped to the stairs. Even in the dark, they looked rickety, as if the wood had been allowed to rot.

That wasn't like Ezra either, to let his cabin fall into disrepair.

She made it up the five steps by sitting down and using her arms and good leg to lift herself backward. The steps creaked and groaned and gave way a bit, but otherwise held. At the top, though, as she was trying to stand again, she grabbed onto the top riser and felt the sting of a splinter as it was driven deep into the web between her thumb and index finger.

"You're going to have to airlift *me* out, Adam Young," she muttered.

It took some doing, but finally she was standing again, a step or two from the cabin door. Balanced there, know-

319

ing she had to hop those last two steps, she envisioned herself breaking through the wood porch and being trapped until morning. But she leaned forward, and braced her arms against the door frame.

"Here comes Peter Cottontail . . . ," she sang grimly, and hopped twice. The plank on which she landed on the final hop wobbled like an old saw, but did not give way. She breathed a sigh of relief and pounded on the door. "Ezra?"

When there still was no answer, she reached for the doorknob, which turned easily. The door swung open of its own weight.

"Ezra?"

Taylor heard an odd creaking, strangely rhythmic, and hesitated as she tried to place the sound. But her tired mind refused to cooperate, and after a minute, she stepped inside.

The air was cool and dry, but it had almost a heaviness to it, pressing in on her in the dark.

Except it wasn't fully dark.

Moonlight shone through narrow cracks in the walls, casting eerie shadows and reaching into the corners with pale fingers. . . .

Her heart began to pound.

The light outlined, from behind, a rocking chair a short distance from where she stood. Someone was sitting there, rocking slowly; the odd creaking she'd heard.

"Ezra?"

The chair continued to rock, forward and back, forward and slowly back.

Taylor could see now, in the blue-hued light, the silhouette of the old man's head, his white hair forming almost a halo. His face remained in shadow.

Why wasn't he answering her?

"Ezra . . ." She took a step forward, wincing at the stabbing pain, and in the sudden breath she drew as a result of it, she tasted a familiar sweetness that had only

320

one source.

Death.

The rocker creaked, forward and back, and this time she heard an underlying sound, the tap of a cane against the wood floor. A cane in a dead man's hand, acting as counterbalance to the momentum of the rocker; together, they formed a ghastly perpetual motion machine.

In the light that played across Ezra's face, she saw that his eyes were opaque, but she felt his stare and if she could have run, she would have.

Part Three

June 18, 1992
Thursday

Chapter Fifty

Sheriff Adam Young called the office at a quarter to six to tell the graveyard dispatcher that he would not be in until after he'd talked to Ezra.

"You may not be able to reach me by radio for a while," he added; the signal tended to get lost in the back hills. "So have Fred take the north county and . . . who else is on duty today?"

"Must be Smitty," the dispatcher said, "or otherwise I wouldn't be looking at his ugly face."

"Is he there?" He'd never known Smitty to be early for work in the four years since he'd hired him. "Put him on, will you?"

There were a series of clicks, and then: " 'Lo, chief."

"What's up?"

"Oh, we had a little altercation in town last night, nothing to write home about."

"You were off duty?"

"Yeah, but it happened right outside my house, so I went on out to give Dudley a hand."

"What exactly happened?"

"Well, it seems there was this fool in a new BMW—you

know the kind with that fake gold trim?—coming up from Frisco, I guess heading to The Park. Anyway, he's out on Old Mill Road, and there are two other cars ahead of him, neither going fast enough to suit him."

"Idiot." At least a couple of times a year, some city driver would run his car off the side of that road, and then they'd have to go out and pick up the pieces. It was never pleasant.

"Right. So he's dogging the cars in front, honking the horn, flashing his lights on and off, and otherwise making a pest of himself."

"Uh huh."

"Anyway, he gets to the straightaway, and zoom, he's passing them, and then, get this, he kind of waves, like 'So long, sucker' and off he goes."

Young had a feeling he knew where this was leading.

"Unfortunately for him, he doesn't know that there's a shortcut a little ways up the road—"

"Ah, an ambush."

"You got it."

"Who was in the other two cars?"

"Kids, chief, coming back from their prom down at the Seaway Inn."

Even the local kids, bless their rebellious hearts, respected Old Mill Road. "I gather the BMW was seriously outnumbered."

"Oh yeah. Eight to one. They blocked him off, and he got out of his car to run."

"That wasn't too bright." There was a chance, a slim one, that the kids wouldn't have broken the BMW's windows to get at the driver. He should have blasted his horn and waited for help.

"They run him to ground practically in my front yard, and there was some serious ass kicking going on by the time I got dressed."

"Was he hurt bad?"

"Nah. He's got maybe a cracked rib, a bloody nose, probably a black eye, but otherwise just the usual contusions and

326

abrasions."

"Anything else I should know?"

"Not that I . . . oh, wait. You might be interested in this. Seems he's a managing editor or something for one of those scandal sheets, come to talk to Rice's sweetie, no less."

"Nancy Chan?"

"None other. She came down to the station to pick him up. Wearing, I shit you not, a trench coat. I didn't hear if they exchanged a password, but something hush-hush was going on. Anyhow, off they went in his BMW, heading back to the city, I guess."

"Well, what do you know?" Sheldon Rice's little bird had flown the coop.

"He refused to press charges, by the way. Said he never wanted to set foot in McKenna's Creek again. Big fucking loss, I say."

Young was inclined to agree.

Rain was in the forecast, and when he went outside he could smell it in the air.

He backed the patrol car out of his driveway, and waved to a couple of his early-rising neighbors. It was clear from their expressions that they were hoping he'd stop so they could try to glean a few of the details of last night's melee—word got around fast if not always accurately—but he wanted to catch up with Ezra before the old man made himself scarce.

Young flat-out did not understand Sheldon Rice's obsession with Ezra—Rice seemed to believe that Ezra was single-handedly trying to ruin him—but he guessed it wouldn't hurt to have a talk with the old man, and warn him to temper his animosity towards Rice and The Park.

Young was surprised to see a car parked behind Ezra's truck, and even more surprised when he recognized it after a moment's thought as belonging to Taylor McKenna.

"What in the world?" he said, shading the glass so he could see inside. He could see the strap of her shoulder bag where she'd tried to hide it under the seat, but otherwise the car was empty.

What was she doing out here? Ezra hadn't a phone, so it was unlikely she'd been summoned for medical reasons.

Rather than waste time pondering it, he set out down the path toward Ezra's place.

When he reached the end of the trail, he was struck by the total stillness. Not a sound did he hear, and nothing was moving that he could see. The wind that dried the sweat on his face wasn't stirring the trees.

Ever cautious, he unhooked the strap on his holster, and then started for the cabin, whose outline he could barely detect through the trees.

As he got closer, though, he saw that someone was standing on the porch, watching him. Another ten yards and he could see that it was Taylor.

"What is it?" he called when he was in hailing distance. "Is something wrong?"

"He's dead," Taylor answered, and the birds that had been motionless until now suddenly took wing.

Adam quickened his step, breaking into a half run, and then slowed again, knowing there was no hurry. He saw the door to the cabin was open, and that rather than standing, Taylor was leaning against the wall.

"I thought you'd never get here," she said as he started up the steps. "I sprained my ankle pretty badly in the dark last night."

"Last night? You came out here at night?"

"It wasn't the best idea I ever had," she conceded. "And I paid for it; I don't think I'll be able to walk out on my own."

"Don't worry about it." He wasn't a doctor, but he could see that she was on the verge of exhaustion, pale and drawn. "Is he inside?"

She nodded. "In his rocking chair."

He went in, and it took a minute for his eyes to adjust to the gloom.

Ezra sat in the chair, one hand gripping a gnarled walking stick, the other folded, palm up, in his lap. His head was tilted back, mouth was slightly agape, eyes open but milky, as though the darkness of his glance had turned inward.

Adam went to the chair and reached down to place his fingers on the old man's throat. There was no pulse—he hadn't expected one—but more telling than that was the feel of the skin, which was oddly reptilian to the touch.

"What the—"

"He's been dead for days," Taylor said from the doorway. "Maybe as long as a week."

He turned to look at her. "That's impossible. He hasn't decomposed—"

"This cabin is built on stilts. The air circulation is ideal, cool and dry. There's no direct sunlight. And for some reason, no insects. He's well on his way to being mummified."

"But Rice swears his security people reported seeing him up on the hill no more than a day ago."

"I can't help that," she said. "Rigor mortis has come and long gone. And a body doesn't dry out like that one in a matter of hours."

"This is crazy. I saw him a few days ago myself—"

"Did you talk to him?"

"No." Young frowned. "I waved, but he acted like he didn't see me."

"I would guess not."

"Wait a minute. You're not suggesting that he's been walking around dead?"

"Of course not."

"Good, because I don't believe in zombies."

"Maybe you only thought it was Ezra."

"I suppose it's possible," he said, although he was far from convinced.

"It has to be," Taylor insisted. "Unless you saw a ghost."

He laughed uneasily. "Right, in broad daylight, driving a Ford pickup."

"There's something else. . . ."

"I don't like the sound of that."

She pointed toward the far side of the cabin. "There's a trapdoor over there."

When he looked, all he saw was the big cast-iron stove and a small table with one chair. "Where? I don't—" But then he squinted and made it out.

"I couldn't go down, not with my ankle, but before my lantern died, I thought I saw bones."

He stared at her for a minute, waiting for his brain to come up with what she'd really said, because the last thing he wanted to hear was "bones."

"Human bones," she said.

Young crossed over to the trapdoor and hunkered down, peering into the darkness. There were lighter areas, here and there, but surely it had to be something other than bones. Reluctantly, he took his flashlight from its ring and turned it on.

There was about a four-foot space between the floor and the ground, which had been dug out to a depth of probably six more feet. A rope ladder had been nailed to a support beam. The planks of wood used to shore up the tunnel sides were gray with age, but it wasn't the wood that gleamed against the dark background.

Many of what he saw were clearly the bones of animals, small and large, but there was no mistaking the origin of others.

"Damn it," he said, flashing the light along what was probably one of the long bones of a human leg. "What the hell is this?"

Taylor made her way across the room, pulled out the chair, and sat at Ezra's table. When he looked at her, she shook her head, then pushed a silver-and-blue plastic ID card — Hawell's long-lost master access card? — across the table to him.

"I found this." She sounded tired.

"We only have got the one missing person," he said, men

tally counting up the bones and trying to assemble them into one—let there be only one—body.

The light illuminated part of a cranium, including the arch above the left eye. The rest of the skull appeared to be buried in the dark loamy earth. A few feet farther in the tunnel, at the edge of the flashlight's range, was a small but perfect skeletal hand, seeming, Young thought, to point the way into hell.

"It can't be," he said. He turned off the light, unwilling to see more, and straightened up. "There has to be an explanation for this. . . ."

Across the cabin, Ezra stared with clouded sightless eyes at the ceiling, keeping his secrets to himself.

Chapter Fifty-one

"Welcome to the Games," Sheldon Rice said. "I am the Game Master."

The gate which separated Level Three from those below began to close, and he waited for it, not wanting to have to shout to be heard. In the meantime, he studied the faces of his first eight players.

It was a nice mix, he thought. Six males and two females the surprise of the draw was that the redhead had racked up more points on the rides than anyone else by nearly a thousand points.

Having the little boy qualify was something he hadn't foreseen—who would think an eight year old would have the necessary endurance—but it shouldn't prove to be a problem. Perhaps he would practice on the child so that when he faced a more formidable opponent, he'd be warmed up.

Of the adult males, the first was Martin, an insurance salesman from Boise—had they anything worth insuring in Boise?—who probably was in his thirties, and getting soft around the middle from pencil pushing. But Martin had a quirky kind of smile that suggested it would be a mistake to underestimate him.

Rice had a suspicion that he might present a challenge, and resolved to take care of him early.

The second man, a Texan named Bowie, had to be fifty if he was a day, but working as an oil rigger had toughened him to a degree that would put most younger men to shame. His forearms were huge, almost malformed, and he had a colorful Popeye tattoo on one arm, an opened can of spinach on the other.

A worthy adversary, Rice fully expected to face him in the End Game.

By contrast, the last of the adult males, Leonard, obviously had peanuts for brains. In his late thirties, Leonard worked in a grocery store owned by his elderly parents, as a kind of bag boy emeritus, a dead branch on the family tree.

Rice wasn't sure Leonard was worth the bother; left to his own pitiful devices, the idiot would no doubt get himself blasted by the Mercenaries within seconds of the start of the game.

Of the others, only the older of the teenage boys looked like trouble. He was powerfully built, but light on his feet, and he had a keen expression that Rice took to mean he had an interest in winning, broken arm or not. His photo ID badge identified him as Max.

"Hey," Bowie said in his raspy voice, "are we gonna get it on or not?"

Rice frowned. He hadn't noticed the gate had finished closing; they were all standing there, waiting for him to continue. He never used to be so easily distracted.

"We are," he said, and turned to an attendant. "Would you get the stun guns, please?"

"Stun guns?" the redhead echoed. "What kind of game is this?"

He looked at her ID badge and smiled. "It'll be fun, Betsy, I promise. Kind of like playing tag."

"I get it," Max said, "it's a war game."

"Well, yes and no."

"Must be a Republican," Martin said in an aside to no one

333

in particular. "Republicans always have trouble calling a war a war."

Rice forced a laugh. "It's more like hunter and hunted," he said to Betsy, who after all had accumulated the most points.

"It sounds violent."

"I wouldn't say that. But tell me, what's been your favorite ride so far?"

The girl, already pink from the sun, blushed but didn't answer.

Which was fine with him; he didn't really give a damn. His motive for asking had been to divert the subject from violence, and nothing more.

The attendant approached just then, carrying a silver attaché case. He placed it on the stone ledge and opened it, revealing ten of the derringer-sized stun guns. Rice nodded, and the attendant handed one of the guns to Martin, who had stepped forward.

"Now what have we here?" the insurance agent asked, turning the gun over in his hands, an avid expression on his face.

"It's quite simple," Rice said. "Each of you will be issued a stun gun. The guns have a mild electric charge which is designed to disrupt the programming of the Mercenaries—"

"The who?"

Rice snapped his fingers, and the attendant went to the control panel to activate the robots, which were stored in a separate gated enclosure.

"You'll see in a moment. As I was saying, the charge, if on target, will render the Mercenaries harmless for the duration of the game. They will be able to transmit tracking information to each other, but a disabled robot can't move, nor can it fire at you."

"Wait a minute, hold on there." Bowie gave him a fierce look. "You're telling us that these robots will be firing at us?"

"Don't be alarmed," Rice said, "it's not what you think. They have dye capsules in their weapons, that's all. It washes off with soap and water. But after you've been marked, you're out of the game, and you must leave the Third Level."

The dark-skinned girl, Celeste, had kept silent thus far, although she'd been watching him as a mongoose would a co-bra, but now she started to shake her head. "There's some-thing you're not telling us."

"Not at all, I—"

He was interrupted by the arrival of the six Mercenaries, who had come from their lair in single file. The robots made almost no sound, only a barely perceptible *thrum*.

"What the fuck?" Max said.

Rice had marveled the first time he'd seen them at how menacing they appeared, how eerily lifelike they were, even with black metallic bodies and glowing yellow eyes. Of all the creatures Wesley had created, these were his supreme achieve-ment.

"Great," Celeste said, "the brothers are here."

Everyone laughed except Rice. He caught the attendant's eye and motioned for him to direct the robots to stop. Clearly, the players needed a demonstration of what they were going up against.

Rice approached Mercenary One. Wesley had shown him how to conduct a system analysis on the robot, and he opened the front panel on its chest, entered a command into its comm-link, and then stood back.

With a grace that belied its origins, the Mercenary whirled, pointed its weapon, and fired at the attendant, who held a tar-get in his hands. At a distance of a hundred yards, it hit dead center, and bright red dye splattered across the board.

The younger teen, Nick, gasped and stepped backward, as if he'd been the one hit. The Mexican kid dropped to a half crouch.

"They're very good shots," Rice said, somewhat unnecessar-ily, but with a great deal of pride. "And they're fast."

"I'll say," Leonard muttered.

"But if you fire at them first and hit them, they will shut down rather than return fire."

"I know guys like that," Max said. "Chicken-shit mother-fuckers."

Rice ignored the provocation. "You must aim at the front or side only; if you shoot them from behind, it won't register.

However, as I mentioned, an inoperative unit can still tell his fellow robots where you are."

Max bounced on his heels. "How do we keep them from doing that? Knock off their heads?"

Rice winced. "I trust that won't be necessary."

"So how many shots do we get?" This was Martin again. "How many do they get?"

"And," Max said, "how do we win?"

"You win by being the last one standing," Rice said, and smiled.

After all the questions had been answered, and each player had been issued a stun gun, Rice sent them on their ways.

"Reload his weapon," he instructed the attendant, referring to Mercenary One. "No sense in giving anyone an advantage."

"No sir."

Rice walked along the line of robot soldiers, feeling like an officer inspecting his troops. With their heat-sensing devices, he expected them to make short work of at least half of the players, but it didn't matter. A weak opponent was no opponent.

What he hadn't mentioned to the hunted was that there was no way any of them could win. The Mercenaries, disabled or otherwise, were to act as his stalkers, leading him to his prey.

The only flaw in his plan was that Bell, who'd assisted him in modifying the soldiers' programming, hadn't been able to undo Wesley's directive that once disabled, they could not come back on-line without a command from 3-C.

Wesley's sense of fair play could be tiresome at times.

"The Mercenaries are ready, Mr. Rice," the attendant said.

"Good, very good." He shaded his eyes and scanned the somewhat hilly terrain. "So am I."

Chapter Fifty-two

Nicholas found a place on the grass that looked reasonably dry and comfortable, then sat down, cross-legged, to wait.

"What the hell do you think you're doing?" Max asked.

"I'm not playing this stupid game," he said. "I'm going to let them get me."

"You what?"

Nick offered his finger to a ladybug crawling up a blade of grass, and grinned at how it tickled when she obliged by making her way to his palm. "I'm outta here," he said, and the ladybug flew away.

"You sure you want to do that?" Max looked from him to Betsy and frowned. "I tell you, I can beat those suckers, and if you stay with me, you will too."

"I don't see any point in being chased all over the damned mountain for some war game," Nick said. "Besides, I'm tired."

"You're *tired?* Hell, try getting around with a few broken bones—"

"Max," Betsy interrupted, "if he doesn't want to play, leave him alone."

"But I've got a plan," Max said, "and I need somebody I can

count on."

Betsy lifted her chin, looking determined. "I can do whatever needs to be done."

"I don't think you know what you're getting into. It might get rough."

"Trust me, okay? I can handle myself."

Nick held out his stun gun to Max. "You can make better use of this than I can," he said.

Max accepted it but shook his head. "I don't understand what you're doing, pal."

"It's just what I gotta do."

"Okay, if you say so." Max tucked the gun into his waistband at the small of his back. "But . . . if you're willing to act as bait, I might as well off whatever comes after you, eh?"

"Why not?" Nick agreed.

It did not take the Mercenaries long to find him. There were two of them, and they flanked him, coming at him from either side. Nick heard a series of clicks—he suspected they were talking to each other—and then the one on his left opened fire.

The capsule hit him in the rib cage, and it stung. Red dye spattered like blood across his midsection, and he had to close his eyes.

Amy.

"Kiss your ass good-bye," he heard Max say, and then there was a noise very much like the laser sound effects in the movies. Once, twice, and the scent of ozone was in the air.

"Direct hit," a mechanical voice said.

"Direct hit," the second Mercenary confirmed.

Nick felt only relief. He opened his eyes and watched as Max approached the first of the robots. Nick got to his feet and dusted off his jeans.

Max grabbed the robot's hand, and somehow forced it to fire its remaining two capsules at the grass, an explosion in red.

"That's in case information isn't the only thing these bastards can exchange." He went to the second robot and did the same.

Nick had to admire his thoroughness.

"Now . . . how do we keep them from yapping?"

In response, the first Mercenary began to make its clicking noise.

"It's too late," Nick said.

Betsy put her hand on Max's shoulder. "Come on, we'd better get out of here."

"Nick," Max said, and fell silent, as though he didn't know what to say.

Nick knew the feeling; all of a sudden his throat had constricted and his chest felt tight.

"See you?"

"Another time," Nick said.

When he neared the gate, the attendant came out from the glass-walled control booth. "That didn't take long," the attendant said with a laugh.

"You win some, you lose some," Nick said.

"Where's your gun?"

"I don't know, I lost it somewhere."

"Shit. I suppose I'll be the one who has to look for the damned thing."

"That shouldn't take long."

The attendant gave him a dirty look, but was distracted as another player—Leonard, that was the guy's name—trudged up, literally dripping red. Nick averted his eyes.

"All right," the attendant said, grabbing the stun gun from the guy's hand. "Get out of here, both of you. Oh, wait. Give me your ID badges."

Leonard did so, but as he unclipped his, Nick hesitated. "Why do you need these?"

"I work here, kid, I don't make the rules. You go down to the hotel, they'll give you back your original badge; this one's only good on Level Three."

Nick had a suspicion that what it was good for was helping

the robots track. He wished he could tell Max that. . . .

The gate had opened just enough for them to exit, and after one last look around him, Nick followed the guy through.

He went to change his clothes, and found the suite empty. Dinah, apparently, was taking advantage of having the five of them out of her hair for the day.

Nick went into the bathroom to wash up, but when he saw his reflection in the mirror, he froze. The dye had dried, and looked even more like blood. . . .

"Amy," he said, and stared into his own eyes.

It had been one of those rare days when the sky was so blue that it almost hurt to look at it, and the air was soft and fragrant.

They had been driving for two days straight, heading from Atlantic City — where his father had dealt blackjack while his mother waited on tables — to Las Vegas, where they would do more of the same. Taking turns driving, they were making excellent time, and so when his mother suggested stopping at a rest area for a while there in Iowa, his father agreed.

They found a spot to park near the trees, which would provide shade for their small trailer.

"You watch your sister," his father ordered. "we're gonna catch up on some sleep."

Amy set out exploring, looking for other kids to play with, but there were only a couple of truckers to be found, and although one seemed genuinely friendly, Nick didn't trust him, and he steered his sister away.

There was a field behind the rest area, and not much of a fence between, so with a glance back to see if anyone was watching, he lifted Amy over. Even as short as her legs were, he had to run to keep up at times.

They wandered back and forth through the tall grasses, playing hide-and-seek. Amy's delighted laughter usually gave her away, but she didn't seem to mind being caught and getting lifted into the air.

When he got dizzy and his sides were aching from turning in circles, he called time, stretched out on the grass, and watched the sky spin. Amy yanked at his arm, urging him to get up and play some more, but he could barely move.

He turned on his side and watched her, making sure that she didn't go too far. The urge to close his eyes and sleep was nearly overwhelming, but with the highway so close by, the big rigs thundering along, he knew it wasn't safe.

After awhile, his baby sister came back and sat beside him.

"I'm hungry," she said.

"Hungry? Look at how fat you are." He poked a finger at her tummy, and she wriggled away, giggling. "You'd better go on a diet like Mommy." Their mother hadn't eaten since New Jersey, because she said her tips went down when her weight went up. Plus, she'd been taking some pills they'd bought off a trucker in Illinois.

The pills made her irritable, but so, she said, did being fat. Dad, who wasn't fat, didn't need pills to make him mad.

"No. No. No!" Amy said.

Her favorite word, in triplicate, no less. "Okay, if you insist, let's go back to the trailer and I'll make you a peanut butter sandwich, but you'll have to be quiet or you'll wake Mom and Dad."

"I be quiet."

The semis had left by the time they got back, and all at once there was hardly any traffic on the road. It was too nice a day, he thought, to be driving. Maybe if he asked nice, they could stay here overnight.

But the minute he opened the trailer door, he smelled the alcohol. If staying meant his parents would be drinking all night, staying no longer had much appeal. He hated it when they drank: They fought like crazy, yelling and screaming and throwing things, including punches that now and then brought blood.

"You wait out here," he said pointed at the metal step that pulled out from underneath the trailer door.

Amy obediently sat down.

The trailer was divided into two halves, a back bedroom that his parents used, and the front kitchen area. The table made out into a second bed where he and Amy slept. There was an accordion-style door that separated the halves, but it had not been fully closed, and he could see that whatever his parents had been doing, it wasn't sleeping.

His mother was sitting at the foot of the bed in her kimono, and she had a glass of her favorite gin in her hand. Her face was streaked with *tears.*

His father standing with his back to Nick, holding the gin bottle by the neck. Dressed in only boxer shorts and socks, he looked, Nick thought, ridiculous.

"I told you," his mother said, "there was nothing going on."

"No? Then why, when I touch you, are you too fucking tired?"

"Because I am tired. We've been driving—"

"We've driven for weeks at a time before, and it never made no difference. Now all of a sudden, it does? Or maybe that Italian gave you a going-away bonus, huh? A little extra something to remember him by?"

"Mr. Martino wouldn't be interested in someone like me," his mother said.

"Oh, he wouldn't, would he? Why is that?"

"Well, I'm not . . ."

"Good enough?"

His mother didn't answer, but bowed her head.

"Let's see if I've got this straight. You're not good enough for that lounge lizard Martino, the greasy bastard, but you are good enough for me? What does that make me? Am I lower than that lizard?"

"I didn't say that—"

"You bitch, I know you been catting around—"

Nick wanted to leave. He could hear in his father's voice that rage was building, and he'd been a witness to this kind of fight before. It would get worse. Maybe, much worse.

He was torn between making his sister's sandwich, and making himself invisible. The thing was, if Amy was really hungry, soon she would start to whine, and if she whined when his father was angry, anything could happen.

He would try, he decided, to distract her somehow, and put some distance between them and the trailer until this all blew over. Maybe he could find a pack of crackers or something in the dash of the car.

But when he opened the door to back out, two things happened at once: Amy ran in, and in the bedroom, their mother screamed as their father struck her hard across the face.

Amy immediately began to cry, and though Nick tried to grab her, she squirmed and tried to run into their mother's arms. The old man was fast, even when he'd been drinking, and he reached down and yanked Amy off her feet. "Whose bastard are you?" he yelled and gave her a

342

vicious shake.

"*Don't hurt her—*"

His father smashed the gin bottle against the wall and held out the jagged glass. "Is this all you have to remember him by?"

Amy, who'd been shocked into a temporary silence, opened her mouth and let out a piercing scream. Nick took a step forward, but so fast, so very fast, his father's hand flew up and the next thing he saw was a fresh spray of blood on the wall. It made a sound when it spattered like rain. . . .

"*Oh God," his father aid. "Oh no. Oh no, I didn't mean to do that."*

Then the sound that filled his ears was the awful gurgling of Amy drowning in her own blood.

His parents left him sitting on a bench with Amy in his arms.

"*We have to go," his mother said. "No one will believe that it was an accident—"*

Nick stared hard at her, but didn't speak.

"*You'd better come with us, Nicky." she said.*

"*I won't leave her."*

"*Nicky, it don't matter now. She's . . . well, it don't matter. Put her down and come on."*

"*No," he said.*

His father, the murderer, had his eyes on the highway, worried about being seen. "We've got to get on the road, Imogene. If the boy wants to stay, let him. He's almost old enough to be on his own anyway. I was on my own when I was his age."

"*I can't be losing both my kids—"*

"*You think they won't take him from you if they find us? Come on, now!"*

Nick watched as they pulled away in a swirl of dust, and then he and Amy were alone. The sky was every bit as blue as it had been, and so were his sister's eyes.

The cop came by later.

Nick blinked, and Iowa was gone.

Until this moment, his life'd had the shape of a Möbius

343

strip, each event leading back to that place in time, that instant that had changed everything . . . only now, having faced it, he was free.

He began to unbutton the stained shirt, and it felt as if he were unburdening himself. It wasn't as much a weight being lifted from his shoulders as a hand releasing his heart. . . .

There was no longer any doubt in his mind as to what he should do.

As soon as he put on a clean shirt, he was going to find Gretchen and Cherokee.

"Are you sure you know what you're doing?" Gretchen asked. She was pale but composed, and eager as all get-out to be heading home to Barstow.

Cherokee was playing with the knobs on the radio, and singing softly to herself.

Nick glanced from child to mother and nodded, pulling the ignition wires from under the dashboard. "I've done it a hundred times."

"Who ever taught you to hot-wire a car?"

"No one," he said, and it felt like the truth. "I was born to it."

Chapter Fifty-three

Wesley frowned, reached over the shoulder of the 3-C communications operator, and turned up the sound on the guy's unauthorized Watchman, which apparently had been patched into the satellite dish on the roof.

"—was killed on the premises of the multimillion-dollar amusement park. Sources familiar with the incident have indicated that the man's death appeared to be the result of a deliberate act, rather than the accident Park officials have reported."

"Who reported?" Wesley muttered. As far as he knew, no press release had yet been issued.

"Referring to a series of lesser incidents which have plagued the amusement park during its Grand Opening week, a former Park employee had this to say:"

The picture switched to Nancy Chan, who was standing on a windswept bluff with the Golden Gate Bridge in the background. Her expression was grave and somewhat indignant, as though what had happened was a personal affront to her integrity.

"There were other guests who were banged up pretty

badly, including at least two that I personally know of who sustained broken bones, but none of the rides were shut down for any significant length of time."

"To what do you attribute this lax enforcement of safety measures?" the reporter asked.

"Management—"

"Bullshit," Wesley said.

"—but what concerns me most is that Sheldon Rice isn't doing anything about it. He's only worried about the bottom line. When he managed to delay the release of information about someone being *killed* at the facility, and essentially chose to endanger the lives of everyone at The Park, well . . . I had to leave."

The reporter peered intently at the camera. "A Park spokesperson refused to comment on Miss Chan's allegations, but state authorities have indicated that an investigation will be forthcoming. David?"

The anchor shuffled papers, smiled, and said, "In other news—"

Wesley reached to turn it off.

The communications operator snorted. "Traitor."

As annoyed as he was at Nancy for smearing him while she was going after Rice, he wasn't sure he agreed that what she'd done was wrong; when Rice refused his request for a twenty-four-hour shutdown, he'd considered going to the press himself.

His primary responsibility, as he saw it, was to ensure the safety of the rides he'd designed, and while he did not believe that safety measures were being deliberately short-changed, he *was* disturbed by Rice's attitude about covering things up.

The truth would come out sooner or later, and trying to hide what had been happening would only make them look worse when it did. What purpose was there in suppressing the news of Homer Goodenough's death, other than to keep potential guests from hearing of it and canceling—or not making—reservations?

He'd come to the conclusion that Goodenough had probably been murdered, although by whom and for what reason he hadn't a clue. Perhaps it was, as Rice insisted, the work of some crazy man trying to close the place down.

Had Goodenough died at the hand of the so-called mountain man, Ezra? Wesley didn't see the old man as a killer. Most of the time, the old guy just stood and stared. And Wesley seriously doubted whether he was wily enough to outmaneuver the cameras, or bypass the computer-locked doors.

No, if someone was tampering, he thought it was someone on the inside doing it.

He realized with a start that the operator was watching him; he'd been woolgathering again. "Don't let the boss see that," he said, pointing to the Watchman. "He'll blow a gasket for sure."

Wesley sat down at a terminal, accessed the command surveillance program, and began to scan it, looking for any signs of an intruder.

The Park's computer system was a closed system, fully self-contained, and thus for all intents and purposes, immune to viruses and hackers. Since it was not reachable via modem over open telephone lines, if anyone messed with the program, it had to be from inside.

He couldn't imagine why anyone would want to change his command program. . . .

"Don't jump to conclusions," he cautioned himself.

But the conclusion he came to five minutes later was inescapable: Someone had gone to a great deal of trouble to rig the system so that when he entered a command—any command, no matter how insignificant—it was automatically copied into the user's file, along with all relevant data.

Which would give the user a head's up on everything he did.

And to add insult to injury, that someone had used *his*

access code as a shortcut into the most sensitive system programs.

It had to be Bell.

"Bell, can I talk to you?" Wesley asked quietly, not wanting to draw the attention of any of the other engineers.

"Absolutely," Bell said, and swung around in his chair. "What's up?"

"In my office."

Bell's forehead creased, and he puckered his lips thoughtfully as he nodded. "We've got trouble?"

"I'm afraid so."

Wesley followed him into the office and closed the door behind them. "I know you broke my access code before—"

"Uh oh, what's wrong?"

"That's what I want to know. Did you alter the command surveillance program?"

"Ask a direct question, get a direct answer. Yes, I did."

"Why?"

"I was told to."

Wesley thought he knew the answer, but he wanted to hear his suspicions confirmed. "By Rice?"

"Absolutely. Who else?"

"Did he tell you why he wanted it done?"

Bell shook his head. "You know how it goes; he tells you 'jump' and if you have to ask how high, you're out of work come Monday morning."

"What about," Wesley said quietly, "the fact that you double-crossed me?"

"Don't take it personally," the older man said, and laughed. "I was following orders."

"Ethics didn't enter into it?"

"Oh, I suppose I may have considered that there could be a conflict . . . I don't remember."

"But it didn't bother you?"

"I can't let it bother me." Bell shrugged. "And if I were

348

you, I wouldn't let it bother you."

"It's not as simple as that—"

"Maybe not for you. You're the fair-haired boy; something happens here, and you've got a dozen offers to choose from. Me, though, I'm too old to be starting over again. I was out of work for eight months before I was hired here."

Wesley felt saddened, because he actually liked the man, but he didn't see an alternative. "Last night," he said, "Rice told me that there was no way to unring a bell. But I think he's wrong. Consider yourself unrung, Bell."

Rice wasn't in his office, and neither was Miss Billingsley. He finally tracked her down in the accounting office on the thirteenth floor.

"Where's Rice?" he asked. "Have you heard from him?"

"I haven't, and I don't expect to. Would you get the door please?" Her arms were full of green-and-white spreadsheets.

Wesley did as requested, then followed her down the hall to the elevators. "Do you know where he is, then?"

"Why, I believe he's up on Level Three."

"What's he doing there?"

"Now, Wesley," Miss Billingsley said with a frown, "I know I sent you a memo, I'm not senile yet. Would you mind punching the call button?"

"Hold it. You sent me a memo about the Games?"

"I did indeed." She pushed her glasses up her nose, and peered at him intently. "You've been working too hard, my boy, if you can't remember a simple thing like that. I put it on your desk with my own two hands. Which, as you can see, are full, so would you—"

He jabbed at the call button. "There was nothing on my desk this morning."

"That is neither here nor there. I put it there, and that's all I'm saying."

He realized that she was probably right, and there was

nothing to be gained by pursuing the matter. "So Rice is busy playing war games," he said.

"I wouldn't call it playing." Miss Billingsley tsked. "I've never seen anyone more serious about a game. You'd think it was a matter of life and death."

Chapter Fifty-four

Hightower had come on duty at noon and had been on patrol for no more than fifteen minutes when all hell broke loose.

At first it didn't really register, that the yelling and screaming drifting in the wind had a different quality to them than usual, but then he turned a corner and it occurred to him that the pods on the Whirling Dervish should not be bouncing off each other and into the tinted dome.

He came to an abrupt halt and stood in openmouthed amazement, watching as the sleek gray pods spun and slammed together. One of the carnival-style rides, the Dervish featured a spectacular light show within its Plexiglas walls, but right now even the lights seemed to be going crazy, and the flashes of purple, blue, and green lasers were so bright that it hurt to look at them. The flickering was so rapid it made him dizzy.

Hightower found his legs, and ran toward the control room, which was located in a plastic bubble at the entrance to the ride. The ride operator, a young woman, was on the phone, with one hand over her eyes and her back turned to the dome.

"Cut the fucker off," she said calmly into the receiver. "I don't care how you do it."

Hightower moved past her, then stood helplessly in front of the control panel without the vaguest idea of what to do. He noted, though, that the big red power switch was in the off position.

Out of the corner of his eye, he saw two of the pods collide head on. Something flew out of one of them, and he saw to his horror that it was a child.

The small body struck the curved Plexiglas wall and slid to the illuminated floor. One leg was bent at more angles than joints could account for, and Hightower could see a pool of blood beginning to collect underneath it.

"Holy Mother of—"

"You!" The ride attendant grabbed his shirt, forcing him to look at her. Her eyes showed too much white and her nostrils flared, and he felt a momentary alarm at how close her face was to his. "You have to do something."

"Me? I don't know what—"

"Listen." She pushed her face even closer. "I can't stop the ride. I've tried everything. Do you understand? It's going to batter those people to death."

He averted his eyes, saw the still form of the child outlined by light, and found he preferred the ride operator's frenzied gaze to witnessing the only possible outcome in the dome; sooner or later, one of the pods would run into the kid.

"I'll go," he said, "and get help."

"Damn it, listen. I want you to go in there with me and help them."

"Go in there?"

"Yes. With me."

"Lady, you're looney tunes." He tried to free his shirt from her grasp, and failed. His hand closed reflexively on the butt of his gun.

"It'll take both of us. I'll be your eyes, and warn you if anything's coming your way, while you help the guests out.

of the pods."

It might work, a voice in his mind said.

"We have to hurry."

He took a step backward, shaking his head, but she clung to him and he could smell the desperation and fear on her. "They don't pay me enough."

From behind the Plexiglas barrier, Hightower could hear the guest's anguished screams along with the screech of metal and the dull thud of the pods crashing into the dome.

A different-sounding thud made him wince and briefly close his eyes. He could not, would not, look.

"You son of a—"

He hit her then, a right uppercut that caught her on the chin, snapped her head back and sent her flying across the control room. She hit the wall and collapsed bonelessly to the floor.

He left hurriedly, holding the front of his uniform shirt together where she had torn off the buttons when he'd hit her.

The frantic voice of the security dispatcher came over his walkie-talkie, and he turned the damn thing off.

He ran along the twisting paths of Level Two, dodging an occasional gawker who seemed transfixed at the sight of this ride or that, operating in an excess of speed and with a fury that seemed almost supernatural. . . .

Hightower wanted out.

He wanted out in the worst way, and if he had to shoot someone to get out, he'd do it.

He ran with his gun in his bruised right hand, his eyes moving from face to face, looking for anyone who might have a mind to stop him. But even as he ran, he could not help seeing the chaos around him.

The pods on the Death Spiral were running *backward,* and had to be doing a cool ninety miles an hour as they looped the loop.

The old-fashioned merry-go-round was likewise operating

353

at a tremendous speed, and through the blur of motion he could see the children, their arms wrapped around their horses' necks as they held on for dear life. Mothers and fathers stood frozen, as though they too had been carved from wood.

Several spiders had escaped the Web and had fallen into one of White Water's more tranquil streams, but their battery packs were sparking and smoking. As he watched, running by, one exploded in a shower of blue sparks.

The Hammer, a cage that was propelled by a weighted counterbalance, was spinning like an electric fan. The tower it was suspended from was shimmying, and—each time the Hammer reached the top of its revolution—emitting an eerily human groan.

A solitary water pod dangled off the side of one of the Water Devil's exterior falls, its rider still strapped in but limp and clearly unconscious.

An elderly woman stood at the entrance to the Graveyard, shredding a handful of bloodied Kleenex and imploring someone to "do something." Inside, a pod had fallen on its side, and Hightower could see a body pinned beneath it.

He ran on by.

At last, *at last,* he reached a security gate. In his eagerness to get out, he dropped his access card, and when he bent down to pick it up, knocked his head on the metal gatepost.

"Hightower," a voice behind him said.

He whirled, raising his gun to hip level as he fell into a crouch.

"What the fuck are you doing?" Beechum had come out of nowhere. "We need everyone working rescue."

"No can do." He hated to hear the tremor in his own voice, knowing it gave him away.

"What do you mean, 'no can do'? It's your job—"

"Not anymore." Hightower pulled the badge off his shirt pocket and tossed it on the ground by Beechum's feet. He took his Motorola walkie-talkie and hung it by the strap on the gatepost. "You can mail my check."

Beechum glared for a second or two, then kicked the badge away. "Fine. Get off the property, now."

"My pleasure." He ran the access card through the reader and the gate clicked open.

At least the gates were working.

Beechum held his hand out and Hightower spun the plastic card toward him like a Frisbee. The security supervisor's reflexes were quick; he caught it in midair.

"It'll be a cold day in hell before you work security again." Beechum's glance moved to the gun, but it wasn't company issue, and he said nothing.

Hightower slipped through the gate and closed it behind him. "Have fun."

But Beechum had already started off in the direction of The Park.

Hightower felt immeasurably safer on this side of the fence, and he wasted no time putting distance between himself and the screams which grew fainter with each step.

Chapter Fifty-five

"Do you hear that?"

Max looked up from massaging his calf, which was cramping from all the climbing they'd been doing, and saw that Betsy was standing motionless, a peculiar expression on her face.

"Hear what?"

"The screaming."

He listened but heard only the wind. "This is an amusement park, babe. Why not screaming?"

Betsy frowned and rubbed her arms, which he noticed were prickled with gooseflesh. "Doesn't it sound . . . real?"

"Ain't nothing real about this place, except this damned mountain."

"And the Mercenaries." Betsy came and sat beside him on an outcropping of rocks. "I think we'd better look for a place where we can rest, somewhere we'll be safe."

Max nodded; he could use a breather himself.

They'd been playing the game for at least four hours now, and he had eliminated only one more of the robots. It had taken him two shots to do it — his casted arm had slipped on the mossy rock he'd used to steady his aim — and they were down to five shots.

Five shots and three remaining robots, unless one of the other players had managed to off one. If so, they had yet to come across it. Plus there was the Game Master—the seventh mercenary—to find and defeat.

It wouldn't be easy, but he still had a few aces up his sleeve.

"Max," Betsy said, resting a hand on his knee. "Why don't I do what Nick did? I'll sit down and when they come for me, and you can get them."

"No."

"Why not? Only one person can win, and I'm not going to be the winner."

"We'll cross that bridge when we come to it. For now, I need you." With a broken arm and a sore right hand, he'd have been robot fodder by now if not for Betsy.

"But I'm slowing you down, and I know it." She wiped her face on the sleeve of her blouse. "I don't want to be the reason you get caught."

"No one's gonna get caught." He looked up the hill and studied the trees, searching for one that would be easy to climb—if there was such a thing—and which would offer some cover.

Betsy's hand gripped his knee. "What was that?" she said, and turned.

He listened and after a moment was able to determine that the sound was coming from their left and that it was probably another player rather than a robot. A few seconds later, the guy from Boise came crashing out of the bushes, wild eyed.

"Hey," the man said, throwing his arms up to cover his face. "Don't shoot!"

"It's cool," Max said, lowering the stun gun.

The man's face was crisscrossed with scratches, as though he'd run headlong through the brush, and there was a swelling high on his cheek that had begun to purple. He fell to his knees a few feet from where they stood, leaned forward, and began to heave, except nothing was coming up.

"Take it easy, man," Max said.

"Shit," the guy said when the heaves stopped. He wiped at his mouth with a hand that was visibly shaking. "I want out of here."

Max and Betsy exchanged a look. "What's the problem? It's just a game."

"I'm not sure," he gasped, and wiped his mouth with the back of his hand. "You know that old guy? Not the Game Master, but the one who came in with us?"

Max nodded.

"I found him . . . back there somewhere."

"What do you mean, found him?"

"I mean I found him. About an hour ago. I think he was dead. He sure as hell looked dead. Face was as blue as a robin's egg."

Betsy gasped. "Oh my God, that's . . . but didn't you check him to see?"

"Hell no. I figured it could've been a trap."

Betsy stood, her hands on her hips. Max noted that she looked cute when she was indignant.

"Trap my ass. What if he had a heart attack or something climbing around these hills? What if he only passed out?"

"Listen, sweetheart, I'm not a doctor. If he did have a heart attack, there'd be nothing I could do for him except sing a chorus or two of 'Amazing Grace.'"

"But if the man needs help," Betsy persisted, "we've got to help him."

"You want to play Florence Nightingale, you go," the man said. "Do CPR on a corpse, I don't care."

Max had about heard enough. "Watch how you talk to her, or I might mistake you for a Mercenary and jam your fucking circuits."

Boise tensed as though ready to lunge to his feet, but apparently thought better of it. "What am I doing? I'm not *like* this," he said. "I'm not a rabid animal. I sell insurance, for heaven's sake."

"Well, I hope you sold it to yourself," Max said, pointing the stun gun at him. "Because I *am* like this, all the time."

He aimed and fired. The guy twitched and fell over in a heap.

"Max," Betsy cried, "why did you do that?"

"All's fair in love and war," he said, taking the man's weapon and checking to see how many charges were left. There was only one, but at least it would replace the one he'd used. "Shit, I should've asked if he got any of the bad guys."

"I don't believe this."

He couldn't believe he hadn't thought of it before. He could have saved everyone some time by zapping the Game Master right out of the starting blocks. "It won't hurt him. Come on, he can be the bait."

"But what about—"

"Later," Max said. "For all we know, his story was bullshit and he was laying a trap for us."

It was clear from her expression that she wanted to believe him. He offered his sore hand and she took it, and they started up the hill.

They climbed up an old oak tree high on the hill and Max stretched out on a thick branch that allowed him to lie down and see in every direction below.

The insurance salesman from Boise came around after a few minutes, but rather than head for the gate, he seemed content to sit and wait to be discovered. When no one showed up after fifteen minutes or so, he got up and began to collect twigs and branches off the ground.

"What's he doing?" Betsy asked.

"I don't know." In fact, he did; the guy wanted to attract attention by setting a fire. Not as dumb as he looked, Max thought grudgingly.

From his vantage point, he surveyed the landscape. He was surprised how far they were from the main gate; he hadn't realized how big this place was. Or how much cover the trees and brush and rocks seemed to give. He didn't see hide nor hair of Celeste and the kid.

Probably they'd already been dispatched, and were back at the hotel having a leisurely lunch. His stomach could use a bite or two right about—

"Max," Betsy whispered, "how come nothing's moving?"

"I don't know."

"Do you think maybe we're the only ones left?"

"It's possible, guess." Down below, the insurance salesman was holding a lighter to the stack of twigs and other rubbish, including some dried leaves that Max thought might be poison oak.

He felt Betsy's hand on his back, and in spite of himself he shivered.

"I don't like this," she said in a low voice. "Why aren't they coming for him?"

"Maybe someone already got the Game Master, and it's just the three of us."

"So then, you'll have to eliminate me?"

Max frowned. He didn't understand why, but the prospect of shooting Betsy disturbed him. "No."

"How else will you win, if—"

"Hush," he said, lowering his face to the branch. "Someone's coming."

The guy from Boise, who was down on one knee fanning the flames, looked up expectantly.

A Mercenary appeared a short distance from where the man knelt, its yellow gaze fixed on his prey. The robot made a clicking sound as it approached, then said, in a synthesized voice, "End game, End game. Obey directive."

The salesman got unsteadily to his feet. "Don't give me any of that 'directive' crap, okay? I'm tired and thirsty, and I've played your silly game long enough, so just shoot me and be done with—"

"End game," the Mercenary said, and as Max had done, lifted his arm and aimed at the insurance salesman's head.

Only, Max saw, there wasn't a pellet gun in the black-gloved hand. . . .

A crackling bolt of electricity came from the creature's fingers, and swarmed over its victim's body in a hundred blue stinging arcs, making a sound like static amplified in Dolby stereo. Wisps of smoke rose from the man's head, and then there was a flash of white-blue light, and he was lifted clean out of his shoes.

Max's mind could not take in the reality of what was happening. Beside him, Betsy had turned away. Thank God she had the sense not to scream. . . .

The salesman twitched in an electric dance, eyes bulging and crying tears of blood. His tongue protruded from his mouth. The veins in his neck were swelling dangerously, and tendons writhed beneath his skin.

The Mercenary lowered his hand, finally, and the man, released, seemed to move in slow motion, staggering backward for several feet before falling face forward onto the ground.

For a few seconds, the Mercenary didn't move. Then it advanced, aimed, and fired again at close range. The body quivered and flopped in the dirt the way Max had seen fish do on sunbaked docks.

Presumably the man was dead.

"Max," Betsy whispered, "oh my Lord, he . . . it killed that man."

"Be quiet, or we may be next."

Max knew that he was out of range to use the stun gun effectively, assuming it would even work. He had several ball bearings in his pocket, but doubted whether they were heavy enough to do any good.

He didn't want to alert the machine to their presence, since there was no question but that the advantage would belong to it. As it was, there really was no way to get out of the tree without being seen; they were trapped, at least until the damned thing went away.

They had to wait it out.

"Oh God," Betsy said, "it'll kill us."

Max narrowed his eyes. "It has to find us first."

Chapter Fifty-six

From her vantage point on the hill, Celeste could look down onto Levels One and Two, and what she saw stunned her. There had to be at least a dozen emergency vehicles — police cars, fire trucks, and ambulances — located throughout The Park, their red and blue lights flashing.

The rides were completely still, and although the arrival of storm clouds this afternoon had brought with them an early twilight, the strings of brightly colored lights which decorated the tracks and buildings and trees had yet to come on.

Thick black smoke poured from one of the ride pavilions, and the firemen trained hoses upon the crackling flames, sending up roiling plumes of steam.

Some of the people she saw were running back and forth, seemingly without purpose, while others tended to the injured who were laid out on the grass. Even at a distance, she could see the blood. . . .

The absence of sirens somehow made it worse.

Celeste felt queasy and light-headed. After a long moment in which she kept expecting the vision to fade, she couldn't bear to look any longer, and forced herself to turn away. She leaned against a tree and sank down until she was sitting on the ground.

Something had gone terribly wrong down there. She had to do something, but what?

Go for help?

Go where, Celeste and ask who?

It was a question she'd never found an answer for in the real world.

She hadn't seen anyone in hours, unless you counted the Mercenary she'd knocked off, but even if she managed to find someone, what could—

Celeste started, hearing a sound like a gunshot, followed quickly by another. She ducked instinctively, falling to one side and covering her head before realizing that it was only thunder echoing through the hills from the darkening sky. For hours the clouds had been threatening rain, and now they delivered, the first fat drops spattering to the ground.

"Damn! That does it. The game's over." She got hurriedly to her feet and turned up the collar of her blouse, not that it made much of a difference. After getting her bearings, she started in the direction of the gate.

The path that would offer the most protection from the rain went through a grove of trees.

The thick growth of trees provided a canopy of sorts, and hushed the sound of the rain. The air was fragrant with eucalyptus and pine.

Celeste walked with her head down, keeping her eyes on the narrow dirt path. She recognized her own footprints from when she'd passed this way earlier, and saw that someone had followed after her. . . .

She glanced back over her shoulder, expecting to see a face in the gloom, but there was no one. Even so, it gave her an uneasy feeling to imagine a presence shadowing her, moving silently among the trees.

The path forked—funny, but she didn't recall it doing that—and she stopped for a moment. Here the footprints were less distinct. She sat on her heels, trying to pick hers out from the rest.

Off to the right, a twig snapped.

Celeste froze, her heart in her throat. Whatever had made the sound wasn't on the path, which meant he, they, *it* was hiding among the trees.

She fought back an impulse to scream. Listening hard, she heard what might have been breathing . . . or the wind sighing through the trees.

Celeste closed her eyes briefly, gathering her nerve, and then took off at a sprint down the left fork in the path. She ducked as she ran, trying to avoid the overhanging branches. One raked across her cheek and tangled in her hair, yanking her head back momentarily before she pulled free.

The path forked again and she went left, into a dense undergrowth surrounding the trees. The path narrowed, until it was no more than six inches across. Tiny red berries had fallen from the bushes into the dirt, but at first glance her mind interpreted them as blood, and she skidded to a stop, nearly falling.

"Shit," she gasped. Her lungs ached for air, and she bent over, hands on her knees, as she took several gulping breaths. She had a stitch in her side, and her cheek stung where it had been scratched —

She thought she heard someone laugh, and that set her to running again.

She didn't even see the web, but ran headlong into it. As delicate as it was, she felt it on her face and arms, and turned in circles as she tried to brush it off. The fine hair on her arms bristled as she imagined the spider whose home it was crawling on her skin. . . .

Celeste blocked the thought, and forgot it outright a moment later when she realized that ahead of her, for perhaps a hundred feet, the path was shrouded with finespun spiderwebs.

She took a step backward.

"Where's the damned gate?" she said under her breath, and turned back the way she'd come.

She hadn't gone more than five hundred yards when she came face to face with a Mercenary, its yellow eyes glowing malevolently in the near-dark.

Celeste raised her stun gun and winced, expecting to be hit with a pellet, but the robot didn't move, although it appeared to scan her. Its weapon was pointed at the ground, where it apparently had fired, judging by the red dye on the dirt and leaves.

Someone had either blasted it or it had malfunctioned, but she approached cautiously nonetheless. It gave her the creeps to be so close to the thing.

She walked around it slowly, wondering if it were truly harmless or if she should try to disarm it. She remembered what the Game Master had said about the robots communicating with one another.

She returned to the front and stepped in closer, thinking that maybe she could open the panel on its chest as the Game Master had done, but when she reached to touch it, it began to make a clicking sound.

Celeste drew her hand back.

The Mercenary's head turned, as though it had heard its name being called. The yellow eyes flickered eerily, and in the base of its throat, what looked very much like the face of a watch lit up, displaying a four digit number.

8 6 8 6.

Something about the numbers seemed familiar. She'd overheard someone reciting those numbers into a radio . . . only they hadn't said eight six, but eighty-six.

"Cancel," she said. "Eighty-six means cancel."

The Mercenary had released its weapon, and was flexing its black-gloved hand.

The display in his throat blinked off and on twice, and then the numbers changed in such rapid order she couldn't keep track.

The robot lurched, taking a step toward her, startling her, and she moved out of its way just as it brought up its hand and—

—blue light shot from its fingers.

365

Celeste fell to the ground and scrambled on hands and knees, taking refuge behind a massive tree trunk. She waited for the robot to find her, but after a couple of minutes had gone by, she peeked around the tree.

At first she didn't see it, but she could hear it clicking, and it was a simple matter to follow the sound. For a robot, the thing was sure making tracks, head turning from side to side, eyes scanning as it moved.

The robot made a sharp right turn and crashed through the bushes as if they weren't there. It was heading, she thought, in the direction of the gate.

Maybe it would lead her out of here.

"What the hell," she said, tucking her weapon in her waistband at the small of her back. "It's worth a try."

She ran downhill through a thicket of trees, trying to catch up to the Mercenary.

The rain had found its way through the trees, and combined with the slick eucalyptus leaves to make her lose her footing. She fell to the ground on her stomach and slid to a gradual stop. Exhausted, she lay motionless.

She felt rather than heard someone come up beside her. Instinct warned her not to move. Not that she even had the strength; she'd never been this beaten-down tired in her life.

A foot nudged her in the hip. "Well, well, well. What have we here?"

Celeste opened her eyes slightly but didn't lift her head. It was quite dark out, but she thought she saw Joey crouching in the bushes . . . and then she blinked.

Joey was gone, if he'd ever been there in the first place.

"Don't play dead, my dear," the Game Master said, reaching down and grabbing her by the wrist. He pulled her to her feet. "You'll take all the fun out of winning."

Chapter Fifty-seven

An ambulance was blocking the paved walkway, its doors gaping open, and Sheriff Young steered around it, driving onto the grass.

The floodlights, part of the emergency response equipment the town had bought after the 1989 quake, illuminated a nightmarish scene: bloodied victims being tended by EMTs who themselves were pale with shock, and bodies lying in a row beneath tarps.

Human debris, Young thought.

He turned off the engine, letting the patrol car glide to a stop near one of the fire trucks that had responded from neighboring towns.

Mason Duffy, head of the town council and volunteer fireman, hurried over in his yellow slicker. "Adam," he said, "we're in trouble here."

Young ignored the understatement. "Where's Rice?"

"Rice?" Duffy shook his head. "I don't know. I haven't seen him, but—"

"How about Davison?"

"Who?"

"The whiz kid."

Duffy frowned and ran a hand through his thinning hair. "Oh, him. The last I saw of him, he was over by the roller coaster —"

"Which one?"

Puffy pointed and Young turned to look. "The Death Spiral . . ."

The floodlights had been aimed up into the framework, and he could see men scaling the structure, making their way toward three of the bullet-shaped cars which were stopped on the track, hundreds of feet above the ground.

He located Wesley Davison in the control room of the Death Spiral. The boy genius looked a little worse for wear as he worked intently at a breaker panel.

"Where's your boss?" Young asked without preamble.

Davison shook his head, not taking his eyes from the rows of breakers, which he was methodically switching off and then on. "Haven't seen him."

"Who's in charge here?"

"I guess I am." One of the breakers was so large that it took both hands to throw it. Davison grunted with the effort, and finally looked around. "But if you want a body count, I can't help you."

"Right now there's only one body I'm looking for, and that's Rice."

Davison moved over to the controls. "My guess is he's up on Level Three."

"Take me to him."

The computer screens on the control panel lit up momentarily, flickered, and went dark again. "Damn it," Davison swore, "why won't it work?"

"I want you to take me to Rice," Young said. He gripped the kid's shoulder, and spun him around. "You understand? I'm going to arrest the son of a bitch."

Davison blinked. "On what charge?"

"Criminal negligence or whatever the fuck else I can think of that might stick. The bastard's gonna pay for what he's done."

Chapter Fifty-eight

Jesus moved back into the shadows. He had heard Celeste running and seen her fall. He wanted to help her, but before he could move, the man had appeared from out of nowhere and captured her. . . .

It was supposed to be only a game they were playing, but Jesus sensed that to the man it was more. Looking into those cold eyes earlier had made him think of a rattlesnake. Many creatures gave warning of their deadliness, and with this man, the warning was in the eyes.

Jesus inched along the ground on his belly, careful not to make a sound. He wasn't close enough to hear what the man was saying, but he could tell by Celeste's expression that the man had frightened her.

Celeste had been kind to him, and she alone had he told the secret of his identity. She had proved worthy of his trust, and now he must prove worthy of hers.

He would find someone to help.

Without hesitation, he turned and, like the snake the man reminded him of, slithered across the eucalyptus leaves toward one of the many entrances to the tunnels.

The skeletons and spiders he had used as markers were less visible than they'd been yesterday, but after his eyes adjusted to the darkness beneath the earth, he found he could make them out well enough to find his way.

The tunnels were narrow in many places where the walls had caved in, and in these places he moved carefully, but there were also great lengths through which he could actually run. And since he was heading primarily downhill, it did not take long to come to one of the many ways out.

He climbed the rusted iron rungs up to the surface, and came out in a thicket of bushes much taller than he. The bushes were blooming with white flowers that seemed to glow in the dark like the faces of ghosts, and, startled, he retreated back into the tunnel for a moment before his sense of urgency reasserted itself.

These bushes had sharp thorns, and he had to crawl underneath to keep from getting stuck, but once he was clear of them, he got to his feet and ran, looking for someone to tell of Celeste's misfortune.

It had to be, he thought, someone in authority; he could not waste precious minutes by being forced to tell his story over and over. But who? Not a guest, certainly, but neither an attendant on a ride.

He stopped to catch his breath and to look down on the rest of the amusement park—he was high on Level Two, above the Death Spiral—and for the first time became aware of the flashing lights below.

Never in his life had he been witness to anything so awful or so unexpected. There were people everywhere his startled eyes looked.

A woman sat on the grass clutching the hand of someone whose upper body was covered by a blanket. She rocked back and forth, tears streaming down her face.

A boy about his own age cradled the bloody head of an elderly woman in his lap.

Two firemen were helping a pregnant woman onto a stretcher, and the white sheet beneath her turned quickly a violent, brutal red.

An ambulance pulled away, its siren wailing and then abruptly falling silent.

Jesus did not know what had happened, but he was nearly overwhelmed by a feeling of hopelessness. He thought of Señorita Fremont, but if she was here, among the injured, he would never find her.

Perhaps he was already too late . . .

Then he recognized a face among the many faces. It was the *agente de policía*, the man whom he'd seen in the lobby two days ago. The *agente* was with the young man who'd had his picture taken with Celeste and the others at the Grand Opening.

Jesus felt his mouth go dry. He stood motionless, seeing them come closer and closer, and his eyes could not remove themselves from the badge, the insignia, on the *agente*'s shirt.

What should he do? If he did not tell someone soon, and something bad happened to Celeste, it would be his fault, and his failure of courage would haunt him for the rest of his days.

And yet to bring himself to the attention of the *policía* was almost certain to result in punishment for the breaking of the law. He would be sent back to Tijuana, perhaps to the very orphanage he had left to escape.

Escape.

Should he save himself or . . .

They were only a few feet away, now, and he made himself stand perfectly still, allowing his last opportunity for escape to pass.

"*Jefe*." he said respectfully, and stepped forward. "*Por favor.* There is trouble, and my friend needs your help."

Chapter Fifty-nine

Rice smiled, reached around behind her, and pulled the stun gun from the waistband of her tight-fitting pants. "Welcome to the End Game."

"You call this a game?" the girl asked. "Those asshole Mercenaries of yours aren't playing by the rules."

"No?" He aimed at the ground a few feet from where they stood and emptied the stun gun of its charge, then tossed it into the trees.

"No."

Her blouse was wet and it clung to her in a very enticing manner. He could see the outline of her breasts and the evidence of her excitement. "Ah, well, that's a pity but . . . you've lost."

Her hazel eyes narrowed. "Good. I want out."

"Are you cold?" he asked with mock concern. "You're trembling."

She said nothing, but looked directly at him, as if to deny her fear.

"If you're cold—"

"Touch me," she said in an icy voice, "and it'll be the last thing you ever do."

Rice laughed. "Now I'm scared."

"Just . . . leave me . . . alone." She spaced the words out for emphasis.

She had, he realized, an edge to her. This was not a shy young maiden, but a wildcat, who might very well go for his eyes.

"You're in no position to be telling anyone what to do," he said mildly.

"Neither are you," a male voice said.

To overreact would be a mistake, and he knew better. He kept his pellet gun pointed at the girl and looked in the direction the voice had come from.

It was, as he'd thought, Max: The other girl, the redhead, stood a pace or two behind and to the right, and both of their weapons were aimed at him.

Of course, from this distance there was no way he could tell if their stun guns still held a charge or if they were bluffing.

"Thank God, Max . . . Betsy," the girl breathed.

Rice discreetly pressed a tiny button near the safety on his pellet gun, calling for reinforcements. Only two of the Mercenaries were functional but they would at least even the odds.

"It's been an exhilarating day, don't you agree?" Rice asked. "Worth the price of admission many times over, but then, I guess you wouldn't know, since you're here as a result of my charity."

Max stepped closer, wild eyed, and aimed the stun gun at his head. "You're one crazy motherfucker. Do you know what your damned robots have—"

"They aren't merely robots," Rice interrupted, not bothering to disguise his disdain. "They're state-of-the-art and beyond—"

"What they are," Max said through clenched teeth, "are killers."

He couldn't help but laugh. "Don't be ridiculous. They're perfectly harmless, I assure you."

The redhead, Betsy, gave a little scream, and he saw from the corner of his eye that one of the Mercenaries had arrived.

Max whirled and fired at it, simultaneously falling to the ground.

The girls hit the dirt.

He wondered if they felt as foolish as they looked. "Overreacting, aren't you?"

The Mercenary came to a halt, but behind it, Rice saw the last of his warriors.

"You've taken all the fun out of it," he said with a frown, and fired a pellet at each of them. "There. The game is over."

Next time he'd make sure that only adults were admitted to Level Three.

"It's coming," Betsy said, sounding panicked. "Shoot it!"

"I think you've forgotten the rules. I can't shoot it," Rice said. "He and I are on the same side. But it won't harm you, not since I've neutralized—"

The Mercenary raised its hand and he had a moment to wonder what had happened to its pellet gun when the first bolt of electricity hit him. The impact forced the air from his lungs and lifted him off the ground.

Rice felt a thrill as the jolt ran through him, and then there was nothing. . . .

Chapter Sixty

Listening to the boy describe what he'd seen, Wesley understood that, like the rest of The Park, the Games and the Mercenaries had somehow gotten out of control. He mentally reviewed the Level Three system, but could think of no way to access and shut it down.

"How'd you get out?" Sheriff Young asked the boy. "No one saw you?"

"The tunnels," Jesus said, and pointed to the ground. "Like a *topo*."

"He means mole," Wesley said, remembering the Spanish he'd learned in grammar school.

"No shit." The sheriff frowned. "This place must be honeycombed with tunnels. That explains how old Ezra worked his magic . . . and why he was so anxious about them digging into the mountain."

Right now, Ezra was the least of his concerns. Wesley bent down so that he could look Jesus in the eyes. "Will you show us?"

"*Sí.*" The boy looked at the sheriff. "But he cannot come."

"Why not?"

Jesus placed his hands on his own shoulders. "He is too big here, he would never fit through the narrow places. But you . . . you will make it."

Wesley glanced up at Young, who nodded.

"I'll get through the gate," the sheriff said, "if I have to blow the damned thing sky high. I'll find you inside. Just . . . stall, if you can."

"Let's go," Wesley said to the boy.

The tunnels, he saw immediately, had been dug many years ago. The wooden supports were gray and riddled with dry rot in spots, and he could see the old flat iron nails, rusting to dust.

There were metal hooks every twenty feet or so, which had probably been intended to hang lanterns, but even that would not be adequate to light the darkness.

Jesus seemed able to find his way, and after a hundred yards or so, Wesley saw how. There were dozens and dozens of the glow-in-the-dark toy spiders and skeletons at intervals along the tunnel floor.

He admired the boy's inventiveness, but right now he'd give anything for a D-cell flashlight. Except maybe he didn't want to see how the ceiling sagged under the weight of the earth. . . .

"Here," Jesus said, when they'd come to a three-pronged fork. "This way."

"You're sure?"

"I'm sure. That way . . . is bad."

There wasn't time to ask why. The tunnel slanted uphill, and rather than walking bent over, Wesley had to get on his hands and knees and crawl. It narrowed several times and was a tight fit getting through, but finally he found himself at the top.

Jesus was already on the ladder which led out into the open air.

Wesley stood up and waited until the boy disappeared out the hole — the ladder rungs looked as though they might separate from the wood wall if they were subjected to too much weight—and then started after him.

He was perhaps two feet from the top when he heard a scream. Above, he saw Jesus looking down and gesturing for him to hurry.

Stall, the sheriff had said. Well, so much for that.

Once out in the open, he sent Jesus back into the tunnel for safety, then cautiously made his way toward the voices. A second later he heard the crackle of electricity, followed by the sound of impact, something heavy hitting the ground.

Thunder rumbled across the sky.

Wesley saw Rice, then, sprawled and quite obviously dead. The others—Celeste, Betsy, and Max—lay facedown in the dirt, splattered with red dye, but otherwise unharmed.

The Mercenary, its hand still outstretched, turned toward him.

"Get down, it'll kill you!" Celeste yelled, and even as he dived for safety behind a tree, he was struck by the quality of her voice, which seemed to hold no fear, and showed no emotion.

The Mercenary's yellow eyes glared, searching for him. It would have no qualms, Wesley realized, about destroying its creator; loyalty wasn't a function of its programming. But then, neither was killing supposed to be.

He peered cautiously around the tree trunk, assessing his options. Theoretically, the dye would serve to eliminate the others as targets—assuming the robot's sensors hadn't been damaged—but he wasn't willing to risk anyone's life by counting on it.

He noted a stun gun lying a few inches from Max's casted arm.

"Does anyone have a charge left?" he asked.

"Sorry," Max said. "I'm out."

"Can you reach Rice's pellet gun?" If it wasn't empty, maybe he could use it as camouflage—

"I can, I think." Celeste rose up slightly off the ground to reach for it, and the Mercenary responded by swiveling in her direction and firing. The electric arc missed her by a fraction of an inch as she rolled to one side.

Lightning flashed, Wesley saw the Mercenary's eyes flicker. . . .

Instinctively, he knew what to do, and he reached into his pocket for the ball bearing he'd found the other day. He waited a few seconds and then, when the lightning flashed again, he threw the metal bearing high into the air.

This time the Mercenary's shot was dead on, and blue light crackled skyward between its fingertips and the bearing . . . and a lightning bolt completed the circuit to the earth, blasting the Mercenary into a thousand tiny pieces, and setting the ground beneath it on fire.

Wesley ran to where the kids lay, helping Celeste to her feet as the molten pieces of metal and electronic circuitry began to rain down.

"Superman," she said, and put her arms around his neck and hugged him. "You know, we've got to stop meeting this way, or I'm gonna start believing in the cavalry."

The DY program director showed up half an hour later to take the kids back to the hotel, but Celeste insisted on staying, even though the rain had begun in earnest.

For a very long time, they simply held hands, because there was nothing to say. When he realized they both were drenched, he put her in the back of the sheriff's car to wait, then walked over to where the lawman stood.

Sheriff Young glanced down at Rice's contorted face before throwing his jacket over the top half of the body. "I guess he finally bought an E-ticket ride," Young said.

Wesley didn't bother to ask what he meant.

Epilogue

Boston, Massachusetts
September, 1992

Dinah Fremont adjusted the portable fan to blow directly at her, and sat back to read, for the fiftieth time, the account in *People* magazine of what had happened this past June at The Park.

It was strange to see the photographs of Celeste and Max and Betsy, to read her own name and a quote attributed to her but which she could not remember making: "These kids are survivors and they're tough, because we as a society have failed them."

Right on, she thought.

But the article — by Nancy Chan, no less — focused primarily on the death of Sheldon Rice, a man whose wealth had allowed him to act out his fantasies on a grand scale . . . and had resulted in his death.

And tragically, in many others: The final toll was eighteen dead—including a security guard who'd been run down by an emergency vehicle as he fled the scene—and fifty-nine injured.

Theories as to the cause of the disaster were varied, and occasionally fantastic, but the most recent speculation was that there'd been a flux in the magnetic field beneath the mountain which disrupted and ultimately disabled the computerized systems.

And, oddly, seemed to have resulted in a huge increase of the insect population.

She hadn't yet been able to forget her last glimpse of The Park. The Death Spiral had been a dark silhouette against the morning sky, and it looked to her like the skeleton of some long-extinct species, frozen in its death throes.

Later she'd sat in front of her television and watched in awed silence filmed footage from The Park. The cameraman had walked along deserted pathways and into the abandoned ride pavilions. There, the camera had recorded the encroachment of nature as it began to reclaim what was, some said, rightfully its own.

It was a haunting image, slender green vines twisting up the metal superstructure of a roller coaster. . . . How could something that delicate ever hope to engulf something so massive?

But it would.

In time, it would.

Wesley Davison had refused an interview request from Chan—a fact that the reporter had made repeated reference to within the body of the article—and when Dinah had asked him point-blank what had happened up there on the mountain, he said simply, "I don't know."

Dinah hadn't given up on getting an answer from him, though; he was seeing Celeste, and flew to Boston once or twice a month. He was trying to convince her and her father to move to California.

"There are some things even Superman can't fix," Celeste said she'd told him. "Running away won't help."

But Wesley was good for the girl, Dinah believed, and she was keeping her fingers crossed. . . .

As for the rest of the first group, Max had recently finished the physical therapy for his broken arm. He'd sent her a cartoon he'd drawn showing him in a medieval torture chamber with—surprise—a redheaded nurse cracking the whip.

She'd gotten a little heat over that; the same nice Mr. Torrance who'd entrusted Betsy to her care, had become something of a raging maniac when Betsy had announced at the airport that she wasn't going home to Mountainair, but intended to stay in Denver for the summer and nurse Max back to health.

Never in a million years had she expected those two to find each other.

Of course, she was far from batting a thousand at anticipating what these kids would do. The young Mexican boy, whose name, according to Celeste, was Jesus Rivera, had up and disappeared the Sunday morning that they were supposed to leave. Celeste denied complicity, but Dinah caught the look that passed between her and Wesley.

She suspected the boy was living in the ruins of The Park, but couldn't prove it.

As for Nicholas, well, all she had from him was the brief note he'd left her when *he* ran away—

"Not having lunch?" Peter Abbott said. He came into her office and sat on a corner of her ever-crowded desk.

"It's too hot to eat." September had been blazingly hot, supposedly as a result of the greenhouse effect. Or the preferred term these days, global warming. Maybe, Dinah mused, a magnetic flux wasn't such a far-out idea after all.

"Hmm." Peter turned the fan toward his face, and closed his eyes in total bliss.

After all the help he'd been to her in the weeks after the

fiasco—as they now referred to it—she could hardly protest. She'd offered to resign, but he'd pointed out to her and everyone else that no one could reasonably have seen what was coming.

Peter relinquished the fan, but then reached across and grabbed the well-worn magazine. "Still worrying at it, I see."

Dinah nodded, knowing it was useless to deny it.

He flipped through the pages of the magazine, and jabbed a finger at a photograph. "Did you read this sidebar on the old man? The one who was grinding up human bones?"

"Ezra, you mean." She'd nearly memorized both articles. "And there was only the one set of *human* bones—"

"—belonging to one Eugene Hawell, whose bleached white bones and security access card were found at the old man's cabin—"

"—and the human bones were *not* ground up."

"Because he hadn't gotten around to it." Peter grinned like a little kid being deliberately gruesome to annoy an adult. "Gotta let 'em dry out first, you know."

Dinah sighed.

"Now to me, that's weirder than anything that happened at The Park. Pounding bones into dust for, what'd they say, fifty years?"

"I guess so."

Peter arched his eyebrows. "Makes you wonder, doesn't it, how someone could do something so weird for so many years without anyone knowing what he was up to."

"I try not to think of it," she said in total honesty.

"Anyway, you sure you don't want lunch?"

"Oh, all right, now that you've really ruined my appetite." Dinah opened her desk drawer to look for her keys and as she grabbed them, the folded note that Nicholas had left fell out onto the floor. She picked it up and opened it, reading again his cryptic words.

I'm not from Iowa, the note said.

Dinah tucked it into her pocket, stood up, and slung her purse over her shoulder. As she passed Peter, who was holding the door for her, she smiled. "I wonder how it is in Florida at this time of year?"